THE PRINCE ADEPT

BY
ROBERT LEO POLL

The Prince Adept
By Robert Leo Poll

A Cornerstone Book
Published by Cornerstone Book Publishers

First Cornerstone Edition 2021
Second Cornerstone Edition 2024

Cornerstone Book Publishers
Hot Springs Village, AR
www.cornerstonepublishers.com

ISBN: 978-1-61342-999-0

Dedicated to my incredibly wise parents, my determined and creative brother, and to everyone who supported and believed in me.

THE PRINCE ADEPT

Prologue

There were once two worlds, one of the heart and one of the soul. The world of the heart was brave, passionate, and daring, while the world of the soul was quiet but wondrous and full of magic. Both existed in the shadow of the other, interacting but never really cooperating. Both scoffed at the inadequacies of the other while secretly envious of their power and achievements. The world of the soul, being intimately tied to the spiritual world around them, began to unveil the songs of the heavens with a grace and majesty that stunned the cosmos. They quickly surpassed the world of the heart and soon found themselves near the pinnacle of perfection, unaware of the precarious spire they gleefully stood atop.

The world of the heart, jealous of their counterpart's lofty height, had only to nudge them.

The world of the soul didn't even realize that they were falling until they burst into a scorching fire that would screech across the cosmos for millenniums. It was a horrifying inferno that would weigh on the souls of humanity with a sadness and misery that became so embedded that its very presence was forgotten — along with the world of the soul.

It is a little-known truth that all life is fundamentally connected, humans even more so to each other and more than one would expect. Even if on a subconscious level, we feel the suffering of others. We are connected. So, it was with one particularly strange day that everyone breathed a deep sigh of relief. It was as if a long-repressed burden had finally been lifted off the chest of every person across the face of planet Earth. Quietly to themselves, everyone sighed. It was a strange occurrence indeed, and very few would ever know what had truly transpired. Few would know what long-standing burden had been lifted, which had been so deep as to be felt planet-wide. Such is often the nature of true acts of good. True acts of good, or miracles, are seldom known to all. And so, it was with a miracle that a deeply profound burden was lifted.

This is the story of that miracle that ended an age of endless, tumultuous sleep.

CHAPTER ONE

The Great City

"Quiet everyone, the wind… it's stopped."

-High priestess Maalen Recean Balerri, Master of the White Arch
Four minutes before the opening of the seal.

Small, gentle snowflakes danced across his face as he sleepily opened his eyes to the dazzling light of midday. Around five white gowned specters looked at him with worry. Each was hazy, distorted, and scarcely any detail could be made out aside from their angelic faces that were haggard by utter exhaustion.

The one closest to him, a woman with vibrant red hair and dark, sleepless shadows under her eyes, bent down on one knee and stared at him intently. Her gaze was a mixture of curiosity and concern. "My brother," she said sympathetically. "You have a terrible journey ahead of you filled with violence and tragedy." She softly dug her hands into the icy snow and pulled out a small, gnarled flower which she regarded with pity, "This world is poisoned. Wake the sleeping master Almerin and tell him that the Prince Adept has fled. Tell him that this might be our only chance."

"They know where we are," one of the ghostly figures announced, causing the rest to form a ring.

"Your armament is nearby. Keep it close. I'm sorry I don't have the time to tell you much, but in your actions, Hiri Handi ebbs." She leaned forward and lightly placed the flower in his hand. "Your memory will return to you in time. Be brave. Keep love in your heart and compassion for those who suffer."

She then stood up as a fog of darkness began to surround them.

Then he blinked, and they were gone. He was alone.

He was leaning against a crumbling gravestone, in the midst of a snow crested cemetery that had succumbed to the unrelenting torrent of age.

He just sat there drawing labored breaths, while trying to comprehend what had just happened. He couldn't. None of it made any sense.

He then tried to remember how he even got here.

Nothing came to mind.

His past?

Still nothing.

Even his name?

Nothing.

Deeper, heavier breaths escaped him as he sat in a state of rising terror. A cold numbness muffled the senses of his body, making movement difficult. He looked down at his gauntlet covered hand and flexed his fingers, trying to get some sensation; the metal plates creaking and groaning as he bent them. His hand tingled slightly, but not much more, at least it was something. Then he looked at his other hand where the little flower rested snugly in his palm. It was pale, wilted, and deeply unpleasant to look at.

He finally glanced down and examined himself. He was encased in battered, silver blue armor adorned with intricate gold enameling and several tiny red capes that fluttered in the wind. A massive gash covered in dry blood ran across the armor covering his chest and shoulder. He took one glance and then looked away with a nauseated groan. The bloody cut in the armor gave the impression that he was almost bisected, and he didn't know if he could bear to look at it. He took a deep breath, exhaled, and told himself that he wasn't currently dying a slow and agonizing death from the gruesome injury, so he should take a look. A horrible, deep scar lay right under the armor. The red-headed woman and her friends must have healed him somehow.

A breeze suddenly swept his chaotically long hair over his face, which he gently pinched with his fingers and brought into focus with his eyes. It was as white as the snow around him, not a hint of color.

He let go and leaned back.

Al… Almur… Al something, he had to find someone named Al something. Did she say Al was sleeping? And why did she call him brother? Was she his sister? His mind felt cluttered and disorganized. Absolutely none of this made any sense.

He wearily gazed around the quiet cemetery. There were no animals, not even any insects, just the wind rustling across the snowy gravestones and through the gently falling snowflakes.

He was truly alone.

Directly across from him in the distance were a series of large, lofty looking buildings connected to a massive tower.

That was probably where he had to go. He took another deep breath and exhaled, the air fogging in the bitter cold. He looked up at the calm blue sky. All he wanted to do was lay by the gravestone and fall asleep.

He softly placed the dead flower into the snow and decided it was time to get up. He braced himself with his arms, and his whole body groaned in agony as he began the arduous task of simply standing upright. He shakily rose from the ground, standing up for a moment before his legs jerked, sending him to his knees with an aching cry.

He was halfway there at least.

He clapped his hand to the headstone behind him, took a breath, and began to pull himself up again. His armor creaked and his body throbbed in protest, but he was standing, bracing himself against the stone slab behind him. It felt like the blood was being poured back into his body, and every limb prickled painfully. As he took a moment to breathe and steady himself, his gaze drifted down to the grave he had been resting on. A fanciful script had been tenderly drawn onto the headstone, weaving in delicate swirls and ending in the soothing image of a flower.

It was definitely some sort of language, but he couldn't even begin to read it.

He glanced over at the other crumbling graves and the etchings, at least from a distance, looked like the same sort of gibberish he found here. Then a reflective glint off to the side caught his eye. It was near one of the tombstones and not at all far from him.

He shook his leg a bit to get some more feeling as he eyed the distance, and whether he could successfully get there. The prickling had mostly subsided now, but he was still unsure if he could walk.

He closed his eyes for a moment, steadied himself, and then staggered away from his support like a struggling infant. Although he swayed and stumbled in desperation for balance, he managed to make it to the next gravestone where he clumsily grappled it for desperate support. He took a moment to breathe, eyed the distance to the next grave, and then set off again, much stronger and steadier now; and he almost made it to the next gravestone before his foot slipped on a patch of ice. He yelped as he collapsed on his side with a muffled thud, moaning in dejection with his face half-buried in snow.

Slowly, he pulled his head out from the icy frost and looked up. Although the object was close enough to see now, it was buried in the snowfall and only a bit of blue and yellow metal stuck out. He clumsily wiped the ice from his face, took a moment to let the aching pain of the fall subside, and then tentatively rolled onto his stomach. With a careful effort, he pushed himself up with his hands and was on his knees again.

The object was just across from him.

He clapped his hand on the gravestone behind him and shakily stood up, being sure to keep as much of a steady balance as he could. Then he let go and shambled over to the gravestone across from him so he could stare down with a profound curiosity at his prize.

It was a sword.

He remembered the redheaded woman mention something about armaments. He slowly got down and gingerly dug his hands into the snow, pulling out a glittering sword, broken mid-way down the blade. It had a single-sided edge and a sizable golden hand guard. The blade itself was a twisting mix of yellow and blue metals. It was fairly heavy, with beautifully intricate symbols covering the entire weapon that nicely matched an empty silver scabbard that happened to be tied to his belt. He held it in his hands for a moment.

It felt familiar, but he couldn't glean anything past that.

He brought the shattered tip of the sword to his scabbard and the blade effortlessly slid inside. It was indeed his sword.

He looked around with a profound sense of triumph, from what was truly a menial task.

The large buildings with the tower still stood expectantly in the distance, and he eyed that as his next goal. He set off slowly and deliberately, using his hands to brace on any object that was nearby. As he stumbled his way across, he gazed around at the striking monuments and meticulously crafted statues of the graveyard. Peaceful women with dark eyes and vigilant men with stoic presence watched attentively over their graves and the silence that gave the place an eerie sort of beauty. The wind and the noisy crunching snow beneath his feet were the only sounds to keep him company.

It was a meditative sort of quiet.

Then he turned the corner and stared down at the shredded corpse of a scavenger, half-buried in the snow with dried blood splattered all over the surrounding gravestones. Its frozen hand clutched a short spear as if still desperately fending off whatever had partially devoured him. The closed dented helmet hid the last horrified moments of life that were undoubtedly etched on the corpse's face, preserved by the frigid cold.

He merely glanced at the corpse and then staggered away in revulsion to lean on one of the nearby headstones not drenched in blood. The silence of the graveyard was shattered as he started to retch in disgust. Then the wind rustled behind him, and he spun around in horror, drawing his weapon, and shakily holding it outwards in a terrified attempt to ward off the unknown.

There was nothing there.

His heart pounded as he turned around and marched onwards through the graveyard with an ever-quickening pace. He flinched at every deceptive rustling of the wind, which now seemed to mask hidden assailants that loomed only in the corner of his vision. Even the benign statues began to look down on him with a malice and hatred for entering a place that wasn't his.

With a hand on his frantic heart and his sword ready to swipe at any threat, he finally walked up to the decaying metal door of the large building that sat as warden of the graveyard. Built of sleek blue and white bricks, its makers took painstaking efforts to chisel in as much sweeping detail as they possibly could while still allowing the building to flow effortlessly out of the ground and into the sky. The enameling, thin pillars, tenderly crafted windows, and even the now disintegrating door were all clearly carved with care. However, everything, the walls, windows, and thin pillars, were now faded, cracked, and lifeless. The building only seemed to hold a small amount of the profoundly magnificent energy it must have once had.

A small, tattered banner pleading for recognition fluttered and quivered along the side wall. It was a solid white flag with a single purple diamond at its center. The heart of the diamond interwove in itself to create another smaller diamond that gave the flag an almost mystical feel. It, like the rest of the structure, might have been very imposing in its day.

He put his hand on the snowy doorknob and turned.

It was locked.

With fury and fear he shook and turned the door handle, then took an irate step back. He had to get in. He didn't want to spend another moment in the cemetery with whatever had killed that miserable warrior half-buried in the snow. He readied his sword and walked over to one of the meticulously crafted windows.

It was beautiful — really a masterpiece despite its age.

He took a moment to breathe it in, and then smashed it to bits with his sword. It wasn't ideal, but it worked. He stepped through the shattered wreckage and stood in a large dark hallway bathed in the light of his newly made entrance. A vaulted ceiling rose up above him lined with lifeless hanging lanterns coated in thick dust. Behind ran the series of meticulously crafted windows that descended down the whole corridor and into obscure darkness. They were almost completely frosted over and served to only let in thin streams of desperately needed light. In front of him was a deep blue wall of shattered mirrors and dusty paintings filled with magical landscapes and colorfully dressed people. The wall was broken by several obscure passageways darting off into the unknown.

It was clear that he was somewhere very expensive and very old.

He stood for a moment, taking in his surroundings with a mixture of wonder and vague unease. That unease quickly turned to startled terror as the uneven whistling of a young girl began echoing through the empty hallways.

He nervously held his weapon close and listened attentively to the odd tune. It came from one of the dark corridors across from him. If he followed, he'd probably end up like the frozen scavenger outside. He had to find Al though. Would this lead him there? Or would it go horribly, horribly wrong.

A horrific, animalistic screech suddenly tore through the hallways somewhere to the far left. The screech froze his blood, but it was the following sound of clattering metal footsteps sprinting toward him that almost stopped his heart.

He wasn't alone and indecision was crippling the precious few seconds he had left. He could flee randomly into the darkness of a building he didn't know only to be hunted down by the screaming metal footsteps. He could also run towards the whistling girl and pray she wasn't allied to whatever beast was charging him. In panic, he chose the gentle whistling.

His legs trembled unsteadily as he pushed forward into the dark corridor, cursing with words meaningless to him. Tracing his hand against the left side of the wall, he unsteadily lumbered his way through the increasing blackness. Something large and horrible crashed behind him causing several paintings and mirrors in the distance to shatter to the ground. It sounded like the creature had slammed into the corner of the hallway, but he didn't turn around to see. He couldn't bear to face whatever was chasing him. He thanked whatever god had granted him this extra moment to flee and continued deeper into the corridor. He stopped when his trembling hand brushed against a doorknob which he frantically wrenched open, revealing a ghastly wall of shadowy blackness. There was no choice. He darted into the room and slammed the door behind him as the stampeding metal footsteps closed in.

It was horrible absolute blackness, but he would rather drown in shadows than face whatever was rushing to meet him. In a fit of hysteria, he ran his hands up and down the door until he brushed a lock and twisted it. The loud snap of the tumblers barely had a chance to click when he was knocked backwards to the ground by the force of the monster slamming into the door.

The creature pounded on the thick wooden barrier a few extra times and then staggered away, either demonstrating a remarkably short attention span or the cunning to find another entrance. It was hard to listen past the frantic battering of his heart, but for this brief moment at least, he seemed safe.

He leaned back on the floor, moaning, as the dull pain of his abused body finally got through to his terror-soaked brain. He shakily sat up, instinctively muttering more curses that seemed nonsensical to him.

There was not the slightest ray of light in the room, absolutely nothing could be seen. The air tasted stale, and he began to feel the paranoia of complete and utter darkness. The sense of safety he briefly enjoyed was quickly evaporating, so he resolved to make this detour short. He ran his hand chaotically across the floor until he found his sword. Then slowly, he stood up and stumbled into the nearby wall. His gauntlet dug into thin wallpaper as he struggled to regain his footing. Though the paper flaked and disintegrated in his hand, the wall itself felt sturdy. Following it was a good way to circumvent the room. He decided to do just that, hoping to find an exit along the way.

As he inched onward, he managed to slightly calm himself using an unsteady train of logic. If there was something in the room with him, it would have surely made its unwelcome presence known by now. He stopped and listened. The continual absence of sound from the room and from the creature outside was a comforting sign. With an insecure nod of satisfaction, he continued along with his sword drawn in his off hand, his right tracing the wall that he desperately clung to for the little spatial awareness it provided him. He shuffled his way further along in quiet solitude until he suddenly collided with some form of desk, to which he shouted more curses.

"Be careful, that's very old."

His heart froze, and he stood in dismayed incomprehension. "Who's there?" he nervously asked the darkness.

"Landala," the darkness replied. It was clearly a little girl's voice, probably no older than ten.

"Landala," he gingerly inquired, "were you…. the one whistling?"

"Yes, the monster was around, and I wanted to warn you."

He would have preferred a warning more direct than whistling, but he wasn't about to argue. "Landala… uh… can you find me a light?"

"No," she simply responded.

"Why not?"

"Because I don't like to see what's left of my body. I died in this room."

He opened his mouth a couple of times to speak, but fear strangled his voice. He didn't know what he was talking to, but it couldn't be good. He took a moment to steady himself, and then chose his next words carefully. The wall he followed must surely lead to a door, so asking *where's the exit* was pointless. He opted to ask for information instead. "Okay… Landala, can you tell me where a man named Al is?"

"I don't know an Al."

"Oh… uh… Almuh?"

"Almerin?"

"Yes," he hastily replied, not entirely sure if it was the right name, but it was good enough for a start.

"He's in the tower. Follow the wall to the door, then go left."

"Thank you… Landala." He made a special effort to memorize her name, he didn't want to offend her; she scared him.

"Okay, but you might need this."

He recoiled in shock when something from the darkness tried to touch his hand.

"It's a gift. Don't you want it?"

"I'm sorry… I just… sure, okay."

He held out his shaky hand, and something unseen provided him with a small, jagged pendant. "What's this?" he timidly asked.

"It's so I can talk to you far away. It's been lonely since everything went quiet."

"Well, thank you Landala," he said, pocketing the small item in a satchel that was tied to his belt, before nervously turning around to leave.

"The monster doesn't like the tower, so try to get there quickly."

"Okay… uh… thank you." He started to leave but then paused, "Landala?"

"Yes?"

"What happened here?"

"They opened the heart of the world, and it hurt everyone."

He had no idea what that meant. He also didn't know how, or even really want, to continue the conversation so he simply muttered, "Alright," and left it there. She terrified him.

He turned around and haphazardly navigated his way past the table, knocking over several objects as he did so. He pressed onward even though it felt like the whole world and everything in it had simply fallen away into the black void around him. The only real things left were the forsaken wall that he desperately clung to and the horrible ghost child he was still keenly aware of. All he could hear was his own haggard breathing in the steep of mounting paranoia. The dark wasn't his friend anymore. He cursed it, and he began to exclaim these curses at low breath when his trembling hand suddenly brushed onto a doorknob, as if the darkness itself had said it didn't want him either.

He slowly opened it to find a dimly illuminated corridor that stretched out towards another hall of windows and hanging lanterns.

He turned back towards Landala. She hadn't said anything in a while, and he couldn't see anything through the blackness. He thought about saying goodbye, but instead closed the door without saying a word. He switched his sword to his right hand and slowly made his way across the new hallway while trying to stifle his nervous breathing and obstinately creaking armor. He peered left and right and saw no sign of the armored creature. On his right, the hall extended further along into obscurity. On his left, it bent inwards slightly and connected to what looked like a bridge outside. Landala had said *left* so he chose the bridge and started making his way left.

His walk was still unsteady, and his chest and back now ached, but he felt more stable overall. He approached the bend in the hall and followed it into a narrow, open bridge lined with patterned white stone balustrades on each side. The enormous tower lay at the end of the bridge on an artificial cliff that jutted out of the landscape. Turning around, it seemed that the other hall followed this same path, making a fork. Then his eyes drifted to the shadowy, indented corner between both paths and noticed an armored monster simply standing there as if to say *you never really had a chance.*

He didn't feel his chest pounding or back aching anymore. He only saw and felt the blank impassive stare of the beast in front of him. Its skin was a colorless black and although it might have once looked human, its painfully malformed limbs, which had shattered out of its silver, angular armor, eliminated any outward semblance of humanity. Its hideously stretched jaw dangled and swayed out from under its helmet, and its spear-like fingers tapped on the floor, trying to maintain some form of balance for its horrifically disproportioned body. The creature took a loud step forward with its only armored foot.

He tore away from the monster and scurried towards the tower as fast as his trembling legs could carry him. He could hear its trampling feet crunching through the snow across the bridge, and he could feel its sickening breath coating his neck as he ran. He felt faint. His head pounded, and his vision blurred, but he kept running while shouting every single curse that instinctively came to mind. There was some sort of gate ahead of him, and he prayed to the high heavens that he could reach it. Then the creature leaped onto his back. It plunged him into the snow as he shrieked in helpless horror.

A shattering crack suddenly boomed across the bridge and then everything was quiet. He kept his face buried in the icy snow, shaking, and paralyzed in utter terror with his ears slightly ringing from the sound.

There was silence.

After a moment or two of not being eaten alive, he shakily lifted his head out of the snow and nervously peered up. A figure, buried in a mass of vibrant yellow armor with blue splotches, stood across from him. It had a vaguely triangular helmet that was almost reminiscent of a beak with a ridiculous, yet somehow impressive, wide blue plume atop its head. It stood unflinchingly still and held a coppery staff outward like a spear ready to strike. He slowly pulled his gaze from the yellow armored man and shuffled through the snow to peer behind at the smoldering carcass of the monster, collapsed in a heap some distance away. He turned back to the yellow man who hadn't moved an inch.

"Almerin?" he coughed.

The yellow man didn't answer.

He waited in the snow for a minute or so. When he was sure that nothing else was about to happen, he achingly staggered up and brushed some of the chilling ice off his face. The yellow man didn't move and still held his staff in a threatening manner.

Cautiously, he approached the yellow man, asking again, "Are you Almerin?" as he crept closer.

The yellow man still didn't answer.

Finally, he stood beside the hulking armored statue. It wasn't breathing or doing anything but standing impassively. He reached out to touch it but then stopped himself. He didn't know if he wanted to wake it up. It didn't look very friendly.

He cautiously maneuvered past the statue and stood before a closed, pale blue gate that wobbled and creaked in the bristling wind. It was covered in brittle glass that warped the scenery behind it, revealing only a glimmer of a courtyard before the tower. Further back was the dizzyingly tall tower itself. It had a spiraling design that was made of faded white brick and marble, which he guessed was a common theme in the city.

He lightly tugged on a frosted circular handle, but it refused to give way. Being gentle didn't work so he began fiercely shaking the gate, hoping that the old metal would break open. Instead, the glass shattered with many loud calamitous cracks. He jerked back in shock and spun around to see if the yellow statue had moved.

It hadn't.

The gate itself wasn't that tall. He might be able to climb it with a little effort. He reached up and then stopped with a groan when his aching body vehemently protested any thought of the concept. He shook the gate again, and nothing happened.

"Almerin!!" he shouted, throttling the gate without any concern for the yellow man behind him. "ALMERIN!!!"

CHAPTER TWO

The Tired Old Man and the Naive Child

"Things haven't gotten better like you wanted it to my love, but at least you're not around anymore to see it. I'm not afraid, my beautiful Eleseney. I can't think of a better way to end than right here beside you."

-The Hopeless Scavenger
Four weeks after the opening of the seal.

He breathlessly stepped back and contemplated his next move. Unpleasant gusts of icy wind brushed through him as he paced back and forth while racking his head for new ideas.

A latch! There must be a latch somewhere!

He shoved his armored hand through the shattered glass and felt behind the gate for any sort of latch. He blindly patted up and down until he finally felt something movable.

"Open! Just OPEN!" he cried as he desperately jostled and wrenched the unseen lever. He couldn't stop here, not here! Not with that monster's corpse behind him. Suddenly, the gate gave a satisfying clink, and he exhaled in relief as it relinquished its path with a hideous creaking. It opened to a small icy courtyard with a single dead fountain and a couple of snow-covered benches. He trudged through and gazed at the multi-level fountain as he passed by. It had frozen midstream, with several crystal arches reaching into the emerald basin below. It had a mysterious beauty that he might have enjoyed had it not been for his recent near-death experience, which painted the ethereal winter landscape in grisly shades of fear. He looked away and stepped up to a splendidly carved dark wood door that stood as the entrance to the tower. He approached the door, put a hand on its silver handle, and tugged and twisted fruitlessly until he gave up and stepped back in a huff. He shuffled a few paces away before turning around and sizing up the lavish door.

He was wearing armor…

How much could it really hurt?

He covered his head and charged, hurling himself into the door and tumbling inside in a heap of shattered wood. He slowly staggered upright with a prolonged groan and unsteadily meandered inside while cradling his aching head, which raged in fury at his recklessness.

The interior was cluttered with magnificently crafted mosaics adorning radiantly green and gold walls. An assortment of dusty gold book stands, benches, and some small tables were strewn every which way, all of which seemed too delicate to touch. Several hanging lanterns hung from a golden ceiling, giving off just enough dim flickering light to dance lazily across the slumbering artistry. His heavy metal shoes clattered across the tiled white and black checkered floor as he slowly walked deeper into the splendid room,

"Almerin!" he called out.

No answer.

His wandering gaze drifted over to a small red door tucked away in a shadowy corner. He tapped a nearby bookstand with his fingers as he contemplated the dangers that might be inside there. How far did he really want to go anyway? Was there anywhere else he could go? He pondered, weighing his options until the rim of the golden bookstand had enough and fell to pieces across the checkered floor. The abrupt clattering in the quiet, slumbering tower startled him. He fearfully eyed every murky shadow and every thin, flickering light as he waited for something horrible to happen. When nothing arrived to investigate the noise, he took a shaky breath and let his shoulders slack.

If anything were going to wake up, he told himself, it would've come after he'd first crashed into the room.

Despite his apprehension, he decided to open the red door. He twisted the knob, which clicked and gracefully swung open. Inside was a shadowy twisting staircase that ascended along the tower's rim, lit by dim wall-mounted lamps and frosted windows. He didn't like the look of it and peered around the room one last time, searching for a more appealing path, before slowly ascending the stairs.

He only trudged along for a short time in the semi-dark before coming to the first door, which was an invitingly pleasant shade of light green decorated by carved flowers. He opened it and stepped into a small garden of dead plants lined in rows along the walls of the room, which were painted to look like a midday sky with a flickering yellowish light in the center of the ceiling to act as a sun. He thought about investigating the plants, but they looked dead and possibly diseased. He didn't want to touch them. He glanced around for only a moment to make sure Almerin wasn't there before moving on.

The next room was some sort of dusty and long unused classroom, much more chaotically jumbled than the downstairs with chairs and desks jostled every which way. It was also horrendously dark, so much so that he only inched his face inside, calling out, "Almerin?" before quickly shutting the door upon a lack of a response.

19

He finally opened a door into a dark and foreboding study, where only the frosted windows illuminated what little of the interior they could. He was about to continue to the next floor when he jolted in surprise at the sight of a dusty old corpse in the shadows. It sat in one of two lofty red chairs before a large burnt-out fireplace, surrounded by piles of papers and books. He hesitated momentarily on the threshold of the room, weighing the possibility of this encounter going horribly wrong. He had to check, though. He'd already come this far. He took a deep breath and puffed out his chest in a frail attempt to exude some bravery. With a marshaled resolve, he inched closer with his sword pointed at the cadaver in case it suddenly decided to jump out of its chair and tear him to pieces.

It isn't rotting like the last dead body, he thought to himself, *so that's good. It moved slightly. It's breathing. It's alive!*

He leaned over the old man and inspected him from his sword's length away, which was what he considered to be a safe distance. The man was covered in enough dust and grime to suggest months or even years of personal neglect. He wore a rimless, flat-topped red hat and a long, gold-braided, tattered red coat.

"Hey," he shook the old man's arm briskly. "Hey, wake up."

The old man continued to sleep.

He looked around for something to wake the old man up with, and seeing nothing, he seized the old man's arm, shouting, "HEY!"

"AH!!" the old man leapt from his chair in a cloud of dust and stumbled to the floor, coughing.

"Almerin?"

The old man shrieked in terror and feebly swiped outward with a hidden dagger at his visitor, cutting nothing but the stale air around him. He scrambled across the floor and over to the corner of the room, where he defiantly held out his dagger, shouting, "St-STAY BACK!" in a deranged frenzy.

The old man's visitor watched with a mixture of alarm and disillusionment.

"Are... you Almerin?"

The terrified old man paused, "Yes, that is my name." He replied in a booming, forceful, and highly polished voice that harshly clashed with his decrepit appearance and craven mannerisms.

They both just stared at each other for a while as they each tried to make sense of the strange, unsettling situation.

"And who are you?" Almerin finally returned the question, still holding out his weapon defensively.

"Uh..." his visitor hesitated. He still didn't remember his name and had no idea how this terrified old man would react to an armed amnesiac. He tried to make up a name, but nothing came to mind, and the stammered words, "I... don't know," just spilled out of his mouth.

The old man suspiciously examined him from afar.

"Oh..." He muttered, his dusty eyes widening. "How very interesting. A Traveler from the other side."

"The what?"

"Do you remember anything at all?" Almerin asked, ignoring the Traveler's question.

The Traveler paused, "I woke up in a graveyard. Some people told me to find you and give you a message."

"What message?"

"Uh," the Traveler paused as he tried to recall what was probably unimaginably important information. "Uhh... they said that someone had left. He was some sort of prince, and this was important."

"What? Did they say it was the Prince Adept?"

"Yes, that might have been it."

"Tell me about these people." Almerin pressed, dropping his guard slightly and letting his meager weapon slide downward.

"They were ghostly, and one of them had bright red hair."

"Probably Maalen!" Almerin spat. "Even in death, she's still as arrogant as ever."

"What?"

"I know what you're here for. You want me to go out there!" Almerin pointed furiously to one of the frosted windows, "You want me," he paused to cough, "to join your horde of hopeless crusaders and suffer in the maw of oblivion like the rest! Well, I won't!! You can leave now." He gestured in the general direction of the door while still sitting in his corner.

The Traveler didn't move. He was still dazed from his encounter with the monster and couldn't entirely comprehend what was happening. "I don't understand."

Almerin stared at his bewildered visitor with narrow, musty eyes. "I'm asking you to leave," he replied more collectedly.

"But... you need to help me," the Traveler whined in confusion. "I don't know what to do!"

"There is nothing to be helped here," Almerin grumbled while staggering up with a groan and meandering over to his chair situated in front of the empty fireplace.

"BUT WHAT SHOULD I DO?!"

"Find a relatively nice place to sit and wait." Almerin collapsed into his chair and leaned his head back.

"Wait for what?!" The Traveler pressed with increasing alarm.

"Death," Almerin answered without looking at the Traveler.

"DEATH?!!!"

Almerin glanced over to his horrified friend and took pity on his utter bewilderment. "Traveler, this malignant city of horrors is cascading across dimensions. It's unsustainable, and eventually it will fade into nothingness. We, and everything in this city, will be dead. I prefer this death to the gruesome fate should we step outside this tower."

"But... the woman... Maalen, she told me that the Prince Adept has escaped!"

Almerin sat upright and answered with a cold bitterness, "She's lying to you. It's impossible for the Prince Adept to leave. It's impossible for anyone to leave!"

"Are you sure? Are you absolutely sure? Because she sounded very certain."

"Traveler, I told you that the city is cascading through dimensions. The only way to solidify the city is to close the seal tied to the planet's heart, the seal that the Prince Adept himself wrenched open to unleash this unholy hell upon us."

"Well... couldn't he close it to leave and have someone else open it after he's gone?"

"It doesn't work like that! It's not a light switch you can flick on and off, and I certainly would have felt if the city had reemerged into a stable plane!"

"Then why did she ask me to tell you this?"

"Because," Almerin answered with mounting impatience, "she wants me to kill the Prince Adept and close the seal, as she's already sacrificed all of her cultist followers to that impossible, reckless task. The city and its people can't be saved," he grimly remarked while returning to the desolate fireplace. "Nothing as unstable and unnatural as this city was meant to exist. It's destined to fade into oblivion. It just needs more time."

The Traveler took a moment to take in this point of view. Almerin's plan to sit and wait for everything to fade away would guarantee death, albeit a peaceful one. However, Maalen's plan to close the seal sounds like near, but not necessarily certain death.

He didn't want to die.

"Almerin?"

Almerin looked at the Traveler.

"Would closing this... seal... thing... kill us all?"

"Closing the seal is impossible. There is a vast metropolis of agony beyond imagination—"

"So, it won't!" the Traveler interrupted with a defiant finger pointed at Almerin, "Then the only option is to close the seal."

"IT'S NOT POSSIBLE!" Almerin stressed to the point where his face turned visibly red, even under the thick layer of dust. "You clearly have no idea what you're doing, and you will bring misfortune upon everyone who travels with you. Get out of my home!"

Almerin returned his attention to sitting aimlessly as the Traveler stood aghast in a speechless stupor.

He stood quietly before meandering over to a window to drag his whirling mind back together. He looked out the window and gazed for the first real-time over the vast expanse of the pearlescent cityscape. The view was extraordinary. Smooth, radiant towers shot across the midday skyline with such grace and beauty that he couldn't help but sigh in awe. The sun joyfully pranced across the teeming white spires, turning them into twinkling stars ready to soar up into the cosmos above. For a moment, he forgot about the horrible monster and the shredded corpse in the graveyard.

It was a pleasant moment to bask in, and the wistful words, "It's a gorgeous city," leapt out of his mouth without much thought.

"It was," Almerin replied with a painful nostalgia.

The Traveler stepped away from the window. He'd stumbled into an opening to talk to Almerin, and he couldn't squander it. "What was this place?"

"The city or *This* particular part of it?"

"This part," the Traveler pointed around the whole room. He wanted to know more about Almerin and his home. Maybe he could find something to help convince him to leave.

"What does it matter anymore?"

"It matters to me," the Traveler indignantly replied. "If I have to die here, I'd like to know its history."

Almerin glanced over at the Traveler and quietly nodded his head. "This whole complex was once a school called the Mistakoen Ordina," Almerin began, his eyes fixed on the fireplace as if it was still burning. "It was one of the most powerful places to harness one's connection to the spirit and the heavens. It was a peaceful place full of love and optimism."

"Who were you?" The Traveler asked, taking a step closer to Almerin.

"I was the Master of the Scarlett Arch, a prestigious honorary title. I was placed in charge of the school for around 40 years, I suppose."

The Traveler paused. If this was a school, then Landala must have been a student. He slowly dug into his satchel and pulled out Landala's pendent, hoping it would strike something in Almerin. "Do you know a girl named Landala?" he cautiously asked.

Almerin's old eyes widened as the Traveler placed the pendant in his grimy hands.

"How do you know her?" his voice faltering into a whisper.

"She warned me of the monster. I asked her where to find you, and she guided me to your tower."

Almerin let his gaze drift downward as he clutched the pendant in his hands.

"Who was she?" the Traveler persisted.

"She was a student of mine. She loved her father, but he never had any time for her. Over the years, I became somewhat of a parental guardian for her."

"Do you know what happened to her?"

"She was killed," Almerin bitterly answered. The Traveler could tell that he was stifling deep pain or regret. He could use that.

"Landala wanted me to give you a message," he lied. "I didn't understand it at first, but I think I do now."

Almerin turned back to the Traveler, who sat in an adjacent chair to speak on Almerin's level.

"She told me to tell you that… it's time to wake up."

Almerin glared at him with a seething suspicion. "Even if that's true, reality itself has become a horrific menagerie of agony, and you are suggesting that we go straight into its maw. Maalen and her followers were reckless, and they paid the price time and time again. The fact that you're here instead of one of her generals means they're all dead or worse. Do you think you could do better? You don't even have your memory yet! You're untested and ill-equipped. You even have a gaping wound in your chest, and you expect to do better than Maalen's trained commanders!?"

"What other choice do we have?"

"Choice?" Almerin replied with a dark shadow across his gaze. "Our deaths are unavoidable, my friend. We are trapped and destined to die, but I've decided to choose the terms of my death here, among my school and my books, at my fireplace. Curse the maw and its horrors! I won't step out to meet it."

The Traveler leaned back with a crushing heaviness in his chest. What was he even doing here? Is the old man right? Is a choice of death preferable to whatever is waiting outside? He didn't know. He didn't know or remember anything except that the redhaired woman told him that the Prince Adept had fled. He stood up with a sickening unease and turned to walk out the door. He didn't want to die. He wasn't ready.

He paused before walking away. He wanted to leave Almerin with a biting comment for filling him with such dread,

"If that's what you believe," he snapped, "then toss Landala's pendant out the window because she believed in you. The Prince Adept has left, and you're sitting here doing nothing!"

The Traveler didn't look back at Almerin. He simply stepped away with a mixture of regret and disillusionment. The bizarre conversation didn't go the way he wanted, and he didn't know where to storm off to. The outside was horrible, so he made his way up the spiral staircase, leaving the bitter old man alone.

The Traveler mindlessly marched some distance up the spiral stairs until he finally decided to enter a random pale white door with a golden handle. Like most of the rooms in the tower, it was incredibly dim, with meager light peering nervously through some of the frosted windows, aided slightly by several faint lanterns gasping at their last breaths of life. Glass casings with all manner of peculiar items and sculptures sat around the silver trimmed room, much in the manner of an exhibition hall.

The Traveler wandered over to one of the casings, which contained a fastidiously carved wooden wind instrument, not unlike a flute.

The Traveler took pride in remembering what a flute even was and felt calm knowing that his memory might indeed return. However, sensing little joy in the memory itself, he decided to move on. The next casing contained a glistening purple gem resting in a delicate silver wire stand. It was large, finely cut, and undoubtedly beautiful, but not much more could be discerned at a distance, so he meandered over to the next casing. Inside, there was a folded white shirt with blue trimmings. It looked old, tattered, and wholly unremarkable without context.

As he leaned away to move to the next casing, his eyes caught sight of a sizeable brass-colored cabinet sitting in a dark corner of the room. The front had strange, illegible symbols carved into a spiral-like pattern. His imagination drifted across all manner of wondrous contents as he investigated it up close. Tapping on it with his hand revealed only that it was indeed made of metal.

Suddenly, the back of the room was animated with a surge of energy. The Traveler jolted around to see the old man standing in the doorway, screwing up the case of a wall-mounted lantern.

"You need a key to open that," Almerin said, tightening the last screw while eyeing the Traveler with visible apprehension.

The Traveler watched in slight confusion as the old man ambled over.

"I keep the batteries in here," Almerin remarked, bypassing the Traveler and standing before the brass cabinet. "I stashed them inside, along with some general tools." He fumbled briefly with the lock before opening it and tossing several bags to the floor with a heavy thud. He handed a coppery screwdriver to the Traveler and said, "I need you..." he paused to look around, "to repair all the lanterns in the tower."

The Traveler remained quiet, trying to figure out what was happening.

"It's not hard; just unscrew the case and replace the batteries." Almerin stared at the speechless Traveler and bluntly asked, "Can you do it?"

"Uh, Yes, yes I can!" he quickly stammered, leaping to the bags with the presumption that Almerin might actually help him.

Almerin ascended the stairs, leaving the Traveler behind in the exhibition room. He wondered what could have possibly changed the old man's mind. It certainly couldn't have been anything he said in their last conversation. He opened one of the bags and pulled out a sizable blue, metallic box, which he hoped was a battery.

It turned out to indeed be a battery, and it took the Traveler a while to figure out how to replace them and even more time repairing as many of the tower's lamps as he could find. At first, he inched his way into every new, dark, and desolate room, prepared for any ambushes, but after around a dozen lamps, he began to drift from room to room and lamp to lamp with little care. Although his body groaned in protest to the lack of rest, he began to develop a subtle exhilaration every time he repaired a new lamp. He would fit in the battery, flip a small switch, and then watch the light dance merrily across the room, animating the beautiful pictures and moldings while casting away a tiny portion of the fears that plagued the back of his mind. Every new lamp confirmed safety and brought out some of the beauty hidden behind the veil of shadows in each room. Then he stopped after one of the lanterns illuminated a mirror. The Traveler grabbed a nearby dusty cloth, blew on it, and swept away the years of grime that blocked his view. He then stood back, mesmerized. He saw the pale, sickly face of a young man, with a hawkish nose, starkly defined features, and a seemingly perpetual look of abject horror. This was not the face of a stranger but one of a long-forgotten friend. He stood for a while, trying to capture any of the foggy memories now bubbling just below the surface. But he couldn't, and with a sigh, he moved on to the next lantern.

As he repaired more and more lanterns, he started to get a better sense of the odd tower he was slowly and meticulously ascending. The lower rooms were mostly simple studies, classrooms, and even a small kitchen. The higher ones were filled with test tubes, crystals, and bizarre machines — the purpose of which couldn't be garnered from a mere glance. The Traveler finally approached a simple door set off to the side, where he heard splashing water along with muffled mutterings within.

"Almerin?" The Traveler hesitantly knocked on the door, with images of phantoms and monsters gurgling at the back of his mind.

"Please tend to this lamp last, thank you," Almerin hollered in reply.

The Traveler continued to the next lamp with a small sigh of relief.

The last room was an observatory with a massive silver telescope aimed at a set of closed shutters. The ceiling was dotted with gold and silver stars glittering over a dark blue background. The Traveler walked across the light blue carpet and unscrewed the matching blue lamp case. He flipped the switch down, pulled out the old battery, put in a new one, flipped the switch again, and screwed the case closed. He then sat on the ground with a protracted sigh, letting himself collapse backward with a muffled thud. He was exhausted from the day's ordeals, and although the carpet was old, it was soft enough to close his eyes and slowly drift away to sleep.

He found himself in a dimly lit room lined with unpleasantly striped dark red and blue wallpaper. The air reeked of smoke and sweat, and the large leather chair he sat in strained his lower back. A large man obscured by shadows sat opposite him, breathing in a cigar and then bellowing out smoke like a dragon. The man lowered his cindering torch and then said in a raspy voice that was somewhere between a choke and a gasp, "Interesting."

The Traveler didn't reply. He didn't know what was interesting, and he had no interest in finding out. The man was evil, and the room was horrible. He wanted to leave.

The Traveler stood up and started to walk out. As his hand touched the cold brass doorknob, the large man called out, saying, "We'll meet again."

The Traveler walked out and shut the door behind him.

He groggily woke up from his unpleasant dream. He was now in a small room, lying atop a surprisingly comfortable wood frame bed with a thin blanket lazily tossed over him. He was still in his shattered armor, only now his sword was missing. He lightly smacked his face to make sure he was awake this time. It stung as it should, telling him this wasn't a dream. With a profound groan of irritation, he let his feet hang over the side of the bed, mustering the energy and willpower to stand up. The meek shafts of light from the nearby frosted window did their best to illuminate the elaborately carved red wood dresser beside him, along with a matching desk and chair, which all now acted as adversarial impediments in the near dark. He sleepily investigated his surroundings from the comfort of his bed until his eyes focused on a note stuck to the door. He should probably read that.

He got up and unsteadily traversed the short distance with the aid of what little light there was. Although he banged his head against the dresser and caught his foot on the chair, he managed to stagger to the door mostly unscathed. He turned on the nearby lantern that he'd repaired not long before and tore off the note.

Although a beautiful script danced on the page, swirling in delicate weaves, it was absolute gibberish. The only understandable part was an arrow pointing down. The Traveler tossed it to the side and opened the door to a small library, now brightly lit by the repaired lanterns. It was filled with books, knowledge, and a lack of both Almerin and his sword. He continued to the staircase and descended in the direction of the arrow. He finally stopped at a door with another note on it, which he didn't bother to read.

"Almerin?" he clamored into the study where he first encountered the old man, who was now standing by the window.

"Traveler," Almerin somberly pulled his gaze from the cityscape and turned to face his visitor. "Please have a seat over here." He directed him to one of the two red chairs before the fireplace. The Traveler cautiously entered the room and stood behind the chair.

It was clear that Almerin had spent some effort cleaning himself up, as he now wore a far less tattered, more regal red and gold coat with the same rimless hat, now dusted off. A weary and furrowed face observed the Traveler, partially covered by shadowy, haggard black hair and beard, cut by large gashes of white.

"I want you to understand that I haven't decided to help you yet," he said with an antagonistic glare that the Traveler felt he didn't deserve. "However, I spoke to Landala, and she also informed me that the Prince Adept might have fled. You're going to come with me to ascertain the true situation. That's all."

"Well, that's a start, I suppose. Now it's your turn." The Traveler challenged Almerin with an antagonistic stare of his own.

Almerin returned the challenge with a confused look. "What's my turn?"

"I delivered you what I hope is vital information. Now, it's your turn to tell me where I am and what all this is?" The Traveler made a grand gesture with his arms to emphasize the scope of his question.

"I am a teacher," Almerin sternly replied. "If you ask a question like that, then be prepared for a lecture."

"I am prepared."

"Then sit down," Almerin waved him into his seat. "Your sword," he quickly fetched it from a cluttered table tucked away to the side of the room, "bears the Royal Vanguard's mark."

"The what?" the Traveler asked, trying to sit in the invitingly plush chair with his scabbard refusing to have any part of it.

"The Royal Order of the Sky was the personal battalion of the Prince Adept. They usually flew atop colossal, magnificent birds known as Rocs and often delved into battle headfirst, earning them the nickname the Royal Vanguards. Does any of this sound familiar?"

"No," the Traveler blankly answered.

"Then I suppose I need to start from the beginning." The old man pulled a curtain across the window and handed the broken sword to the Traveler, who had now removed his scabbard entirely and tossed it to the floor so he could sit down. He moved past the Traveler and over to the room's lantern, which he turned off, plunging them both into darkness. The Traveler nervously glanced around at the overbearing blackness with a rising sense of terror that pounded away at his fragile constitution until Almerin struck a match that highlighted the harsh, tired creases of his face. He moved over to the adjacent red chair and tossed the small match into the fireplace, which suddenly roared with more passion than it had any right to, before sitting down and turning to the Traveler.

The Traveler put his weapon to the side of his chair and started to lean forward to give Almerin the proper attention, but then his muscles reminded him of what he put them through, and he leaned back with a wince. Until now, he'd been pushing through the aching pain with nothing but blind fear and adrenaline, but now that he had a moment to stop, his body would hear of nothing else.

Almerin looked at the exhausted Traveler and then fumbled around in one of his upper pockets before producing a jagged green stone that glittered in the firelight. He held the stone to his forehead, closing his eyes and muttering a prayer before passing it over to the Traveler.

"Your injuries have gone beyond the physical for the most part. You need energy. Take off your gloves."

The Traveler clumsily pulled off his heavy gauntlets, and the old man gently placed the stone in the Traveler's pale hands. "Hold onto this until you feel better."

He closed his frigid hands around the craggy, lime-green rock, which suddenly melted away the coldness with an odd warmth.

"Hmm, let's see. Where to begin?" Almerin muttered while stroking his beard and letting his eyes drift across the crackling fire.

"This used to be a great and powerful city known as Hiri Handi," Almerin began, "in a great and powerful kingdom called Itzalla, which translates to those who delve enough into deep history as The Shadow," he explained with profound reverence. "It didn't mean shadow as in darkness or evil," he corrected, "but it meant darkness in the sense of shade. It was supposed to be a place of respite for when the sun had been beating on your head too long." He said with a light smile that quickly faded as fast as it came.

As he talked, the fire began moving in synchronicity, which then slowly became a swirling disconnection of peaceful images.

"It didn't use to snow like this, though. It used to be a pleasant and temperate place."

The Traveler's eyes clouded as he watched an aged city form in the fire, nestled in and around a massive canyon, with merchants from distant lands coming and going like the ebbing tides of the sea.

"Although this was one of many kingdoms, it was the most advanced and influential. We sat atop the world's heart, a point of power that allowed us to almost unlock the secrets of the heavens themselves. To help us harness this power were our two monarchs, the Coronated Speaker of the Ordena, the guide and oracle of our faith, and a powerful and distinguished commander known as the Prince Adept."

He paused with a frown at the word as a powerful, imposing figure with the head of a hawk arose in the fire, flanked by a jackal-headed woman and a man with a long, pondering raven's head.

"The Prince Adept was a sacred title in reverence to Ecrea, the goddess of the moon who watches over all that we built and who witnessed it crumble to dust. The title Prince Adept meant *the best of our people chosen to act as Ecrea's hand*." He paused to let the phrase settle in the surrounding quiet as a ragged, weeping woman swirled in the fire. "The Coronated Speaker of the Ordena acted as Ecrea's voice and wisdom. Far below these giants of power and prestige was I, Master of the Scarlett Arch, an honor for my heroic actions while tending to the wounded in war. For my deeds, I was appointed head of the Aclamartom Sanctuary and Academy in Hiri Handi." He said while straightening up with a small amount of pride.

The Traveler saw a mangled man arise in the fire with the twisting head of an ostrich and a ram.

"The Prince Adept, all of us really, became obsessed with unlocking this world's deeper powers and secrets. Our obsession and haphazard methods caused unimaginable devastation to this realm and the sun plane."

"The sun plane?" the Traveler interrupted, pulling himself out of a foggy stupor.

"Ah, yes. We exist in a dual realm where one gently affects the other. What's left of this world was often called the moon plain due to our deep connections to magic and energy. The other was known as the sun plain for its burning will and deep passions."

Almerin leaned forward and carefully eyed the Traveler, who winced apprehensively. "I feel that you must have come from the sun plain, my friend. I have trained eyes, and although my memory has been dulled, my instincts and vision are still fairly decent. To my eyes, it is abundantly clear after spending this time with you. Although how someone from the sun realm became a Royal Vanguard and how you even came to this realm, as I was under the impression that the portal between our realms was sealed, are both profoundly interesting questions. I can scarcely imagine what chaos is transpiring in the sun plane." Almerin leaned back and let out a protracted sigh. He didn't continue immediately but instead sat quietly, either trying to rediscover his place in the story or marshaling the will to continue.

The smoldering fire, even the room, seemed to wait in bated breath for the old man to speak, and the Traveler found himself slowly drifting away, back into the swirling embers of the fireplace.

"We were able to tap into the heart of this world," Almerin continued at what now seemed like a distance to the Traveler. "The device of which is somewhere near the center of the city, deep within the high palace. For ages, we could carefully draw our power and wisdom from this seal. It held boundless energies, and even high masters from the sun plane would come here to see and experience this phenomenon. It was a gift from days older than time, and then inevitable war engulfed us," his face contorted with a miserable look as the low thumping of cannon fire suddenly rattled the room. "The other nations became jealous that our kingdom sat atop the single most important spot in the world. We tried to play the neutral party, mediating disputes without involving ourselves in military conflict. Unfortunately, as we grew more powerful and arrogant, the other nations began to seethe. A brutal, long, generational war engulfed us. Political radicalism thrived, and the devious traders from Posiid, an island nation which lay in the sun realm, began to buy more and more influence from us by selling armaments." The Traveler looked down at a golden rifle with a hard iron barrel, wrapping his fingers around it with glee.

"As the war raged on, the Prince Adept and his allies started to become callous, brutal, and eventually merciless against their foes. The Posiidians whispered poison in our ears, and we strode down the darker paths, which yielded tantalizing victory after victory."

The Traveler gazed across a dense crowd chanting, "Blood for blood," with such a terrifying ferocity that even the earth seemed to quake in fear.

"Finally," Almerin continued, "the Prince Adept marched on the seal, flanked by local and foreign supporters, determined to end the war with the power he felt the Coronated Speaker was hoarding. Although I had sealed myself in this tower when they bled our world, I could hear her cries as she was slain over the seal."

A single distant shriek cut across the room, and Almerin leaned forward with an empty look of destitution as everything suddenly grew quiet. No chanting crowd, no crackling fire, just quiet. A terrible, empty quiet.

"We suddenly gained a horrifying power that devastated all who stood against us as we upheaved the very ground with our fury. We leeched the very life around us to fuel our vengeance, and when the sun dwellers saw what was happening, saw the life in us slowly trickling to a stillness as a slow and insidious insanity began to rip us apart, they fled. They fled through their portal in Posiid and collapsed the bridge between our worlds. I don't know what became of them, only that they would never come again until now." He said, carefully regarding the Traveler. "Here, endless snow fell, and all life in the capital… well, slowly transformed into the monsters that hammer at my door, but I had special training. Training that allowed me to keep my faculties and slowly, over time, re-center myself."

The old man leaned back reflectively. The fireplace had grown dim but still stubbornly crackled with the last flickering ashes. "I simply watched everything around me burn from afar. Our entire world was not only thrown into chaos but was bludgeoned into near obliteration, and I honestly haven't left my tower since. It is a nightmarish affliction that we have created and which you are about to tread into." Almerin gazed across what little was left of the fire as he said, "Are you truly willing to face such a gruesome and horrific death for this cause?"

The near darkness frightened the Traveler, who took a pensive breath and then replied, "Is there another option?"

"Stay here and wait," Almerin let the sentence trail off.

"I think…," the Traveler paused with an unexpected hesitation. He wanted to say something brave like, *if I'm going to die, then I want my death to have meaning!* The truth, however, was that he didn't want to die. Staying here was accepting death. Going out was grasping at a chance to live, even if it was a slight chance. "I think we should go," was all he could muster to say.

"Then you should follow me," Almerin said as the fire's last embers withered into nothingness.

Almerin guided the Traveler down the winding stairs of the tower to the main entrance, where the suit of peculiar yellow and blue armor stood guarding the threshold of what little was left of the front door that the Traveler had thoroughly decimated earlier.

"How interesting," Almerin mused, approaching the armor while the Traveler kept a healthy distance behind. "It's almost like he knew it was finally the time."

"The time for what?"

Almerin kept his eyes fixed on the suit as he somberly answered, "To finally bury the past."

He suddenly turned to the Traveler, "This will be your armor now, and since it will become a metaphorical part of you, you deserve to know its history. Inside that suit," Almerin glanced over with a pained look of pity, "is the remnants of a man called Estrin. He used to guard this place, and when his life ended, I…" he paused with a look of shame, "reanimated what was left, so he could continue protecting the tower. It was an unholy and heinous endeavor, and I now must personally dig the grave that he deserves."

It took a moment for the Traveler to realize that he was being given a suit of armor containing a corpse, probably a rotting corpse. Before he could process a response, Almerin gestured toward the mortified Traveler and asked, "Can you fill the bath on the upper floor with scalding water? I will need to sterilize the armor. Please don't come back down here until I find you. It's not your burden to see what's become of Estrin."

The Traveler waited momentarily as a flood of questions and concerns rattled around his head, each vying to be blurted out first. What's so special about this armor? How did Estrin die? Should I wear anything that has to be sterilized? He finally settled on,

"Why this suit?"

Almerin looked at the Traveler with surprise, then at the armor, and back to the Traveler.

"Draw your sword."

The Traveler did so.

"Now, take a breath and close your eyes."

The Traveler hesitated with fear and uncertainty before finally shutting his eyes.

"Now concentrate on your sword."

"What?"

"Just focus on your sword," Almerin prompted.

The Traveler collected and marshaled his tired, nebulous mind to the sword and waited for anything to happen.

"Now open your eyes."

The Traveler did so and beheld his sword glowing a faint bluish color before tossing it to the checkered floor with a shriek.

Almerin muttered something disapprovingly before walking over and collecting the weapon. "Your sword is made of a very rare material, prized for its highly conductive properties. It's sensitive to energy, especially that of the creator, and is crafted to increase its effective cutting by a magnitude if energy is poured into it. The armor will respond in kind."

He respectfully passed the Traveler his sword and said, "Very few swords and even fewer suits of this composite were ever made due to the rarity of the metals. Your armor's hardening properties will be invaluable if you are intent on this mission."

The Traveler gingerly sheathed his no longer insignificant shard of a weapon as Almerin once again approached the suit of armor.

"You should find the bath on the upper floor. I have work to do."

CHAPTER THREE

The Outside

"I honestly don't know what the point of existing is anymore. Sometimes I think about taking a long walk outside, and letting the beasts devour me..."

-*Estrin Geanta*

Six months after the opening of the seal.

The helmet sizzled as Almerin dipped it into the scalding water. He swished it around the delicately carved bathtub with two long metal prongs and a pair of heavy gloves. He then gingerly pulled it out, took a deep breath, and, to the Traveler's astonishment, blew several puffs of fire over the helm.

Almerin glanced over to the mesmerized Traveler, sitting in a wooden chair he'd dragged into the door frame to watch.

"I'm surprised you haven't seen this type of magic before."

"I don't remember much of anything really."

"You clearly still have impressions. Your memory will return." Almerin blew several more puffs of fire and then dipped the helmet back into the water.

"The old teachings dissuade most uses of magic," Almerin began while letting the helmet soak. "They taught that miracles are true divine expressions of love, guided by your higher self, your spirit. Magic is the formation of a miracle via the ego, not guided by the higher spirit, and thus is inherently dangerous."

"I don't understand," the Traveler vacantly replied.

"It's okay. Miracles are complex affairs. We are mortal, bound to the world in our bodies, and our sight is limited because of this. Magic is performed with our limited sight, which means that any magic, even magic with good intentions, can be chaotic and damaging because we can't see the whole picture."

"Is what you're doing right now magic?"

"Yes."

"Then, isn't that bad?"

Almerin gave a pained smile, "I guess we thought we could see enough of the universe to perform magic safely, and I'm not sure if anyone even noticed when the quick use of magic superseded the sophisticated and deeply complex use of miracles. It doesn't matter much anymore, though. I've lost the ability to commune with my higher spirit, so chaotic magic will have to do." Almerin somberly gazed into the boiling tub of water as he muttered, "There's an irony that I've survived this long. I always was of the more reckless ilk. Well, until now." Almerin then turned to the Traveler. "Did you know that digging Estrin's grave was my first time outside in… well, I can't recall how many years? It was absolutely terrifying. The howling wind, the isolation, I didn't use to be a coward. I was actually near the front lines of a battle once. Maybe that's what sapped my constitution. I've heard that war hardens a person and gives them true strength. I never saw that. All I've seen war do is instill a bloodlust in some while sapping the life out of others, like a parasitic tumor."

Almerin glanced over at the Traveler, who hadn't spoken in fear of derailing this brief window into his new companion's soul.

"Kick over that armpiece, will you?"

The Traveler nudged the arm piece closer to Almerin, who grabbed it with the prongs and dunked it in the water.

"Can you teach me magic like this?"

"I shouldn't have to," Almerin replied while putting the helmet aside in a separate pile. "Royal Vanguards are usually taught some level of magic. It'll come to you along with your memory. If you want to speed up the process, I suppose you can meditate at the Sanctuary when we reach our destination. Speaking of which, I have a task for you," he suddenly announced.

"Uh, okay, sure."

"I need you to start taking inventory. I have a master list on my desk, near where you found me. Retrieve it and make sure the supplies are still there. This will be essential to our travels."

"Yeah, I can do th—" the Traveler stopped. At every turn, he only found this gibberish of a language. He, unfortunately, seemed to be illiterate. "Oh... err... actually no. I can't read anything."

Almerin gave him a surprised look, which quickly faded into an understanding nod. "That makes sense. After all, you're a sun dweller, and this isn't your natural language. Very well, I'll finish up here while you sort through and familiarize yourself with what gear you already have."

"I'll do that." The Traveler stood up and walked away as Almerin removed the arm piece from the boiling tub of water and blew another puff of fire.

The two later gathered in one of the upper floors of the tower, a spacious room with many windows that Almerin defrosted by placing his hands on the glass and melting away the ice. They revealed a stunning view of the glorious metropolis as Almerin unrolled a massive timeworn map on a heavy dark wood table that proudly crowned the center of the room.

"We are headed to the Aclamartom Sanctuary," he said, pointing to a tiny spot on the horrendously complex map. "It was a center for meditation and should offer me a clear sight to look across the city. Here's the path," he pointed to another tiny spot, which the Traveler struggled to even see.

"Do you have any bigger maps?" he finally asked. "This is complicated."

"I only have more complicated maps. Focus, here's the path," Almerin pointed again to the tiny spot. "We are cutting across the Student Chambers, the Archives, and finally the Sanctuary. Memorize this path!"

"How? I can't see it."

Almerin looked around, grabbed a pen, and drew a few lines to mark their journey.

The Traveler leaned over, tracing his finger across the map while carefully eyeing the path. Surprised, he pulled back and said, "This doesn't seem too far away."

"It isn't. The Sanctuary is right over there," Almerin pointed toward the school that sat right outside the window. "However, even that short distance could be fatal. We must be on our guard at all times."

The Traveler nodded in acknowledgment, and the two began gathering their gear. After reviewing their supplies one last time, they exited the tower through the front door that Almerin had hastily replaced with a spare wire gate that he had stuffed away in some corner of his tower.

Almerin shoved the gate open and moved outside into the faint orange glow of dusk with a somber, melancholic step. He took the lead, brandishing a spiraling gold staff with a bright red tip. The Traveler lumbered out in his new ill-fitting, cumbersome yellow and blue armor, a small blue cape fluttering behind him. Despite the weight and the hampered eyesight from his plumed helmet, it did fill him with a greater sense of safety than his old armor. He felt like a slow-moving wrecking ball, which gave him some small sense of calm in the treacherous environment he was now descending into. The Traveler lifted his visor and stood for a moment to bask in the pleasantness of the evening sun. He took a deep breath of the biting cold air and, feeling faintly nauseous, shut his visor and decided that he hated the outdoors. He continued walking to keep pace with his guide.

Almerin had provided him with rations, canteens, a small map, and some other minor objects that the Traveler didn't already have when he finally took the time to search the satchel and bags tied to his old armor. Although he didn't find a name buried in the clutter of stuff, it was clear that he did arrive in Hiri Handi well prepared. Even with the added provisions and the assistance of what appeared to be a very powerful sage, he felt vulnerable, anxious, and slightly dejected for having this monumentally perilous task placed before him.

As they walked halfway across the bridge, the Traveler froze in shock.

The monster's carcass was gone.

"Almerin?!"

Almerin stopped, "Yes?"

"Th… the… the bastard is gone!"

"The what?"

"The monster!"

Almerin gazed wearily at the Traveler, "What monster?"

"It was a giant *Thing* with giant *Fingers*! It attacked me before, and the guy who had my armor shot it!" The Traveler feverishly pointed down to the impression of the creature in the snow, "It died right there!!"

Almerin followed the Traveler's finger to the impression and took a hesitant breath. "By now, I thought you understood what you're walking into. Look over the side of the bridge and tell me what you see."

The Traveler was fearful and confused, but he tentatively bent over the ledge. His eyes beheld the metropolis again, which devoured his gaze with curiosity and awe.

The whole city seemed to be built in a massive canyon. The tower and other important-looking structures were either built along the edge, tall enough to rise up on their own, or built above other buildings on what looked like platforms. It was a beautiful yet jealous clutter, with all the towers desperately vying to be the tallest. In the distance, he saw the looming behemoth that he assumed to be the palace. It was a complicated network of spires, buttresses, and a few massive bridges that soared across the sky, all surrounding a foreboding central bastion.

He tore his gaze away and peered down as Almerin said. Below them was the rest of Hiri Handi, clouded in a thick darkness. The Traveler squinted to see any detail, but all he could make out were distant buildings and what seemed like rustling beneath the blanket of shadows. "Mostly darkness, although I think I saw something moving."

"What do you feel?"

"Feel?"

"Yes, focus on the shadows below."

The Traveler looked back down at the darkness and focused.

"Do you feel anything?"

"I don't know. Scared, hungry maybe."

Almerin snorted a half-chuckle, and pulled out a small, purple foil-wrapped bar from his bag and handed it to the Traveler. "Here, this might satiate and calm you."

It had bizarre lettering on it that the Traveler couldn't read. "What is this?"

"A snack bar, Omos, used to be my favorite. I would often carry at least one on me at all times. I packed a few more in your satchel."

The Traveler cautiously lifted his visor and then pulled away the foil to reveal a dark, blue-colored candy bar. It smelled pleasant enough.

He bit into it and tasted bitter richness with a very thin layer of syrup in the center.

Almerin glanced down at the city as the Traveler was greatly appreciating the blue candy bar.

"I can't tell you what that creature was. I've never seen something like that before, but I can tell you what I feel. Even though you meant yourself, you are not wrong. There is a hunger, a starvation down there."

Almerin looked up at the orange setting sun and directed the Traveler to follow his gaze. "The sun, moon, and ground beneath our feet are sources of energy, our life force," he began. "Although in this realm, we often rely more on the moon's influence than the sun. They are both powerful and gentle sources of energy."

"However," Almerin looked back to the Traveler, "when the seal was ripped open, it gushed out a massive amount of life force, imbuing our people with enormous power before it bled dry, shriveled, and pulled the whole city in with it. In this place, we are severed from Ecrea, heaven, and any other life. Energy is scarce, almost nonexistent. Therefore, the need is far greater, and the effects are far greater. Think of it as if everything and everyone is parched, and the sun and moon are the last droplets of water. Where we are, how we are, we can feel and receive both the sun's and the moon's energy. That was why the most important structures were built higher, although it was, in fact, selfish on our part to cover portions of the city. Normally, this would have been only an inconvenience, and people would have had just to travel higher every so often to adequately recharge. But now, it's become a haven for unimaginable terrors."

"Things that couldn't receive or were incapable of receiving the subtle droplets of energy left from the sun and moon clearly turned to more primordial forms of claiming energy." Almerin walked over to the Traveler and peered over the side of the bridge.

"When I look down there, I feel a horrible, painful starvation. There are things now that will do whatever it takes to get life force. Even cannibalize their brethren to feed at the denser energies contained in the body." He pulled his gaze away from the shadows below and steadied himself on the railing, looking as though merely glancing down had taken something from him.

"Opening the seal affected everyone differently," he continued. "I imagine that those who operated on a baser level of existence, who operated on a level of impulse rather than forethought and compassion, found themselves becoming…" he looked over to where the creature had been and let the sentence trail off. "We must remain as high as possible, for my friend, I fear the darkness below."

The Traveler now understood why Almerin was so hesitant to go. He didn't even want to leave now! The Traveler took a terrified mouthful of Omos and looked back down at the darkness with visible dread.

There was a moment's pause as they both contemplated how much they didn't want to be there.

"You might not know this," Almerin began, in a markedly lighter tone, "but the bridges that extend from the palace took longer to build than the palace itself — seventy years, in fact."

"Seventy years?" The Traveler knew what he was trying to do and was thankful for the distraction, "Why on Earth would you build anything that takes seventy years?"

"On Earth? That's an expression I haven't heard before."

The Traveler stopped and realized that he had indeed used the word Earth and with some vague understanding of what it meant. It felt like his home or something similar.

Before he could follow this train, Almerin continued. "The four bridges that extend from the palace are known as the Sovereign Roads. Those bridges were the height of human engineering and achievement. Not even the Posiidians, sun dwellers who had surpassed us technologically, although not spiritually, had built anything like this. A magnificent, monumental, and outright unnecessary colossus of engineering! Flying would have absolutely been simpler," he said while tracing his hand across the sky, "but we instead built bridges that you could walk across for hours and hours without getting exhausted or even winded. You could even go barefoot without any pain or discomfort! Although appallingly inefficient, it was a marvelous masterpiece." Almerin had a distant look in his eyes, and the Traveler simply didn't know how to respond to his enthusiasm. "Come," Almerin finally motioned. "You'll get to see this bridge firsthand when we get there."

The Traveler shut his visor, and they continued onwards with a forced air of optimism that thinly covered a deep apprehension. They crossed the tower bridge and entered the main complex. Almerin led the way, pausing every few steps to brush his hand over a cracked mirror or gaze at a faded painting with a broken frame. He stopped and grimaced at the shattered window that the Traveler had broken in through. "This place used to be cleaner," he thoughtfully remarked while stepping over some shattered glass.

The Traveler didn't say anything, and they continued on. Dark corridors shot out every few steps, and the Traveler nervously peered down each one before passing by, looking for any sign of the monster that was no doubt lurking somewhere nearby. They moved deeper into the dark and desolate academy until a sudden lack of windows stopped them.

"Do we have a light?" the Traveler inquired, suspiciously eyeing the wall of blackness ahead of them.

"Something of a light, yes." Almerin tapped his staff on the ground and created a frail, luminous orb atop its tip that gave off enough of a thin glow to let them see ahead. They marched on through the increasingly narrow passageways until they came upon a large dark wood door with tarnished hinges and peculiar etchings. Almerin turned a grimy doorknob, and nothing happened.

"What?" Almerin exclaimed in disbelief.

The Traveler nervously leaned forward, "What's the matter? Are we in danger?"

"No," Almerin replied, hastily feeling around in his pockets. "At least not that I'm aware of. The door is just locked!"

The Traveler quietly stood by as Almerin pulled out a substantial key ring and fumbled through the mass of keys for the right one, trying several into the lock that didn't fit.

"This is why the door was never supposed to be locked," he bitterly muttered.

The Traveler had nothing to do or say except watch the old man's increasingly desperate attempts to open the door with a fading sense of safety.

"Ah ha!" Almerin finally proclaimed in victory amidst the satisfying crack of the tumblers. He pushed the heavy door open, revealing a grey brick circular room with a pale ceiling, a soft grass floor, and a delicate glass fountain in the center trickling water into a crystalline basin. Two passageways shot off on separate sides of the room, lit by a series of small round lights built into the construction of the walls.

Almerin slowly stepped inside while gasping quietly to himself.

"Is everything okay?"

"This… this is the Labyrinth." he started in bewilderment. "The Labyrinth is supposed to be far below us with the rest of the training center!"

"I don't understand." The Traveler stepped inward, and suddenly, as if it had been waiting for this very moment, the heavy door behind them slammed shut with a skull-rattling bang. Almerin spun around in horror while the Traveler shrieked, "We're TRAPPED!" and scrambled to the door in a fruitless effort to wrench it back open.

"Traveler, step aside!"

The tip of Almerin's staff was leaking a furious red glow, and it was aimed at the door like a cannon ready to fire. The Traveler hastily slid out of the way, and they both inched backward until they hit the end of the room behind them. Almerin took a deep breath and then discharged an ear-cracking bolt, followed by a concussion blast that punched both of them into the cold, unyielding brick wall. They groaned and staggered upright as the cloud of dusty rubble that once was a door slowly settled.

The dark and musty academy corridor they came from had quietly morphed into another simple grey brick passageway, utterly unremarkable in form yet absolutely terrifying to the Traveler, who cried, "Almerin, what's happening?"

Almerin straightened up and stared with fearful bewilderment at the new corridor. "The Labyrinth..." He weakly answered, "Has made its way into the upper academy."

"WHAT IS THE LABYRINTH!?"

Almerin turned to the Traveler and took a shaky breath to calm himself before answering, "It's a tool used for training precognitive abilities, and the only thing you need to solve it is a good intuition or," Almerin dug around in his pocket and pulled out a golden triangle, "a key."

"So, we're safe?" The Traveler wearily ventured.

"No, not in the slightest. But we're not trapped." Almerin turned away from the Traveler and took a cautious step forward to take in the environment as if to glean some elusive secret. "The Labyrinth doesn't grow," he mused. "It doesn't extend past where it was built. So how would this be possible?"

The Traveler had nothing to contribute, so he stayed silent and watched the old magician muddle through the problem.

Almerin walked over, put his hand on one of the walls, and thoughtfully bowed his head. For a moment, the Traveler thought something incredible might happen. He held his breath as Almerin stepped away with a defeated sigh. "I don't understand what's happening here," Almerin admitted, "so we should be cautious during our escape. Expect some sort of attack."

The ghastly monster with the hanging jaw crawled across the Traveler's imagination. He stepped closer to Almerin, who held out the golden triangle and pressed it into the wall, causing a luminous yellow line to suddenly cut across the room and down one of the corridors.

"That's our exit," Almerin announced. They both began following the line.

Their shoes crunched into the short grass floor as they weaved and swerved through the featureless narrow passageways. It darted and twisted along the claustrophobic channels until it suddenly broke into a startlingly open space. A tall grey ceiling arched over several thin, willowy trees wisping out of closely trimmed grass. Short grey bridges connected passageways far above while scattered tunnels and pits broke apart the ground at their feet. Despite the unnatural environment that confused and unsettled the Traveler, the line never wavered. It simply zoomed across the walls, jumping past false corridors and ducking into the one true path. They devoutly followed the line across the stark clearing and slid further into the depths of this strange construction. They marched on and on for what felt like ages through similar passageways that all began to blend into a featureless mess of confusion. The Traveler didn't know how far in the maze they were. He liked to think they were deep within the cold and baffling Labyrinth, maybe even near its heart, and it wouldn't be much longer before they reached its end. In truth, he had no idea. They could have only scratched the surface of a system of madness that stretched out for years.

He started to ask Almerin if he knew how far they were when a disgusting scent suddenly assaulted him. He stopped, gasping and coughing.

"What the hell is that!" he sputtered.

Almerin looked around, trying to catch the direction of the scent, and then took a few steps to peer around the corner of a false passage that the line was bypassing. He ventured further into the corridor and away from the main path, with the Traveler hastily following behind. Almerin followed the scent to an intersection with a large, wilted tree that aggressively branched outward with a fierce, dominating presence that protected a lump of something at its base. Underneath was its charge, a creature that had sought safety under the tree's grand presence. A corpse was sprawled atop its wide roots, ripped open and torn to pieces with blood and gore splattered everywhere. The Traveler took a morbid step closer, and had it not been for the grand shadows of the tree that blanketed the horror, he would have vomited on the spot. He staggered a good distance out of sight from the grisly spectacle and leaned on a wall to collect himself.

Almerin approached him from behind and placed a hand on the Traveler's shoulder.

"Did the monster do that?" the Traveler weakly asked.

"If not, then something similar did. We are not in a place of..." Almerin suddenly stopped mid-sentence to gaze guardedly at his surroundings.

The same thought barreled through the Traveler's mind like a train wreck. "Do you think the monster changed the Labyrinth?"

"I don't know how that would even be possible. But..."

"So, what do we do?" the Traveler whined.

"Get to the exit. Kill the manifestation of primordial hunger if it approaches us."

"That isn't a plan!"

Almerin put his hand on the Traveler's shoulder. "We can't out-hunt it, not in here, at least. All we can do is march with a clear purpose and intimidate it. Either we bluff the creature, and it leaves us alone, or it makes an attempt on us, in which case we kill it thoroughly."

The Traveler gawked at the forest of paths surrounding them, uttering a slight whimper. He hated this place.

"I'll lead," Almerin announced. "You keep hold of my hand and watch behind us. Pay attention to the corners."

The Traveler nodded and grasped Almerin's hand like one might grasp a life raft at sea. They slowly slid away from the gruesome scene and once again began following the yellow line that was gracious enough to extend itself to Almerin's detour.

No monster yet.

Although they continued to weave and turn through the passages, they now walked at a nervously subdued pace, with Almerin cautiously peering around every corner they came to. The Traveler anxiously held his sword outwards to ward off any attacks. He didn't know if it would actually help him, but it made him feel a little better.

Still no monster.

At every corner, the Traveler envisioned that monstrous, deformed hand reaching out to pull him in. At every lengthy corridor they walked through, he imagined turning around to suddenly find Almerin gone, without a trace. Out of the corner of his eyes, he could almost perceive movement in the distance, but he was never entirely sure. However, the worst part for him was a subtle tapping in the back of his head that told him the yellow line wasn't leading them anywhere. The Labyrinth had changed, so why wouldn't the line be altered as well? He stuffed the thought into a small closet in the depths of his mind, where it restlessly rattled about, waiting to jump out.

Still no monster.

They continued inch after painful inch, wading through the burning swamp of prolonged paranoia that slowly wore down and frayed the Traveler's constitution. The fight-or-flight instinct is a powerful and integral tool for survival. However, when you can do neither for hours at a time, it suddenly becomes vital that you're able to calm yourself and stifle the instinct. Otherwise, it insidiously eats away at the mind and can cause you to make terrible mistakes.

Just as they passed a four-way intersection, a clank suddenly echoed out, and the Traveler screamed and spun around, swinging wildly in the air.

Almerin quickly grabbed his arm and halted his vigorous assault before either of them was injured. He didn't say a word but just stared at the Traveler with a fierce glare, who, in turn, relaxed and lowered his sword. Almerin pointed to the left path, one that the line was avoiding, and then pointed straight ahead, motioning that they should keep following the line. They carefully bypassed the left path, the Traveler keeping watch over the rear as they went.

Finally, they marched up several steps, and Almerin released his hand. He quickly whirled around to see a large, deep blue door built into the labyrinth wall.

Almerin tried to open it, but it didn't budge. This couldn't be how it ended, stopped right at the exit by a locked door. The Traveler swallowed his raging fears and waited for Almerin's next plan.

Almerin turned to the Traveler and whispered, "I have the key to unlock the door. Just keep an eye behind us as I unlock it."

The Traveler nodded and nervously twitched as he turned around to keep watch, expecting the very worst to befall them.

No sight of the creature.

Almerin turned the handle again and nudged it, but nothing happened. He mumbled at low breath as he once again pulled out the key ring and, to the Traveler's horror, began to sift through each key again.

"Don't you remember the key?" the Traveler hissed.

"Yes, it's the same one I used to enter."

"Then why..."

"Because I put it back on the ring," Almerin quietly retorted.

"Why!?"

"Because force of habit. I'll have it open in a moment. Just keep watch."

"Can't you use magic?"

"I don't know what will happen if I blow it open. I'll have it in a moment."

With an unraveling psyche, the Traveler turned his full attention back to the Labyrinth and continued to keep watch. Nothing of the monster could be seen, but it had ample space amidst the myriad of passageways to hide. The Traveler tightened his grip around his sword and gazed across a large room filled with thin, willowy trees and perilous corridors. It only took a few agonizing minutes, but without a word, Almerin swung open the door. They both darted inside, shutting it with a thud and locking it behind them.

CHAPTER FOUR

The Autumn Colored Garden

"Do you know what's wrong with the Labyrinth yet?"

"It's not being manipulated by the Prince Adept. I think it might be alive..."

-The Expedition Party, on orders to ascertain the nature of the Labyrinth's change.

Forty-three years after the opening of the seal.

They came out into a large, empty hallway illuminated by a series of more reasonably proportioned windows, all desperately endeavoring to let in what was left of the feeble light of dusk.

The Traveler leaned against a musty wall and took a moment to recover from his most recent traumatizing experience.

Almerin took a few frail steps inward and watched as the Traveler fumbled around his bag for something to drink. "This was just the first of many encounters," he warned.

"I know," the Traveler grumbled, straightening up slightly. Knowing didn't help, though.

A tattered blue carpet rolled aggressively across the relatively barren hall. It didn't so much direct but demand all attention be brought toward two enormous dark iron doors. The doors boasted black carvings of trees and plants. It towered above them with a foreboding presence amplified by the dimness of the room and the unsettling lack of ambient noise. The doors emanated a profound power that deeply unsettled the Traveler.

He lowered his canteen and asked, "Are you sure this is the right way?"

"Fear not Traveler. This is a place of rest. It is ancient and has defenses, but none that will harm the peaceful-minded. Some even say it was built before the city itself as a refuge for the tired and weary."

Almerin approached the doors, put both hands on them, and, to the Traveler's astonishment, pushed them aside with ease. A few apprehensive steps forward, and the Traveler was able to peer inside.

It was a garden filled with massive twisting trees, winding stone paths, and quiet streams that had yet to freeze over despite the blistering cold of Hiri Handi's endless winter. The ceiling was domed with paneled glass. It seemed that little, if any, snow had collected to block out the fading orange sunlight that bathed over the ancient benches and bridges scattered every which way across the tranquil garden. The Traveler stepped inside with a quiet reverence. It was somewhat chilly, although not nearly as much as outside or in the academy. All the garden's trees and plants had lost most of their leaves, which were sprinkled across the ground in vibrant orange, red, and yellow colors. In truth, the garden felt more asleep than lifeless. All he could hear was the water from the streams quietly trickling away.

"Incantations and miracles require a steady, calm mind," Almerin explained, talking in a respectfully low tone. "This is the Aclamartom Sanctuary, where all practitioners would come when the burdens of the physical world became too much to bear. It brings back many fond memories, even if this place has slipped into a deep slumber." Almerin softly wandered into the garden, "Take some time to meditate, maybe even practice some magic. This is a peaceful place, and nothing here will hurt you. I must gaze across what's left of the city to see where we stand."

"Wait, how do I practice magic?"

"Just focus on what part of the world draws you and see if any memories return."

And with that, he meandered over to the garden's edge, passing through a thin wooden door which he gently closed behind him.

The Traveler gazed around at his invitingly mysterious environment. The wooded paths and small shrines dotting the area stirred an unexpected desire to run around and explore, while the trickling streams and silent trees invited rest and healing. He did feel safer now, so much so that he raised his visor, which until now had remained firmly shut. He took a deep sigh, one which seemed caught in his chest, and allowed himself to close his eyes for just a moment and bask in the peacefulness of a room that seemed to sweep him up with promises of safety and peace. He opened his eyes in search of a nice bench where he could relax and jolted at the sight of two figures sitting far away at the opposite ends of the garden.

"Almerin." the Traveler shouted. "We aren't alone!"

Almerin didn't respond, and the Traveler quickly shut his visor again, which filled him with a mixed feeling of despair and agitation.

He paused momentarily as something deep inside beckoned him forward, almost whispering in his ear. Against his better judgment, he drew his sword and cautiously approached with his weapon held outward. He took soft steps as he neared the leftward individual, wishing not to make much more noise than he already had. As he guardedly approached, he could perceive the form of a man dressed in similar armor to what he himself had woken up in. His blond hair was disheveled, and a thick beard covered a narrow face with a sickly pale complexion. He was perched on a stone bench with his hands held outwards while quietly muttering to himself in a way that projected insanity. The stranger slowly looked up at the Traveler, who nervously stood on the other side of the thin dirt path that separated the two. The Traveler held his shattered weapon to the side in a guarded stance as the stranger gave a pained laugh and rhetorically asked the Traveler, "I didn't do well, did I?" The stranger's trembling hands were covered in a shocking amount of blood, but the man himself had no wounds.

"I don't think I did well at all," the man lamented. "I'm so sorry I couldn't help you..." And with that, he faded away.

The Traveler stood alone in silence. He felt so sure he knew this person. It wasn't a loving connection, like a sibling, but it still twisted something deep inside him. A friend maybe? He quickly glanced to the side and saw that the other individual was still sitting at the far end of the garden. He swiftly hopped over a patch of bushes and darted along the stone paths much less quietly and carefully than before, with his weapon sheathed. As he made his way across the faded roads and through the leafless thickets, he came close enough to perceive a woman dressed in a similar armor as him and the other man, but it was brighter and far more regal than his or the bloody stranger. She, too, looked battered and bruised but not as sickly as the man before. She had dark brown hair, sharp hazel eyes, and a robust but bitter face with lines too deep for her age. She sat staring blankly into the sleeping garden. The Traveler slowly approached and sat beside her, unsure if he should say anything. She turned to face him with a startled shock that quickly sank back into an expressionless apathy.

"I'm sorry," she said with a biting indifference, "For what happened to you, but you were never the one we really needed."

Her statement was resolute, and her eyes looked hollow and empty. The Traveler stared into them as she faded into nothingness, leaving him with a chilling sense of dread. He got up and resolved to find Almerin. Backtracking his way through the sanctuary, he caught sight of the little wooden door Almerin had disappeared through. He approached the door, twisted the small, rusted handle, and found it unlocked. The door opened to an undecorated stone staircase that he quickly jogged up, hastily tracing the side of the sanctuary until he reached the top, where he was met with another thin wooden door.

He opened it slightly. "Almerin?" he tentatively asked, peeking his head inside a pale beige room.

"It doesn't make any sense," Almerin weakly replied.

The Traveler took a breath of relief and stepped through the door. It wasn't a large room; maybe four people could comfortably fit inside. Almerin sat on a small, ragged carpet surrounded by a few burning candles. Before him was a massive, black framed window overlooking the vast expanse of the city.

"It doesn't make any sense. He should be here," Almerin distraughtly muttered to himself.

"What doesn't make any sense?"

Almerin turned with such a look of profound dread that it seemed to wither the thin light of the candles and quake the fragile walls of the claustrophobic room. The Traveler took a frail step back as the old man said, "I can't sense the Prince Adept, Traveler. I should be able to sense something, anything from him, even his rotting corpse! But I can't feel him at all!"

"What does that mean?"

"It means he did the impossible. Not only did he survive opening the seal, but he truly left the city."

"So does that mean Maalen was right?"

Almerin bowed his head and took a moment to center himself. He then looked out over the cityscape and said, "I cannot adequately express the severity of the situation. From here, I even feel his influence swathed over my tower. He wanted me there." He looked back up at the Traveler. "For someone to survive what he did with his faculties intact and to be able to not only manipulate but leave the city entirely, which is falling between the cracks of dimensions as we speak!" He took a breath to calm himself, "Presents a grave threat to all realms, including yours. We must get to the seal at once and close it. I sense the Prince Adept left what remains of his personal guard, Bakar, to watch over the seal, and we will have to overcome him. After that, I really don't know what must be done, but I'm sure we will find it along the way." To the Traveler's surprise, Almerin leaped up with a robust energy fueled by utter terror. "We must move quickly, my friend. Let us depart at once!" and then he darted down the stairs with the Traveler struggling to keep pace. They wound past the sanctuary's sleeping trees until they finally came to its end. They stood before two startlingly massive, black metal doors covered in indiscernible markings. The colossal doors towered in size over them, making the Traveler feel small and insignificant as he stood with his head bent back to take it all in. He looked over as Almerin approached the door and touched his finger to the tip of his staff, which gave a soft red glow. He then drew a series of luminescent symbols on the door with his hand. The Traveler couldn't even begin to understand what he was looking at as the symbols seemed to shift, change, and squirm across the door as if Almerin had suddenly created life. When he was done, Almerin stepped back, and the doors hummed and chimed. They suddenly began to swing open with a deep rumble that made its way through the Traveler's bones, a rumble which could have easily been interpreted as a warning.

The sun split through the cracks and poured into the room until the doors finally parted to the snow-laden courtyard of the Aclamartom sanctuary. A wide-open space blanketed by a thick layer of pristine, white snow stretched out before them. Lofty houses and sweeping, elegant structures lined the periphery, with several frozen fountains lined in rows leading to a bridge. Directly ahead was one of the Sovereign Roads, a massive bridge that shot straight to the palace a great distance beyond. The palace seemed to shimmer and weave unnaturally like some sort of echo that wasn't quite there. The Traveler nervously eyed their far-flung destination while Almerin stepped outside and took a deep breath.

"It's been far too long since I've been here," he somberly reflected.

They both stepped out of the warm and welcoming garden of the sanctuary and into the frigid, bitter cold of Hiri Handi. They steadily approached the bridge directly ahead, the thick snow crunched beneath their footsteps as they marched. A disturbing quiet surrounded them. Even the lightly tumbling snow and softly swaying wind seemed hushed in anticipation. The Traveler uneasily glanced at Almerin, who apparently shared his anxiety as he glanced nervously around the expansive courtyard.

A sudden clank rattled out, and they both froze and whisked around to quickly identify the noise. A small, tattered white flag with an interweaving purple diamond at its center trembled atop a flag pole off to the side.

"How odd," Almerin quietly mused as the flag, having finally been acknowledged, stopped moving.

The Traveler pointed up at the banner and said, "I saw something like that at the cemetery. What is it?"

"The flag of Itzalla, our Grand Banner," Almerin proudly answered with a bitter touch of irony. "It represents the perfect balance between the masculine, symbolized by the pyramid, and the feminine, symbolized by the delta. It also depicts the ideal government, commanded by few on the top, balanced by many in the middle, leaving few on the bottom. The center is interconnected to represent the divine harmony when such a balance is achieved."

The Traveler almost remarked that if the flag represented perfection, then why were they standing at its grave, but he quickly caught himself when he saw Almerin mournfully gazing up at the motionless banner.

Almerin sighed, took a few steps forward, and held out his staff, which sparked and singed through the rope tying the flag to its mast. It fell with a muffled thump into the snow, and Almerin walked over and began to respectfully fold it into a diamond.

Even though Hiri Handi had so far done nothing but project pain and agony onto the Traveler, a part of him couldn't help but feel some of the same reverence for the city that Almerin did. He didn't believe he'd ever lived here, but he could easily see its former brilliance peeking through its hollowed husk. As he watched Almerin fold and then set fire to the flag with the solemnity of a funeral, he suddenly understood how much Almerin was part of the city, sharing in both its former majesty and its current decay.

They marched on and quickly reached the beginning of the bridge, which was only covered in a light layer of snow, unlike the rest of the courtyard. It was tremendous, as if expecting a horde of people to suddenly rush upon its flawless, slightly glossy surface. Almerin gently stepped onto the bridge and looked back at the Traveler with a hopeful elation.

"It works! All this time, and it still works! With this, we can easily reach the palace."

The Traveler also stepped onto the bridge and felt the dull aches in his limbs fade, and his energy strengthen. He optimistically looked ahead and saw the looming, shadowy fortress in the distance. It was a clear path, but a bitter, sobering draught of cynicism washed over him, and he turned to Almerin. "What if it's a trap?"

"Judging by our experiences in the archives, a trap is certainly a distinct possibility. My friend, I think we both feel the looming danger. But this is the most direct and safest path to the palace. All others might force us below the darkness and put us in even greater harm."

Almerin began to walk onwards but stopped when the Traveler didn't move.

He turned back and said, "This is the safest way. I assure you."

"Well, what about help? Shouldn't we look for allies?"

"Traveler, I've felt what little was left in this great mausoleum of a city," Almerin said with a grim shadow across his face. "There is only madness, pain, and horrors that would eviscerate the both of us. Any forces that we could potentially pull out of that seeping abyss would be mangled, broken, and near useless. I'm sorry to say this, but it's just us."

The Traveler walked a few paces forward and clasped his hands on the bridge's perfectly molded railing. He bent over the side of the bridge and peered down, trying again to see for himself what was lying below them. No detail could be seen, but he thought he saw movement again in the murky black soup beneath them. He stepped back and nodded, "Alright, what should we expect from the trap then?"

"The palace has defenses in the form of massive black birds that rest atop the spires and buttresses. These birds can not only do horrendous damage themselves but can also bring stonework warriors who do equal, if not more harm. If they come, stay close to me. My powers are more effective against them than yours, even with your armor."

The Traveler glanced over the side of the bridge again and, feeling faintly nauseous, looked back at Almerin.

Almerin faintly smiled and led the way as they began their journey across the bridge.

The Traveler expected to be exhausted or at least winded after walking half of the enormous bridge, but surprisingly, he was still as fresh and invigorated as when he first set off. Almerin had not exaggerated the bridge's unusual nature. They walked quietly for much of the time. It wasn't an awkward silence, where neither knew what to say, but rather a restful, peaceful silence. They were far above the horrors below them, walking across this great sturdy bridge that propelled them onwards to the heart of Hiri Handi itself, the palace. The

Traveler didn't fear whatever monsters might pour out its wretched gates. They were prepared, and their might would surely cut through any beasts that came to face them. He gazed around, taking in his surroundings with a swelling pride in his chest while Almerin occasionally hummed a small tune that only barely reached the Traveler's ears. Almerin was in remarkably good spirits as well, despite his panic back at the sanctuary. The Traveler's mind drifted back to the two disturbingly familiar apparitions he met in the garden and thought that this was as good a time as any to ask Almerin about it. "Almerin?"

Almerin turned his head, "Yes?"

"I saw two people in the sanctuary after you left me alone. A man and a woman."

Almerin raised an eyebrow.

"They felt so familiar, but I can't remember who they were. Do you think they're ghosts?"

"The sanctuary is a point of incredible power," Almerin answered after a moment of consideration. "And it draws many entities under those great trees. Did they come to you with a specific message?"

"Yes. The first one I met was wounded and told me he was sorry. The second one gave a half-hearted apology and then said I was never the one they needed."

Almerin huffed. "You have a very cold acquaintance, my friend. If they are from your current life and not some ancient incarnation, then I'd imagine they were apologizing for whatever incident caused your scar." Almerin pointed to the Traveler's breastplate, under which was the horrific scar the young adventurer woke up with.

The Traveler instinctively moved his hand over his chest. Whatever happened to him must have been grisly to cause that wound. This made him suddenly indignant that he only got a feeble apology from the woman he spoke to. Surely, he deserved more than that!

"Do you remember anything else about them?"

The Traveler shook his head. "Not really, no."

"Well, you've come from the sun realm," Almerin began following a thread of logic. "But you have a sword from the Royal Order of the Sky. That means you've been in contact with the people of this world while you were here on whatever mission you set out to complete. They clearly thought highly enough of you to make you a Royal Vanguard and, though this is only an assumption, felt regret at whatever catastrophe led to your near demise." Almerin pointed at the Traveler's chest again. "After that, Maalen and her ethereal fellows healed you and then sent you off to find me and close the seal. That's, at least, my working hypothesis so far."

"But are those two people I met still alive? And what was my mission to begin with?"

"I have absolutely no idea," Almerin resigned. "It's your memory, not mine. If either of the two apparitions you met are still alive, I'm sure your memory will jolt if we meet them. Other than that, I don't really — " A tremor rippling through the bridge stopped him mid-sentence.

"What was that?" the Traveler glanced over at Almerin, who was struggling to make out something in the distance. The bridge rippled again, and the Traveler saw a cloud of smoke erupt far ahead of them.

"Run!" Almerin shouted. "Run, boy, RUN!!!" and Almerin suddenly bolted back to the sanctuary. The Traveler scrambled behind him as the bridge shook again, and again, and again. With each shake, a louder thundering boom got ever closer and closer. The Traveler ran faster than he thought possible, even with his cumbersome armor, keeping closely behind Almerin, who ran with what felt like inhuman speed. No matter how fast they ran, the thundering boom kept closing in. The Traveler turned to catch a glimpse of what was happening and saw the bridge erupting behind him as clouds of debris went flying every which way.

And the explosions were gaining on them.

He shrieked and continued trailing Almerin, who was shouting a symphony of blasphemies. The end of the bridge was in sight, and they both hastened as quickly as their exhausted, wheezing bodies could take them. The Traveler felt small rocks from the explosions lightly pattering off his armor. His ears were ringing, and his chest and legs felt like they were about to crumble into mush. They made it to the end and leaped off the bridge into the snowy courtyard of the sanctuary, where one last explosion blew a cloud of smoke and dust over them both. They were huddled in the snow, still shielding their heads in shock, gasping for air.

Then, after a moment or two, Almerin struggled up with a cough and stumbled to the edge of what used to be the bridge. The Traveler was too tired and stunned to get up, so he watched from the ground, still gasping for breath.

Almerin gazed in a destitute silence over the broken bridge until finally he muttered, "One hundred years… One hundred years to build, and you destroy the wretched bridge!" he roared at the empty air before him.

"You! You Foul Machination of Stupidity! Curse you!! ETERNAL DAMNATION UPON YOU!!!" He then moaned and slumped to the ground with his face in his hands.

The Traveler marshaled what little strength he had left and stood up with several aching curses. He then stumbled breathlessly over to the battered old man. "Almerin?"

Almerin turned to him with a look of bitter melancholy.

"Are you ok?"

"To be perfectly honest," he exhaled. "I've been much better. I had a lot of memories tied to that bridge. Just fond memories to ashes. Like everything else."

Then, something far across the broken bridge caught the Traveler's eye. In the distance, a black swarm of something hazy was approaching, and the Traveler's stomach sank at the sight of it. "Almerin?"

"I see it. Those would be the palace defenses." Almerin shot up off the ground, startling the Traveler while shoving a green stone in his hand. "Quickly, we haven't much time. Into the Sanctuary!" Almerin bolted across the frozen courtyard towards the sanctuary, with the Traveler following closely behind, clutching the green stone until its power faded and then tossing it to the side. Once inside, Almerin and the Traveler heaved both great doors shut. Almerin banged his staff several times, and the same runic symbols appeared. The doors creaked and moaned, then stood silent.

"That should buy us a moment at least."

"What, are we just going to wait here?" the Traveler protested between haggard gasps for air.

Almerin banged his staff on the ground, this time away from the door. The Traveler looked up in shock as the whole garden groggily awoke from its deep slumber. Trees began to creak and crack as they flexed their branches, and hordes of luminous blue insects crawled out from their ancient bark and began to make sweeping passes above in swarms. "That's exactly what we are going to do," Almerin declared. "Now, go to the largest tree. Dig your hand into its bark, and if fate be kind, you'll pull out something. Go, quickly!"

The Traveler didn't even begin to understand this bizarre order, but he obeyed regardless. He dashed into the garden, passing under shifting trees and ducking away from terrifying swarms of luminescent bugs. He found what he considered to be the largest tree in the center of the garden. Though it had few leaves, it towered in might and bulk above the rest. He stood at its base and, as Almerin instructed, burrowed his hand into its trunk. To his wonder, it broke apart easily. He felt something gooey within its aged bark and carefully drew it out.

He held in his hand a disgusting heart made from wood and oozing sap. It was an unsettling thing that he could almost feel beating as if it were alive. He didn't have much time to study the horrible artifact when a loud crack from above froze his blood. Massive charcoal black birds carrying stone knights flew over the glass dome covering the sanctuary. One by one, they dropped the warriors onto the glass, who then began to hammer it with their spears and swords. Although Almerin told him to expect this very assault, seeing it firsthand was an entirely different matter.

The Traveler was not brave. He didn't want to be here. All he wanted to do was find a small room and lock himself inside until the many terrors around him went away. He would have gladly stayed with Almerin in his tower had it not been for his nagging compulsion to survive. He gawked at the stone knights, screamed, and flailed back through the shuddering trees, under the swarming insects, and returned to Almerin, sputtering and stammering breathlessly as he tried to chaotically recount what he'd seen.

"I know, I know. My friend, be calm. Did you pull anything out of the tree?"

The Traveler showed him the oozing, sappy heart.

"Incredible. You'll have to let me look at it when this is over." Before the Traveler could ask what it even was, the door behind them banged and creaked. "We don't have much time," Almerin shouted over the noise. "Stay close to me. If we're together, then we have a chance to survive this."

The Traveler stuffed the wooden heart into his satchel as the door boomed again, and the glass above began to crack. The Traveler shakily readied his sword while Almerin closed his eyes and muttered what seemed like a prayer.

The Traveler didn't want to die.

The glass above broke first. The stone knights fell in droves, with many being caught and torn to shreds by the hordes of insects and the thundering branches of the trees. Almerin pounded his staff on the ground, which sent out a flurry of red bolts hurtling toward any fighters that had made it to the garden floor. The Traveler watched in horror. He felt insignificant and fragile, even with his hulking yellow armor. The doors behind them boomed and shook louder than before. Immense birds hurtled through the garden, and a troop of warriors who had survived were now hacking their way through the thickets to Almerin's position. Then the doors broke open. A horde of the fighters poured through like a tidal wave and fiercely slammed against a hastily made energy barrier that Almerin struggled to keep up. He shouted something to the Traveler, but the novice fighter couldn't listen.

This was it, the Traveler thought to himself. They were going to die. He had to make a choice...

The Traveler's mind spun in terror as he scrambled away from Almerin's cries to come back and barreled into the mess of the sanctuary. He tripped on a moving vine and tumbled over. Everything was spinning, and he felt sick, but he found his sword and sluggishly stood up.

Chaos surrounded him. Massive birds were now pulling off whole tree limbs, and stone warriors were slashing and dodging at their base. All the while, the trees were thrashing and upheaving the ground around them. He was scared, scared with the deep type of fear that sinks past your nerves and into your soul. He stood motionless as the melee swirled around him. His mind was collapsing inwards.

A vine suddenly swept under his leg and pulled him to the ground, saving him from a colossal branch that flew right over his head. This jarred him enough to bring him back to his senses.

He had to move fast!

In a fear-pitched haze, he scrambled across the embattled sanctuary, trying desperately to find a way out. He quickly cut across the garden and suddenly stood face to face with four stone warriors. He didn't have time to think. He slammed his sword into the closest one with all the force he had. The blade landed clean on the warrior's neck and just sat there pulsating with the Traveler's energy. It barely made a crack. The Traveler bolted in the other direction quicker than the warriors could respond. He ducked and dodged his way through the battle as the clattering footsteps of the fighters closed in on him. Had it not been for the old masters who prioritized strength and endurance over speed and agility when creating these soldiers, the Traveler would have been quickly overcome and killed.

Finally, he saw a door and quickly ducked inside, slamming it shut behind him. Straight away, he recognized the passageway and staircase leading to the beige meditation room he had found Almerin in earlier. A spear from one of the warriors tore through the door, and he took off up the stairs. It wasn't long before he heard it shatter completely, but their inability to perform menial tasks like opening doors gave him seconds at least.

He dashed up the stairs into the meditation room and found himself cornered. He had remembered the room and had a desperate, frantic hope that he would find a door or passageway he'd overlooked last time, but there was nothing. Nothing except the large window Almerin had sat quietly in front of. Heavy footsteps clamored up the stairs, and he panicked. It was a mistake! Everything was a mistake! He was trapped and didn't know what to do. In frantic desperation, he pulled out the old pendant from his satchel and dropped to his knees, begging desperately for help.

"Jump!"

It was Landala's voice, and he didn't have time to dispute it. It was insane, and every rational voice in his head told him not to do it, but the footsteps were nearing, and he was afraid. He leaped through the window and fell in a mass of fear and broken glass. He fell past the sanctuary, past the upper city, and into a misty darkness.

As he tumbled downward, he heard Landala's voice shout, "Crush the pendant!"

He crushed it and waited to smash into the bottom of the city. There was a horrific thud and the sensation of landing in thick mud. For a moment, he thought he was dead. He struggled out of a small hole, his armor glowing and a small ball of light sputtering around him. He curled into a ball, shaken and disoriented. The faintly glowing orb did its best to push the infringing blackness away from all sides. But it was quickly fading, and the darkness was inching closer.

"I don't have much time here," the light began. It was unmistakably Landala's voice. "Listen closely. This isn't just darkness around you. It wants to destroy you! You must rely on yourself, on your own powers. Every Royal Vanguard has some energy training. You may not have a memory, but you have to find your power, or else the darkness will kill you. I can't do this for you. Everyone's energy comes in different ways. Think of what draws you: water, fire, nature, anything! Quickly!"

And with that, Landala's light faded. The glow dispersed, and the Traveler gagged at the sudden wafting smell of rot as the encroaching darkness pressed on him from all sides. His mind raced. What did he feel a connection to? Water, fire, nature, none of these made a significant impact. He was lost and didn't know what to do. He was in absolute blackness now. It was almost suffocating. And then, in terror, he realized that he was suffocating! He coughed and grasped at his throat as the pungent air became too thick to enter his lungs. His heart pounded, and his mind frantically darted from empty solution to empty solution as he searched for something, anything at all. He ripped out the slimy wooden heart from his satchel and shook it fervently as his concentration started to cloud and his vision blurred. The heart did nothing. He wheezed and dropped the useless thing. As he began to slump over, desperately gasping for air, he heard something. It was a memory, almost like a dull scratchy recording. It was the sharp tones of an older man's voice.

"Light! Light is the most useless of miracles! What good can you possibly do with that?"

And the Traveler held out his shaking hand and created a small, timid ball of light. He heard the darkness retch and retract away, releasing its grip and allowing the precious air to once again fill his strained lungs. The Traveler rolled onto his knees, lifted his visor, and heaved onto the floor. He held the fragile light close to his chest and trembled.

CHAPTER FIVE

The Shadows that Move

"My love, this is the bridge where we first met. Where I first saw your beautiful eyes and pretended to ask for directions so I could talk to you. On our bridge I ask you now, will you marry me?"

-Almerin Arnaz Telith

Forty-five years before the opening of the seal.

The Traveler took a moment to breathe what he could of the thick, humid air that reeked of spoiled meat. He slowly looked around, taking in his new environment with paralyzing dread. He was in the maw now, a place that Almerin himself wouldn't dare venture. It was dark, utterly outrageously dark. It was also hot, and not in a pleasant way like Almerin's fireplace, which was comforting and vibrant. No, it was a muggy, damp heat that covered him in sweat and irritation.

The small light he held in his hand illuminated the spot where he stood but didn't extend an inch past that, where unsettling noises slithered inside the surrounding blackness. He reached for his sword but only patted an empty scabbard. It was gone! He desperately tried to stifle the rising panic in his chest as he crawled across the grimy, snowless pavement, patting the ground for any trace of his weapon. His hand stumbled over something, and for a moment, he thought the universe might be kind to him. No, it was just the useless heart-shaped piece of sappy wood. He quickly cloistered it away in his satchel and unsteadily stood up to scan the ground for his sword. He couldn't see anything but horrible darkness.

Something was watching him, though. He could almost feel it on the back of his neck. He had to find his weapon. There was simply nothing else he could do. He was defenseless without it. Feeling weak and faint, he raised his hand and poured some more energy into the orb of light. The orb expanded and shined over the murky ruins of an old town district. The mossy, slightly melted buildings around him silently loomed over as if disapproving of his existence.

He looked away. He just wanted his sword back. He expanded the light a little bit more and caught sight of that beautiful glimmer of metal. It sat in the middle of the open street, almost outside of his view. He dimmed the orb to conserve energy and strode over to the weapon. A sickening wall of shadow stood just beyond the sword, a wall that the orb couldn't banish. He tentatively put his foot down and felt the sword. It was clearly right there, but he couldn't move it. Then his blood froze as a low, raspy breathing began to rattle in front of him. It just breathed in and out in the most horrible way, and his heart lurched with the realization that he was standing face to face with something, something standing on his sword. He tried his best to steady himself as he considered his situation. If a monster was in front of him, then why didn't it attack? Was it sleeping? Surely not with all the noise he'd been making.

He took a few shallow breaths just to make sure he was still alive before reaching out his hand and strengthening the orb's power.

The light wasn't enough. The wall of blackness was still there.

He poured all his power into the orb's light and gave a small cry as his trembling hand began to burn. The melted buildings and cracked roads of the district were pulled out of the shadows and into the semi-sun that he created. The wall of shadow evaporated, leaving him alone on an empty street with no monster in front, behind, or anywhere around him. He didn't know what was worse, that he knew something was there or that he couldn't find any trace of it.

He quickly grabbed his sword, along with the last bits of sanity that were leaking out of his head. He dimmed the burning sun resting in the palm of his hand to just a tiny light that peered nervously through his fingers at the overwhelming, claustrophobic darkness. It was a small light, but if what Almerin said about the lower city was true, then he wouldn't be recovering much energy here. He had to conserve what he could. He picked a street and began walking. He didn't have the courage to venture into any of the appallingly decrepit houses yet, so a random street would have to do.

It was more than simple darkness that swallowed the city around him. It felt like a copious fog rather than an absence of light. Maybe it was both, or something else entirely. Walking beneath its surface, he could almost feel it writhe and shift like a living thing. It was a disgusting feeling, and the more he was aware of it, the closer he held the orb of light, which made walking nearly impossible. Several times, he mistakenly kicked or stumbled over something in the street.

While turning a corner, he suddenly bashed his foot so hard against a craggy, pale column that his leg reverberated. He cursed bitterly, which was quickly replied to by a shuffling from a nearby house. He raised his hand and poured some energy into the orb to increase its brightness. Something behind a partially unhinged door squirmed away into the shadows, leaving him with a sickening fear that he tried to subdue by taking several deep breaths of rotting air to calm himself. He quickly gagged and felt even worse. He dimmed the orb and quietly said, "You can have the house," while continuing on his miserable way.

His mind aimlessly drifted to Almerin back at the sanctuary, wondering if he had gotten out alright. He didn't know if leaving Almerin was the right thing to do. When the moment finally came, he realized he didn't fully trust Almerin. Almerin had carelessly led him across the bridge after all. What if staying to fight in the sanctuary was also a horrible mistake? He still felt conflicted, though. He had abandoned Almerin in a moment of need, and he had no idea if the old man survived or not. He hoped he did. How couldn't he? Almerin not only wielded untold forces of magic but had the whole sanctuary on his side.

Though, if it was that clear cut then why did he abandon Almerin during the fight?

He bashed his foot again and cursed. Absolute obscurity consumed everything around him. Although it was calming to occupy himself with something other than the horrible present, it was becoming clear that he couldn't allow his mind to wander while trying to keep aware of potential dangers.

He carefully pressed onward, knocking his foot or running into large obstacles from time to time, making more noise than he would like. He suddenly stopped when he heard a shifting behind him. The Traveler bathed the area in a fierce light to catch whatever was following him by surprise.

Nothing.

He didn't want to use up too much energy, but he simply couldn't walk blindly anymore. He kept the light dim but increased the brightness just enough to see around him.

He continued on and wondered why he had ever chosen to come to this city in the first place. Almerin said something about it being a choice, but why him? Why was it him? Surely, there was someone braver and more qualified to be here. Or maybe it wasn't a choice. Maybe he was forced here against his will... He couldn't remember. Really, anything could've happened.

Then his thoughts shifted to the two apparitions he'd met in the garden. He knew them, but he couldn't remember from where. The bloody man and the cold woman both unsettled him. The Traveler fiercely shook his head and knocked his fist against his helmet to try and keep focus. His mind kept wandering to anything but the present, like something was trying to drag him away. He needed to focus. He trudged on through the malevolent fog, shoving distractions out of his head while trying to keep a firm grasp on what he was doing.

He turned a corner and stopped in view of a small light that aggressively seized his attention. A window on the first floor of a partially melted house was faintly glowing. The house blended into the other murky, lifeless buildings around it, save for the single tantalizing fire in the window. It swayed and danced provocatively across the blackness, promising the Traveler life, safety, and help.

He dimmed his own light so he wouldn't be seen quietly approaching the window. It was nearly impossible to see through the mold-tinted glass, but the Traveler was able to make out just enough to discern that there were no signs of movement. He waited patiently for a few moments and then reached for the nearby disintegrating door, gingerly turning the greasy door handle. The handle was cold, an odd cold that pulled the very heat through his gauntlets and out of his hands, but it was unlocked. The Traveler cautiously entered with his sword leading the way. The inside was desolate. Piles of garbage and bits of food were splattered across the ground. Brightly colored chairs and sofas sat with a thick coating of rot, and the blue and white walls of the house were peeling. The place looked disgusting, and the Traveler started to turn around to leave when a withered voice called from the shadows, "Wait!"

The Traveler lit up the orb in shock. The whole room burst with light, and every crack and crevice was revealed to him.

Something shrieked and slithered away into another room, screaming, "The light! Turn it down! Turn it down!" It was a coarse and horrible voice, somewhere between a man's and a woman's.

The Traveler dimmed the light slightly, but only slightly.

"You're not like the others. Who are you?" the voice whimpered from the shadows.

"What others?" the Traveler asked, the creature's timidity giving him a sense of courage to pursue the conversation.

"The mindless beasts that wander the streets. I keep them away with my light. You're different, though. You're not a monster. Where are you from?"

The Traveler hesitated, unsure of how much he wanted to tell this creature. "I came from the Aco... Acla... the sanctuary up above."

"Aclamartom?"

"Yes, do you know a way back?"

"I might indeed," the voice mused, "but you'll need help from the Golden Band."

"What's that?"

"You don't know? That is extraordinarily surprising," the voice paused. "I'll help you, but I need to ask you for a favor in return."

"What do you want?" A sense of danger was slowly starting to creep up the Traveler's neck. He didn't want to spend any more time here than was necessary. It was only his good experience with Landala, the creature's timidity, and his own desperation that kept him here this long.

"My light," the creature explained, "the one sitting on my windowsill needs energy to burn so it can keep the monsters away. I normally use my own, but you seem strong, and you're glowing with power. Give some of your energy to my light, and I'll tell you what you want."

The Traveler looked over at the small burning candle on the windowsill. It seemed unremarkable, and the light it produced was meager. "If you need light," the Traveler suspiciously retorted, "why are you so fearful of mine?"

"You have too much light. I've been without it for so long that it burns me," The creature whined. "I just need a little of your energy to keep my candle burning."

The Traveler didn't know what to do. He needed the creature's help, but what if that tiny little candle sitting on the windowsill somehow sucked out his very soul?

"Why should I trust you?"

The voice paused, and then said, "I understand. Just wait here for a moment."

The Traveler saw a formless shadow whisk into a dark hallway at the edge of his orb's light. He heard some rustling in a back room, and after a few seconds, a scroll flung out from the hallway and gently rolled to the Traveler's feet.

"It's a map of the district," the voice said. "I circled this house and a concert hall filled with allies and music." A small, pale wind instrument covered in bumps and engravings suddenly rolled out from the darkness and bumped the Traveler's foot. "If you play this at the doors of the concert hall, you will meet the few members left of the Golden Band. They are better able to help you than I. Now...," the voice hedged, "go and find them. After you see that I'm telling you the truth, would you promise to come back and keep my light burning?"

The Traveler was all too eager to take the deal. He grabbed both the map and wind instrument and promptly left with a "Yeah, okay, sure."

The Traveler doubted he would ever come back. He walked out the door and carefully navigated his way through the cavernous lower city with the map the creature had provided. Twisted street signs and slightly melted shop names suddenly became meaningful as he matched their names to the map, using them to guide his journey to the Golden Band. As he walked deeper into the heart of Hiri Handi, he slowly began to hear the soft harmonies of a string instrument delicately winding its way through the city and gently brushing past the Traveler, who tilted his head up slightly to hear better. Up until now, part of him had been wondering whether the creature had tricked him. He seemed to be going in the right direction, but the fear that he was walking straight into a trap that would end with his mangled body being used as fuel for that monster's candle hounded him. The music gave him a tangible hope. Surely, no demon could make that. It had to be the Golden Band.

He tenaciously followed the sound and continued through the twisting streets and winding alleys until the distant music became clearer. It was sharper now, and he slowed down to a meandering pace until he suddenly stopped altogether, letting the harmonic melody wrap itself around him like a warm, fluffy blanket. There was only one instrument playing, but it was played beautifully. The music was soft, peaceful, and touching. For a brief moment, the Traveler forgot that he was surrounded by a horrible blackness that was simply biding its time until he ran out of energy to keep his light burning so it could devour him. For just a moment, he felt calm. The feeling was fleeting as his rational mind quickly obliterated this serene trance with the sledgehammer of fear and paranoia. Still, he pressed on with even more determination to meet the Golden Band than before. He followed the map through a weaving, claustrophobic alleyway that suffocated his movements until it finally gave way to a wide-open space that gave reverence to the grand, extravagant, arched structure that soared up and out of the murky shadows like a rainbow. It was the music hall.

The hall was lined with enormous, decorated columns. Faded lights illuminated the sides of the building, which were covered in rolling murals of angels, clouds, and music. At its base were two separate entrances at each foot of the rainbow-esque arch, both with a sprawling set of blue tiled stairs that were reminiscent of a winding, colorful river. The Traveler listened to the deep, wistful sound still emanating from inside the building and eagerly ascended one of the stone rivers up to the entrance. The rusted silver doors of the music hall had large colorful windows, though too opaque to see anything on the other side, and a white handle, which the Traveler gingerly grasped.

It was locked. Why wouldn't it be? he thought to himself. He placed the orb of light beside his shoulder, which, to his satisfaction, stayed, and pulled out the wind instrument. Sticky goo dripped off the little flute, and he hesitated to blow into it. Something must've leaked in his bag, but now was not the time or place to check. He was so close to help and fear was acting as a powerful, chaotic motivator. He shook some of the sap off with disgust, lifted his helmet, and softly blew into it to make sure it still worked. The sound was clear and piercing. He stepped back, listened to the gentle music to try and understand its rhythm, and then blew into the instrument with all his might.

It was horrible, more like a dying animal than anything else.

Then, the music inside stopped. It must be working, he thought, and he blew again, shifting his tone as best he could to create something less grating to the ears.

He couldn't.

Then, something suddenly slammed into the doors and part of the wall above it, cutting an enormous, terrifying crack into the stonework.

"No, no, no!" he spat aloud, backing away from the door. "No, you can keep your music. I don't want any of it!" He shut his helmet and bolted back down the river of stairs as something slammed into the wall again, creating another horrible crack.

The Traveler scarcely had time to reach the bottom when the doors suddenly broke open, releasing a horrible mass of shadows that leaped straight over his head and disappeared into the darkness. From the little he glimpsed, it had an animalistic, primordial shape.

The Traveler stood dumbfounded, staring into the darkness where the creature had fled. As he stood in silence, considering whether or not it was a good idea to hide in the music hall, an armored man carrying a small cannon under his arm sprinted out of the broken doors. He stood at the top of the stairs and hollered, "YOU! GET UP HERE NOW!!!"

The Traveler wasn't going to argue. He clamored up a few steps toward the music hall when a shadow quietly swiped the man aside, tossing him into the surrounding blackness without even a single shriek. The Traveler's soul sank into the deepest pit of his stomach as the shadows melted into a towering black monstrosity.

In reality, it was only a second, but it seemed like an eternity to the Traveler. The tangible mass of horror peered down the stairs and examined its brightly colored prey. It was a featureless black thing, a blackness that was more of an abyss than a color, with the face of a sickening skull that shifted in and out of focus like moving water.

The Traveler's mind couldn't comprehend what he was staring into, and he simply stood there facing down the goliath, lamenting a life poorly spent. Although it felt like an eternity to the Traveler, the creature only observed him with something similar to curiosity for a mere moment and then decided that the Traveler's presence was unsatisfactory. It lurched forward while stretching its arm outward to claw him into oblivion.

Having neither the agility to dodge nor the speed to run, the Traveler took his last seconds of life to place his right foot behind him and raise his laughably small sword with a cry that resembled the squeal of a pig.

As he prepared for death, a shrill, ear-piercing gash of sound that bore into his skull rang out from the music hall and caused the horrifying goliath to turn away and gawk at the ungodly noise.

Now was his chance. He wouldn't get another.

He ran.

He ran back towards the first alleyway that he could see and darted inside as the goliath behind him began to bellow and slam the ground. He barreled into the alley, weaving and skirting past every insidious obstacle that leaped out from the darkness to entangle him and shot out the other side into an open street. A house quickly melted into view, and he rocketed for the front door with a dizzying speed. He covered his head and, rather than take the precious time to open it, blindly hurtled himself into the door, shattering it to pieces.

He clumsily stumbled up, grabbed his sword, and darted straight across a hallway into a kitchen, rattling some scattered dishes as he awkwardly tore by. Despite the pungently decaying food stifling his breathing, he slid under one of the counters and began frantically muttering half-formed prayers, hoping the monster wouldn't find him. For a moment, there was silence, and he cocked his head up to listen.

Nothing, not even a murmur of noise.

The Traveler shuffled up a bit, knocking his exceptionally protective armor against the cupboards as he gingerly peered over the counter. It was no use; everything was black. He was keeping his light too close, fearing that he might be spotted. He slid back down and continued muttering gibberish until the floor suddenly jerked and the house trembled with the hideous crack of shattering metal and wood.

It had found him.

He shrieked and covered his head in bewildered terror as everything around him shook, dishes crashed, and the deafening calamity of noise got closer. He could run. There even appeared to be a window at the end of the kitchen that he might be able to fit through, but he couldn't move. His legs, his entire body, had stopped obeying him and just simply gave up. All he could do was cover his head in horror.

Then, another abrupt shot of terrible noise masquerading as music rang out, and he heard the behemoth screech and then cascade down the street in a thunderous madness.

He didn't move for the longest time. He just listened. A light pattering of footsteps dashed into what was left of the house and then stopped just before the kitchen.

"Hello?" an appallingly cheerful voice inquired. "Are you still alive?"

The Traveler wearily peered over the counter to see who or what was talking to him. A spidery, gangly woman dressed in a mishmash of bags, battered patchwork armor over a dirty white coat, and a gold sash stood in the hallway. A purple veil covered her entire face, and her head, which was cocked slightly to the side in an unsettling way, was completely wrapped in white cloth. Her gloved hands held onto a bow and a stringed musical instrument.

The Traveler stayed behind the safety of his counter and asked the peculiar individual from afar, "Were you the one making that…" He hesitated at the word "…music?"

"I was," she proudly answered, fidgeting her stance to make her small instrument more obvious. It was white with green flowers painted over its fragile construction, and it perfectly matched the thin bow she held in the other hand. What was the name? It was familiar. The violin? It looked different, though, like it was only inspired by the violin. He didn't know how it could have made such a horrific noise.

An uneasy silence drifted across the room as the Traveler suspiciously eyed the strange woman.

"Are you part of the Golden Band?" he finally asked.

"I am! My name's Yslawna," she said with a slight bow that felt reminiscent of a theater performance. "And it's my job to safeguard humanity from the evil spilling out of Hiri Handi. We exist to protect people and remind them of the divine cord that connects us all."

This felt rehearsed, or at least insincere, and it made the Traveler wonder how trustworthy this person actually was.

"What's your name?" Yslawna suddenly asked.

"I don't remember."

"Oooh, I see. Well, did you wake up in that armor?" she inquired, tilting her head slightly with curiosity.

The movement disturbed him, and he hesitated with a confused, "What?"

"Your armor, I've seen it before. Do you remember where you got it?"

"Uh..." the Traveler was still shaken from the day's ordeals and had to work hard to pull any information from the muck that was now his brain. "A man called Almerin gave it to me. I'm on a mission." He boldly announced from behind his kitchen counter, trying to sound as official as possible in the hopes that he might enlist this individual's help. Trustworthy or not, she clearly hadn't tried to murder him yet, and that seemed like a good sign.

"I'm trying to regroup with Almerin and close the seal in the palace."

"Wait! Wait, wait!" Yslawna energetically interrupted, waving her hand unnecessarily to add even more emphasis. "You work for Almerin?"

"Y-yes," he tentatively answered, unsure where this was headed.

"And he's finally decided on a whim to just close the seal?"

"Uh... can we talk somewhere safer?"

"Oh, that monster is going to be gone for a while," she casually remarked. "I really drove it crazy and sent it off on a fake chase. It's much safer at the chapel, though. We can talk there."

"Where's that?"

"In the Music Hall. Just follow me, and I'll show you," she invited with an optimistic jaunt that was wholly unsuited to the surrounding environment.

The Traveler's new friend pranced away while he stayed be-hind his counter, with most of his body still unwilling to move despite the increasingly nauseating smell of rotten leftovers.

Yslawna quickly returned and started pulling bandages and other medical supplies out of her bag, saying, "I'm so sorry. I didn't realize that you might be injured. Where are you hurt?"

"I-I'm not hurt. I just…" The Traveler tried to describe the sensation of overwhelming doom and terror, but the more he dwelt on it, the less he could actually talk.

"Ohhh, I see," Yslawna muttered, understanding the unspo-ken message of fear. "Well, we can stay here if you really want to, but the chapel has food and beds and doesn't smell as bad. I'd recom-mend a change of scenery." She extended her hand to the Traveler, like an adult might do to a lost child.

He looked at it for a moment and, with a profoundly twisting sense of both hope and dread, took her hand. He slowly stood up and moved away from the limited safety of his counter and over to his new acquaintance, who packed up her violin-ish instrument into a thin black case which she slung over her shoulder. With a small metal lantern in hand, she led the way out of the shattered house and to-wards the music hall.

Chapter Six

The Golden Band

"It's up in the sky where I feel free, not down here in the filth. I should have been a Royal Vanguard. Those giant birds looked amazing."

-Awhet Ebarria

450 years after the opening of the seal.

"It's always exciting to meet new people!" Yslawna gleefully remarked while leading the way back through the cramped alley. She had an odd way of walking that was somewhere between a strut and a lurch, and she moved her hand in dizzyingly exaggerated gestures while talking. "I'll need to give you a proper tour of the hall!"

"I look forward to it," the Traveler cordially replied while stepping over some garbage as he tried to keep within the pale light of Yslawna's lantern. He wasn't actually interested in a tour as his opinion of the city and its various marvels was currently plunging into the deepest possible chasm. However, his new friend was amiable. If he was nice, she would probably help him get back to Almerin.

He might even be able to convince her to join his group if she seemed stable enough.

The hall once again melted out of the shadows as they approached. The outdoor stage lights that once glorified the structure's magnificence now detailed the twisting carnage of the left entryway where the enormous monstrosity first broke out. As the Traveler followed Yslawna to the base of the flowing river of stairs, the murky wheels in his foggy brain slowly turned to the shadowy creature that tossed him the map and wind instrument.

Why was he instructed to play music here? Why did that monster attack him?

He stopped as the dots began to sluggishly connect, and Yslawna turned to face him with a tilt of curiosity and asked, "Is something wrong?"

"It was a trap..."

"What was?"

"There was a strange creature that I met, and it said I would find help from some sort of band if I played music here. But that *thing* only attacked after I played the music."

Yslawna stood quietly for a moment and then slowly put her hand on the Traveler's shoulder. Although her face and expression were concealed, the next words she spoke held the weight of the grave, "What did it look like?"

"I don't know. It stayed in the shadows."

"Do you still have the instrument it gave you?"

"Uhh... No, I dropped it when the monster attacked. I think I was somewhere at the foot of the stairs."

Yslawna spun around a few times, searching the ground for the instrument. "Go search that way," she suddenly pointed to the right.

The Traveler created another small orb of light as he began investigating the enormous grounds of the music hall for the tiny flute-like instrument. He didn't seriously expect to find anything, but he was the cause of this mess, so he didn't want to be perceived as unhelpful. As he sauntered around the area, gazing across the ground, he looked back at Yslawna, who was zigzagging back and forth in a bizarre and unsettling manner. He had no idea what she was doing, but it looked important, if not insane. He turned away. He didn't like watching her.

"AH HA!" She suddenly shouted,

"You found it?"

They both returned to the foot of the stairs where Yslawna held out the victory prize, the small flute.

"Just as I thought," she exclaimed, "it's broken. You couldn't have played this if you tried… This is going to be a very unpleasant reunion," she muttered to herself. "Do you still have the map?"

"Yeah," the Traveler dug in his satchel and pulled out a slime-covered map.

Yslawna gingerly took the map with as few fingers as possible and asked, "Was it like this when he gave it to you?"

"No, something must have leaked in my bag."

"Thanks," she sarcastically mumbled. "The music hall is right over there." She pulled a key off her belt and tossed it to the Traveler, who fumbled but didn't drop it. "Go straight in and keep going straight all the way to the back of the stage. Find a staircase somewhere behind the stage's left side, and then just follow the arrows until you reach a door. Use that key to enter. That's our chapel." Yslawna suddenly bolted off, shouting, "Just wait for me there!"

The Traveler stood alone in the empty darkness with a million questions sitting on the tip of his tongue, questions that would clearly have to wait until later. He looked over at the enormous, shattered entrance of the music hall, which stood atop that sprawling set of stairs, and passively exhaled before climbing all the way back up. When he reached the top, he staggered over to a bit of cracked wall and began quietly cursing. The day weighed on him, and he needed a minute to collect his thoughts. He gazed around at the city from the heights of the music hall but couldn't see anything except that horrible darkness. He sighed weakly and stepped through the gaping hole where the front doors used to be and into the main hall.

The inside boasted a depressing sort of beauty. Deep blue was the primary color, but a heavy heaping of silvery white with gold trims accented the interior. Like most of Hiri Handi, the entryway was crafted meticulously with love and care. However, like the rest of the undercity, it was depressingly faded at best. The room could only barely boast miserably about its past as darkness, filth, and the erosion of time tore and besmirched the grace it once had. What used to be magnificent was now ghostly and depressing.

The Traveler walked straight, as Yslawna had said, passed a cracked ticket booth, warped from the pervading humidity, and entered a theater that stretched far and wide past the limits of the Traveler's orb. He cautiously made his way through the peripheral darkness that shrouded the edges of the theater, moving past the rows and rows of seats that sat expectantly towards the front stage where an empty chair sat alone. At each end of the stage were two massive, black-tipped crystals, some ritually arranged candles, all extinguished, and a few chalk symbols drawn across the ground. The Traveler didn't know what the crystals were or why they were there, and he didn't really want to touch them in case they were dangerous. He paid the crystals their due notice and continued on.

He stood before the stage and had trouble deciding whether Yslawna had directed him to the left side of the stage or the stage's left side looking out, which would be the right side. He paced hesitantly across a soft red carpet and then decided to follow whatever stairway had arrows on it, starting with his left side. He marched up the side of the stage and passed through a velvet blue curtain, which presented him with a cheery, bright orange arrow mounted to a cracked beige wall. It pointed up, and the Traveler obeyed, starting his ascent up a narrow, painstakingly crafted, black-tiled stairway with white swirls and wrought iron rails filled with birds and forestry, all of which were tucked away in a dark corner of the music hall that few would ever actually walk up, let alone stop to appreciate. The orange arrows guided him higher and higher, past countless wooden doors that a small part of him wanted to open, with a much larger part objecting wholeheartedly on the grounds that he didn't know what was on the other side. The doors remained closed, and he continued marching up.

He was tired. His legs ached, and his armor made it worse, but he finally reached the one orange arrow that pointed sideways instead of up. He opened the door and stood slack-jawed at a blood-soaked hallway painted with dried gore and deep gashes that cut into the drywall. The hellish corridor stretched out to a heavy metal door with an orange dot. He cautiously entered the grisly scene, his heavy feet creaking on some loosened floorboards, and then shut the stairwell door so nothing could attack from behind. It was a battleground, with no sign of the participants. All of the side doors in the hall were bricked up, and it seemed that whatever came here was forced into this single corridor to be slaughtered. There was a clear, straight path to what he assumed to be the church, base, or whatever Yslawna was using to live in, but he still hesitated. Every instinct in his body told him not to walk down the blood-spattered hallway, but he didn't really have a choice.

The Traveler drew out his sword, cautiously inching his way past the carnage and over to the reinforced metal door. He pulled out Yslawna's key from a small side bag and opened the door. He took a few steps in and was once again greeted by that horrible darkness. A rusty lever sat enticingly close to the entrance, which the Traveler absentmindedly pulled, too fast for his brain to warn that it could trigger an alarm, trap, or any other catastrophe. He jumped as the lights snapped on with a bone-twisting crack. He was in a small, makeshift chapel with frail wooden pews of different styles and construction all lined up near the center of the room. At the end was an altar with decorative ornaments arranged on a covered table. Behind it, were two prominent banners with the same purple diamond and white background, the flag of Itzalla. Draped over the altar itself was a black cloth with a single gold line across the middle.

The chapel seemed mundane enough, and then he looked up. Across the entire arched ceiling were rows and rows of brightly decorated bed sheets and tablecloths, strung together in a thick, colorful web of madness. The construction of spiraling insanity was enormous as it was intricate. Stunning patterns in the web were created through knots and weaving the different cloths together. So many patterns were weaved into the web that it was difficult, even dizzying, to look at. The time and effort devoted to this creation was startling enough to give the Traveler pause. He took a tentative breath and then tore his attention away from the web of madness to softly close the door behind him. With a few slow steps into the room, he hesitantly shouted, "Is anyone here?"

No one answered.

The chapel was somewhat oval-shaped, with four doors clinging to the edges. The subtle but pleasant aroma of baked bread drifted from an open door on the left side of the room, distracting the Traveler from his nightmare-soaked paranoia. He made a sharp left to follow the scent into a small, disheveled kitchen where two half-eaten meals of drinks, bread, and bowls of white congealed somethings sat at a table covered in maps, books and one broken, silvery sword, all of which sat under a meandering ceiling fan that lazily swayed back and forth. The Traveler moved towards the table but stopped when his gaze was pulled aside by the far wall, which was covered in a ludicrous number of decorative dinnerplates mounted with profound pride. Like the web of madness, the dinnerplates were thoughtfully placed together to create new patterns that sprawled across the wall. It wasn't as stunning as the cloth web, but it was still a startling sight to see. Stacks of plates, maybe less prestigious or unsuitable for some grand design, were placed in piles at the bottom of the wall.

The Traveler walked in, took a weary notice of the unsettling arrangement, and then grabbed a piece of what he could only assume to be bread off one of the half-eaten meals. He didn't bother touching the white mush. He smelled the bread, which was nice enough to entice a bite. It wasn't wholly unpleasant, but it was dry and flavorless despite the attractive smell. He put the bread back and decided to finish scouting the area first before stealing more. Returning to the center hall, he began investigating each corner of the chapel to indulge his paranoia, which skyrocketed in equal proportion to both tiredness and general bewilderment. The other door on the left side opened to an elongated storage room filled with rows of splendidly crafted cabinets and wooden lockers. He only took a moment to admire the woodwork before noting the absence of any monsters and promptly shutting the door.

He moved to the door on the right of the chapel hall, which opened to a hallway with more doors and rooms that needed to be investigated. He started walking down the hall, compulsively opening and then shutting the doors he came across.

Bedroom.

More storage.

Armory.

Bedroom with a little girl....

He paused in delayed shock as he stared down at the darkhaired child dressed in a faded nightgown.

"You need to sleep, or you're going to collapse," she said with concern.

He knew that voice. That innocently soft voice which deeply unsettled a profound part of him, as if she was going to suddenly leap across the room and chew his neck open. "Landala?"

"I brought a new necklace for you too."

"A what...?"

She tossed the necklace, and the Traveler recoiled in horror, egregiously fumbling the catch but not dropping it. It was a small, pearled necklace that glittered in the orb of light that the Traveler refused to put out.

"It's safe here," Landala continued. "Light a candle and sleep before you pass out."

The Traveler looked up from the necklace to ask a storm of questions, but Landala had disappeared, leaving him with a mixed sensation of both disappointment and relief that she was gone. He stood there momentarily gazing down at the glittering necklace before slowly stuffing it in his satchel. The bedroom looked quiet and inviting. He shuffled into the room and gently shut the door behind him. He lit a small, readily available candle that sat beside a fluffy bed where he settled in and closed his eyes. His helmet stayed on; he refused to remove it or his armor, but the pillows were soft enough that he was able to quickly drift away into a shallow, restless sleep that was barely able to leave behind all the terrors around him.

The Traveler was suddenly at a dinner table, beholding a fine piece of toast. It was gloriously cooked to crispy perfection, and all that it needed was a soft, rich slab of butter to be spread across its golden surface. The Traveler took a thin, silvery knife, gently cut into the creamy butter, and began to spread it over the toast with great satisfaction. All he had to do now was eat it. He paused and tentatively gazed down at the toast. It was perfect, too perfect. Something terrible must be about to happen! The Traveler leaned back in the sunlit kitchen of his scrupulously clean house, staring down in confused horror at his breakfast.

The toast just sat there.

Something must be wrong with the toast. It couldn't just exist like this! SOMETHING WAS WRONG!!!

His hand trembled as he held the buttered toast, and he began to scream in terror as the toast refused to reveal its true sadistic nature. He sat there screaming until his pleasant kitchen began to spin in a dizzying circle that made him want to vomit until it slowed and then finally stopped.

He was in that awful dimly lit room again lined with the unpleasantly striped dark blue and red wallpaper. The man obscured by shadows sat opposite him, still breathing in a cigar and then bellowing out smoke. The man lowered his cindering torch and said in his strangled voice, "I imagine you haven't taken to the city."

The Traveler didn't reply. The room was still ugly, and the man was still horribly unpleasant, except now he was becoming an inconvenience for interrupting the Traveler's imaginary breakfast.

The Traveler stood up to leave, and the man called out, saying, "Do you know what your friend is doing right now?"

The Traveler didn't care. He just wanted his breakfast. He started to walk to the door when the man said, "She's bathing in the blood of her enemy."

The Traveler stopped.

"And she's relishing it," he continued. "Although revenge is an effective anesthetic, it can be addictive and corroding. Watch her."

The Traveler tried his best to ignore the awful man by walking straight over to the door. Right as his hand touched the cold brass doorknob, the man called out, saying, "We'll meet again."

The Traveler stepped out and shut the door behind him.

He woke up with a start and stared blankly at the door as the slow realization that he wasn't dreaming anymore trickled into his foggy head. The Traveler clumsily rolled out of bed and, with a sudden craving for buttered toast and a hatred of cigars, meandered out into the hallway, where a trail of bloody footprints splattered across the length of the floor.

"YSLAWNA!?" the Traveler belted in shock.

Some dishes clattered in the distance, followed by light footsteps pattering across the chapel. The hall door swung open, and Yslawna darted in, shouting, "What? What happened?"

"There's blood everywhere!"

"Oh," she sighed in relief. "Oh, I thought we were under attack. No, there's just lots of blood around here. You eventually get used to it."

The Traveler's face contorted with a look of apprehension and confusion, but his visor obscured all of this from Yslawna, who took a step out of the hallway and asked, "Could you come with me to the kitchen? I wanted to ask you some questions, if you don't mind."

She strolled back to the kitchen while the Traveler took another disturbed glance at the bloody footprints before following behind. As he passed through the chapel hall, he stopped at the altar, which had been redecorated. A funeral black cloth was draped over, and three burning candles and an elegant silver plate rested on top. A thin golden ribbon had been gently placed in the center of the plate.

Yslawna leaned out of the kitchen, looking for the Traveler, and caught him examining the new arrangement. "It's for Awhet," she explained. "I can't find his body, so those candles will have to do."

The Traveler's chest tightened as he suddenly realized that Awhet was probably the man who tried to call him into the music hall before being batted away into the darkness by that enormous, skull-faced monstrosity.

The Traveler stepped away from the funeral arrangement while letting a painful sigh slip out. He had known something was wrong with the shadowy creature that had given him the map and flute, but he thought he could outsmart it. Maybe had he not acted so carelessly, then Awhet might still be alive… He didn't want to think about it. He entered the kitchen, where Yslawna pulled out a chair for him to sit and then moved over to one of the counters, where she began to assemble some form of breakfast, humming merrily to herself as she worked.

The kitchen tried its best to create a warm and welcoming environment, but every aspect of the room was just slightly off-putting. The table was massive, and odd gashes were sprinkled over its top.

The entire wall of plates was disconcerting, to say the least, and finally, there was Yslawna. She didn't move like a normal person or even like Almerin, who was sluggish but deliberate. Her movements were sudden and jerky, as if her limbs were moving before consulting with her conscious mind, and the song she was singing was far too merry to be sincere.

The Traveler jostled the old, thin wooden chair Yslawna had pulled out and then he looked down at the enormous bunker that was his suit of armor. Sitting in that chair wouldn't end well, so he decided to lean against the wall instead.

Yslawna turned around with two bowls of unappetizing white mush and then stopped and stared at the Traveler's awkward lean. "You don't want to sit?" she asked with a tilt of her head.

"I uh… I don't think the chair would survive."

"Oh, I see," she muttered. She handed one bowl to the Traveler while sitting down with the other herself. "The chapel isn't dangerous, you know. You don't have to wear all that armor here."

"Well," the Traveler hesitated, not wanting to reveal how little he trusted this place or Yslawna. "What if we have to leave in an emergency? It's better to be prepared."

"True. But always wearing armor and always being ready for battle can slowly erode your sanity. Normalcy is important for a healthy mind."

The Traveler glanced over at the wall of dinner plates and looked back over to his wiry, veiled companion. "There's nothing normal about this place," he grumbled.

Yslawna laughed in a twisted way that made his skin crawl. "You're right," she conceded, "But it's important to create a sense of normalcy when the abnormal becomes your entire life."

"Doesn't that make you complacent?"

"It can if you're not careful," she explained while the Traveler slowly stirred the mush with his spoon to try and make it look more appetizing. He lifted his visor and took a cautious spoonful. It was bland and pasty, and he immediately regretted trying it.

"You're not from Hiri Handi, are you?"

The Traveler looked up in surprise, "Almerin said that too. How can you tell?"

"Well… To start, you talk with a heavy accent like you don't quite know how the words sound."

The Traveler was astounded that he never noticed this.

"And you're overflowing with energy like people were in the early days. I'm surprised you weren't swarmed while trancing around under the fog."

"The fog?"

"It's the blacker than night mist that suffocates the lowest parts of Hiri Handi," Yslawna explained while twittering both her hands apart to represent the layer of fog.

"Oh, that fog."

"The fog doesn't cause the evil here, though," she continued. "It just forms when there's a high enough concentration." She paused, "I guess you might be intimidating to the lesser creatures. How many encounters did you have before coming here?"

The Traveler mentally sifted through his recent escapades, which all blended together in a swirl of unpleasantness. He pulled two significant encounters. "There was one monster near Almerin's tower, but that was before falling into the fog. There was also that creature that gave me the map. Did you ever manage to find that thing?" He asked, taking the opportunity to explore the dream man's horrible prediction.

"Oh him…" Yslawna seethed. While her purple veil did succeed in completely hiding her expressions, her animated voice betrayed her emotions. "He won't be harming anyone else. I made sure of it."

The horrible old man with the cigar might've been right, and he hated that. Part of him wanted to ask if Yslawna's engagement with the creature had anything to do with the bloody footprints in the hall. He hesitated, however, and she swiftly took the opening to change the subject.

"So, I guess you're wondering who I am and what this place is."

"Uh... yes, yes I am," the Traveler answered while again glancing over at the wall of plates.

"I am a member of the Golden Band," she said with enough pride to fill every single plate on that bizarre wall next to them. "We are a band of protectors who exist to fight against the evil here. We act to remind people of their humanity and to safeguard the defenseless!" she said while theatrically tapping her hand on the table. "The name refers to the divine cord that connects all life together. All life is connected," she demonstrated this by clasping her hands together, "and is as precious as your own life. We are one, and we depend on each other. We live and die for each other."

She stopped talking, and it took the tired and battered mind of the Traveler far longer than was comfortable before realizing he was supposed to say something.

"So, you're not a musical band?"

Yslawna laughed, "No, although I'm a musician."

The Traveler slowly nodded and looked around the room before asking, "Where is everyone?"

"Probably dead," she replied with a shocking banality. "But I can't be sure. I've lost contact with the entire order."

The Traveler didn't know how to respond to this. It sounded like she was the last vestige of whatever order she was so proud of, and he wasn't sure if he was more startled by the statement itself or the way she said it.

"So, you mentioned needing help when we first met?" she asked, changing the subject again.

"What? Right, yes. Almerin and I were separated at the Acla... Aclo..."

"The Aclamartom Sanctuary?" she completed his thought.

"Yeah, that one. Can you help me get there?"

She thoughtfully leaned back in her chair while the Traveler took another bite of the mush to see if it had gotten any better.

It hadn't.

"How urgently do you need to get back?" she finally asked.

"I don't know. Almerin was in the middle of a battle the last time I saw him."

"A battle? With who?"

"Stone knights and a lot of giant black birds."

"That's not good. I'm guessing you two tried to walk to the palace."

"Across the bridge that exploded, yes."

Yslawna thoughtfully tapped her fingers on the table and then said, "I have a half-functional ship that can fly us there quickly, or we can try to walk, which would take quite a while. I'll let you decide."

The Traveler almost blurted out, the ship, but his instincts caught him. "What do you mean half-functional?"

"It was nearly obliterated during a very long fight with the Commander of the Reliquary," she stopped at the Traveler's vacant expression and then clarified, "He's this terrifying guardian that harasses ships that venture out too far into the open sky. He speared the engine with an arrow, but Awhet and I had gotten it working a couple of times since then. It *Should* get us safely to the sanctuary."

The Traveler quietly wrestled with the task's urgency against the dangers of flying the 'half-functional' ship until he finally answered, "We should take the ship." He had a bad feeling about Almerin, and he'd already wasted enough time sleeping.

"Ok! It'll take a few minutes to get it ready. Why don't you take some time to sift through the supplies until I'm done." She pointed to the storage room as she stood up, "and then wait for me here."

"Do you mind if I pay my respects to Awhet's altar before we go?" the Traveler felt guilty about the man's death and wanted to make a small gesture in his memory.

"Of course!" Yslawna said with a twinge of surprise in her tone. "Awhet gave his life to try and warn you. He was a good person like that…" Her voice cracked slightly as she ended the sentence, and her head slowly slid down to gaze at her untouched bowl of mush.

"Yslawna, I…"

"He named the ship the Dancing Star," she suddenly cut him off with a startling jolt of cheerfulness. "I think it was named after an actress he liked, Isrina. She was a perfect blond with a perfect face, voice, fame, and plenty of admirers. Awhet never stood a chance!" She said with a hearty chuckle.

All the Traveler could do was give a fake smile while Yslawna stuffed down her misery into a tiny ball that she tucked away somewhere in the depths of her soul. She picked up her bowl of mush and said, "Alright, I'll be right back." On her way out, she stopped before the altar, bowed her head, and said a short prayer.

She took a few steps away and then stopped and turned to watch the Traveler do the same. He couldn't think of a formal prayer to say, so all he said was a very quiet, "I'm sorry."

CHAPTER SEVEN

Ghosts and Echoes

"Darkness is only truly within us, and the world is a reflection of us. So, it is within us that we find the light to brighten the world."

-From the Book of Worlds.

There is a quietness that pervades across the decrepit city of Hiri Handi. It is an utter lack of ambient noise, a soundlessness reminiscent of death itself. A predatory, merciless game of hunting and hiding has been playing out across Hiri Handi for longer than most can remember. Whatever entity is brazen enough to make noise and expose itself has either lost the will to live or is truly a force to be reckoned with.

These were the thoughts of the creatures that watched the blindingly energetic Traveler from afar with terror as he staggered and clattered his way across the cavernous streets of Hiri Handi, and these were their thoughts as a golden boat high above burst into flames, screeching across the midnight sky with a deafening roar. It was a golden, boat-shaped spectacle of a thing with an old iron chair bolted to the bow and a tall rod, capped with a pink crystal, jutting out from a central windowed cabin where two figures screamed and flailed as they sprayed foam over bursts of fire.

"THE CONSOLE! SPRAY THE CONSOLE!!!"

The Traveler aimed the canister and showered foam over the cockpit and Yslawna, whose sleeve was beginning to catch fire.

She quickly lunged back over to the steering wheel and began to steady the ship through a thick layer of foam, yelling, "You need to climb into the engine room and put out the fire!!"

"I can't fit in there!"

"THEN BLANKET THE ROOM FROM THE HATCH!"

The Traveler hurtled out of the cabin and onto the rear deck, where he hauled open a heavy iron hatch with a backbreaking groan. Smoke and fire bellowed out of the shaft, along with the reeking scent of oil and doom. He pulled away from the pungent fumes to cough and then vigorously emptied the canister into the engine room. The smoke diminished, but before he could even give Yslawna a weary thumbs-up, a sudden piercing whistle cut through his ears, and Yslawna slammed open a cabin window, stuck her head out, and shouted, "YOU NEED TO RELEASE THE PRESSURE VALVE!!"

"WHERE!"

"FRONT!!"

He dropped the canister and bolted to the front of the ship, where a pipe on the floor had blown open and steam was pouring out.

"TURN THE RED WHEEL!" Yslawna leaned out, pointing to a jerry-rigged wheel attached to the front of the cabin.

He ran over and slowly, painfully, twisted the unyielding wheel until the horrid whistling stopped. Then he collapsed with a profound exhalation of relief. After a moment to catch his breath, basking in the feeling of relative safety, he lumbered upright and stumbled back into the cabin. He shut the door behind him, which closed with the stiff creak of neglected hinges, and slumped into a red velvet bench near Yslawna, who was fiercely wiping foam off very important buttons and levers.

"This ship is going to need a good wash after this," She remarked, glancing over at the Traveler.

"Does this normally happen?" The Traveler asked through panted breaths.

"No, the engine doesn't usually catch fire like this, although Awhet was really the one who could pull the most from her." She brushed some more foam off her veil while spinning the ship's worn, red padded steering wheel to the right so they could land at Almerin's tower.

Although the sanctuary was the last place Almerin had been seen, the current plan was to quickly search the tower first. After that, they'd sweep their half-functioning ship as loudly as possible alongside the length of the academy, to get Almerin's attention if he was hiding inside, and then land in the courtyard of the sanctuary. They'd then search inside and figure out where to go from there. It was a simple but solid plan.

The Dancing Star staggered and lurched its way to the tower bridge, where it parked with the unsubtle grace of a walrus. They both exited the cabin and huddled around an extendable side ramp that Yslawna struggled in vain to wrench open. She quickly gave up with an exasperated sigh and climbed down a narrow side ladder instead. The Traveler very cautiously followed, keeping track of each cumbersome foot placement until Yslawna helped him with the final step onto the bridge. He took a few paces forward and gawked at four of the stone soldiers from the sanctuary battle. The life had drained out of them, and they had become inert statues frozen in the middle of battering down the wire grate Almerin had set up as a makeshift front door. The statues were quiet, though. The wind was still, and not even the racketing calamitous approach of the Dancing Star seemed able to disturb this slumber. The Traveler guardedly took his eyes off the warriors and looked up at the tower as the moonlight gently wrapped itself around it in a ghostly embrace as if to say, it's mine now.

Yslawna started to walk forward, and the Traveler quickly grabbed her shoulder, saying "No, those statues are vicious!"

"It's okay. I've seen them before. They can only last a certain amount of time before the magic wears out. They're harmless right now. Watch." She scooped up some snow, packed it into a ball, and hurtled it at one of the statues. It hit square in the back of the head, and the warrior responded with motionless indifference.

"See?" She continued walking forward while shouting, "Almerin! We've come to rescue you!"

There was no response.

The Traveler started to walk forward as well when a hand from behind tugged on his shoulder. "Don't go in!" Almerin distraughtly whispered, "I'm already gone..."

The Traveler whirled around to see nothing but the entrance to the academy behind him. "YSLAWNA!"

Yslawna froze mid-step on the threshold of the tower's gate and then quickly turned around and darted back to the Traveler. "What happened?"

"I heard Almerin's voice. He said he's gone..."

She paused and then asked with two fingers pointed at the Traveler for emphasis, "What exactly did he say."

"He said don't go in and that he was already gone."

She quietly looked up at the tower. A curtain in one of the higher rooms fluttered, and she tentatively asked without turning, "You mentioned a monster near Almerin's tower. Did either of you ever kill it?"

The Traveler's stomach quaked with nausea. He stumbled back, bracing himself on the bridge's balustrade and shivering uncontrollably as horrible images of Almerin's fate flashed across his mind. The burning guilt that maybe he had caused this by running away during the sanctuary fight sapped any strength he had left.

"We should go," Yslawna announced, putting her hand on the Traveler's shoulder and pulling him towards the ship.

He didn't budge. His legs were too weak, and he felt sick.

"You have to move! I can't carry you unless you're willing to shed all your armor."

It was too much. It was all hitting him at once. The monster, the labyrinth, sanctuary, under-city, and the ungodly behemoth with a skull face were all cascading down on the Traveler in a parade of terror.

He tried to speak, but all that came out was a feeble gasp.

Yslawna ransacked one of her satchels and pulled out a foamy red vial. She poured and measured the amount into another vial, opened the Traveler's visor, and said, "Drink this, but don't spit it out. It's horrible."

The Traveler took the vial, drank, and gagged at a flavor he imagined similar to licking wet mold off the floor. He felt slightly numb as all his fears and doubts began to drift away into the ether.

"Can you move?"

He sluggishly stood up and stumbled slightly as they made their way back to the ship. They ascended the ladder and departed as quickly as the ship's sluggish, foam-filled engine would allow. As the Dancing Star puttered back towards the music hall, the Traveler took one last glance through the cabin window at the cold, isolated tower.

He bowed his head and sat on one of the lavish red benches in a vague stupor. It was a pleasant numbness that let him drift and ignore both everything that had happened and everything that might. His uncomfortably heavy armor felt feather light, and as he gazed around, he noticed for the first time how truly beautiful the Dancing Star's cabin room was. The colors were vivid, and the gold lining the ceiling was incredibly shiny. He closed his eyes, let his head lean back, and drifted away until Yslawna tapped him and said, "Drink this, and you'll feel even better."

He sluggishly grabbed the orange vial, slurped it down, leaned over, and vomited. "What did you do!?" He bawled as everything came back into a sharp focus that hurt both his eyes and head.

"I neutralized the potion. It's very powerful, and I was worried you would start needing it to function."

"I DO! Give me the vile!" The Traveler reached forward to seize Yslawna's bag, but she simply stepped back, and he hunched over with a groan. "God Damn," He muttered through clenched teeth as tears trickled down his face. "I never asked to be here…"

"No one ever does."

"What the hell do you know," the Traveler vehemently spat. "This place is your mess, not mine."

Yslawna sighed and knelt down. She placed her hand on his shoulder to comfort him, saying in the sweetest and most soothing voice possible, "Friend, my family was butchered, my skin was seared off, and everyone I've ever known has been slaughtered."

The Traveler looked up at her impassive purple veil with an expression of profound anger and shock that sharply projected the words — *stop now. You are making this worse.*

"But I've managed to mostly stay sane," she continued, with her appalling joviality, "so I can help you do the same. What do you say?"

A disturbingly significant part of the Traveler wanted to reply with, *just throw me off the ship now so I don't suffer later,* but his nagging compulsion to survive wouldn't allow it. "Okay," he miserably mumbled.

"Come with me," she waved him up as she opened the cabin door.

The Traveler sullenly followed Yslawna out to the front of the ship while grabbing onto everything he could along the way to brace his unsteady, nauseated march.

She brought him to the old and somewhat cushioned iron chair bolted down to the ship's bow. "I'm going to detour a little while we go back home. I just want you to sit and watch the cityscape fly past."

Home, the music hall was his home now… The thought upset his stomach, so he stuffed it down while he made himself comfortable in the old iron chair. He leaned back and watched the cloudy night sky wisp over the sparkling towers of Hiri Handi as the ship meandered its way back home.

Yslawna was determined to make the music hall a peaceful place for the Traveler. It had been the refuge for many members of Yslawna's old order for a very long time, and now it was the Traveler's refuge, too. After they landed, Yslawna brought the Traveler to one of the many theater halls in his new home and settled him in. Her music was soft and soothing. He was drenched in anxiety, fear, and paranoia, but in this moment, he was able to let the plaguing thoughts of death slip away while he leaned his head back against the soft theater chair. He allowed the delicate music sweeping across the small auditorium to wrap him up and carry him to a quiet place of safety and calmness.

Yslawna sat on a simple stool, alone on the stage with her violin-ish instrument. She had started off with a quiet introductory performance, but as the song rose, a chorus of other instruments began to emerge without any sign of the musicians themselves. He would have to ask her later about it, but they harmonized well enough that he didn't really care at the moment. The thin, pale lights of the deep blue auditorium, accented by red chairs and curtains, were just bright enough that he wasn't particularly scared of anything creeping up on him while also being dark enough to comfortably close his eyes, which he did, and he quickly started to drift off to sleep. It was in the strange twilight of sleep and waking that the empty auditorium suddenly filled with people. Some in armor, some in robes, many were sad, but all were quiet as the innocent and gentle music suddenly juxtaposed itself against the surrounding horror of Hiri Handi to create something that dug at the sorrow in the deepest part of the soul. It was only a brief window where the music suddenly clicked in a way that the Traveler could catch a glimpse behind Yslawna's true mask, but he could only fully appreciate it for a mere moment before drifting off entirely.

He later awoke with a start as Yslawna jostled his shoulder.

"Brahhh... What happened?"

"You fell asleep," she said with a laugh while sliding into an adjacent chair.

The Traveler started to stammer out an apology, but she stopped him. "It's okay! Falling asleep was the point of the song. It was to soothe your unsettled mind," she said, lightly tapping his helmet. "But now..." she held out a colorful remote which dimmed the room's lights and then began digging around one of her many bags until she produced two grayish, unappetizing sandwiches.

She handed one to the Traveler, who started to ask, "What's thi —" but was cut off as Yslawna bounced up with an animated, "Oh, I forgot to set it up!" She quickly bolted down the aisles and disappeared somewhere behind the stage.

The Traveler looked down at the ugly sandwich, which already nauseated his stomach, and then nervously glanced around the darkened auditorium, keeping watch for any distant shadows that might be moving by themselves until Yslawna returned to reclaim her seat.

She suddenly bounced back up the isles and sat down. "Okay!" she held out the colorful remote and pressed a large yellow button, which caused a dazzling display of colors to suddenly dance across the solid blue backdrop of the stage.

"The dark," the Traveler started to protest as Yslawna handed him some sort of ceramic thermos to accompany his ugly gray sandwich.

"Don't worry," she waved her hand while leaning back in her chair. "The room is sealed, and monsters don't often attack the music hall outright, and if they did, I would sense it. You can relax." She

110

turned away to take a bite of her sandwich and then returned her attention to the radiant display of colors.

The Traveler took a breath to calm his anxiety before lifting his visor and following Yslawna's lead by taking a bite of his own sandwich. It was dry and tasteless but better than he expected. He took a sip of his drink, which was only slightly nicer, before turning to Yslawna and saying, "Thank you."

He didn't really care for the sandwich, drink, or bizarre light show, but he appreciated the effort she made, and he didn't want to insult one of the few people left in Hiri Handi.

"You're welcome! I needed a break as well, and the colors are always relaxing."

The Traveler settled in with another bite of his sandwich.

They sat through the light show in what slowly became a mesmerized stupor, quietly watching the shifting display of colors that danced and twisted in hypnotic movements while eating and drinking barely acceptable food. They didn't say much of anything. They just sat for what could have easily been hours until the colors finally faded, and Yslawna turned on the lights.

She guided the Traveler back to the chapel through dismally depressing corridors and morose stairwells, which were all given a brief injection of life by her passionate comments on art and history. When they finally returned to the chapel, they prepared a toast.

"To Almerin and Awhet."

"To Al-Almerin and Awhet." The Traveler choked slightly on Almerin's name, but he raised his mug with Yslawna, who sat across from him, and he drank while she turned around to do the same in privacy.

He thought about asking if her injuries were really that bad, but he hesitated. Her sweet voice was clearly insincere, and her body language was twitchy and unsettled. Even the way she held her mug was somewhat jerky. He didn't know what sort of psychological land mines sat just below the surface. So, instead of trying to learn more about his new companion, he settled on simply staring down and swirling his hot, almost pleasant milky drink. He didn't need to know her. He just needed to work with her until the job was finished and he could find a way out of this place. He sank into the cushioned iron chair that he and Yslawna had taken from the ship and pulled into the kitchen so he wouldn't have to worry about shattering any of the chapel's fragile wooden chairs. While the thought of taking off his armor had crossed his mind, it had already taken a significant amount of courage to completely remove his helmet, which sat at a mere arm's length away on the kitchen table. Removing his armor would have to wait until he was more adjusted to his surroundings or possibly when his lack of bathing prompted Yslawna to say something.

"It's never easy to lose someone," she sympathized in an unusually subdued tone, "But it helps to know that they're never really gone. He'll come back in another life, and maybe you'll both rekindle your friendship there."

The Traveler somberly looked up, "What do you mean?"

"He'll reincarnate."

"What does that mean?"

Yslawna paused as she realized just how little the Traveler understood what was happening around him. She held up her hand. "The finger is you, your soul," She pulled on one of her fingers to make the point clearer. "The other fingers are your past souls. Like your current incarnation, your finger can move independently from the other fingers," she twittered her fingers to make this point as well. "However, they're all connected by the palm of the hand, which is your spirit. The goal of living is to learn, so your spirit creates different souls," She pulled on her finger again, "to experience life in different ways so it can learn. Do you understand?"

"No," the Traveler plainly answered.

"Well, you've been through a lot lately. We should explore the subject more after some time has passed."

"I think I killed him." The words just sort of spilled out of his mouth uncontrollably. Yslawna leaned forward and replied, "Whatever you think you did, you probably didn't."

"But I —"

She put her hand up to interrupt him. "Things happen, often very terrible things. You don't look like a murderer, though. I've seen murderers. Whatever mistake you might think you've made, you learn from it, and you move on. These things happen, I can tell you from my own horrible experiences." she said with a small, bitter laugh.

The Traveler sighed. He understood that he wasn't directly responsible for Almerin's death, but indirectly… "You have to help me finish our mission," he pleaded.

Yslawna put her mug down and said, "Why don't you start from the beginning."

The Traveler began to recount his fever dream of a journey. Being greeted by the red-headed woman, discovering Landala, Almerin, and their preparations to go to the palace and close the seal. Yslawna stopped him once when he mentioned the name Landala, but she couldn't pull the recollection and another time when he got to Almerin's meditation in the sanctuary.

Almerin told you that the Prince Adept left?"

"Yeah, he was really shaken up about it."

"Actually left?"

"He said that…" The Traveler leaned back as he sifted through the muddled gibberish that was his memory for the exact conversation, which Almerin's look of sheer terror helped to etch into his brain. "He said that he couldn't sense him at all, not even his tattered corpse."

Yslawna paused in contemplation and then quietly leaned forward and put her head in her hands.

"Are you okay?"

"No," she weakly replied. "No, I can safely say that I'm not. This is very bad. It's what we always feared might happen." She looked back up to the Traveler, whose perpetually bewildered expression hadn't changed, and she asked. "Do you know what the sun realm is?"

"Yeah, Almerin mentioned something about that. This is the moon plane or realm…"

"The terms don't matter too much."

"Oh, well, he said I came from the sun plane."

"You come from the sun plane? From the *actual* sun plane?"

"Yeah," he answered with a cautious twinge of uncertainty. "Is that bad?"

"Not bad, but incredibly bizarre. I thought you were from one of the tribal kingdoms outside Hiri Handi. I didn't realize you were *that* much of an outsider." She leaned back in profound thoughtfulness as she stared at the Traveler.

He responded to this uncomfortable reevaluation with a nervous sip of his drink.

"The leaders of the Golden Band," she suddenly began, "had long felt the Prince Adept was looking to project himself into a new kingdom. We've felt for a while now that he had been using the terrors of Hiri Handi to create some sort of… abomination of an army, or at least some sort of unholy mass of demons that he could simply unleash to devastate any adversary. I think he's looking to unleash that force on what little is left of this world."

The Traveler sat up and said, "I don't understand. I thought the whole world was already like this place."

"No, no," Yslawna hastily corrected. "Hiri Handi, sitting in the heart of the storm, is falling between dimensions."

The Traveler still didn't comprehend what that meant, and he conveyed this to Yslawna with a blank stare.

"Imagine that this city is a bubble, filled with monsters and evil," she explained, "but we've caught glimpses of the outer world.

It's certainly not a happy place. It's crawling with power-hungry warlords and savagery, but it's not at all like this! If the Prince Adept unleashes Hiri Handi on the rest of the world, it would be a slaughter."

The Traveler wished he could sympathize, but the stakes felt distant to him. He didn't know any of these people. Almerin even said he wasn't from this world at all. Was it so terrible that he just wanted to find a way home and let everything here sort itself out? He knew that wasn't an option. He knew he had to save those savage warlords outside the city and what few, if any, people were left in Hiri Handi. He had to do what was right...

"And now that you've said you're from the sun plane, I have to wonder if the Prince Adept is targeting your home too."

"What? Why?!" the Traveler sputtered, his unempathetic disconnect shattered.

"Why else would someone from the sun plane journey into the abyss?" she said, while demonstrating the act by raising her hand and then plunging it below the table with a dramatic flair.

He knew she might be right. Why else would he be here? It didn't fill him with a courageous sense of duty, though, just dread and a feeling of entrapment. She waited for him to respond while he went to take another sip of his drink. It was empty, and he set it on the table with a small, defeated groan. He looked back up at Yslawna, and the single phrase she casually mentioned when he first sat down with her finally penetrated his cognitive thought. The weary cogs of his mind began to turn. "You said you belong to a group, the Golden Band?"

Yslawna tentatively slid back in her seat as she replied, "Yes, but not many of us remain."

"But you said you weren't sure. Some of you might still be out there, right? Are you certain they're all dead?" he persisted, the small tinder of hope beginning to burn in his chest. "Maybe we can find them!"

Yslawna sighed, not a normal sigh, but one that rattled out from a deep and dark place. "No one has responded to my signals for a long time, and I think it might be dangerous to go looking for them. It might be better to do this on our own."

"No. Almerin and I tried to go by ourselves, and now he's dead. We need help." The Traveler wasn't willing to play this isolated game of self-sacrifice anymore. They were going to get help and build an army, and that was that.

She looked down, either in deep thought or some other emotion that he couldn't perceive, and said, "I only know of two who might be left, and I don't even know what shape they're in. But you might be right," she conceded with an outward gesture of her hand. "We do need as much help as we can get, and we also could use some special maps if we're going to break into the palace."

"Almerin had some maps in his tower."

"Then that's a second place to look. I have a good idea for the first. But we should have spiritual guidance before any of this."

"How do we get that?"

"I lost the ability a long time ago, but…" she stared at the Traveler and then enthusiastically pointed to him. "You said you spoke to a spirit called Landala?"

"Yeah, she helped me several times. She gave me a necklace, too." The Traveler pulled Landala's necklace out of his satchel and placed it on the table with a disgusting, slimy plop.

"AH!" The Traveler stood up in confusion and wrenched off his sap-covered gauntlet, which clattered on the table. "Why is this happening!?"

"What is—" Yslawna started to point at the ooze-covered necklace, but the Traveler cut her off by pulling out his satchel and dumping the contents onto the table, which slowly slid out in a horrible, congealed pool of slop. An oozing wooden heart slid out on top of the mess, and the bizarre experience with the tree that he had shoved into the depths of his mind as something unsettling that he could deal with later rushed back into his forethought.

Yslawna aimed a shocked finger at the heart and shouted several blasphemous exclamations that would've surely earned a hearty slap from her moon goddess.

"I... uh..." the Traveler struggled to put into words something he barely understood himself. "I pulled it out of the giant tree in the sanctuary. Do you know what it is?" he asked, turning to Yslawna, who hadn't lowered her finger.

"No, I've never seen anything like this! You pulled it out of the Aclamartom tree?"

"Yeah, Almerin told me to."

Yslawna put both hands on the table and leaned closer to get a better look at the heart. The Traveler did the same.

It was still oozing sap, and the Traveler was almost sure it was beating.

They both stepped back and looked at each other, each waiting for the other to come up with an idea.

Neither of them could.

"We need guidance." Yslawna declared.

The Traveler agreed with a fierce nod.

"Can you pass me the necklace?"

He sifted through the pile with one finger, drew out the gooey pearl necklace, and gingerly passed it to Yslawna, who immediately turned to the kitchen sink.

"Did Landala say why she gave it to you?" She asked while grabbing a thin hose attached to a ceiling-mounted water canister.

"She said it was to communicate with me."

"Fantastic!" She turned a knob on the canister and eagerly began washing off the necklace.

The Traveler sat back down and started to sip his drink, which was still empty.

Yslawna turned slightly and asked, "Do you know anything about the spirit?"

"Not much," the Traveler sighed at his own inattention and put the empty cup back down. "Her name is Landala, and she was one of Almerin's students."

"Can you describe her?"

"Um… small, dark-haired."

"And she was one of Almerin's students…" Yslawna repeated to herself. She grabbed a cloth to help scrub off the slime, "How old was she?"

"I don't know, less than ten, maybe."

She slowly pulled her hands away from the faucet and began tentatively tapping on the sink.

"Almerin said he had been something of a guardian for her," The Traveler continued, noting Yslawna's sudden agitation, "and that her real father was distant. That's all I know."

Yslawna mumbled something under her breath and began fumbling through her bags for something.

"Is everything okay?" he asked as Yslawna started opening cupboards in the kitchen while cursing under her breath.

"I'm trying to find a history book." She opened a cabinet in the corner of the room and pulled out a hefty red book, which she began fiercely speeding through.

He waited for some sort of dramatic revelation, as seemed to be her style. Unfortunately, the revelation was far more dramatic than he anticipated, and he jolted in shock as Yslawna suddenly hurled the necklace across the room, where it clattered against the wall.

"Yslawna?!"

"Don't talk to her again!" She snapped with a fierce finger aimed at the Traveler's face. "Landala was the daughter of the Prince Adept, and she's as decayed and corrupt as he is!"

"But—"

"He could be using her to try and get to both of us. That's what they do here. They corrupt others and use them to destroy or corrupt even more. DON'T TALK TO HER AGAIN!"

The Traveler wanted to argue that Landala saved his life when he fell from the archives, but Yslawna was leaning over the table with such a terrifying ferocity that he feared she might turn on him if he said even a word of this. He instead simply asked, "What do we do then?"

"We get rid of the necklace, we store…" Yslawna pointed to the beating wooden heart, "that thing… and we continue with the plan to find some allies."

"Okay, I'll get rid of the necklace then. Where's a good place to throw it?"

"The hanger is fine," she replied, completely oblivious to the Traveler's extremely transparent plan to keep the necklace. "When you're done, you should come back here so we can talk."

"Sure." The Traveler slid his helmet on and took a sideways glance at his slimy gauntlet. He would have to leave with his right hand exposed until he washed it later. He started to walk away and then compulsively turned around to put his disgusting gauntlet back on while trying not to look at Yslawna, who had sat back down, watching him. He collected the necklace and then walked away with absolutely no intention of getting rid of it. Landala was a creepy child, but she was the one who saved him. He was also certain that she was the one who talked Almerin into leaving. It couldn't have been any of his feeble arguments. It must have been her.

CHAPTER EIGHT

A Nice Little Detour

"It is understood that the nature of life is cyclical, with the purpose being the continued evolution of the spirit. Many have asked, if life is cyclical then why should death have any meaning? The answer, in my opinion, is simple. If the purpose of physical life is learning, then how many of us would comprehend the true value of life without death to contrast it? How many of us would understand light without dark? Today, we will explore these concepts."

-Almerin Arnaz Telith, Master of the Scarlett Arch and head of the Aclamartom Sanctuary and academy in Hiri Handi. Lecture on the nature of death.

Twenty-two years before the opening of the seal.

The Traveler made his way through the chapel, down the bedroom hallway, and up a little staircase tucked away in the corner. He retraced his steps as best he could, only coming across two dead ends where he had to turn around. He soon found himself in the chapel's hanger, nestled somewhere in the upper part of the music hall. The metallic skeletons of old, dismantled ships were stuffed into the shadowy corners of the room, all picked apart to service the Dancing Star, which pridefully sat in the center. It was battered, dented, clawed, and many of its panels were missing, leaving delicate wiring and mechanisms exposed. Despite the scarring injuries and its fire-prone engine, it didn't seem to sink into feebleness. Instead, it sat proudly in the center of the room with all its age and debilitations like a venerable matriarch who could still upheave the world if given the right chance.

The Traveler gave the Dancing Star its due acknowledgment and approached the hangar doors. The colossal iron entrance that rose up to the ceiling and spanned to the far edges of the hanger was closed to both help protect the ship when it wasn't in use and limit intrusions into the chapel.

He nervously hovered his hand over an innocuous control panel as he mentally retraced Yslawna's relatively easy steps to open the door.

"The red lever on the left side..."

He thought it was overly dramatic to open the two massive doors just to toss out a necklace, or rather pretend to, but Yslawna had been frighteningly insistent. He wanted to be sure she heard the doors open.

He gave the red lever a solid tug, which stuck slightly and then thumped downward. The whole room rumbled in a way that made his teeth want to jump out of his mouth as the doors slowly and painfully slid open with an arthritic effort. Suddenly, the vast, terrifying midnight cityscape of Hiri Handi once again sprawled out before him.

He paused, allowing himself to be absorbed by the sheer enormity of the landscape, which never ceased to amaze him, before shoving the lever back up when fears of attackers started pecking at his fragile state of mind. After the aged doors finished closing, he descended back into the heart of the chapel. He backtracked to the kitchen with the necklace safely in his satchel, where he found

Yslawna leaning over a ragged map set out on the table. She looked up and tentatively asked,

"Did you do it?"

"I took care of it," The Traveler lied. "I've seen the Prince's handy work. I don't need his daughter hanging around looking to take a chunk out of my neck."

"What?"

"She just looked... scary," The Traveler added while sitting back down in the iron chair. He hoped that detail might solidify his lie.

Yslawna gazed across the table at him momentarily and then pointed behind her, saying, "The heart is in the sink. I have no idea what it does, but it won't stop oozing, so I put it over there. Carrying it around is going to be tricky." She hedged slightly and looked back down to the map, "I also wanted to apologize for my... anger earlier."

"Oh, don't worry about it," the Traveler dismissed. He really wanted to stop talking about the necklace.

Yslawna sat down and massaged her head as if to alleviate an endless migraine. "It's been a terrible time for me lately. I've seen many deaths, and Awhet's is still very fresh for me..." She paused and looked up at the Traveler, who was terrified she somehow sensed the presence of the necklace with psychic forces that he couldn't comprehend.

"Do you want to go for a walk?" she suddenly asked, perking up slightly.

The concept was absolutely appalling to the Traveler. Not only was he still nervous about keeping the necklace from Yslawna, but any walk beyond the protection of this little fort could easily result in a horde of monsters devouring him. He decided to venture for specifics. "Do you mean around the chapel?"

"No, I mean outside the music hall."

It was worse than he thought. Outside the music hall was completely unacceptable.

"S-Sure," he compulsively answered, not wanting to arouse suspicion. He hated himself.

"Great!" Yslawna hopped up and enthusiastically skipped over to the exit, slowing down her pace for the Traveler, whose complete lack of enthusiasm had made getting up from his chair an arduous task. He followed her outside the reinforced door, which she shut with a dull thud and locked behind them.

He could change his mind. He could say he was too tired.

She looked over at him with a glowing cheerfulness and announced, "Okay, I'll lead the way!"

The Traveler just nodded.

They walked out of the shattered entrance of the music hall. Yslawna strolled down the river of winding blue steps like a gleeful child while the Traveler wearily followed behind, taking in the utter blackness with dread. He had almost rehabilitated his sense of smell from the time he spent above the darkness, but now it was once again brutally assaulted by the pervading rot. Through a fit of choking and gagging he launched a final desperate appeal, "Don't you think we should start looking for allies," he paused to cough, "and then search for a way to enter the palace?"

"Absolutely, but morale and unity are important to success. A walk would do us good!"

"What about the horrible giant monster that tried to eat me? Isn't it still around?"

"It won't be back for a long while, and I'll sense it when it comes."

The Traveler wasn't convinced and would have persisted in arguing if Yslawna's mood hadn't unexpectedly shifted to a such a lighter tone. He couldn't tell if it was fake or if being out in the rotting, suffocating lower city was actually benefiting her. If the pungent, stale air helped stabilize his new companion, then maybe something good would come from this horrible trip after all.

"Okay," he resigned. "But I'm trusting you."

"Trust is always the first step!"

He gave a weak nod and continued following. She led them down an empty boulevard lined with dead trees and malevolent houses that melded in and out of the shadows when Yslawna's lantern was able to cast its faint light across them.

She finally stopped before a particularly derelict shop with shattered windows and an illegible sign barely hanging onto the building.

The Traveler stood next to her and asked, "Is something wrong?"

"No. This has always been a good place to look, so let's start here."

"Look for what?"

"Trinkets!"

The Traveler thought he could see a beaming smile under her usually impenetrable veil. She enthusiastically bounced into the store with the Traveler nervously trailing behind. They stepped into a wide entry space that braggishly directed his eyes towards aisles and aisles of moldy clutter.

The shadows suddenly squirmed and contorted as creatures darted away from Yslawna's lantern.

"We're not alone!" The Traveler quickly drew his sword and prepared for an attack.

"Relax." Yslawna put her hand on his shoulder, "They're just lesser beings."

"But —"

"I can tell if something bigger is coming. I've done this for many, many years."

"I thought you said you lost the ability?"

"I said I lost the ability to commune with spirits," she replied, taking in the miserable scenery with an incomprehensible anticipation. "I would be dead if I lost all my senses."

The Traveler lowered his sword but refused to sheath it while Yslawna began rummaging through the aisles. "What sort of objects do you like?" she inquired while brushing aside some old cartons.

"Um, I don't know," The Traveler distractedly answered, still keeping watch for those creatures that ran away. "I haven't really thought about it."

"You should. A hobby is a great way to maintain positivity, especially when things get rough. Awhet would go nuts for new plates, especially if they had little intricate designs on them."

"I guess the wall was his doing."

"You guessed right."

She pulled out a nasty, ragged blue and white checkered cloth, which she flapped twice before discarding it to search another pile of junk. The Traveler quickly deduced that Yslawna was responsible for the chapel's cloth web of madness.

"You should find a hobby," she continued while sifting through some soggy boxes. "It's important to find something to occupy your time with."

"I think I'm okay. I just want to close the seal and get out of here."

She paused her search and slowly looked up at the Traveler. "It's not good to think like that."

"Think like what?"

"Like you're absolutely going to succeed. Like everything is going to be okay."

The Traveler was taken aback. "I don't understand. You think I should plan for failure?"

"Yes, without question. You need a backup plan, and you need to temper your expectations. Otherwise, defeat will destroy you."

"I…" the Traveler hesitated while trying to wrap his head around the concept of failing. "What kind of backup plan do you mean?"

"How are you going to survive in Hiri Handi if we fail? I might be killed, and you might be left alone. How are you going to stay sane?"

"Well, I..." he wavered again. The concept of simply living in this hellish nightmare of a place, alone, without any immediate goal or purpose, was completely incomprehensible to him. It couldn't be done. "I don't have a backup plan," he finally admitted. "We have to close the seal, and that's... just it."

Yslawna stared at him for a moment before pushing the soggy box away with a sigh. "You have an inflexible mind."

"What? No, I don't."

"Then go find a hobby."

"What?"

"Go look around this place for something you like." She gestured to the cluttered junk piled on either side of them. "Take it and bring it back to me."

The Traveler started to sputter out a confused rejection of the senseless task but stopped as Yslawna just stared at him again. He was probably proving her point. "Okay," he relented. "Fine, I'll look around for something nice. But be sure to warn me before anything tries to attack us."

"Absolutely. Try looking at the far wall over there. There's a few fancy ornaments still intact."

The Traveler left Yslawna, who returned her attention to her pile of garbage. Following her directions, he gazed up at an entire shelf of ugly clutter and half-melted trash. Ghostly figurines, rotten cartons, twisted metal bits, and shattered pottery ran across the whole wall. He didn't want any of it. When he reached the end of the shelf, he glanced around a little before wandering into the next aisle in a methodical order.

More and more garbage...

The next aisle, more and more garbage...

Next aisle, just garbage...

Next aisle, Yslawna sifting through some shelves. "Did you find anything?"

"Not yet," he mumbled.

He ambled into yet another pointless aisle, stopped, looked around, and stared at nothing but trash. "There has to be something around here," he muttered to himself as he pushed aside the grime and junk on the shelves in the hopes that something worthwhile might be hiding behind a rotting carton or a bent can. He couldn't find anything, so he randomly grabbed a partially melted boat to keep Yslawna off his back and went to the shop entrance, where he waited for his companion to finish whatever she was doing.

She came strolling out not long after him with a bright yellowish tablecloth, which she triumphantly held out to the Traveler, who took in her sheer joy at the simple object with visible unease. It was mostly intact and embroidered with what looked like various fruits.

She tied her cloth treasure across her waist and asked, "What about you? Did you find anything?"

"I did." He apathetically held out his melted piece of trash.

Yslawna examined the boat with more interest than the Traveler was comfortable with and then looked up and asked, "What does it mean to you?"

"What?"

"Why did you choose this? What does it mean?"

The Traveler blankly stared at her as his mind scurried around for some sort of answer. "Uh, it represents… freedom, blue skies, and open seas."

"No, it doesn't," Yslawna accused with a finger pointed at his face.

The Traveler sighed and discarded the little boat. "Okay, I couldn't find anything. But it's been a long day, so maybe another time will be better." He paused as he realized with horror that he just extended an invitation to roam around this nightmarish city a second time.

"Let's sit," Yslawna suggested, settling down on the shop steps and waiting for the Traveler to do the same.

"I'd rather not."

She just looked at him and patted the step next to her. He wasn't getting out of this easily. He took an apprehensive breath and sat down with his back exposed to any monsters in the shop behind him and his front exposed to anything else lurking in the surrounding darkness.

"I gave you a test," Yslawna started, "I wanted to see where your psyche was."

"I guess I failed."

"It's not a test you can really fail... but yeah, I guess you did. Let me try and explain. I used to be an inquisitor of sorts..."

The Traveler quickly glanced over at Yslawna, suddenly terrified of his companion.

"The brethren of the Golden Band were going insane," she started, "so I would be sent to investigate murders or evaluate problematic individuals to make sure they weren't a threat to others. The trinket thing was a test. The choice of object was always a good indicator of someone's mental health."

"Are you... going to try and kill me?"

"NO," Yslawna jolted in shock. "NO, of course not! I'm just concerned for your wellbeing. I'd never murder you!"

He gave a slight nod, followed by a quick effort to derail the conversation, "Okay then, can we go back to the Music Hall?"

"Not yet. You still chose nothing as your trinket."

"What does that mean?"

"It means you don't accept the circumstances."

"How can I? Look around," the Traveler exclaimed with an outward gesture toward the horrible void of blackness in front of them. "Look at what's been happening. How could I ever accept any of this?"

"You need two psychological anchors to survive in Hiri Handi," she explained while softly pushing his arm down. "You need a sense of calmness in your life and a strong purpose to keep you grounded. What you're doing right now is rejecting any possibility of calmness by only focusing on how you want things to be, not how they are."

"I don't understand. How do I NOT focus on the monsters trying to eat me alive?"

"If you only focus on what's wrong and horrible around you, then the long-term psychological toll will eat you alive like one of the actual monsters. Believe me, I've seen it many times."

"You're worried I'll have a mental breakdown?"

"Worse than just a breakdown," Yslawna said, slumping slightly as if the words were pulling her down. "You'll start down an ugly path by focusing more and more on the gnawing agony deep inside you because you're always losing far more than you can ever gain. You'll first blame the amorphous circumstances of the world around you, then the people in it, and finally, yourself because you're too weak to make things how you think they should be. Then, some-thing starts whispering in your ear and pointing out your failures. It will tell you that you're weak and starving because the bonds of love that connect us actually make us fragile and dependent. That true power comes from absolute self-sufficiency, and that true independ-ence only comes from the realization that everything exists to either serve or hinder you."

The Traveler nudged backward as Yslawna leaned closer.

"When you start to believe that you are hurting because you deserve to BE hurt, that the weak deserve to suffer and the powerful deserve to prosper because it is the natural order of things. When you resolve to no longer be weak, to no longer exist in the shadow of oth-ers but instead make THEM exist in your shadow, you begin to give credence to the darkest impulses of your being. You slowly become a ravenous predator, an animal that only seeks to satiate its starvation. You become one of the beasts of Hiri Handi."

"You think I'm going to become one of—" The Traveler's indignant anger caused the sentence to stick in his throat. The thought of those monsters, let alone becoming one, was unthinkable to him.

"I've done this for a long, long time," she explained. "This entire place is a recruiting ground to build an army of horrors that will go on to spread more pain and misery, and it devours people just like you," she said with a firm hand on the Traveler's shoulder, "If you continue like this, then it will either spit out your corpse or turn you into a mockery of your former self."

The Traveler looked away. He didn't know what to say. He didn't know if there was anything to say.

"What's your purpose?" Yslawna suddenly asked.

The Traveler was caught off guard and gave a confused, "What? My purpose?"

"Yeah, what's driving you? What's pushing you forward?"

He looked back to that infernal wall of blackness in front of him and replied with, "My purpose is to close the seal and escape this hell."

"Why?"

"What? What do you mean why?"

"Why close the seal? Why not just try and escape?"

"How could I possibly escape any of this on my own?" He said with a profoundly sarcastic laugh that was drenched in fear and pain. "I was hoping you would take me out of this city with you after the seal was closed."

"What if I gave you a way out now?"

He paused. He didn't know what sort of psychological test this was, and Almerin made it seem like leaving wasn't really an option. "How?" he cautiously asked.

"I could bring you back to Almerin's tower. We'll kill the monster that murdered Almerin, so you'll be safe there. I'll try to close the seal myself, and that will bring the city onto a stable plain of existence. Then I'll come back and take you out of the city with me."

"That's a false choice," he huffed. "If I don't help you, then you might die, and I'd just wither away in Almerin's tower."

"It's not a false choice," she sternly retorted. "I'm scared that you're too focused on the task and you're not taking the time to adjust to life here. I'm scared that you're not even able to adjust to life here. And if we failed in our mission, if we were forced to bide our time and wait for another opportunity while existing in Hiri Handi, it would destroy you. You don't have a fundamental purpose to keep you going other than the single-minded resolve of the current mission at hand. You have one feeble anchor of purpose, and you're not even able to accept the anchor of calmness at all. You're just drifting from place to place, looking for an escape. This makes you vulnerable."

The Traveler didn't respond. Part of him knew she might be right. But how could he ever empathize with these people or this quest? Everything here was disgusting and evil, and they did it all to themselves.

"Can you tell me why you would die for this cause?"

"Because…" He almost said something noble like, *the fate of the world rests in our hands*. He truly wanted that to be enough. He wanted a sense of empathy, a sense of good, and justice to be enough to die for. It wasn't, though. He didn't know these people. He had no connection to this world and wasn't ready to die. He hated this place, and no amount of philanthropic idealism could ever persuade him otherwise. "I can't," he answered.

Yslawna didn't say anything. She simply sighed and stood up to leave, with the Traveler doing the same.

"When we're ready, we'll be going to the Grand Library," she announced. "That was the stronghold of the Golden Band, and there might be a survivor left inside. However, you're going to see nightmares in that place, horrible nightmares."

The Traveler twitched at the concept of something worse than what he'd already encountered so far, "What do you mean?"

"When the seal was opened, the pain was just too great, and the population slowly lost their minds. Evil used this and the instability of the bleeding seal to spread its power and convert many into monsters who would then go on to destroy everything around them. Upon the rise of this darkness, the oldest and strongest spirits incarnated in our land gathered as much of the population as they could to shelter them. These people were raving, insane, and dangerous. We lined the library with their cages and prisons to contain them as we tried to heal what was left of their broken minds. This was where I," she pointed to herself, "and almost all of the order came from. We could only heal a few, however. Their pain was deep and treating the mind is a difficult thing. Their screams and cries filled the library like a chorus of anguish. If you go, you're going to witness this, and I wanted you to understand before stepping foot in that building. It's a sight that can often break people."

"All of those… people are still there?"

"Yes, and with little to no members of the order left, they likely have run of the place. This, among other personal reasons, is why I haven't been back for so long." Yslawna walked up to the Traveler and looked through his visor at his tired, frail eyes. "I want to give you a choice. Up until now, circumstances have been pulling you along. You can choose to come with me to close the seal and face the myriad of possible gruesome fates that lie at the end of your short life in the service of humanity. Or I can take you back to Almerin's tower. I'll kill the monster that slayed your friend, and you can take Almerin's place. You'll be safe, and nothing will ever harm you. If I succeed, I'll come back for you and take you out of the city."

"I..."

"Please don't answer now," she stopped him. "Sleep on it, and when you awaken, come to me with your answer. Please understand that there's no dishonor if you choose to stay behind. This needs to be your choice, not something you do because circumstances are forcing you to."

The Traveler started to call out to Yslawna as she walked away, but he didn't. He didn't know what to say. The trip back to the music hall was quiet, unpleasant, and sprinkled with minor small talk that only served to avoid retracing their previous conversation.

The Traveler spent a large part of that night pacing in his little bedroom while trying to come to terms with what Yslawna was asking of him. How could she even ask him, though? He didn't need a profound purpose beyond the mission. There was absolutely no way he was going to stay in Hiri Handi.

He sat on the bed, which gave a complaining groan to the weight of his armor, and he pulled off his helmet and shoved it onto the nearby nightstand. He pulled off his gauntlet and massaged his aching face.

He could stay in Almerin's tower like the old man wanted in the first place. A quiet death. Maybe he wouldn't even die. Yslawna would carry on the torch with or without him, and she seemed capable enough. It was clear that he'd found someone to give the mission over to, so why didn't he? He thought about Almerin in his tower and wondered if he would end up like him. Scared, isolated, and waiting forever in vain for an outcome that might never happen. Would Almerin's death be in vain if he stayed behind? He forced the old man out of his tower and then abandoned him during the sanctuary battle. Did he owe it to Almerin to keep pressing forward and assure that the seal was closed? He could lie. He could tell Yslawna that he'd thought about it and that he was committed to the wellbeing of the world. All they needed to do was finish the mission. He wasn't going to stay here for any length of time.

Time...

He sighed and let the constant tiredness seeping into his muscles drag his head downward. Why was he lying to himself? This mission wasn't going to end quickly, if at all. He might be stuck here. The music hall might be his home now.

He put his head in his hands and trembled as the sickening concept took hold of him, no longer allowing him to bask in the pleasantness of a perfect world where he would close the seal and leave Hiri Handi to retire in some majestic countryside with great mountains and thick green trees.

Was she right? Was he on a destructive path? Could he survive in the long term? Did he even want to? The thought scared him. He shook his head, pulled off his other gauntlet, and leaned back on his pillow.

He wondered what Yslawna must have been like before Hiri Handi ate her alive. She was probably less twitchy, more even-tempered, and less emaciated and disfigured. Was he going to end up like her? Twitchy, deformed, starved on tasteless food and enamored with dirty tablecloths. She was able to survive, though, in a way that he didn't think was even possible. She was able to survive while still keeping some amount of empathy for the world, even a world that did this to her.

He closed his eyes and hoped the horrible fat man didn't invade his much-needed sleep. He wanted to dream about buttered toast again, and he wanted to eat it this time.

CHAPTER NINE

The Grand Library

"This isn't like the old wars where you can butcher your enemies on a jointly agreed battlefield. This is a war of the mind, a war where psychology and paranoia are the weapons, and the true damage is self-inflicted."

-Enekoat Arzako, High Commander of the Golden Band
1,930 years after the opening of the seal.

The Dancing Star sluggishly pulled away from the music hall and set course for the old headquarters of the Golden Band, the Grand Library. The Traveler fidgeted in his seat as he struggled with what to say to Yslawna about last night. Instead, he hid behind the sounds of the rattling engine, the surging winds pressing against the windows, and the rattling dials cluttering the cockpit. He gazed outside and lethargically watched the glistening, early morning cityscape sweep past. He was tired, and the only sleep he could get was shallow and unfulfilling. He looked over to Yslawna, who was perched in her captain's chair, pulling some levers while keeping the large navigation wheel steady.

She hadn't asked him what his decision was during their breakfast, and she wasn't saying much of anything now. He wasn't sure if she was simply waiting for him to speak first or if she had grown concerned about him and was quietly contemplating what to do. Either way, it would cause problems down the road if he never mentioned Yslawna's question. He hesitantly exhaled, "Yslawna?"

She spun her chair around and looked at him.

He hedged as he considered lying to her with a story about some sort of profound realization of self-sacrifice for the greater good. However, instead of spinning a long meaningless yarn of deception, he stared at her dirty purple veil, which covered the damaged face of a profound individual. It wasn't the shallow power of muscle and force that emanated from his companion. No, sitting before him was someone with courage, an iron will to get up every day knowing that this endless nightmare was waiting right outside. If he wanted that same will to survive in Hiri Handi, then he couldn't off-handedly dismiss her. He bent his head down as he took a moment to reflect and then meekly began with, "I hate this place. I'm scared of everything, and I don't want to be here. You were right before. I'm drifting from place to place, and if I found an escape, I would probably take it. I know that might not be noble, but it's how I feel."

"Why are you traveling with me to close the seal then?" she asked in an uncharacteristically even tone.

"I don't know. I guess it seems safer fighting monsters with you than to try and hide away somewhere."

"I'll drink to that!"

"What?"

Yslawna leaned over and opened a small metal cupboard with a half-filled bottle of dark liquid. She sniffed it and reared back with disgust before pouring it into two small silver cups that had been tucked away nearby. She handed him the cup of dark liquid and leaned back in her chair with her cup raised, "to mediocre companions in a world of horrible choices!"

The Traveler chuckled in the wonderfully ungraceful way that comes with unexpected humor and said, "I don't understand what's happening. You're absolutely crazy."

"I wanted you to start thinking about everything happening here. You didn't give the answer I would've liked, but you're thinking about stuff now, and that's the first step."

The Traveler shook his head in confusion. He didn't understand Yslawna, and it was possible that he never would. She was clearly trying to help him, though, and that meant something to him. They raised their glasses in unison. Yslawna untied the bottom of her veil and brought her cup to a horribly disfigured mouth that gave the Traveler a chilling pause. He didn't dwell on it and quickly joined her in an unhealthy swig of the drink before they both spit it out, cursing in shock at what they had just allowed in their mouths.

"What the hell was that!" the Traveler sputtered.

"I don't know," Yslawna coughed and spat. "Awhet used to make and drink this all the time. He said he kept a special one here for emergencies." She refastened her veil and wrenched open the cupboard doors to shove the tainted bottle back in while the Traveler vigorously flushed his mouth with water from his canteen.

He glanced around the small cabin for a bucket. Finding none, he spat onto the floor instead and looked over to Yslawna, who was preoccupied with a crumpled note. "What's that?"

"I found it in the cupboard. It says, (*Note to self: this is a medicinal tonic, NOT alcohol. Do not drink!*), and then it gives instructions on how to use it."

"What? Is this going to kill me?"

"No," Yslawna reassured, "but we probably shouldn't drink anymore. I guess Awhet really did—"

A sharp, piercing squawk suddenly cut her off as it echoed across the vast distance of the city. There was a pause of horror before the Traveler scurried to the window to scan the horizon while Yslawna quickly began pulling levers to send the ship deeper into the city. With a sudden thump and a roaring of the rickety old ship that was barely holding itself together, they lurched deep under the nauseating fog that shrouded the hollow edifices of Hiri Handi.

"Why are we going under?!" the Traveler cried in terror. "What was that noise?"

"That was probably the Commander of the Reliquary."

The Traveler vaguely remembered the name that Yslawna had mentioned in passing and shouted across the sudden pounding engines, "Wait, is that the guy who attacks ships? I thought you and Awhet killed him!"

"I never said that."

"Well, I assumed since you didn't make a big deal of him!"

"Okay, that might have been my fault. However —" Another piercing squawk from above cut her off again, and she quickly began pressing some more buttons and pulling more levers as the sluggish craft continued its descent. "We need to stay low. Keep your eyes and ears open," she warned. She snapped on a pair of switches that triggered a dim set of floodlights to illuminate the alarmingly abyssal path ahead of them, "This is what we used to call *The Trap*."

"What?"

"The Commander will force the ship deeper into the city," she continued, snapping some more switches and turning on a few dim, orange lights around the ship. "Then he'll wait until the ship needs to resurface. That'll happen if the monsters of Hiri Handi swarm onto the ship and rip it to pieces. I need you to get the spear mounted on the outside of the cabin."

"But —"

"Go! Quickly," she shouted while waving him away with her hand. "Get it and come back!"

The Traveler stumbled out of the cabin, pulled a hefty brass-colored spear off its holster, and slid back inside. "Yslawna?"

"Shh," she hushed him with a single finger to her mouth as she turned the nobs on the different cockpit dials, silencing them and plunging the cabin into an uneasy quiet. The ship slowly meandered with a hum rather than a deafening screech, and the normally gushing wind was only gently whipping past. "Listen closely," she whispered, dimming the interior lights and allowing them to see a little better outside.

The Traveler stood still and listened. A light pecking somewhere outside caught his attention. "Yslawna."

"I hear it too. Go outside and spear it, then come back here. And don't stay out too long."

The dim orange lights illuminated only the bare essentials, which did little for him as he stepped outside and ungraciously slid his way across the cabin wall towards the pecking. He gingerly leaned over the ship's railing and illuminated the lower side with an orb of light. A scrawny little creature was picking at the side panels and looked up in terror. Its horrible sunken-eyed features looked human-ish; maybe it once was. Whatever it might've been, it couldn't stay on the ship. He hefted the spear up and struck the creature off into the blackness with a quick and vicious blow. He stepped back and basked in the power he suddenly had over these little beasts. If this was all he was facing, he could do this. Then another little beast jumped on his head, and he shrieked in all-consuming terror as it feverishly clawed at his helmet.

"AAAHHH!!!!"

He struggled and wrestled with the thing until Yslawna opened a window and tossed a thin, silvery bolt of magic that splattered the creature. The Traveler stood motionless, dripping in gore, as he tried to reclaim his scattered senses.

"Are you okay?" Yslawna leaned out the window.

"Not really," the Traveler called back, still frozen in terror.

"Are you hurt?"

"I don't think so."

"Then come back inside before something else jumps on you!"

He grabbed the spear, which thankfully hadn't rolled off the side of the ship during his panic, and ducked back into the cabin, being mindful to shut the door behind him. He staggered over to one of the red benches, sat down, and waited. Out the window, horrible husk-like buildings slowly crawled past. The meager sight illuminated by the faint yellow lights of the Dancing Star was upsetting enough, but the pair of eyes that would occasionally look back at him was just too much. "Yslawna, something's watching us."

"A bunch of stuff is watching us. Just keep aware and listen."

He kept listening, and it wasn't long before he heard that horrible pecking again. He marched outside, struck the beast off the ship, and then ducked back into the cabin. Then he heard several peckings at once. He marched outside and struck both beasts off the ship, then ducked back in. As they ventured further and further along, the peckings became clawings, which eventually turned into screaming bashings. The Traveler spent hours striking these little creatures and even slashed one that tried to jump on his head again. He lost track of time and only focused on massacring the swarm of monsters that now brazenly tried to tear the ship apart. He had become so focused on hacking his way through these horrible abominations that scrambled onto the ship like insects that he didn't even notice when the Dancing Star had finally passed back above the fog until Yslawna opened a window and shouted, "You can come back inside, we're out of danger."

The Traveler stopped, still dripping in blood and gore, and realized he could see the sun again, which greeted him with its typical blinding glare. He shakily wandered back into the cabin, let the spear slip out of his hands, and quietly sat down where he waited until they finally arrived at their destination. The Dancing Star tentatively circled around the Grand Library as it searched the area for any obvious signs of danger. The building was much more of a series of intermingling cathedrals than a single entity, which together far surpassed the size of the music hall in a dizzying display of grandeur.

The general form was different than the other sleek but striking towers of the city. The library was intricate and disorienting, with pale spires and obelisks sprouting like weeds from every corner. A healthy heaping of gardens and courtyards was also tossed over the complex for good measure.

The Traveler pressed his face against the cabin window and peered down at the mess of buildings to try and see if anything particularly terrible was waiting for them. Although he couldn't discern much of anything, let alone a threat, the place had a foreboding feel to it. He leaned back and whimpered, "I don't like this at all…"

"You shouldn't," Yslawna replied while turning the navigation wheel and steering the ship around a corner. "Toward its end, it was filled with crazy people, even crazier than me."

She piloted the ship down to a suitable landing spot that rested above the blanket of shadows and then flipped some switches that let the engine slowly shut down with a winding purr. She walked over to the Traveler, who remained seated. Protecting the ship had taken an unexpected toll on him, and he was still marshaling the will to go on.

"I'll be out in a second," he shakily said without looking up. "I just need to… catch my breath."

Yslawna slung her kaeta over her shoulder and said, "Take all the time you need. I'll check the area outside."

The Traveler stayed in and watched Yslawna through the window as she once again tried to open the draw bridge, whose stubborn refusal to give way forced her to climb down the side ladder instead. The cold isolation of Almerin's tower began to look more and more appealing, but he couldn't second guess himself now. He had to keep going. After a minute or so, he sighed, pulled himself up, and walked out of the cabin to join Yslawna.

As he descended the side ladder, his foot slipped, and he jerked violently before barely recovering his position. He took a quick glance down at Yslawna, who nervously fidgeted as he struggled to secure his footing. He indignantly shouted, "Why isn't there a door at the bottom of this ship?"

Yslawna took a cautious step back, "It was broken, so we welded it up to stop intruders. Please don't fall!"

The Traveler took note of her disheartening backstep. It was understandable. If she tried to catch him, he'd certainly crush her under the weight of his ridiculous armor. He cursed his heavy bunker of a suit, which was starting to become far more problematic than helpful. He still couldn't bring himself to take it off, though. He needed all the protection he could get. Carefully, step by step he climbed down while keeping track of every foot placement until he finally stepped onto the platform. Yslawna greeted him with a profound enthusiasm that, had he not known her, would have been easily interpreted as patronizing.

The small side entrance to the landing was rather subtle compared to the rest of the library. A simple wooden door sat under a decorative arch depicting a sky filled with birds soaring over white, fluffy clouds. The entryway was small but surprisingly warm and inviting, a feeling that was contrary to the rest of the library's intimidating exterior. They both walked up to the door expecting some kind of resistance, but to their surprise, it was unlocked and smoothly swung open as if eager to invite them inside. They cautiously entered and wandered onto a large balcony overlooking a stunning palace of a room. Towering bookshelves made of topaz and marble loomed over scattered clusters of classroom tables, chairs, and drawing boards covered in distant scribbles. Tall pink walls capped with white trimmings and a bright blue rug sprawling in four directions across a yellow carpeted floor gave the room a youthful, adolescent feel.

Yslawna wistfully leaned on the balcony railing and sighed, "Welcome to the children's wing. Not much has changed since I left."

The Traveler started to absentmindedly copy Yslawna and lean on the railing beside her with his incredibly heavy armor, but he quickly stopped himself before any damage was done.

Yslawna pointed down at some of the tables and distantly commented, "I studied down there."

"You guys had a school set up?"

"More than that. Most of us were often so mentally damaged that they had to reteach us how to perform simple tasks like reading and cleaning. They took us to the children's wing of the library and turned it into a place for rehabilitation. It was a peaceful time. We were protected from the outside world, and all we had to worry about were things like eye-hand coordination and how to speak."

The Traveler looked across the bright and beautiful room and could easily see the source of Yslawna's profound nostalgia. The place wasn't as peaceful as the sanctuary, but it was close. "I can understand why you'd want to stay here," he remarked in an effort to connect with his friend.

"Yeah, it was nice. At first, I didn't want to leave when my recovery was over, but I quickly realized that I had a job to do…" She sighed again and tapped her hand on the railing while stepping back, "If anyone is still here, then they're probably deeper inside the library. I'm surprised that there isn't any sign of the patients." She pointed across the room, "They should be running all over the place!"

"This looks like a big complex. Maybe they're hiding somewhere else?"

"But look how organized the room is! This place should be a disaster." She slid her finger along the railing and swept aside a decent amount of dust.

The Traveler looked around, "Organized but not clean…" He paused when he suddenly realized what he was inferring.

"Someone was here, but they haven't been back for a long time," Yslawna finished his thought.

She nervously tapped on the railing a couple of times before descending the flight of stairs that ran from the balcony down to the bright blue carpet below. They stepped off the stairs and followed the rug across an eerily silent room.

"This way," Yslawna pointed ahead, and the Traveler followed behind her unusually subdued pace.

Up close, the room was no longer inviting. It was beautiful and well-organized but also empty and quiet. The childlike, youthful energy had morphed into something destitute and painful, especially for Yslawna, who slowed down to look at a crate of old toys tucked under one of the classroom tables.

"Are you okay?" the Traveler asked from behind as Yslawna discarded some stuffed animals to the side.

"Yeah, I'm just looking for some memories. How's your memory been doing?"

"It's still mostly gone, but I've been getting more glimpses."

"Don't worry. They'll come back to you," Yslawna reassured while tossing another toy to the side.

"The memory loss doesn't bother me too much. I usually forget about it."

It took Yslawna a moment for the joke to impact, but once it did, she gave a chilling, cackling laugh like it was the first joke she had heard in years. "That was well done," she giggled as she struggled not to tip over.

The Traveler slowly backed away and gave Yslawna her space. The joke wasn't that good, and her unhinged laugh was unsettling. He meandered past a light wood table singled out from all the others by the clutter of books and maps tossed in a haphazard pile. He stopped before the mysterious pile to take a closer look, hoping that something on it might be useful. If this was the only spot that wasn't organized, then maybe someone had been here.

He brushed aside some scrolls and pulled out a particularly colorful map that made absolutely no sense whatsoever, and the fact that he couldn't read only made it more incomprehensible.

"I remember that! I always loved the colors of this map," Yslawna suddenly chimed in, leaving the crate behind and striding back to the Traveler with a stuffed yellow star in her hand.

He glanced at it and asked, "Did you find your memory?"

"I did," she tucked the star away in one of her bags and pointed to the map. "This was an attempt to record an experience in one of the higher dimensions and involved one of the more famous mental expeditions. It's a jumbled mess, though," her tone turned darker, "and the explorer ended up losing his mind."

The Traveler looked over at Yslawna and nervously put the map down.

"The ego is fragile," she continued, "and without the proper preparations to ground you or a robust willpower, many journeys into the higher or lower plains can blur the line between this reality and others. Usually, this is simply too much for anyone to handle."

The Traveler nodded. "Got it. No trips into the higher plains for me."

"It's a good skill to have. You just need to know what you're doing. But why is this table the only messy thing here?"

"That's what I was wondering," the Traveler stepped back as Yslawna began sifting through the papers and scrolls.

"These are all about the mind…"

"Is that bad?"

"I don't know." She put one of the maps down and grabbed another, "Maybe someone was looking into how to stabilize minds." She put down the map and turned to the Traveler, "Maybe Jalmi had been up here. That was his area of expertise, after all."

"So, he might still be here? Is that who we're looking for?"

"It's possible," she answered with a sudden jolt of enthusiasm. "I think the sanatorium is the first place to look. Follow me."

She gestured with her hand, taking off with the Traveler following behind.

As they descended deeper into the library, the magnificently bright walls of the children's wing were replaced with wood and then finally a pale blue that had aged poorly, turning cloudy and grey. The lights dimmed, and the ornamentations dwindled until only the absolute essentials remained. Still, there was no sign of any active life, not a single noise or a haphazardly discarded book.

Finally, they stood before a horrible grey door in the deepest depths of the library.

"You've seen the nice part. Now, welcome to the sanatorium," Yslawna sarcastically announced before pulling open the door to unveil a dark and twisted mirror image of the kind and high-spirited atrium they entered through. They stood on a balcony overlooking a space filled with hanging rusty cages and shredded wallpaper that exposed the heavy stone underneath. A sea of bookshelves built out of dark green quartz littered the ground floor, interspersed with what looked like operating tables and the occasional broken cage. Far in the center of the room was a monster of a creature cloaked in black and wearing a beaked helmet with glowing white eyes. It hunched over a bloody table, sifting through books and scrolls. Oddly though, the hanging cages were empty, and not a single soul other than the cloaked beast seemed present.

The Traveler stood aghast at the sight of the thing, and he jolted in horror when Yslawna casually strolled over the balcony edge and shouted, "Jalmi!"

The monster looked up at Yslawna and then quietly back down to its work.

"Maybe you should do the talking," Yslawna whispered to the Traveler, who was still stunned by the sight of the room and the horrible creature in it. "I don't think he's forgotten what I did."

"What did you do?"

"I ripped someone's heart out..."

"WHAT? You mean ACTUALLY...?!"

"Look, it was a complicated situation, and I've paid dearly for it since then. You should be the one to talk to him, though. You did start this off after all," she proclaimed with an encouraging pat on the back.

"Well..." he hesitated, "can you tell me anything about him?"

"He oversaw healing and rehabilitation. He's a kind soul with a great empathy for life."

"He doesn't look it," the Traveler replied, glancing over to the beast he had to talk to.

"He spent his time in Hiri Handi delving into countless mangled minds," Yslawna explained. "And it left its mark on him. Just be nice, and he will be too."

The Traveler nervously nodded while eying the imposing creature. "Okay," he muttered, "I can do this." He marched down a nearby flight of stairs to meet the ghastly thing while Yslawna followed a fair distance behind.

The air seemed thicker as he stepped off the stairs and onto the ground floor. The Traveler coughed at the sudden stench of mold as he made his way through the unsorted bookshelves, past bloody tables, and up to the looming monster who tapped twice on the table with a horrible metal claw of a hand while flipping through the pages of a grimy old book.

"Hello, Jalmi."

Jalmi didn't even look up.

The Traveler hesitated briefly before continuing, "I would tell you my name, but I honestly can't remember it," he said while walking forward, attempting to project both confidence and humility. "What I do know is that we desperately need your help."

Yslawna approached and watched from behind a bookshelf.

"And I know you have problems with Yslawna," he turned briefly to his friend, who gave a timid wave, "but we need your help,

Jalmi. We're going to close the seal. We're going to finally end this nightmare."

Jalmi didn't respond. He didn't even seem to acknowledge the Traveler's presence.

"Jalmi?" the Traveler cautiously asked, taken aback by the creature's utter silence.

He continued to flip through the pages.

The Traveler glanced behind at Yslawna for help, who gave him a thumbs up at a distance.

He turned back to the creature and said, "Jalmi, we NEED your help. People are dying. Please stop looking at the book!"

Jalmi ignored him and continued to flip through the pages.

The Traveler glanced back to Yslawna, who promptly darted over and put her hands on the book, which stopped Jalmi from turning the next page.

"Jalmi!" Yslawna shouted, and the creature replied with the blank, impassive stare of its beak-like mask.

She slowly relinquished her grip, and the creature simply stared at the two, its mask covering any hint of thought or contemplation.

It then resumed flipping through the pages of the book.

The two bemused recruiters walked back a reasonable distance, where the Traveler whined, "What's wrong with him? It's like his brain is melted!"

Yslawna turned around a couple of times as if looking for an elusive answer fluttering just out of sight and then suddenly stopped and looked upwards.

"There," Yslawna pointed.

The Traveler followed the direction of her finger and saw a thin pair of eyes veiled in shadows atop one of the hanging cages.

"What the hell is that?" the Traveler whispered, profoundly distraught that it had been watching them this whole time.

"Something that shouldn't be here." Yslawna pulled a heavy book from one of the shelves and hurled it at the creature with astonishing precision. The entity squirmed around the cage as the book narrowly missed its target, flying harmlessly past the creature and landing somewhere in the library with a solid thud.

Yslawna and the Traveler stepped back as the thing began screeching with a horrid wail that twisted the Traveler's eardrums until they wanted to duck inside his skull.

Jalmi suddenly stopped, and the two trespassers took another cautious step back with the Traveler readying his sword.

"Jalmi?" Yslawna gingerly asked as the creature stood in silent contemplation for a moment before picking up its table and heaving it at the both of them. They quickly ducked behind separate bookshelves for cover.

The Traveler scrambled up and shouted to Yslawna, "You said he was FRIENDLY!"

"He was!" she hollered back as Jalmi began lifting one of the quartz bookshelves.

They both cursed in unison and bolted back to the exit. The bookshelf collided with another right beside the Traveler in a terrible crash of smoke and stone that caused him to tumble to the ground. Yslawna grabbed his arm and helped him stumble out of the open main aisle and behind the cover of the surrounding bookshelves.

"MOVE!" Yslawna shouted as the Traveler slowed down, thinking they might be safe behind the fortress of bookshelves. They weren't, and another shelf crashed into the one next to them, causing a domino of cascading crashes that they narrowly managed to duck away from.

They weaved and turned their way through the aisles and away from the hurtling shelves that pounded any area they stayed a moment too long in until the stairway back up to the exit finally came into view. It sat there, out in the open and completely exposed. In the few seconds to make a decision, Yslawna screamed, "LEFT!" and the two darted to the side, away from the tantalizing exit that quickly received a hurtling bookshelf, collapsing the staircase into rubble. They darted back into the maze of shelves and continued making their way leftward.

Amidst the surrounding explosions and the dizzying dodging from left to right, the Traveler lost track of Jalmi's location. They finally shot out of the devastated isles and began barreling towards a small side door when Jalmi's horrific claw of a hand reached out and batted the Traveler to the side. He didn't know how that lumbering mammoth had moved so quickly, and he cursed life itself for being so unfair as he slid to the side. But he was alive. It was instinctual. He didn't plan it, but when he saw that claw, he poured every ounce of energy he had into the suit, and it locked up and saved his life. His horrible, cumbersome bunker of a suit had kept him alive when even the monster thought he should be dead. Jalmi turned away as Yslawna cried out in horror, and he saw an opportunity. He clamored up as the monster began to rip out another shelf, and he poured what little energy he had left into his sword and dug it into the monster's back. It screamed in a nauseating, ungodly way, dropping the shelf and staggering. The Traveler wrenched out the sword and scrambled to the door along with Yslawna, who bolted it shut behind them.

CHAPTER TEN

The Gated Waltz

"Never underestimate the power of books. The entire wealth of knowledge of our species at our fingertips, and we still somehow find ways to create hardships."

-Jalmi Yabeen, Librarian of the Grand Library
Twelve years before the opening of the seal.

The Traveler's eyes blurred, and he coughed as breathing suddenly became harder. Yslawna rushed over as he stumbled into a wall, and dragged him onwards, shouting, "NO! We need to keep moving!"

Then, a bookshelf collided with the door, and the whole passageway behind them collapsed. They barreled forward and crashed into the ground, only narrowly avoiding the cave-in. Everything turned dark, and the Traveler passed out.

He was in that awful dimly lit room again, lined with the unpleasantly striped dark blue and red wallpaper. The man obscured by shadows sat opposite him, still breathing in a cigar and then bellowing out smoke. The man lowered his cindering torch and said in his irritatingly strangled voice, "Welcome back."

"Fuck you," was the Traveler's reply. He hated this man, and he hated that he'd just been slapped by the horrific claw of the supposedly gentle and peace-loving Jalmi. He was not in the mood for this.

The man laughed in a croaking way that made the very walls squirm uncomfortably. "Indeed," he chuckled, "and I imagine you feel the same way about the whole world right now." He puffed on his cigar and lowered it, spewing out smoke like an old chimney.

The Traveler didn't know why he was listening to any of this. He stood up and began to walk to the door.

"It's a mistake to help Jalmi," the horrible old man said. "Not everyone wants to be saved."

The Traveler stopped. He'd be stupid to listen. The man was clearly evil. He put his hand on the cold brass doorknob as the man called out, "You'd have to use the heart."

The Traveler stopped again, wearily turned around and asked, "What do you know about that?"

"I can teach you how to use it. It's the only thing that might possibly reach your... new friend," he said with a disgusting chuckle.

"No thanks, I can figure it out myself." He turned back to the door.

"I should at least warn you about the heart."

The Traveler guardedly turned around.

"As an investment towards our budding association."

"Speak!" the Traveler didn't know why he was even listening, but he resolved to only listen for a moment and then leave.

The man puffed on his ridiculously fat cigar and then bellowed out smoke like a burning house fire, savoring his brief power over the Traveler's attention.

"The Heart has the power to enter memories — skin to skin, heart to heart," he said in the most unpleasant way. "When you enter Jalmi's memories, make sure to pay close attention to his state of mind, or you'll suffer dearly."

He was clearly being manipulated, and what made it worse was that the Traveler entirely expected it and had walked into the trap anyway. He thought about cursing the demented chain smoker but felt too tired and dizzy. He instead settled for walking out the door and slamming it behind him.

He blinked several times as the shapeless blur of the room slowly came into focus. "UUhhh, AAahhhh...."

"Yeah, you're going to feel like that for a while." Yslawna's distorted form slowly solidified, sitting at his feet while looking up from a partially disintegrating book. "You spent a lot of energy in that fight, and the medicine I just gave you is temporary. If we want to look on the positive side, I'd say our encounter was a partial success."

"How do you figure?"

"Well, no one died."

The Traveler sighed. That was a horribly depressing metric to judge success by. He leaned up as much as his sore muscles would allow and looked around. He was sitting in an alcove in the wall with one of Yslawna's cloth blankets tucked behind his head. The room was somewhat small, damp, dark, and colored with that ugly blue-grey wallpaper, which meant they were probably still in the depths of the library. A couple of stray bookshelves sat at the other end of the room, along with some dark wood doors and scattered tables.

He leaned back down with a groan, "What do we do now?"

"Well, I couldn't carry you far, so I didn't do much scouting. I didn't want anything to eat your face off while I was gone."

"Thanks."

"You're welcome! So, while you were unconscious, I came up with a plan," she announced with a sparkling enthusiasm that somehow scared the Traveler. "I think we could try and reach out to Jalmi."

The Traveler twitched.

"I think that creature is manipulating him," she continued, "probably to slowly siphon his energy. That means he's not completely lost. I have my kaeta with me, which I can use to soothe him while you keep his attention—"

"I can't really move," The Traveler interrupted.

"Don't worry, I'll give you a chunk of my own energy along with some crystals to boost you. So, here's my plan. The library used to house an armory. If we can get there, we might be able to grab a rifle that you can use to snipe the creature controlling Jalmi. If you miss, then I'll play a song to soothe him while you run around and keep his attention away from me. Your armor will help in case you actually get hit, but we avoided his attacks before, and I'll be slowing him down. Once he stalls, you can target the little parasite again."

The Traveler nodded. Maybe it was the utter lack of energy that clouded his tired mind, but the perilous plan actually seemed reasonable enough. If he could just shoot the creature controlling Jalmi, then everything would be over quickly. "Do you know where the armory is?"

"I believe I remember, but first, let's get you on your feet." Yslawna pulled off her glove and held out a hideously gnarled hand covered in deep burn scars. The Traveler hesitated at the sight of her deformity but then quickly pulled off his own gauntlet and grasped her hand. It felt like a weight had suddenly been lifted off his chest, and he breathed out in relief as Yslawna hunched over slightly.

"Ok," she said while sluggishly getting up. "Let's get moving."

Yslawna picked the far-right door, and they both ascended a winding staircase bathed in the now meager light of Yslawna's partially damaged lantern, which now flickered from time to time until she finally gave it a good whack.

"Why am I losing so much energy?" the Traveler asked between haggard breaths. "I thought you said I was full of energy."

"You were, but you're not accustomed to this type of environment. This door," she directed, pausing to enter a pale, thin door that led to a series of slightly nicer wood-paneled hallways. "Nor are you trained to protect your energy," she continued while walking. "You also drained a chunk of your power into that suit. I wouldn't use it again unless absolutely necessary."

"But…" The Traveler hesitated as they turned a corner and continued walking. "That was the only saving grace of this dump truck of a suit. It's heavy and slow."

"What's a dump truck?"

"What? Oh, I think it's a truck that collects garbage."

Yslawna turned around and cocked her head slightly in confusion.

"It's a thing with wheels that rides on the ground… and collects garbage."

"Oh, like the old vehicles before we built ships. This path up here," Yslawna led them up another stairwell. "Why does your suit collect garbage?"

"What? No… that's not… I'm just getting tired of it, especially if I can't use its power without nearly killing myself. I guess it's better than nothing, though. What happens if I run out of energy completely?"

"Hmm… this door here." They stepped off the stairwell and through a metal door into another wood-paneled hallway. "You'll probably pass out before you drain completely," she answered, stopping briefly to look at a painting of waterfalls before moving onward. "If you run low on energy, you become disoriented and confused, which will cause you to make mistakes, and then monsters will eat you."

"Oh," the Traveler nervously remarked while taking note of his constant bewilderment and disorientation.

"You run too low for too long, and then you run into *Real* problems. You'll lose your psychic senses as well as your common sense. Let's see…. organ failure and disease will be likely, and you'll be easily preyed on by the dark forces here, which will try and coax you down darker paths that will eventually turn you into one of the monsters."

"Okay, well, what's a good way to regain my energy?"

"Good questions." Yslawna applauded while turning a corner and passing through a wide, multi-level, carpeted room filled with bookshelves, tables, and an assortment of odd-looking devices. "Meditation is good. If you still have your psychic senses, then finding and resting at a peaceful location that feels nice is also good, although those are few and far between in this city. Hmm… positivity is also important."

"What?"

"When people die here, their spirits will often stay behind and send energy to us fighters. They can only do it if you have a peaceful mind, though. Upset disrupts energy. So, if you stay calm, the old masters can lend a helping hand from the ethereal plain."

"Is that the anchor you were talking about before? Calmness?"

"It is. Continual disappointment and upset will drive you insane, regardless of how strong your purpose is."

"Can you really stay calm with all of this happening?"

"Sure… take this set of stairs up here," Yslawna led the way as they walked up several flights. "You just need to find a way to relate positively to your surroundings, even if your surroundings are a burning pit fire. A good thing to do is create stillness inside you, a sense of peace that allows you to disassociate from the surrounding chaos. Personally, I like to imagine a little garden with fantastic, bright colors."

The Traveler eyed his ragged, jittery companion as she began to describe her imaginary garden full of waterfalls, rainbows, rolling clouds, and vibrant trees with such a joyful enthusiasm that it pained the Traveler to think she might never see it in reality.

"What happens if you can't find inner peace?" the Traveler asked after stepping off at the top floor and following Yslawna onward.

"Well, that means you can't anchor yourself. I guess you go crazy then!" she said with a startling laugh that froze the Traveler's blood.

The Traveler kept a slight step behind Yslawna who guided him across the expanse of the library and finally to a large iron door in an unsuspecting little hallway. Yslawna reached out to bang on it but froze with her fist hovering near the door.

The Traveler nervously leaned forward and asked, "Is everything alright?"

Yslawna put one finger to her mouth and hushed the Traveler, who readied his sword. "Feel like fighting a monster?" she whispered.

The Traveler vigorously shook his head 'no' while Yslawna unpacked her kaeta.

"Don't worry," she stepped back behind the Traveler. "I'll be helping you. Just keep your sword ready and cut the beast to pieces when it attacks you."

"Wh-What?!"

Yslawna started playing with slow, sweeping rhythms that felt like an introductory performance.

The Traveler took a sharp breath as he realized Yslawna was asking him to face the monster alone. He stood before the iron door and shook his head. This was stupid. It was ridiculous and dangerous! He took another breath and gripped the door's clunky, stiff handle as the music softly propelled him onward.

He wrenched the heavy door open and stood before a disgusting monster that watched him from across the other end of the old forgotten armory. It was a hideous thing with clawed hands, a vaguely humanoid body covered in dark, sludge-green scales, and a stretched-out mouth with a long, curling tongue. He expected the abomination to suddenly charge at him, but it didn't. He and the beast began to cautiously circle each other as the music morphed into a waltz of death, with each sizing the other up before the main performance began.

The Traveler calmly breathed, in and out, as the beast gave a low guttural growl that twisted its deformed mouth, bearing a nasty set of black teeth.

The Traveler didn't want to look at it. Its very presence unsettled his mind to the point that it made him want to run away screaming. He couldn't look away, though; he had to watch its every horrible movement, so it didn't get the upper hand.

The waltz continued to swirl through the room in a way that gave the Traveler a sudden bizarre sense of confidence. It didn't feel at all like a fight but a dance that he somehow knew the steps to.

"You can leave if you want to," the Traveler shakily called out to the beast.

It replied with a vicious snarl, but its bloodshot yellow eyes betrayed a fear in them. It broke the waltz first and charged the Traveler, who sliced its throat before being slammed into a wall. The beast sprayed horrible black blood on him while trying to bite his head off.

Yslawna cut a strong, vicious strike into the melody of the waltz, a strike that the Traveler felt in his bones, giving him the power to kick the beast away. It slid across the floor but quickly squirmed upright, and they once again began circling each other. The Traveler, cautious with his sword held outward, and the beast, wounded and clutching at its throat. The waltz picked up in speed as the two circled faster and faster in a rhythmic flurry. They both knew that they were reaching the end.

The wounded beast kept its distance from the Traveler, eyeing him with rage. Then its horrible yellow eyes suddenly darted towards Yslawna, who stood outside the armory. The Traveler knew what its deeply poisoned mind was thinking, so he stopped in front of the exit to block its path. It looked at him for a moment, then screamed in fury and charged at Yslawna, trying to bypass the Traveler entirely. He stepped to the side and cut his sword deep along the monster as it sprinted past. Both he and Yslawna were drenched in a shower of black blood as the beast fell to the floor in a horrible mess.

He looked down at the carcass and basked in the power he didn't think he could ever have. "I did it!" he shouted. "I actually did it!!!" He gleefully looked up at Yslawna, who stood dripping in the tainted blood. "Oh… uh… sorry," he stammered.

"Better it than us," she said while pulling a cloth from one of her bags and gently wiping the copious amounts of black blood and gore off her kaeta. "You did good in there. The Gated Waltz is a complicated song, but you picked up the rhythm quickly. This bodes well for our next fight with Jalmi."

The Traveler twitched again at his name and nervously looked around, asking, "Are there any more monsters here?"

"No, I don't think so." She folded the cloth up and tucked it in one of her bags. "I think this was its home."

"What do you mean?" The Traveler turned around and caught sight of the farthest wall of the armory, which he had completely missed while focusing all his attention on the abomination he had danced with. The walls were stained in bright red blood near a nest of bones scattered across the floor. He glanced over at the black blood on Yslawna and then back at the red blood in the armory, "why is the blood different?"

"Because," Yslawna explained while packing up her kaeta. "It probably found red-blooded prey. When something is that poisoned the blood often becomes black. Don't drink black blood."

The Traveler pulled up his visor, giving Yslawna a deeply confused and startled look.

"Not that you'd ever drink blood!" she quickly corrected, "but especially don't drink that blood."

He concernedly nodded while Yslawna quickly scanned what few weapons were left in the monster's nest. The armory, while clearly having a large capacity for all types of weapons imaginable, only had a few broken armaments.

"I guess this wasn't unexpected," she noted while sifting through what little was left of the inventory. She grabbed two busted rifles, popped them open, and, in a blur of movement, quickly replaced some parts to make a functional weapon. She turned back to the Traveler, "Ok, let's go!" They stepped out of the armory and slammed the iron door shut.

"Don't you need ammo for that?" the Traveler pointed at the gold-rimmed gun she held.

"Nope," she handed it to the Traveler. "It's a winding gun!"

"What?"

"Here," Yslawna grabbed the gun back from the confused Traveler and explained, "You wind this wheel back to create the charge." She grabbed hold of a gold handle attached to a wheel on the side of the gun and wrenched it back with a loud click, causing the middle of the gun to glow a discomforting blue. "And press this button to extinguish the charge if you don't want to fire." She pressed a red button on the top of the gun, and the blue light faded away with a soft purr. "This gun is old, so don't fire and charge too quickly. The last thing you need is for this to explode in your face. Count to three after you fire, then charge the wheel. It's easy as that!" She handed the gun back to the Traveler.

"Shouldn't you be the one to use it?" he asked, jostling the rifle a little to get a feel for its weight. It was heavy and solid, something he could easily use to bludgeon a monster if it stopped working.

"I'm the backup plan," Yslawna said with her thumb pointed at herself for emphasis. "And besides, I've always been better with my music."

Yslawna picked up the large black case holding her kaeta and asked, "Are you ready?"

The Traveler wanted to say a strong and powerful, *I'm ready!* But what actually came out was a timid "ok."

CHAPTER ELEVEN

The Dreams We Choose

"Why do I feel like we're on the losing side despite victory after victory? I know we need these guns, but I feel that we've sold our souls. I don't trust these Posiidians! I don't trust them, and I don't trust their depraved leaders!"

-Casadarious Markelm, Grand Chancellor of the Itzalla Empire
Three years before the opening of the seal.

Yslawna poked her head out from behind the door to Jalmi's lair, and seeing an absence of hurtling objects, she waved the Traveler behind her as they both cautiously entered the room. The gold-plated rifle the Traveler nervously held was old but sturdy. All he needed was a good shot. He wrenched back the charging mechanism and followed closely behind Yslawna, who quietly weaved and turned through the maze of shelves. She finally stopped and motioned the Traveler to get ready while she ducked back into the maze. The Traveler had a perfect sight on Jalmi, who had made himself another makeshift table off slightly from the center of the room. He was once again preoccupied with reading, and the shadowy puppeteer was still hanging above him.

The Traveler lifted his visor to aim better. He peered through the half-rusted iron sights of his rifle at the parasite up above. If he couldn't kill it, Yslawna would start playing her music to slow Jalmi down and give him another shot. Hopefully, Yslawna wouldn't be needed. All he had to do was just line up the shot... He squinted his eyes as the crosshairs drifted slightly from left to right with every anxious breath. His heart began thumping louder for every second he hesitated, every second he had to contemplate failure. The creature up above squirmed slightly. It was getting a better view of him. He had to fire now!

He lined up the crosshairs as best he could, held his breath, and pulled the heavy iron trigger. There was no recoil, but the deafening crack pounded his ears and shook his head. A plume of exhaust exploded along the side vents of the gun. He strained his eyes to see through the smoke before diving to the side with a shriek as a table flew across the room, nearly crushing him into nothingness.

He had missed.

He clambered up and back into the maze of books while Yslawna's song began to echo in the distance. Its rhythmic, captivating tune gracefully tranced across the library as the Traveler dodged shelf after colliding shelf. His eyes became heavier as he darted in and out of the maze to avoid Jalmi's increasingly disoriented aim. A haphazardly flung shelf suddenly soared far over his head and landed somewhere in the distance. Jalmi was losing control. The song was working! He then slipped and fell to the ground as the overwhelming tiredness that he'd been ignoring finally began seeping into his limbs.

The song was working on them both!

With a sleepy groan, he staggered up and stumbled slightly while trying to keep his balance. The music had swelled into some sort of orchestra. He had no idea how that many instruments could be playing, but there was no way he could aim with the way he felt, at least not without something to lean on. He staggered to an over-turned shelf and rested his gun on its back for stability. It wasn't perfect, but it was all he had.

The little creature controlling Jalmi was still up there. The Traveler shook his head as the room began to spin. What was he do-ing again? He felt so tired... The parasite!

He clumsily pulled back the charging wheel and lifted his vi-sor to aim through the sights. The creature was swerving back and forth, making it difficult to shoot. He gritted his teeth and cursed his unbearably drowsy eyes as his sights refused to line up with his tar-get. If he didn't shoot soon, he was going to pass out. It had to be now. He held his breath and lined up the target as best as he could.

Then, the creature suddenly fell and hit the floor with a dull thud.

The Traveler paused and blinked a couple of times to make sure he'd seen that right. He hadn't fired. Yslawna's song must have put it to sleep. The music slowly stopped, and the Traveler looked around for any sign of flying shelves or metal hands looking to bat away his skull. There was nothing. The room was quiet. He slammed his visor shut and darted over to where the creature fell, and there it was, splattered on the ground in a pool of black blood. He tried not to look too closely at the thin, deformed ghoul. He still couldn't really tell what it was, only that it must surely be dead. He started to walk away but froze after a few steps, turned around, and shot what was left of the creature just to make sure it was dead. It didn't move.

He made his way back to the center of the room where Yslawna was perched on an overturned bookshelf with her kaeta in hand and Jalmi motionless on the ground.

"Is he dead?" the Traveler asked with a few nervous steps for-ward.

"No, but he's shut down," Yslawna sighed, kicking her feet back and forth. "This might be harder than I thought it would be."

"You didn't tell me that your music would affect me too."

Yslawna stopped, "Did it? I tried to shield you, but I guess my song was slipping. Sorry."

"It's ok," the Traveler exhaled, "at least we got the worst part out of the way."

"True." Yslawna hopped off her perch and stood beside the Traveler, both of them looking down at the giant heap of robes and metal that was Jalmi. "Always look on the positive side!"

The next day was spent trying to reach the unresponsive behemoth who, not long before, had been hurtling bookshelves at them. The Traveler and Yslawna both agreed that they needed all the help they could get if they were going to launch an assault on the palace. However, despite all their efforts, he remained stubbornly comatose. Their victory prize was tossed into the corner of the room, in the upper part of the library, high above the insidious fog that infested the city. The Traveler and Yslawna sat at a small table nearby, sipping on tasteless drinks while they seriously considered the possibility of Jalmi never waking up.

"We might have to leave him," Yslawna finally admitted, setting down her cup at the distasteful notion. Neither of them wanted to say it, but they had both been thinking it for a while. "We don't have unlimited time here."

"I know," the Traveler answered after taking a sip. He glanced out of the window next to them as the evening sun slowly drifted down through rippling clouds of purple and orange. It was already getting dark, and they'd wasted too much time trying unsuccessfully to reach Jalmi. He didn't even know how much time they had left. Almerin made it seem like closing the seal was extremely urgent to the point that he marched carelessly across that horrible bridge. However, he wanted to use every other option before turning to the words of the fat old man who plagued his dreams.

He looked back at Yslawna and asked, "So, there's nothing else we can do?"

"Nothing quick," she answered between sips through the bendable straw sticking out of her cup. "Every possible method would take weeks, possibly even months, just to get him to wake up. And I'm not even qualified to perform these techniques. He was," she pointed over to the slouched heap in a corner.

This wasn't what he wanted to hear, and the Traveler meekly hid behind his cup as he confessed, "We haven't tried everything."

"What do you mean?" she leaned closer in a way that slightly unsettled her tired and beleaguered friend.

"I've been seeing this horrible man in my dreams." The Traveler tentatively began. There was a nagging fear in the back of his mind that Yslawna would somehow turn on him if he gave her a reason to feel that he was somehow compromised. Even if her intentions were good, she wasn't very stable. "He recently told me how to use the wooden heart… thing."

"You don't trust him?"

"Absolutely not!" the Traveler scoffed. "He's horrible, but I guess it's our only option right now."

"Why would he do that?"

"Probably to gain my trust. I don't trust him, though," he quickly added.

"What did he tell you to do?"

"Skin to skin, heart to heart, I have no idea what that means, but he said I could use it to enter memories."

Yslawna took a thoughtful sip from her straw. "It probably means you have to be touching him and then maybe put the wooden heart on his heart. That was done in an old fable with a princess, some little people, and a magical fish… I think."

"What?"

"It's the only suggestion I have."

"Well, guess that sounds easy enough to try." The Traveler nervously glanced back over to Jalmi, and Yslawna noted his clear apprehension.

"I would offer to do it for you," she hesitantly said as the Traveler stood up. "But I don't think Jalmi wants to see me. He saw me at my worst, and I don't know if he's ever forgiven me."

"The way he was tossing those bookcases, I don't think he's forgiven anybody. Just stay close to me in case it goes bad."

Yslawna gave a slight nod in agreement and added, "I can pull you out if anything looks or feels wrong."

They moved over to Jalmi and stopped. He was indeed an intimidating sight. Even unconscious and lazily tossed in a corner, he somehow invoked the primordial fears of death. He was massive, cloaked in black with a horrible beak-ish mask, and if he decided to wake up at this moment, they would probably both be dead. If death had a form, the Traveler expected it to look like Jalmi.

The Traveler dug in his satchel and took out the heart, contained in a clear sealable bag that Yslawna had provided him to protect his various tools from the heart's leakage. It was almost completely full of that awful goo, so he pulled out the disgusting artifact and then emptied the slime-filled bag onto the floor with a loud, stomach-churning *slop.*

"I hope this will be enough contact," Yslawna grunted while trying to remove one of Jalmi's sharp, bloodstained gauntlets. "I really don't want to try and remove his armor." The glove stubbornly resisted her efforts until it finally relinquished and clattered across the floor.

The Traveler pulled off his own gauntlet and knelt beside the giant.

"Flesh to flesh," he grasped Jalmi's cold, coarse hand, "and heart to heart." As he pressed the oozing wooden heart into Jalmi's chest, the room began to dip and spin in a way that made him want to vomit.

It took a few moments for the dizziness to fade. Everything was swirling around in a nauseating spiral, but it was slowing down. He? Was he himself? He didn't know. His head hurt. He slowly crawled out of the cindering wreckage that used to be a building and out into the icy night air. Small burning embers drifted among the snowflakes as heaping fires flared all around him.

He? Who was he? Everything hurt; he couldn't think. He tried to remember. There was an attack. A gift? No, a trap. Someone broke into the museum. No, they were let in. The intruder stood before the leadership as they were in counsel. They were surprised. He shouldn't have been able to get that deep inside without anybody knowing. The intruder said something. What was it? "Humanity is irredeemable, monstrous. Your self-deluded lies have only led to death. Now I bring you yours." He then retreated, and there was a fight. Were they winning? Yes, he remembered they were winning, and then a bomb went off.

He trudged across the snow, one aching step at a time until he slumped against a cold wall. He gazed across the burning inferno with a blank stare. His mind couldn't comprehend what had happened. It was too painful to process all at once.

Everyone was dead.

He still couldn't remember his name. What was it?

It was Jalmi.

He took a pensive breath and then collapsed to the ground, weeping in horror and agony. It was Enekoat! He remembered his face, full of rage and bitterness as he stepped out before the leadership: Enekoat, the quiet strategist who had dearly held the lives of so many in his hands; the man who Jalmi had found sobbing quietly after the abysmal first charge on the palace where a third of the Band was slaughtered; the man who fiercely fought against the shrewd commander Casadarious, and the notion of sacrificing lives to achieve a greater goal. How did this happen? Had the leadership broken him? Had his years laying out more and more vicious but effective battle plans, his years choosing who would live and who would die, finally corrode his very identity? Did the Band even notice or care?

The fires burned and slowly engulfed what little was left of the museum. It was grisly, but Jalmi was glad it was a fire. Fire was clean and purifying. He hated the idea of his family being left to rot and decay out in the open air. This was clean.

He tearfully bowed his head in misery. He should have died with the rest. It was his armor that saved his life — the massive, accursed suit that he wore to tend to the raving mad. He should have died, and someone more worthy should be standing in his place. He wasn't a fighter or tactician. Even as a healer, he needed the support of his family, the Golden Band, to do his job. He was nothing now.

Movement in the distance caught his eye, and his weary head lifted up. Some figures far across the fire were standing before the blaze.

It might have been Enekoat and the monsters he brought with him. If it was him, then maybe there was a chance he could be saved! Maybe if he could just speak to Enekoat to show him a better path.

Jalmi staggered up and moved toward the figures. He kept to the shadows and snuck up behind the group to see what he was walking into.

It was Enekoat. His pale, sickly form seemed to twist in the crackling light of the inferno. He tossed some wood into the wreckage and seemed to be speaking to someone. Jalmi was too far away to hear the words, though. Then something darted out from the darkness and tore Enekoat to pieces while he wasn't looking. Blood sprayed into the air, and his monstrous slaves tried to intervene. The attacker quickly stole Enekoat's swords and tore them to pieces too. Jalmi recognized her energy, even as malformed as it was.

It was Yslawna. He didn't know how she was even able to survive the blast, but she was mangled and disfigured now, both in form and energy. She looked up from the carnage as a man darted away in the distance. Then Jalmi saw her do the unthinkable. She ripped the energy from Enekoat's body. It was disgusting, and Jalmi looked away as his stomach flipped from the gruesome scene. Then she followed the survivor, leaving bloody footprints in the snow, while Jalmi pursued from the shadows.

A radiant moon peered down through dark, misty clouds as the man clad in a bluish variant of the Band's battle armor hurdled through a gate and out onto a snowy, isolated bridge. He frantically hammered against the opposite gate in a desperate attempt to wrench it open when he suddenly heard a rattling behind him and spun around.

Yslawna was perched atop the entrance, just staring down at him.

"He forced me to let him in!" he shakily shouted across the length of the bridge.

Jalmi recognized that voice and energy. That was Asier, an insecure fighter with a habit of following anyone he felt was stronger. His energy was weaker than Yslawna's, but then again, it always had been.

"He was going to kill me!" he desperately pleaded. "I didn't know what he was going to do there! Please, I didn't KNOW!"

Yslawna was going to murder him. She had to stop.

"Yslawna!"

Jalmi stepped out from the shadows and stood at the foot of the bridge, staring up at Yslawna through the pale glowing eyes of his beaked mask. "Yslawna, don't kill him." He begged, his deep voice booming across the bridge. "He could be innocent, and there has been more than enough death today."

"It wasn't me!" Asier continued to plead. Yslawna spun back around, her gaze piercing through the blue-tinted eyes of his helmet, causing him to stutter slightly. "It… it wasn't me. They forced me to let them in. They forced me to watch. Yslawna, please!"

Yslawna glanced back at Jalmi. He knew what she was doing. She was evaluating whether he would intervene, and she knew the answer. She paused for a moment to drink in the moonlight, then jumped onto the bridge and charged Asier, who shrieked and readied his sword and shield.

The fight was short and savage. Asier desperately battered Yslawna with his shield once or twice but failed to land any significant blows with his sword. Yslawna assaulted him with a horrific fury that drowned out Jalmi's cries to stop. She finally cut through his armor, and he fell to the ground, pleading desperately for mercy. Jalmi screamed from a distance as she lifted Asier by the throat, ripped off his breastplate, and tore out his beating heart. She held it to the moon's light and then crushed it, letting the blood run down what was left of her arms.

Jalmi just watched. When she crushed Asier's heart, she also crushed what was left of his. It was that moment of absolute certainty that he knew everything was lost. They had failed, and there was no point to existing anymore. He stepped away in a stupor of disillusionment and wandered back to the wreckage, leaving Yslawna behind with the corpse of Asier.

The next of Jalmi's memories became more and more disconnected as he fell deeper and deeper into despair. He fell to the point where the Traveler regained his own sense of self while drifting across the shattered memories of the broken man.

Jalmi sought refuge in his old home of the library, where he tended to the mangled souls of Hiri Handi in a sort of thoughtless daze. One by one, the final remnants of the Golden Band drifted away until Jalmi was left alone, still tending to the agony of the library's inhabitants, still trying to bring what was left of these hollow shells back into the light, back to their true selves.

Finally, the last surviving commander, Casadarious, arrived at the library's hollow doors. He berated Jalmi, saying that it was foolish to try and repair the damage that was done to these people. He explained that in order to save them, they needed to forget their past and forge a new identity through a new purpose. Jalmi was too weak to argue and Casadarious left with the frenzied victims that the Band had so carefully gathered.

Jalmi was, for the first time, truly alone.

It was in his aimless wandering that he came across a creature that had broken into the library's atrium. It was a small, pathetic thing that was desperately trying to attach itself to stronger creatures to feed off them. However, like most monsters in Hiri Handi, it had completely lost its own sense of self in the process. It, like Jalmi, was empty.

When it came scurrying through the library's cold, desolate halls, starving and weak, it approached Jalmi, and he embraced the creature. He wanted to drift away into nothingness, and the creature offered him exactly that — no thoughts, no feelings, just the assured-ness that everything would drift away.

The Traveler stood before Jalmi in the depths of the healer's beleaguered mind. The bloody, beating red heart of the Aclamartom Tree rested in his hand, no longer made of wood and sap, and the corpse of the creature Jalmi had cherished laid at his feet.

Jalmi was slouched in a corner, dressed in ragged black robes without any shoes. He slowly looked up at the Traveler with the great effort that comes from soul-rending apathy and asked, "Why did you kill it? I was happy…"

"It was a parasite, Jalmi," the Traveler softly replied, glancing down at the bloody carcass.

"I…. know it was," Jalmi stared at the corpse and then looked up at the Traveler with tired, weary eyes. "But it… was my choice…"

The Traveler knelt down and studied the broken man. He was bald with sturdy features that were chipped away by a pale and sickly complexion, covered by a look of sorrow so deep that it seemed etched into the build of his face. This was a man who wanted to die.

"Tell me what happened," the Traveler asked while settling down on the floor.

Jalmi let his gaze slide downward and just mumbled, "Everything…"

"Yslawna's come back, though. She's here and wants to help you."

Jalmi shook his head, "Doesn't matter anymore. We've already lost everything."

"And we're looking for other survivors," The Traveler persisted. "We're going to attack the palace and finally stop this nightmare."

"It's impossible…" Jalmi's expression sunk further into an apathetic emptiness. "It will always end the same… This is destiny. I understand that now. We did this to ourselves because we were unworthy to exist. The universe, Ecrea, is purging us away."

"That's not true. How could the universe be purging us if it gave us this opportunity to survive? Not only survive, but *Win!*"

"It won't work…"

"But the Prince Adept has fled!" The Traveler put a strong hand on Jalmi to try and counteract the utter lack of willpower he was facing, "and he left the seal vulnerable. Jalmi, this is our chance!"

He was embellishing, but he felt it was what Jalmi needed to hear.

Jalmi didn't even look up. He just mumbled, "It doesn't matter… none of it does…"

The Traveler got up and stepped away to collect his thoughts. Jalmi wasn't budging. He was basically talking to a wall at this point.

The Traveler turned back to Jalmi and said with a sharp wave of his hand, "How can it not matter! Yslawna came back, and more are coming."

"It doesn't matt-"

The Traveler picked Jalmi up and shoved him up against the wall as he shouted, "STOP SAYING THAT! You think I don't think about that every waking moment!" The Traveler barked, trying to pull out the barbs Jalmi was unintentionally sticking into his fragile mind. "The possibility that none of this matters, that nothing here can change…" the Traveler suddenly looked at the broken man, whose expressionless apathy had transformed into sheer terror, and he let him go.

The Traveler stepped back and took a shaky breath. "Maybe you're right," he exhaled, trembling. "Maybe the universe is purging us away because we're somehow unworthy to exist. But what if you're wrong? What if the universe is actually sending us chance after chance to fix this, and all we have to do is keep seizing those chances until one of them works? I'll be damned if I'm going to squander one of those chances because I'm disillusioned!"

"There's no good here," a dark cloud passed over Jalmi's face as he spoke. A cloud of destitute resolution that the Traveler refused to see. He was going to pull Jalmi out of this stupor, and he was going to do the same to everyone else until they had an army to fight the Prince Adept with.

The Traveler nodded, "I see what this is. You're low on energy, right? Yslawna said it can make people go crazy. Well, here, take some of mine."

The Traveler extended a hand, which the broken man grasped and nearly ripped him to pieces. Jalmi took nearly everything, and the Traveler collapsed to the ground right as Jalmi's bloodstained claw swept in a flash of motion and stopped right before the Traveler's face. The Traveler just stared at its sharpened tip, which hovered right before his eye. It shimmered slightly in the light in a way he'd never noticed before.

He looked up at Jalmi. Yslawna was holding his arm back while her thin silver sword dug into the base of his neck. A steady stream of red blood flowed down Jalmi's black armor and over Yslawna's white and violet arm. She hefted him back and tossed him to the floor while the Traveler just sat and watched.

"Are you ok?!"

The Traveler didn't reply. He could still see Jalmi's claw, even though the giant was now a dead lump on the floor.

CHAPTER TWELVE

The Master of the Skies

"Jalmi, every day I have to decide who to sacrifice so that the larger army can survive. If you'd seen the things I have. If you'd seen the choices I had to make while the leadership does nothing but ask for more and more, then you'd understand my destitution. I don't believe in the Golden Band. I'm just not capable of it anymore."

-Enekoat Arzako, High Commander of the Order of the Golden Band

2,450 years after the opening of the seal.

The Dancing Star hobbled away from the library with its crew eager to put some distance between them and their devastating defeat. Although Yslawna tried several times to coax the Traveler into opening up about his experience using the heart on Jalmi, he remained mostly silent. He wasn't actually judging Yslawna or even thinking very much at all. He was too exhausted and confused to think. He just sat, allowing everything to sink in. Then, the all too familiar squawk of impending doom echoed across the drowsy evening sky.

"What was that?" The Traveler asked, lifting his head out of the stupor he'd slipped into.

"The Commander of the Reliquary," Yslawna shouted over the sudden roaring of the engines. She pulled some levers, and the ship began descending. "He normally isn't this tenacious."

The Traveler glued his face to the window as the Dancing Star once again dipped below the city and under the sickening fog. He knew what was coming next, and his stomach quaked at the thought of it. Even though Yslawna had given him another chunk of her energy, he no longer possessed the willpower to patrol around the ship in the crushing blackness again. He pensively waited for her to give that horrible order, but she didn't. Instead, she cursed with an uncharacteristic anger and slammed the console, breaking off one of the thin levers.

"What's wrong?"

"We're being boxed in," she replied while fastening the cracked switch back in the console. "It's not just the Commander that's attacking us. A soul horde is on its way too."

"A what?"

"It's the massive beast I first saved you from. The giant skull-faced thing composed of a thousand raging souls with the single-minded purpose of death and feeding," she explained while massaging her head to focus.

It took a moment for the Traveler's tired mind to pull the corresponding memory, but when he found it, recalling the monstrosity that killed Awhet and had him trembling in a rotting kitchen, he jerked in horror. "Shit!"

"That's accurate…"

"Can you play your…?" the Traveler was even struggling find simple names, so he just sighed and gave up, "musical instrument thing… and make it fall asleep?"

"My kaeta?"

"Yes!"

"No," she stopped the ship with a lurching halt and spun her chair around to give him her full attention. "The beast is very agitated, and I don't have enough energy to pull it off. I'm exhausted."

"Then what do we do?"

"We need to decide whether to stay under the fog and contend with the soul horde the hard way or go up and fight the Commander of the Reliquary."

There was an awful silence that hung in the air like the nauseating fog that surrounded the ship. Neither of them knew what to do, and each was waiting for the other to make a suggestion.

"No, ideas?" Yslawna finally asked. "Ok, well, it's bad either way. What if we flip a coin?"

The Traveler's skin prickled more and more as he thought about that gigantic monstrosity. He'd take anything but that horrific monster.

"I..." the Traveler hesitantly began, "can't fight the... soul... what did you call it?"

"The soul horde."

"I can't face that again." He said with his head hung in cowardice. "Maybe we should fight the Commander. Almerin told me that I'm a member of the Royal Vanguards. Maybe that will help us somehow."

"Almerin said that?"

The Traveler drew his sword for Yslawna to see for herself.

"He said there was some sort of symbol."

She got up and gingerly took the sword. "It's not the usual forging. It's more chaotic and clunky," she remarked, twisting and turning it around in her hands to give it a thorough examination. "It's the right materials, though, and there's the royal symbol." She returned the sword and sunk back into the captain's chair. "So, we face the rider," she announced with a subtle, "Ecrea save us," added under her breath. She pushed some levers forward and raised the ship out of the fog and into a dwindling sunset that filled the Traveler with a morose sense of finality. She then pressed some buttons and walked away as a red light enveloped the cockpit.

"Grab your gun. We'll have to fight from outside."

The Traveler grabbed hold of the rifle he'd haphazardly tossed into a corner of the cabin and followed Yslawna out onto the deck. She opened a hatch at the stern of the ship and, with the Traveler's help, hefted out a bizarre cannon covered in glass panels.

"What is this thing?" the Traveler grunted as the two heaved the shockingly heavy gun over to the leftward railing and latched it on with sturdy metal clamps. "This..." she spoke between panting breaths, "is an old defensive weapon. I don't have time to explain how it functions, but Ecrea have mercy that it still works."

"Wait, what?"

A creature in the distance suddenly barreled out from a batch of silky clouds. It was a horrific, enormous black bird with heinous red eyes. It soared across the sky and let out a ghastly screech as it spread its wings to let everything know it had arrived.

So, this was one of the Rocs Almerin had talked about; the Traveler thought to himself, marveling at the physical incarnation of doom beelining for their ship. He wondered if he ever had one of those before he lost his memory.

Atop the shocking bird was a man covered in a ludicrous amount of capes, feathers, and regalia, all colored white and violet. The Traveler assumed him to be the man Yslawna had illustriously called "The Commander of the Reliquary." His very form seemed to glimmer and reflect in the sunset like a divine entity stepping down from the very heavens to pound Yslawna and the Traveler into a fine mist.

Yslawna cursed and slammed a bolt on the cannon, which extended four massive glass panels that sat like delicate shields on the tip of the gun.

The Commander flew alongside the Dancing Star, where he brandished an enormous black bow which, to the Traveler's horror, he began to draw back with what looked more like a spear than anything that could be considered an arrow.

He aimed it at the ship and let it go.

The fiercely wisping air around them cracked with a shudder as the arrow shot across the sky. Yslawna fired her cannon in response, which contorted the air and batted the arrow aside into one of the towers below.

The Traveler watched the explosion in mesmerized terror until Yslawna snapped, "What are you waiting for? Fire your GUN!"

The Traveler jolted out of his trance, hastily readied his rifle, and fired in the general direction of the Commander. He missed, and the Commander pulled another spear from his quiver and began to draw back.

"Shit!" the Traveler furiously wound back the charging wheel, hoping to get in another shot before the Commander fired, but he was too late. The spear seemed to not fly but cut across the sky with another sickening crack. Yslawna fired her cannon just moments before the spear impaled her to the side of the ship. It was at this moment that the Traveler realized with utter horror what was happening. Yslawna wasn't creating a shield that would effortlessly block attacks. She was firing her own weapon at the same time as the Commander, which negated his blows. This meant she had to time her defense carefully.

Which meant her defense could fail if she was a moment too slow.

The Traveler brought the rifle up to his shoulder. Through the old iron sights, he could see the Commander pulling another spear out of his quiver. He lined up the sights with the rider's chest and fired, but the Commander waived his hand and diverted the shot. He then drew back as the Traveler wound his gun and hesitated momentarily before sending the spear hurtling towards Yslawna.

The hesitation was enough to disrupt her. She barely deflected the spear, sending it cascading into the ship's cabin, where the

Traveler watched it crash through the side windows and embed itself into the cabin wall.

He quickly looked back as the Commander drew another spear and slid it into the massive black bow. The Traveler didn't fire. He was playing his game now. He wanted to fire when the Commander couldn't deflect.

The Commander drew back and then stopped. It was a feint! Yslawna fired too early, and then both the Traveler and the Commander fired at the same time.

The Traveler's shot hit him square in the chest, causing him to jerk and slide limply off his Roc, which screeched in rage, while the Commander's spear barreled into Yslawna, impaling her through her stomach into the side of the ship.

The Traveler tossed his rifle to the side and scrambled over to Yslawna, who was clutching the spear in agony.

"Cut… the BACK!" she gurgled between gasps. She slid forward with an agonizing groan and exposed the blood-soaked, ungodly black spear that burrowed into the wall.

The Traveler drew his sword, poured energy into the blade, and sliced into the spear, freeing Yslawna.

And then the Roc attacked.

It flew straight into the Dancing Star, ripping off the mast and tearing into the cabin. Shards of metal cascaded around the Traveler, who quickly leaped over Yslawna to shield her from the debris. He staggered up as the ship unsteadily teetered back and forth and looked down at Yslawna, who was still clutching the spear in agony. She pulled a pocketed blue rock out of her bag and looked at the Traveler. "When I say *now*, rip out the spear."

The Traveler didn't question. He grabbed hold of the spear with one hand and braced Yslawna with the other.

"Now!"

She screamed as he tore out the spear, drenching him in a spray of bright red blood. She crushed the rock into her wound, and it foamed and hardened over the area.

Then he heard the Roc's screech again.

He picked her up and stumbled into the cabin, strapping her into the only undamaged bench. He then lunged into the cockpit and strapped himself into the chair right as the Roc made another pass across the stern, sending the ship spiraling out of control and back into the darkness of Hiri Handi. The Traveler blinked several times as everything slowly came into a sickening focus. The ship wasn't moving anymore. They had stopped. He slowly looked around as much as his aching head allowed him to. The Dancing Star was a mess of twisted carnage, with a single crimson light from the cockpit washing over the horrible scene. Yslawna was still strapped onto the red bench, but she wasn't moving. The Traveler unstrapped himself and slid out of his seat and onto the ground with a thud. He pulled himself up with a nauseated groan and then carefully navigated his way to her, mindful of the jagged gaping hole that used to be the center of the cabin. He knelt beside Yslawna, pulled off his gauntlet, and tried to take her pulse. There was something weak, but he couldn't be sure. He didn't really know what he was doing.

"Yslawna, can you hear me?"

She didn't answer.

He slumped down beside her and just watched the crimson light bathe over the wreckage. This seemed very much like the end, and he didn't know what to do...

Landala!

He ransacked his satchel, found the necklace, and began muttering frantic prayers in a fit of hysteria, hoping she would answer.

Nothing.

He quickly glanced around. They were in the darkness. Maybe she couldn't talk to him here. He had to get higher! He put on the necklace and his gauntlet, unstrapped Yslawna, and started to carry her out of the ship when her bag spilled open and leaked all of her things onto the ground, including the peculiar stuffed yellow star. The Traveler cursed, bent down, and gingerly grabbed the yellow star before leaving. It seemed to be the most sentimental item to Yslawna. He carried her out into a large street with his small orb of light hovering on his shoulder, flickering with the meager energy that he could barely pour into it. It was too dark to see where the tallest building around him was. It was too dark to see anything at all.

"Left."

He knew that voice. It was Landala! He stumbled leftwards until a large mammoth of a house covered in green mold and centuries of decay loomed out of the shadows to stare down at him. The front door was unlocked, so he carelessly barged in and began searching for the nearest flight of stairs. A filthy, partially unhinged sign hung over one of the far doors, and as he walked over, his aching, battered heart lifted slightly. It was some illegible words below the image of stairs. He passed through the rotting wood door and began ascending an endless grey stairwell. He marched higher and higher, step after step, up the cracked and peeling stairs until his legs and arms ached and slowly became numb.

Eventually, he lost count of the stairs and just mindlessly staggered higher and higher until he heard a scurrying from behind. Something had followed them.

He slowly put Yslawna down and spun around, reaching for his sword. A giant insect of a creature with many teeth and eyes watched with amusement as he tried to draw a weapon that wasn't there. He froze in terror when he suddenly remembered discarding the sword somewhere in the Dancing Star after cutting Yslawna free. All he could do was shriek in terror as the insect leaped on him in a savage biting frenzy. He screamed, howled, and wailed as the beast tore at the solid plates protecting his fragile body. Finally, he grabbed hold of one of its eyes and blinded it with a burst of light. The bug squirmed back and gave the Traveler only a flash of an instant to scramble up and pull out Yslawna's silver blade. The bug lunged forward again and impaled itself on the sword, squirming and screeching until the Traveler shoved it over the railing and into the abyssal darkness below. A satisfying splat confirmed the insect's death, and the Traveler breathlessly collapsed. He started to get up, but his body pounded with aching exhaustion. He didn't know if he could keep going. He didn't even know if Yslawna was still alive…

"Yslawna," he gasped, more to himself than his unconscious friend. "I think this might be the end for both of us. I'm sorry you never got to see your garden."

"Me… too." Yslawna suddenly murmured.

"Yslawna!"

"I'd say… it's been fun…" Yslawna paused. "But it wasn't. I'm gonna rest now…"

"What? No!" The Traveler jostled her, but she said nothing else.

"Ah, god!" he cried as the profound sense of desolation that he'd been pushing down finally flooded over him. Through his weeping sobs, he glimpsed a haggard figure a few steps below him. He looked down and stared into Almerin's tired old eyes.

"Saving her will have a heavy price."

The Traveler pulled himself up slightly and said, "Tell me how."

"Keep climbing higher. Use one of Yslawna's energy stones."

The Traveler blinked, and he was gone. He pulled off his battered gauntlet and stopped to watch his sickly hand twitch with nerves and fatigue. He ignored it and sifted through Yslawna's bags until he found the last green stone left. Its warmth was soothing, and for a brief moment he was reminded of his old bed from long before Hiri Handi, with heavy sheets and thin pillows that were neither too soft nor too hard. He shook his head to brush away the painfully nostalgic memory and hauled Yslawna up with a brief and fleeting surge of power. His agonizing march continued higher and higher.

Eventually, he stopped to take a nauseated breath and then gazed into a wooden door unblemished by age or mold. This might be it! He shifted Yslawna around so he could open the door and then stepped into a long, beige corridor filled with leafless plants and dusty paintings. A large window along the wall showcased a musty old lounge with a balcony outside.

This was what he needed.

He staggered through a slightly nicer glass door, marched past the dusty velvet chairs of the lounge, and stepped out onto the balcony, where he laid Yslawna down in the pale moonlight.

Almerin and Landala sat beside him as he took off his helmet and looked at them in utter desperation.

"You have to perform surgery on her to repair the damage," Almerin explained. "It's extensive, so this isn't going to be easy."

"HOW?!"

"Don't worry," he calmly replied. "You'll be guided. But it's going to take a lot more energy than you have. My friend, I'm afraid it will probably kill you."

The Traveler blinked a couple of times, letting the statement sink in, and then slowly looked down at Yslawna, mangled and blood-drenched.

Almerin watched him and then said, "You've already made the decision before coming here, haven't you?"

The Traveler quietly nodded, with a couple of tears trickling down his cheeks. He slipped his hand to his satchel and pulled out the stuffed yellow star Yslawna had taken from the library. He had witnessed what was probably her darkest moments firsthand. No one would ever blame him if he said the price for saving her was too high. Though, as he looked down at her, he didn't see a gruesome monster. All he could see was that gentle song she played for him in the music hall. That quiet, peaceful song drowning in the chaos and madness of Hiri Handi. A song she played to soothe him despite his rash actions that led to the death of her friend. She was a good person who was strong enough to weather this hellish place. He couldn't leave her like this, even if he wanted to. He gently tucked the star under her arm so she would have it when she woke up.

"I've seen many miracles in my time," Almerin explained to the Traveler, who looked at the old man with exhausted, fragile eyes. "Though, I've scarcely ever seen such a profound miracle of thought. The Golden Band came to me many times for help, and each time, I sent them away. I didn't believe in them, and I didn't believe that things could change. I made a mess of everything, and I could've helped Hiri Handi in so many ways." Almerin gazed at the Traveler with a slight smile and pointed to Yslawna, "You've made a different choice. Are you ready?"

"Yes." The Traveler answered for the first time with clear resolution and not feeble indecision.

"First, look for Yslawna's red bag."

The Traveler found and detached a red satchel.

"Inside, you'll find surgical tools and bandages."

"Don't my hands have to be sterile?"

Almerin shook his head, "I can handle that. Pull off your gloves."

The Traveler pulled them off and offered Almerin his hands. To his shock, the old man grabbed them and extended out a warmth that wrapped around until all the unpleasantness that he'd been through melted off.

"How?" the Traveler muttered.

"Landala. She is mediating this with her necklace. She has a special connection with you."

Almerin let go of his hands, and the Traveler looked at Landala, who was quietly sitting on the side, and he asked, "Why her?"

"She used to be your daughter in another life," Almerin said with a sideways glance at the child.

"I don't understand."

Almerin paused thoughtfully as he considered how to explain this. "The purpose of existence is the evolution and change of your immortal self," he carefully began. "When the Prince Adept murdered the Coronated Speaker and opened the seal, his body became drenched in too much sin and blood to be useful for the spirit. His spirit fled from his body and reincarnated as you. You're his reincarnation. You carry the same spirit as the Prince Adept."

The Traveler was at a loss for words and was about to protest vehemently when the sudden pungent smell of smoke wafted from behind him. He didn't turn around. He already knew what deeply unpleasant person was sitting behind him.

"No," he whimpered. "No, I'm not the Prince Adept. That's..."

"You're not the Prince Adept," Almerin cut him off. "But you are part of him."

The Traveler gazed down as what little sense and understanding he had assembled of this horrible world finally seemed to fall out from under his feet. "How did I get here then?" he weakly asked without looking up.

"I understand it as a cascade of ill-intentioned errors. Individuals outside of Hiri Handi wanted to liberate the Prince Adept, not understanding that he was just an empty, spiritless shell. They summoned you to this world by mistake and then used you as a sacrifice to free the husk of the Prince Adept from the prison of Hiri Handi. That's how he was able to flee, and that's how you gained that scar." Almerin pointed to the Traveler's chest.

"Am I... a monster then?" he weakly asked.

"No, but you do carry a debt with you."

It was too much to think about, so the Traveler shook his head to toss away the incomprehensible concept assailing his delicate, tired mind. He looked up to Almerin and asked, "What do I do first to save Yslawna?"

Almerin began directing which of the crystalline tools to lay out on a white blanket tucked inside the satchel.

The surgery itself was horrific. Almerin carefully guided the Traveler as he cut into Yslawna while using crystals charged with what little energy he had left to repair the extensive damage. His vision eventually blurred, and his head pounded, but he stubbornly continued until the very end. When the surgery was finished, he let the tools slip out of his hands and slowly leaned back as everything clouded into darkness. He smiled, though, knowing he could finally sleep soundly and that he would be leaving what was left of the world in good hands.

CHAPTER THIRTEEN

The Empathetic Bridge

"A Roc is no ordinary creature. They are remarkably particular to which rider they allow into their minds; but once a mental connection has been established, they will move the very ground itself to aid its rider. Pity to the person who kills its most trusted companion."

-Asontzo Ilseea Delis, Commander of the Reliquary, Royal Order of the Sky Seventeen years before the opening of the seal.

The Traveler meandered his way across the murky streets of Hiri Handi in a dazed stupor. He didn't die, which was a positive for him, but he wasn't quite right either. Up seemed down, left seemed right, and whenever he walked close to a building, it stood up and walked away. Finally, he found a house that would stay put. He even had a new roommate, but they got into a fight, and the Traveler evicted him… or it, he wasn't really sure. As the Traveler sprawled out across the floor, he looked up and noticed how many doors were in his house and how they all danced and moved about in a most displeasing manner.

He began barricading them to create a protective fortress, but it wasn't enough. There would always be more entrances, more doors, more places to be attacked from. Realizing this, he halted his efforts to close up the house and instead began creating a shell around himself. Nothing would ever bother him. Nothing would ever hurt him.

As his shell neared completion, he suddenly heard the loveliest melody from outside his walls. He tried to ignore it at first, imagining the dangers and terrors that lay on the outside, but as the gentle harmony continued, the feeling of a long-forgotten home began to bubble up inside him. Not the harsh and ugly home that he'd been building, but a soft one. One from his oldest memories that dug up a painful yearning deep in his chest.

He poked his head out from a crack in the wall and shouted, "WHO's there?!"

Yslawna slowly stopped playing her kaeta and let the instrument rest on her lap as she sat with her back against the living room door.

"Remember me?" she tentatively asked her former friend, who was huddled inside a cocoon of rotting garbage and broken furniture. "I'm Yslawna, your musically inclined friend."

The Traveler paused as he tried to pull the associated memories. "I KnOw you! You're that crazy woman who likes bED sheets and CanNibAlizeD, that guy on the BRIDge!"

Yslawna hesitated at this unexpected insight into her past, "How do you know about that?"

"Jalmi's MEMORIES! The Traveler shoved the oozing wooden heart out of the shell with such chaotic force that it slipped out of his hand and plopped on the floor. "Oh..." he muttered at his lack of coordination. "Doesn't MaTTEr! NOw, HOW did you find me?"

"You saved my life. So, I tracked you down to help you."

"YoU will not Address ME as YOU! I Am Aaron Hodges! Of the UniTEd STatES of VirGinia...wait, that doesn't sound right."

"The United States of Virginia? Was that your home?"

"YES!" he shouted back, aghast that she'd never heard of it.

"Why don't you tell me a little about it?"

He paused again as the memories drifted by, almost but not completely out of reach. "The Trees," he wistfully muttered, "were so many bright colors... yellow, red, orange... with big blue mountains everywhere..."

"It sounds wonderful," she coaxed, trying to draw out as much nostalgia in him as possible. "Why don't you come back with me so we can take a trip there."

"No!"

"Why not?"

"BeCausE I'm INSANE!" He shouted as dramatically as he possibly could, confused that she hadn't noticed the shell of rotting trash around him. "And I'm the PRInce AdePT, MasTER of DOOM!!!"

"What?"

"I'M ThE PRInCE ADEPT!"

"Don't you think you're a little... young to be the Prince Adept."

"I'm his rei... ra... reincar..." The complicated word confused Aaron.

"Reincarnation?"

"YES, ALMerin exPLAINed it to me while I healed YOU."

Yslawna buried her head in her hands as she tried to process this. "That would explain why Landala contacted you," she muttered, more to herself than her half-crazed friend. She hesitantly looked up and weakly asked, "Then why did you save me?"

Aaron angled his head up as if the memory was trickling in from the ceiling. "I uh... I couldn't bear to see you go off like that, bloody and helpless. You didn't deserve that, not after everything you survived. And I didn't see myself surviving either way." He shook his head as the brief spout of lucidity vanished, "Now, go AWay. I build MY shell!"

Yslawna just stared blankly as Aaron tucked his head back inside the cocoon and sealed up the hole with some more garbage. She sat quietly for a moment, contemplating their exchange, before she finally set down her kaeta, walked over to the cocoon, and began tearing it to pieces until she was able to drag Aaron out. He screamed and shrieked as she ripped off his helmet and suffocated him with a chemical cloth that caused him to lose consciousness.

As he drifted off to sleep, he found himself in that awful, dimly lit room again, lined with the unpleasantly striped dark blue and red wallpaper, which was now peeling and cracked. The large man obscured by shadows sat opposite him, still breathing in a cigar and then bellowing out smoke like a broken oven. The man lowered his cindering torch and just looked at Aaron, who eyed him with a new suspicion.

"Is it really that much of a shock?" the man snorted.

Aaron leaned back with a tremendous amount of shock. He stood up and pulled the chain of a dusty old light that hung lethargically from the ceiling, illuminating a large ugly man dressed in the purple and white colors that once paraded across Hiri Handi with pride. He had a coarse, bloated face with sunken eyes filled with pain and regret.

"You're the Prince Adept!" Aaron accused with a fierce finger pointed at the fat old man.

"Obviously, but I'm the only part of the Prince Adept that mattered," he smugly retorted. "I'm a part of you. The part connected to your spirit. The other part lurching around outside is nothing but a hollow shell, a shadow."

Aaron stood up in a rage. "You're not part of me!" he roared. "This is a trick! A trap to try and enter my mind and possess me!"

The fat old man chuckled in the most sickening way before pausing to puff on not a cigar but something close to it. It was some sort of drug to ease physical pain. Aaron shook his head to brush aside the recollection.

"You know it's not a trick," the Prince Adept said between puffs. "You can feel it in the deepest depths of your soul. The sins of your past life manifest in person!" he exclaimed with an outward gesture of both his hands.

"No," Aaron shook his head as he backed away. "No, I couldn't do the things you did. I could never do the things you did. You turned everything inside out!"

The Prince Adept held his cigar-like drug between his fat fingers and gazed at it as he said with a frailness that Aaron thought was beyond him, "Everything I did was out of weakness and fear. I wasn't strong enough to walk the long, right paths. Paths of mercy and charity, paths that would leave me vulnerable. I instead chose to cover my fear and weakness with brutality and ferocity. I didn't think it mattered how dark the roads I walked were. As long as there was a bright light at the end of it, then everything would eventually be justified."

Aaron stared at him with a simmering hatred and growled, "Was it justified?"

"Of course not," the Prince Adept plainly admitted. "But you've made an extraordinary choice this time around. Like Almerin said, a miracle in thought. To sacrifice your own wellbeing for the welfare of another, leaving you weak and feeble to the chaotic forces around you. And what is truly remarkable is that it seems to have paid off."

Aaron sleepily awoke in a dark pool of warm water. He sat upright and groaned as every part of him ached with the unceasing abuse Hiri Handi had thrown at him. He clutched onto his sickly, pallid arms and cradled himself to alleviate some of the throbbing pain. He felt the bare, unprotected skin on his shoulders and then patted his uncovered helmetless head.

His armor was gone!

He started to scream and thrash around in terror as all the monsters he'd ever come across suddenly lurched out of the water and began to slowly descend upon him with a horrifying rage. He shrieked and closed his eyes while he waited for death, but it didn't come. He waited a few extra moments just in case death was taking its time, but it still didn't come. He finally allowed his eyes to cautiously open and glance around.

He was curled as close to a ball as his body would allow inside a large, dark chamber filled with knee-high, surprisingly temperate water. A dim lantern was perched on a mossy stone altar at the far side of the room, built into a wall covered with old exotic carvings of religious depictions. At the other end of the pool was Yslawna, who sat by the door silently watching him.

"Yslawna?" Aaron weakly asked.

She didn't say anything. She just sat, draped in shadows, with the terrifying stoicism of her impenetrable veil.

The uncharacteristic silence confused Aaron, whose fragile mind immediately turned to the surgery he had performed on her and a fear that it had gone horribly wrong. "Yslawna," he coughed while inching his way closer. "Please... don't be dead!"

"So, you're the Prince Adept's reincarnation," she mused.

Aaron stopped. He vaguely remembered telling Yslawna something about that. Fear pulled his body backward in a scrambling panic as he suddenly realized that his life, not hers, was the one in danger. He crawled back until he hit a damp wall and then tucked his body into the shallow water as if it would somehow transform him into a fish that could quickly swim away. He tried a couple of times to say something, but all that came out was muddled, cowering gibberish.

Yslawna tilted her head with curiosity, "I always thought meeting the force behind the Prince Adept would be more... intimidating."

Aaron didn't respond. He just watched from as far away as possible.

The disfigured, psychologically frail warrior dressed in faded white and violet leisurely stood up and meandered closer to Aaron, who slunk further into the corner of the pool. She stopped and looked down at his terrified face, which barely poked out of the water. "Relax," she dismissed with a wave of her hand, "I'm not going to murder you."

Aaron didn't say anything. He just cowered.

Yslawna extended her hand to Aaron and said, "Dance with me."

"W-what?"

"Dance with me."

Aaron was drowning in both water and utter confusion, but he cautiously extended his hand and accepted Yslawna's invitation. She pulled him to his feet and guided him to the center of the pool. She placed her hand on his wet shoulder, the other grasping his pale, brittle hand, and they began to slowly sway back and forth to the gentle sounds of a soft, slightly uplifting piano.

"What's happening," Aaron whispered.

"We're dancing."

"Where's that music coming from?"

"Shhh," Yslawna hushed. "It's magic. Just dance."

Aaron stared into Yslawna's grungy veil with a slowly subsiding paranoia and allowed his feet to stagger sloppily through the water in a semi-rhythmic fashion.

"Wh-what happens now?" he asked with a twinge of fear that strangled his words.

"I don't know," she quietly answered. "Tell me about your home. You started talking about it while you were insane."

Aaron took a wistful breath as nostalgia crept up inside him. "I think… I used to live up near these big blue mountains covered in trees and winding roads. In autumn, the trees would change into these vivid colors that would light up the world as you drove by. When I was younger, I'd build a pile of leaves and hide from my older sister. I'd mess up her room and then hide in the leaves. She'd always find me, though. I don't know why I bothered hiding there."

"What was your house like?" Yslawna asked, still guiding Aaron as they lazily swayed in loose circles.

Aaron glanced over to the side as the memories danced within reach for the first time. He mentally plucked the memory and held it in his hand. "Smallish, a single-story house with a small living space and a big yard. We lived there with our mom after our parents divorced. We'd sometimes stay at our father's, but his house was always cold and stoic."

"What happened when you grew up?"

"I uh…" He unexpectedly hesitated as regretful memories suddenly shoved their way forward. "I let my dad buy me," he admitted. "My mom declined from the pressures of raising us, and my dad would just swoop in with money… and he swept me away with him."

"What about your sister?"

"She stayed with my mom and struggled. She got married eventually but didn't invite me to the wedding."

"What about you?" she continued to prod.

"I did well for myself, but I guess I never realized how distant everything had become until I heard about the wedding… That hurt, and it hurt more to know it was my fault." He sighed and turned his head away from his regretful choices. "I was eventually sucked into all of this. Literally, I think. I remember something about the floor sucking me in and a bunch of depressed, feudal mountain dwellers raving about their great heritage."

"Is that where you got your sword?"

Aaron nodded, trying to remember the bizarre span of time between his normal life on Earth and the ugly horror of his journey in Hiri Handi. He didn't just appear inside this hellish city. It was clear he had spent some time in the world around it. "I think they were the ones who trained me," he continued a little hesitantly, following impressions rather than actual memories. "I can only remember bits of it, though. But the feelings I do have of them are… sad. I think they were a miserable people. We ended up traveling to Hiri Handi, but it's all still a haze."

"It's alright."

"Can I ask, why we're dancing like this?"

Yslawna spun Aaron in a loose arc and said, "I need to see if I can stand to be around you after learning what you are. You're part of what ruined me."

"I, uh… ok."

"You're also a terrible dancer."

"Oh…"

"But you're building an awareness of right and wrong, and I can work with that."

Yslawna abruptly let go of Aaron and stepped back. She walked away toward the door, leaving Aaron alone in the middle of the pool with a horrible pit in his stomach that said everything was not alright and that it wasn't going to be alright. However, the feeling suddenly lifted like a tremendous anchor when he looked over to Yslawna, who had stopped with her hand extended to help him out of the pool.

He just looked at her as a myriad of emotions welled up inside him. He wanted to say something profound that expressed how deeply he was affected by what had been happening the past few days, but all he could muster was a fragile "Thank you."

She helped him out of the pool and brought him upstairs to a cozy little room with a small wood-framed bed to settle in for some much-needed rest.

Aaron groggily awoke sometime later, though he had no way of knowing how much later. He sat up in his bed, surrounded by a dark, quiet, wood-paneled bedroom. A simple nightstand with a burning candle sat between him and another bed, completely stripped of its sheets.

He leaned back into his over-fluffed pillow and stared at an old ceiling, webbed with small, jagged cracks. The room was hushed and peaceful. The little candle beside him somehow gave off enough of a glow to push back the looming darkness without being too bright or disruptive.

Then, a sudden rattling downstairs stirred all the nightmares crawling in the back of his mind, and he bolted upright. It was probably Yslawna, but he'd better make sure.

His gear sat snuggly in the far corner across from his bed. He carefully got up, mindful of how weak he still felt, and then slowly staggered over to his armor while accidentally kicking his sopping wet clothes across the floor. He reached down to his helmet and brushed his hands over the thick coating of blood and grime that obscured its brilliantly bright colors. It also boasted quite a few more obvious dents than he expected. He softly set it down and began to buckle his belt and sword when he looked at the empty scabbard where his blade used to be. He sighed and put the belt back down with his armor. He'd have to ask Yslawna for one of her swords and maybe some more clothes, too. A humble little dresser rested next to the door, so he stopped there before leaving and pulled out a loose-fitting shirt and some brown pants. He sluggishly put them on and quietly stepped out of the room. A little stairway to the side led down to where a Crunch Crunch Crunch emanated from below.

He peeked down and looked right at Yslawna, who sat at a modest dinner table with a spoonful of cereal shoved into her scarred mouth. Unsurprisingly, the night blue sheets from the bed next to him were strung across her shoulder.

"Mmm, gud mrning," she greeted through her spoon. Aaron staggered down the stairs with heavy, fatigued steps while Yslawna pulled down her veil and nudged a suspiciously off-colored box closer to Aaron. "Have a seat. I found some cereal that's still edible," she cheerfully beamed. Aaron was too exhausted to tell if her mood was genuine or fake.

A thin candle sat in the table's center, under a dull ceiling fan that swirled in a drowsy circle. A bowl and spoon were already prepared for Aaron, who slumped into his chair and poured the shriveled, flaky bits that pretended to be edible into his bowl.

Yslawna leaned over and poured some water from her canteen into his cereal, making it even more unappetizing.

She twisted the lid back on her canteen and boasted, "It's not often I find cereal. This is a treat."

"Thanks. Is this expired?" Aaron asked, gazing into the watery cereal and watching the shriveled flakes soften into mush.

"Extremely, but it's safe to eat."

Aaron gave a weak nod and began to stir his cereal absentmindedly with a spoon.

Yslawna watched him stir over and over again for quite a while until she finally asked, "What do you want to talk about first?"

Aaron looked up, "What do you mean?"

"A lot's been happening," Yslawna said in between a spoonful of cereal she shoved under her loosened veil. "My old companions would always talk everything out during quiet moments like this. So, what do you want to talk about first?"

Aaron paused to consider this. Such a menagerie of unpleasantness had consumed his life that it was difficult to choose one thing to focus on. He thought he'd start with the obvious first. "Can we talk about the… reincarnation thing?"

"No," Yslawna answered shortly.

Aaron twitched nervously, "Uh... ok." He apprehensively tapped on his bowl until he finally settled on the next thing that squirmed in the back of his mind. "Jalmi."

Yslawna gave a short, surprised nod. "What about Jalmi?"

"He affected me."

"Yeah, I imagine he did. He pulled out a massive chunk of your energy."

Aaron hesitated as he tried to put into words the strange experience using the heart on Jalmi. "It wasn't just that. I WAS Jalmi for a while. I saw what he saw, felt what he felt. And watched Jalmi choose that thing, that parasite, over us."

"You mean he cared for it?"

Aaron slowly nodded, "Yeah, I think he did."

Yslawna leaned forward, "You saw into his mind and felt what he felt. You tell me why."

"I don't know. I guess it offered him something he needed: safety, assurance, stability. But at such a cost... I don't understand why I couldn't reach him."

"Sometimes you just can't. Believe me, there are MANY people I would have done anything to save. Sometimes, it's just not meant to be. It's not a lacking on your part, though," she said while pointing her spoon at him.

"Jalmi thought humanity was irredeemable..." The words just seemed to spill out and hit the ground like a boulder.

Yslawna paused with her spoon in her mouth.

"Do you think he was right?"

She softly set her spoon down. "Do I think humanity is irredeemable?"

"Yes."

"No."

"Why, though?" Aaron asked with an animated fervor, bubbling up out of the fear and nihilism that had made a comfortable home in the dark places of his psyche. "Look around us, look at what's happened here!"

She shrugged, "Doesn't matter."

"How can it not matter?"

She aimed her spoon at him and calmly explained, "If there's ever a little bit of good left, even just a speck, then humanity is redeemable. Like right here in this little room," she gestured around at the quaint little dining room that they found themselves in. "The two of us eating cereal, not destroying each other. This is good." she scooped up a spoonful of mushy cereal and waved it around while she spoke, "There's always good, even in Hiri Handi. It might be just specks, but it's there. And if there's always good, then humanity is always redeemable. That is why forgiveness exists: to be a bridge between good and evil. Hm… this reminds me of the chapel," she wistfully remarked through another mouthful. "Awhet and I would spend so much time talking about events."

Aaron let out a heavy sigh and looked back down to his cereal. It looked distasteful, but Yslawna was going out of her way to be nice. He took a mouthful of it.

It tasted as he expected.

He nudged the bowl away and pouted, "Nothing tastes right here!"

"I know. You get used to it eventually, though."

Aaron froze as a hopeful thought lightning bolted through his struggling mind. He leapt up and startled Yslawna who choked slightly as he began to vigorously dig through one of his satchels for the beautiful gift Almerin had left him.

"What are you doing?"

"AH HA!" Aaron triumphantly held two purple foil-wrapped Omos candy bars.

Yslawna stood up and gawked at the exquisite treasures. "Where did you get this?" she breathlessly whispered as Aaron reached across the table to hand her one.

"Almerin packed me a couple. They were his favorite, apparently."

"He was sitting on that stash? No wonder he didn't want to leave that tower!"

They both unwrapped and bit into the candy bars. It was like giving the sweet nectar of water to one parched so thoroughly that death had become their neighbor. They both said nothing. They just ate in silence, relishing the all-consuming experience of generously sweetened food from a long-gone age of decadence and plenty. They licked the wrappers to the bare foil and then basked in the memory of the experience before it slowly fizzled away.

Aaron was the first to speak, as Yslawna had been deprived of such a treasure for far longer. "What's our plan now?" He asked with an exasperated flare of his hand.

"I don't know," Yslawna answered through a sugar-fueled daze. "I'm thinking about raiding Almerin's tower for more Omos bars, though."

Aaron couldn't help but let a smile break through the sour depression that had begun to harden across his face. He chuckled slightly and added, "That'd be a worthwhile expedition. But what's our plan now? We don't have a ship anymore."

"Some visitors came by. I sent them away, though, until I was sure you'd be back on your feet."

"What, more survivors!?"

"Not really. It's something I haven't seen in Hiri Handi before, and I've seen a lot. They wore sacks on their heads and asked if I'd follow them. Wouldn't answer any questions."

"That sounds foreboding."

"I know, but they came in peace, which is something very rare in Hiri Handi. I need to investigate this, especially since our options for getting into the palace are thinning out."

"Ok," Aaron groaned with his hands in his face at the obviousness of the danger. "But this is probably a trap that will try to kill us."

"You might be right." Yslawna lifted her veil slightly to take a mouthful of cereal, which she immediately regretted and pushed away. "I'm going to have to re-acclimate my mouth to garbage again."

"Don't worry. You get used to it eventually."

Yslawna rolled up her candy bar wrapper and tossed it at her grinning companion.

CHAPTER FOURTEEN

The Caretaker of the Forgotten

"Do you feel it? The Energy here? It's places like this that form the bulwark of our defense. When you find one of these locations, mark it! They can often deter the most stubborn of pursuers."

-Marceon Ecra, Clinician of Medicine, Order of the Golden Band

1,320 years after the opening of the seal.

The two tired, bashed, and beaten fighters cautiously traversed the ever-watchful streets of Hiri Handi to the last place Yslawna encountered the odd survivors, the wreckage of the Dancing Star. As they neared what was left of their old ship, splattered across several buildings and a courtyard, Aaron perceived the faint images of three people sitting by a fire near the bulk of the wreckage.

"That's them," Yslawna pointed, raising her makeshift lantern to get more light.

Aaron readied the silver sword Yslawna had given him just before leaving. The two stopped a short but safe distance away, and three figures rose in the flickering firelight to greet them. They were emaciated, dirty, rag-wearing scavengers that carried rudimentary spears and axes. All three had cloth sacks tied over their heads, completely obscuring their faces.

"Will you follow us?" one of them asked in a blank, toneless voice.

Aaron immediately hated them, the rigid way that they stood, and the unnatural way the man spoke.

"Yes," Yslawna answered. "Lead the way."

The three gathered torches from the fire and began to leave, not even checking if Yslawna and Aaron were following.

"Yslawna!" Aaron whispered, signaling her to slow her pace and lag a good way behind the survivors so they couldn't overhear them.

"These guys don't seem right in the head, and why are they wearing those masks?"

"I wear a mask."

"W-well, they're different."

"They're under something's influence," she subtly gestured to the group that continued to march ahead. "Just stay close and keep a clear and calm mind. Mental intrusions can only happen if your mind is agitated and disorderly."

Aaron nodded and turned his attention back to their three guides.

The odd group led them through a short journey across Hiri Handi. They weaved around and through houses with a surprising awareness of their surroundings. Only once did Yslawna and Aaron hear a snarl from the ruins of a miserable old house, but the creature, possibly being small in stature, thought better of attacking the group and allowed them to march onward. Their guides eventually led them to a massive entrance leading underground.

"This is the Mausoleum," Yslawna whispered as the odd group hopped over an old black fence and darted into the entryway, disappearing below.

The entrance of the Mausoleum was closer to the Grand Library's complex architecture, rather than the smooth, elegant motions across the rest of Hiri Handi. It, like the library, looked like a relic from an older time and seemed determined to fill every inch of space with carvings and statues. The massive entrance sheltered a wide stairwell that proudly descended into obscurity.

They approached a timeworn, modestly small gate that meekly guarded the grandiose stairwell.

Yslawna jostled the gate, which was locked and refused to budge, stubbornly clinging to its last purpose to keep people out. She gracelessly kicked it off its hinges and trudged through with Aaron, who wearily scanned what he could of the area around them for any signs of a trap. The two gingerly descended into the grand entrance and down the old stairs. They soon stepped off into a darkened cave of tombs with faint lights dotting the graveyard like fireflies. Though the air was stale, it was far less putrid and oppressive than what was on the surface. Aaron took a greedy breath of the better air, but it still assaulted his lungs all the same as he quickly descended into a series of vigorous coughs that racketed like cannon shells across the silent graves. When he was done, he paused and looked over to Yslawna, who just stared at him.

"Sorry," he bashfully apologized.

"Eh, at least you didn't do this." She pulled out a small handgun, aimed it up, and fired a large flare. It screeched across the Mausoleum and then bobbed up and down far above their heads.

Aaron stood aghast for a moment but then realized it was probably for the best. Whoever wanted them there already knew they'd arrived. They weren't going to be surprising anyone.

Yslawna took a confident step forward and proclaimed, "When in doubt, light everything up."

Aaron couldn't agree more. In the flare's unpleasantly orange light, he was able to take in the dizzying full scope of the Mausoleum. It wasn't merely rows and rows of graves around them but an entire underground city filled with colossal statues and massive tombs, all dedicated to the dead. Aaron approached one of the tombs in fascination. It was large and squarish, but it came to life with colorful, flowing images of flowers and weaving clouds that soared high above all the problems of the mortal world. A string of beautifully crafted words was written on the front, but he couldn't read any of it and stepped away with a small sigh.

"This was left over from an older age," Yslawna said, noting Aaron's obvious curiosity. She stepped beside him and explained, "We used to build intricate monuments to death before we began to treat it as a passing rather than an end. We eventually discarded the tombs in favor of simple burnings, but I still think these are beautiful. A tomb like this commemorates life, while a burning only helps us forget about the loss. Even if life is cyclical, every life lived is important."

She cut herself short when another group of survivors, all wearing sacks over their heads and one wielding an enormous burning staff, scurried out from the tombs. They stopped ahead of Yslawna and Aaron, stood there, and said nothing. Then, the group abruptly turned around and marched back the way they came.

Aaron pensively watched them and said, "I guess someone's getting impatient."

"You're right. They don't seem too smart, though. That can work for us." She pulled off the large black case holding her kaeta and tapped Aaron on the shoulder. "You follow them, and I'll provide support."

She darted off into the maze of tombs, leaving Aaron alone before he could even comment on the plan. He stood there befuddled and confused before setting off after the welcoming committee, afraid that he might lose them entirely. He found them a good distance ahead and slowed his pace to follow from afar. As he skulked behind, Yslawna's gentle music began to drift and sway across the

Mausoleum, giving him a sense of confidence that recalled his victory over the ugly monster he danced with in the library.

He trailed the sack-wearing fellows for a while as they wound their way across the twisting roads that stretched out in bands like a spider's web before finally coming in sight of a large, parched fountain. The group halted next to a man who had been sitting on the edge of the fountain, gazing lethargically at where the water used to be.

Aaron nervously approached the man, who refused to even acknowledge him. It felt like a profound power play to demonstrate Aaron's insignificance compared to the might of this man's ego. He was balding with a long, narrow face that seemed stretched over his skull. He wore a dirty black and gold long coat and a faded gold cape. The man said nothing and just continued to gaze into the water until Aaron had enough. Marshaling his fragile sense of confidence and self-assurance, he staggered out a weak, "Hello?"

The old man jolted and looked up, "Ah, what? Who are you?" he asked in a tired, thin voice drenched in uncertainty and confusion.

Aaron blinked a couple of times while processing the baffling response. For a moment, he saw Almerin in the old man's eyes, but the familiarity was fleeting. Almerin's tower felt like a refuge, while this place felt agitated and dangerous. "Uh, my name is Aaron," he finally replied. "I thought we were invited here. Do you know who's in charge?"

"OH, of course," the man quickly gave a frail bow. "My name is Casadarious. I am in charge, and yes, I invited you and your friend here."

Aaron eyed the old man's minions, who shuffled around the periphery. More were probably hiding around the tombs, but Yslawna was still playing somewhere in the distance, and this encouraged Aaron to keep going.

"I'm a member of the Golden Band," Aaron reciprocated the bow, "and we've come at your request."

"You don't wear the Band's colors," Casadarious mused, pointing at Aaron's armor and then pulling at the gold and black of his own coat. "But your colors are familiar. Wait, I have a sword. Does this happen to belong to you?" Casadarious vigorously motioned one of the sack-wearing minions until it brought over a twisting blue and yellow sword broken halfway down the blade.

Aaron looked at it with wide, eager eyes and a slack-jawed mouth, but his helmet obscured this from Casadarious. "How did you find it?" Aaron asked in a suppressed, flat tone, possibly too suppressed to be taken as genuine.

"Its energy was strong and not hard to track down. It also seems to match your armor."

"Yes," Aaron quickly answered, "it does belong to me."

Casadarious motioned the servant to hand over the blade, which Aaron snatched before the old man could reconsider.

"I've asked you to come —" the old man's eyes drifted to the side as he struggled to keep his train of thought. Aaron awkwardly waited, wearily watching the sack-wearing minions who began drifting closer until Casadarious snapped back into focus. " — to come because of shifting events in Hiri Handi," he continued. "Something great has changed in the city, and suddenly, Yslawna is out again in that racketing old ship. We need to council, and I need information."

"What is this?" Aaron asked, pointing first to the sack-wearing servant and then to the minions standing off to the sides.

"These are my people," Casadarious pointed around at his work, not with pride but with a bitter melancholy. "I've been keeping them passive. I'm sure you can appreciate the dire nature of our situation."

"Why do they have bags on their heads?" Aaron nervously asked. He didn't want to play games. He wanted to know what was happening before he got any deeper into this.

Casadarious sighed, "The evil in Hiri Handi is only getting stronger, and the few willing to oppose this are dwindling. We've nearly lost the fight, and there's almost nothing left to save."

He was beating around the bush. Aaron pointed at the sack-wearing people again and repeated his question, "What is this?"

"The product of desperation," Casadarious answered with a grimace. "The Golden Band used to carefully tend to the madness inside their hearts. They'd draw out the insanity and heal their pain while stabilizing their minds. We don't have that power anymore. I've wiped their minds entirely, their past, their pain, and bound them to my will."

"That's..." Aaron faltered as Jalmi's memory came crashing back through his head like an avalanche. Casadarious was the one who stole everyone away from the library, leaving Jalmi alone.

"This was necessary," he continued with a sharp, resolute tenor. "We don't have the means to properly heal these people anymore."

Aaron pointed at the old man, "This is brainwashing."

"These weren't even people anymore. They were dangerous to themselves and everything around them."

"Why did you abandon Jalmi in the library?"

Casadarious's eyes lit up in surprise. "So, you've seen him? What's become of Jalmi?"

"He's dead."

"How?"

"We... were forced to kill him."

Casadarious sat on the fountain's edge and hunched over as if he'd been punched in the chest. He closed his eyes and weakly swallowed. "Then you understand. You just don't want to admit it."

Aaron didn't say anything, and Casadarious looked at the battered yellow knight with profound sadness.

"Opening the seal drove these people insane. They have become animals, and they need to be saved." He pointed to one of the sack-wearing survivors. "I put these bags on their heads to help them forget their own faces. I know it's horrific. But when they look in a mirror and remember who they are, the insanity and pain takes hold, and they become savages. I wanted to bring Jalmi with me." he pounded his hand on his chest. "But he was broken, a shell. There was nothing I could do for him without wiping his mind like everyone else here!" he stopped as rasping coughs seemed to sap the life out of him. He sat back down on the fountain's edge with a weak sigh. "You tried to save him," he said with cold, narrow eyes, "and you discovered the cost. What I've done is the only way left."

Aaron glanced at the dirty rabble around him. Masked, barefoot, and quiet. It didn't feel right to purposely keep them like this. The way they watched, though, peering from behind the tombs in great numbers as if they'd suddenly surge forth and tear him to pieces, struck a primal fear in Aaron. He looked away.

"I want us to work together." Casadarious slowly stood up and took a step closer to Aaron. "We're allies. I can provide you with provisions and a replacement ship, and you can tell me what's happened."

"It's a long story," Yslawna suddenly cut in from right behind Aaron, who jolted in shock.

"You're too quiet," Aaron gasped with a hand on his heart. He didn't even notice when her music had stopped.

"Good to know I haven't lost my touch," she said with what was probably a wide grin under her veil. She pointed to the withering old man and explained to Aaron, "I know Casadarious. He was a commander for the Golden Band and a good person."

Casadarious gave a grateful smile to Yslawna and then turned to Aaron. "Believe me," he pleaded. "I would want nothing more than to tend to each person's madness and bring all of them back to sanity. But this just isn't possible anymore. We don't have the power, and we're out of options." Casadarious looked back to Yslawna. "It's been a long time," he said with a profound tiredness, "and we have a lot to talk about. I have a home not far from here. Why don't we talk at length over there?"

Yslawna gestured for him to lead the way, and he did so. Aaron followed behind with a nervous glance back at the minions, who suddenly scattered away into the forest of tombs. Casadarious led them through the heart of the Mausoleum, where more and more of his sack-wearing people began to appear until the area morphed into a languid town of sorts. The citizens of this dreary settlement muddled around burning campfires and small crops of fungus plants growing out of dirt graves. Pale lanterns hung on every few tombs, giving off a thin, ghostly light as Yslawna's flare finally faded away. Occasionally, they would pass a survivor or two handing out bowls of mush and small cups of water to anyone who approached. Despite many people passing by, that horrible quiet still pervaded. No one talked, not even to each other. No one cooperated on tasks or even interacted with anything outside of whatever they were lethargically attending to.

Casadarious finally stopped before an aggressively large tomb with sharp edges and wide columns. The body had been hollowed out and reused as a manor that vigilantly loomed over the rest of the town. Across the street was what Aaron assumed to be the first militarized guard he'd seen so far. A villager in mud-smeared armor bearing a small lantern stood on the opposite side of the street, directly across the manor, in such a rigid pose that Aaron thought he might be trying to become a streetlamp. Casadarious gave the guard a sharp, unfriendly grimace before motioning to a nearby minion who wordlessly heaved open two heavy iron doors, allowing them to step inside the manor.

They turned right and strolled into an unpleasant little dining room with stark grey walls and a massive table made from a tomb door placed over some large stones. Horrific poverty was nothing new to Aaron here, but the chapel had been able to turn it into something warm. This was cold and stoic. Casadarious lit a few thin candles and invited everyone to sit on cushioned blocks around the table so Yslawna could begin recounting their journey. As they talked, some servants shuffled around the periphery of the room while providing food and drinks. The food was some sort of greenish fungus paste, and it looked almost as disgusting as the frothing sludge in dark ceramic cups that they slapped onto the table.

Aaron didn't go near the drinks, and he nudged the food away.

Casadarious shot him a concerned glance. "It's certainly nasty," he admitted. "But it's the best we can do. It's got most of the vitamins you need and is simple enough for the people here to harvest and make."

"I'll pass for now, thanks."

Yslawna took a bite and then nudged her bowl away as well before continuing their tale. Aaron shifted nervously as Yslawna approached the part where he admitted to being the reincarnation of the Prince Adept, something he still didn't really understand. She explained how Aaron saved her life while risking his own well-being and then, surprisingly, omitted the unsettling revelation entirely. Aaron quietly exhaled in relief and then glanced over at Yslawna with sincere gratitude. Up until now, he had been trying to peg how much or how little Yslawna trusted him. This omission spoke volumes. Casadarious was looking down, absorbed in thought, but Yslawna caught Aaron's glance and returned it with a slight nod. She then continued all the way to the Mausoleum.

Casadarious didn't say anything at first, not even to comment on the bizarre properties of the wooden heart. He quietly massaged his head to brush aside the nightmarish images that encircled his imagination, written vividly across his frightened eyes, until the frail words finally leaked out of his mouth. "So, the Prince Adept has truly left the city." he weakly mused. "Then we don't have a choice. We'll need to strike soon."

Yslawna agreed, "You have an army of sorts, but moving across Hiri Handi to even get to the palace will greatly thin out your numbers. That much movement might even draw several soul hordes."

"You're correct, but we have two advantages. If the Prince Adept has left, then the palace will be much weaker. I don't think I'll need many of my forces to overcome their defenses. Second, I've found a secret entrance that will take us straight to the palace."

"You've found a what?" Yslawna asked, not even trying to hide her astonishment.

"I... uhh..." Casadarious's eyes glazed over, and he began muttering disoriented gibberish.

Yslawna and Aaron exchanged nervous glances. Although they both wore masks, the feeling of concern was painted in their body language and tentative breathing. Yslawna leaned forward, pulled off her glove, and snapped her fingers in Casadarious's face until he awoke with a start.

"Ah!"

Yslawna looked him over and said, "You've seen better days."

"Both of us have." Casadarious rubbed his tired eyes. "Holding everything together has taken a greater toll on me than I thought it ever would. It doesn't matter though. Do you remember the labyrinth, Yslawna?"

"Yeah," she replied with a startling bitterness at the recollection. "Yeah, I remember it."

"The secret passage is in the labyrinth." He turned to Aaron, "The one you and Almerin recently passed through. I have a key." Casadarious took the hand of a servant to help him stand and walked out of the room with a visible frailness haunting his steps, leaving Yslawna and Aaron alone with a servant who stood off in the corner.

Yslawna pointed to her bowl and asked, "Do you have anything better to eat?"

The servant said nothing.

Casadarious came back, muttering something about the palace while holding onto a familiar golden triangle. "The city is falling between dimensions." He placed the triangle on the table. "The Prince Adept has somehow dislodged the palace to make it slip a little from the rest of the city. Entering is exceedingly difficult but not impossible. However, I've found a way in." He proudly tapped the triangle. Yslawna and Aaron looked over the delicate little thing that shimmered like sunlight while Casadarious proudly boasted, "I had to comb everywhere for this, but it was well worth the effort. Although its reliability is somewhat," he hedged, "erratic, as the labyrinth has grown in ways I can't even fathom. I believe it is consistent enough to bring us to the palace. If it falters, then we can resort to a chemical stimulant to excite our psychic minds to bring us the rest of the way."

Yslawna shook her head, "That's a dangerous thing to do. Stimulants like that fry the brain, and neither of us have much brain left to fry."

"Your friend might," he pointed at Aaron, who instinctively leaned away. "We shouldn't need them, though," he quickly corrected, noting Aaron's vitriol reluctance. "I strongly maintain that this is the best way to enter the palace," he tapped the triangle again for emphasis.

Aaron sank into his uncomfortable stone block. He had pushed the labyrinth to the back of his mind in the blissful hope that it was just some horrible eccentricity that he'd never have to visit again. He had no desire to go back to those unnatural corridors and spar with whatever might be lurking there. Although, the idea of an allied army foraging a path and cutting through any monsters that might be hidden away did give him a little bit of confidence. He looked over at the meager servant, scrawny and wasted away by years of underground living, and felt that confidence plummet.

Casadarious's plan might just be wishful thinking. Then again, hasn't everything he and Yslawna done so far been wishful thinking, too?

Casadarious stepped back from the table and proclaimed, "This is the time to finally end this nightmare. I'll show you to your rooms where you can rest and prepare. I'll need time to marshal my forces." He began to lead the way out of the room but stopped on the threshold of the door. "This house is safe, but my hold over the residents here is… tenuous at times. Please don't venture around without being properly armed and prepared. They can be unpredictable."

CHAPTER FIFTEEN

The Scarecrow

"The chaos of the bleeding seal clouds their minds and actions. It's not enough to bring them back to where they were. They need to be elevated spiritually, so they can overcome the world's cry. It's a beautiful sight when they awaken though, like a child seeing the world for the first time."

-Jalmi Yabeen, Master of Medicine, Order of the Golden Band
543 years after the opening of the seal.

Casadarious led Yslawna and Aaron up a flight of jaggedly cut stone stairs to their rooms. The grand tomb Casadarious made his home in was segmented into burial chambers emptied out and furnished with only the bare essentials, including several small windows cut into the walls to allow some degree of airflow.

Casadarious looked at the pitiful accommodations and said, "I'm sorry, but these rooms will have to do. Luxuries are rare here. I need to meditate before we set off. If you need anything or have any questions, speak to the fellow in white standing outside the front door. He'll guide you to my garden."

Yslawna and Aaron thanked Casadarious, who turned and disappeared down the stairs.

Aaron looked around his barren room with unease. A stone acting as a chair, a fragile wooden table, and some blankets and sheets mushed into a pile to act as a bed were all that was provided for him. Aaron meandered inside and gracelessly collapsed into his pile of sheets.

"What do you think?" Yslawna asked, standing in the doorway and looking down at Aaron as he pulled off his warped helmet that was discolored and stained with god only knows what.

Aaron exhaled, "If he can pull himself together, I think we might have a chance at closing the seal."

Yslawna nodded, "He's reached his limits. Casadarious was one of the high commanders for the Golden Band and always had a profound well of strength to draw on. Let's just hope his sacrifices here haven't been in vain."

"So, you trust him?"

Yslawna hesitated. It was small, but enough to turn Aaron's head. "I know Casadarious very well. We were both commanders. He was one of the first to challenge Enekoat's brutal pragmatism and would constantly sacrifice his own well-being to help others. What Casadarious has done here is… disturbing, but I don't see any other way."

Aaron pondered stealing that golden triangle, but it felt too risky. "Okay," Aaron leaned back with a sigh and stared at the ceiling.

"I also tested my music on the minions while you two were talking."

Aaron sat up again, "What?"

"I can exert some control over them if I have to."

Aaron grinned at Yslawna, "Okay, good to know we have a backup plan."

She stared at him in a way that made him uneasy and then gave a joyful clap as a wonderful idea occurred to her. "I need to check my bed for any sheets I don't have!"

She darted off, and Aaron gazed at the empty door frame for a while after she left, wondering if Yslawna would ever manage to fit all the sheets in Hiri Handi inside that old chapel. He leaned his head back down but didn't close his eyes. He just gazed at the ceiling as an uneasy feeling of doom slowly suffocated his ability to think. Over in the door frame, the Prince Adept was sitting comfortably in his wheelchair and smoking his drugs casually like nothing was wrong.

"YOU'RE NOT SUPPOSED—" Aaron caught himself before his screams caught anyone's attention. He swallowed and took a few shallow breaths before continuing in a subdued but anxiety-riddled tone, "You're not supposed to be here while I'm awake."

"I'm just here to remind you of my evilness," the disgusting old man laughed.

Aaron blinked a couple of times in disbelief. "What? I already know you're evil."

"And yet you've allied yourselves to Casadarious. Have you learned nothing from my tale of self-obliteration?"

"We don't really have any choices left," he vehemently protested. "And besides, what evil has Casadarious done here? Yslawna agreed that we couldn't save these people. I tried to save Jalmi, and he almost took my head off!"

The Prince Adept scoffed and then puffed on his drug in a theatrically dramatic pause before answering with a sharp, "You know better than this."

Before Aaron could stagger out a stunned retort, the Prince Adept continued, "Casadarious bound an enormous amount of people to his will. Do you think that such an act is done without ego? To wipe away someone's identity and declare yours so infallible and pure as to be a grand anchor is the very height of ego, my friend."

"But these people are insane," Aaron shot back.

"Who draws the line of insanity? Who declares what is best for the whole, and what inevitable sacrifices must be made? Do you think that Jalmi, who had mastered medicine of the mind, had simply never thought to subjugate the raving lunatics around him before Casadarious scooped them all up?" The Prince Adept narrowed his eyes and glared at Aaron with a piercing coldness, "When you place yourself at the very top of a machine of such desperation, then you'll quickly find the purity of your soul tested as you're pushed to sacrifice more and more to keep that machine moving. You've ignored very obvious cracks in this machine. I advise you to take a walk."

And with that, the Prince Adept was gone. Aaron stayed still, quietly contemplating the exchange in a slow stupor of apprehension until he heard someone talking to Yslawna in the room next to him.

"Casadarious requests your presence."

He heard Yslawna follow the woman as their footsteps trailed down the stairs and faded away into nothingness. Aaron stared at the ceiling for a little while longer until the Prince Adept's warning stirred him to do something. He got up, put on his dented helmet, stepped out of the room, and began snooping around the makeshift house.

Casadarious's room was barely better than his. Books on fragile wooden shelves lined the sparsely furnished room. He had a dirty old mattress on the floor rather than a pile of sheets, which seemed to be the only comfort he kept for himself. Aaron couldn't read any of the books and found nothing evil about the mattress, so he continued his search around the house. He meandered downstairs and began rummaging through a rudimentary kitchen with a couple of pale boxes tossed in a corner, counters stained with green fungus paste, and old, musty jars lining some thin shelving. He opened one of the jars, smelled something putrid, and then quickly put it back. He couldn't bring himself to open any other, so he left the kitchen and walked across the main hallway to re-enter the dining room.

Then he caught sight of the front door, which sat ajar and partially opened.

This was unacceptable.

Aaron stood before the door, grabbed it firmly, and tried several times to close it, fighting against the old, warped hinges, which refused to line up properly with the rest of the door frame. He stepped back and swung open the door to get a better look at the hinges. Out of the corner of his eye, he saw that guard again. He was still standing across the street in the exact same spot with a small lantern in hand, providing a meager illumination to the surrounding crowd of sullen figures meandering back and forth to whatever activities they mindlessly attended. Aaron stood against the door and peered out. The guard was like a statue, unmoving and even forcing other minions to walk around him. Aaron cautiously opened the front door and stepped outside. The guard still didn't move.

"What do you want?" he shouted across the street.

The servant dressed in white standing just to the side of the door startled Aaron by answering, "To serve the Golden Band."

"Not you!" Aaron hushed the man and pointed to the guard still standing across the street. "What do you want?"

The man didn't answer and still didn't move. Aaron started to go back inside but stopped as the Prince Adept's warning once again squirmed in the back of his mind. It might be dangerous to go over there, but it might be even more dangerous to ignore this. He anxiously looked around, wondering if he should find Yslawna first. It would take too long, so he cursed and walked across the street over to the guard. He stopped before the human streetlight and asked, "Why are you out here? What do you want?"

"Help..."

Aaron took a startled step back.

"Help," the man begged in a withered gasp.

The guard stumbled around and began to lurch through the thick maze of tombs and graves. Aaron drew his sword and cautiously followed before he could disappear. The two waded deeper into the Mausoleum and further away from the town until not another sack-wearing minion was seen.

They stopped before one of the tombs, indistinguishable from the others around them. It didn't look significant in any way, but the guard just stopped there, gazing at a locked door.

Aaron stood next to the man, sized up the door, and asked, "Do you need me to open this?"

The man just stared into the door.

Aaron nervously glanced around in case anything was about to ambush him and then jostled the door's handle, which unsurprisingly refused to budge. He readied his sword but hesitated before pouring any energy into it. He was still weak, and spending energy was no small thing right now. Something important might be inside here, though. He took another look at the miserable guard, who just quietly stared at the door and then poured a small amount of energy into the blade. With a swift cut, the lock hit the ground with a clang. He kicked the door open, releasing a staggering smell of rot that surged out of the tomb. The smell throttled his lungs, and he stumbled back and gagged. The guard seemed completely unaffected. Aaron held his breath and peered inside at several bodies piled atop each other in the dark. He couldn't really see them in the dim light of the guard's lantern and was glad he didn't.

He stepped away from the tomb and turned to the guard, "Is this what you wanted to show me?"

The man didn't answer. He just stared at the shadowy mass of bodies.

Aaron eyed the guard suspiciously and wondered what would happen if you brainwashed someone who wasn't insane. He yanked off the sack covering the man's head, expecting something extraordinary to happen.

A dirty, dark-haired man with a pale, bony face just looked at him with glassy eyes. Aaron took a nervous breath and dug into his satchel for the bag containing the wooden heart. It would be extremely reckless to use it on this man…

He wearily gazed down at the heart and began to reconsider and put it away when the man weakly muttered, "Help…"

Aaron pulled out the slimy heart and emptied the bag on the ground with a horrible *plop* that he never ceased to find nauseating. He took another breath and exhaled while pulling off his gauntlet — flesh to flesh, heart to heart.

The room spun in that familiar, sickening way as the ground slowly opened up and swallowed him.

Aaron stood in the middle of a dark, humid bog of sludge and sickly weeds. It was a bog that stretched out endlessly in all directions until it met a large pale moon sitting on the night horizon. The guard Aaron wanted to help was curled up next to a large rock. He cradled a crooked walking stick with a lantern tied to the end and was the only source of light other than the moon.

Aaron sat down next to the man and asked his name.

"Enatt," he weakly replied. He pointed up at the moon and said, "No matter how far I walk, I can't escape it. It's following me everywhere, making me forget things."

Aaron nervously looked up at the moon and wondered how anyone could possibly escape such a thing. The bog was flat and offered no shelter of any kind. There would be no hiding from the colossus peering down at them. Aaron took Enatt's emaciated hand and helped him stand up. Together, they trudged through the humid bog, searching for anything that might destroy the moon. The goal seemed hilariously futile, but Aaron couldn't think of anything else that might work. After hours of quietly trudging through the muck, Aaron stopped to rest on a small hill that protruded out of the flat terrain like a boil. Enatt stabbed the lantern stick into the soft ground and sat down with Aaron to mull over ideas on what to do now.

"I tried walking," Enatt explained, "and I've tried to build a home out of the mud, but it always collapses."

"How much of your life do you still remember?"

Enatt paused to think. His eyebrows furrowed, and his eyes sharpened momentarily, but then it was gone. "I can't remember anything," he admitted. The lantern's yellowing light traced the utter fear that twisted in Enatt's frail face.

Aaron looked away. It was too hard to watch. "You brought me to a tomb filled with bodies," Aaron prodded. "Do you remember any of that?"

"No," Enatt shook his head.

"Do you remember the Prince Adept or the Golden Band?"

Enatt shook his head.

"What about that lantern there?" Aaron pointed at the lantern stick. "Do you at least remember where that came from?"

"I found it after being chased by something in the darkness."

Aaron's eyes darted to the shadowy landscape around them. This was supposed to be Enatt's mind. There couldn't be monsters here… could there? "What chased you?" he hesitantly asked, his eyes fixed on the distant shadows.

"I don't know. I never saw it. I heard it, though, and it doesn't like the light. It never bothers me while I have the lantern."

Aaron looked at the yellowing light cast by the lantern. It didn't look or feel good. In fact, it felt just as sickly as Enatt. Aaron looked over to the side at a particularly large shadow circling the hill. It was difficult to see, but it was there.

This is Enatt's mind, Aaron thought. There shouldn't be monsters here. He unhooked the lantern from the stick and then cracked the end to make a sharp spear.

Enatt's eyes widened, "What are you doing?"

Aaron considered for a moment if he really wanted to fight that thing. He didn't have any weapons other than this makeshift spear, and whatever was lurking around the hill looked big. He also wasn't brave or strong.

He looked over at his pale and withered friend and said, "You have to help me fight this thing."

"I can't," Enatt looked away. "I'm too scared."

Aaron sighed. He had finally found someone more terrified than himself. He looked down at the beating heart he held in his hand, which again was no longer wooden. He didn't remember carrying it all this way. But he had it now, and that gave him a surprising sense of courage. He thinned out the end of his spear a bit more as he watched the distant shadow. There didn't seem to be any other options. He had to fight the monster or erode into nothingness like Enatt.

Enatt stayed behind with the lantern while Aaron marched down the hill to meet whatever was watching them. The beating heart of the tree pounded in his hand with the fearful rhythm of his own heart as he approached a large mass of shadows that rose from the ground like a tower of smoke. It didn't say anything. It just looked at Aaron with snow-white eyes tucked into a featureless form.

Aaron held his spear close and presented the heart to the creature. "W-what do you want?" he timidly asked. He had hoped he could project a sense of power and confidence, but that clearly wasn't going to happen.

The creature snarled, and in its white eyes, he saw pain and suffering. Images and scenes drifted in its eyes with greater and greater clarity the longer Aaron looked at it.

"You're not a monster..." Aaron muttered as the realization suddenly hit him. "You're Enatt's memories."

The monster whimpered and lowered its head.

Aaron looked back at Enatt, still huddled on the hill with that lantern. He charged up the hill, surprising Enatt, and smashed his lantern into pieces.

"WHAT DID YOU DO!" Enatt shrieked.

"I'm giving your memories back."

Enatt cried in terror as the monster tore up the hill and leaped on him with a horrific fury.

Aaron pulled Enatt out of the bog, and they both stood in the Mausoleum before the rotting, defiled tomb in the twisting light of Enatt's lantern.

"They're all dead," he sobbed with tired, bloodshot eyes.

"I know, I know." Aaron stepped closer to comfort him but stumbled back as the man covered his face and screamed in a blood rage.

"No, no, no!" Aaron frantically hushed him as the broken man began to tremble in fury.

"Nakinee!" He suddenly shouted. "She's still under his control!"

"I'll find her. Don't worry." Aaron picked up Enatt's sack and handed it to him. "Wear this to disguise yourself. We'll find Nakinee and Yslawna."

He took the sack with unease and looked up at Aaron. "You have to kill him. He has to die!"

Aaron didn't answer. He just pointed and said, "Put the sack on and lead me to Nakinee. Then we'll find Yslawna and figure out what to do next." He had no interest in fighting Casadarious. He just wanted to escape.

Enatt put on the sack, and the two strolled back into town as inconspicuously as they possibly could after experiencing such sudden trauma. Nakinee wasn't hard to find. Enatt led Aaron to some fungus gardens growing out of several dirt graves. The two marched past the oblivious workers shuffling around the farms and up to Nakinee, who was on her hands and knees digging in the dirt.

Enatt tapped her several times to get her attention and then pulled off his mask.

She dropped her tools and just looked at him.

He knelt down and began talking to her in a low voice while Aaron stood guard. The crowd of workers didn't seem to care at all until Nakinee started screaming and weeping.

Suddenly, the crowd around them stopped working and just stared at the three of them.

"Uhh… Enatt, Nakinee!" Aaron drew his sword and tapped the two to get their attention. "I think we should go!"

Enatt stood up and gawked at the massing numbers of slaves. "We won't be able to fight our way out."

"You two put on your masks," Aaron directed as the slaves continued to stare in the most hostile manner possible. "Try to blend in and find Yslawna. I'll distract Casadarious until she can put these things to sleep."

Enatt and Nakinee put on their masks and slipped away into the mass of people as Aaron began waving his arms and shouting to the crowd to draw their attention.

"Hey, you brainless sackheads!" He screamed. "Bring me to Casadarious! I demand to see your leader!"

The group followed Aaron as he marched all the way back to the manor.

Casadarious was waiting for him with a gaping mouth and a mixed look of surprise and terror as Aaron strolled up, a massive swarm of sack-wearing slaves following behind.

"What happened!" Casadarious reeled. "I told you to be CAREFUL outside the manor!" The old man then turned to the crowd, and upon making eye contact, they began to lazily disperse. He looked back at Aaron with an angry twinge. "Well?"

"I tripped over some tools, and they all freaked out. Where's Yslawna?"

Casadarious blinked several times at the pitiful excuse. "She's in the armory, inspecting the weapons." Casadarious motioned one of the sack-wearing slaves, who then sauntered over and whispered in his ear.

This wasn't good. Aaron glanced around and saw several slaves peeking out from behind the tombs. The crowd didn't disperse. They just hid away, possibly waiting for Casadarious to give the word to attack.

Aaron tried to stifle his nervous breath and stay as calm as he possibly could.

Casadarious nodded and dismissed the man, who then ambled away in a random direction. "You have no idea what you're digging up," he said with a venomous glare.

Aaron needed more time. He didn't know how much, but hopefully, Enatt would reach Yslawna soon. She would then start playing her music and save them. That is, if Enatt and Nakinee could even find her and if they weren't already captured. Aaron shook his head to jostle the horrible thoughts away.

"Then explain it to me!" Aaron shouted back, trying to bide more time. "I don't understand why you've done this."

Casadarious sighed and stepped closer, "What have those two told you?"

"Enatt led me to a tomb full of bodies. I gather that you were responsible."

"Enatt and Nakinee are damaged," he said with a sad shake of his head.

Aaron staggered back, "What? Was everyone damaged because there were a lot of bodies in there?"

"The mental decay was infectious. I told you before that we don't have luxuries here. We are fighting for our very existence. I discovered early on how frail the mind is. How easily it can be manipulated, and how quickly the darkness can seep into them and this last holding of light. The group that came with me was being poisoned. They were becoming corrupted by the darkness!"

"But you murdered them."

"Because I had to! Inegos opened the door. He was frail and becoming corrupted. He spread murder and fear to the rest. He damaged them. Made them vulnerable, and one by one, they began to turn against me and against our last hope of survival. I did what I had to do. I subdued their minds and executed the ones that the darkness took hold of, the ones beyond my capacity to help. I had to, for everyone's sake! I doubt you would have the courage to do the same."

Aaron almost shouted back, "But if everyone's dead, then what is there left to save?" but he caught himself. He was vulnerable here and had to keep Casadarious engaged until Yslawna could start playing her music.

"I actually understand," Aaron feigned.

Casadarious skeptically furrowed his brow, but he had a slight twinge of hope in his eyes.

"Jalmi was beyond my help, too," Aaron continued. "I tried to save him, and it almost cost me my life. I understand what you've done, and I understand the poison that can infect the mind. But… we can't just kill people. It's immoral and goes against the good we've been fighting for. I saw the sanity in Enatt, but you say the darkness has taken hold of him. Let's find Enatt and speak to him. If you can show me that he's…"

"Stop," Casadarious put his hand out. "I've only ever heard words as silky from the Prince Adept himself. You should be proud."

This made Aaron physically sick.

"But I'm not going to prove anything to you. I haven't survived here by second-guessing myself. You and Yslawna will leave."

Aaron paused, "Just leave?"

"Yes, I want you both gone. Forever! Take Enatt and Nakinee with you, too. Deal with their madness," he said with an outward fling of his hand.

Aaron took a step back, "Uh… okay. Sure, we'll leave."

Suddenly, a familiar, striking melody began to rhythmically thump across the Mausoleum in a way that made Aaron's stomach lurch. Casadarious glanced around in terror as all of his slaves looked toward the source of the noise.

"That would be Yslawna," Aaron said, taking several steps toward the terrifying music. "She's securing our exit, so I'll be leaving then."

"No, wait," Casadarious begged with a look of terror in his eyes that froze Aaron's blood. "I know that song. She's about to kill us all!"

"What?"

"Stop her!" Casadarious pleaded. "She's going to break my hold and drive everyone insane. They'll rip us to pieces! STOP HER!"

Aaron bolted away towards the music to stop Yslawna. He didn't have to question if Casadarious was lying because he also recognized the distorted melody of the Gated Waltz. That song, which had given him the courage to confront a nightmarish monstrosity, now propelled him speedily past all the slaves who stood gawking at the increasingly base and almost primeval music. It was a sound that seemed to dig at the lower instincts in a way that scared the deepest part of Aaron. He shoved several of the slaves aside as he hurtled through the twisting paths of the dead to the one tomb that stood in an isolated patch of dirt with three figures sitting atop its roof. Aaron frantically glanced around, looking for a manageable way to climb up. "HEY!" he shouted while waving his arms around like a maniac.

A figure shuffled over to the roof's edge and kicked down a rusty, extendable ladder. Aaron hastily climbed up and pushed past Enatt and Nakinee, who greeted him with rejoicing praise.

The rhythmic music pounding across the Mausoleum began to reach its peak. Aaron found Yslawna perched on a stool near the roof's edge, dragging her bow across her kaeta until it wanted to scream. He grabbed her shoulder and shouted over the reverberating music, "Yslawna, stop!"

She gave him a surprised glance and scaled the song back into a continuous rhythm.

"Yslawna, don't kill them. Casadarious said we could leave. Your music even gives us a way out. We don't have to kill everyone."

"Not everyone," Enatt answered for Yslawna, who was still keeping the rhythm. "We'll survive up here, but Casadarious and his evil will die."

Aaron knelt beside Yslawna and pleaded, "Don't do this. We can't become the monsters. Too much depends on us!"

"We won't," Enatt interjected again. "Because we're doing what's right."

"HOW IS THIS RIGHT?!"

"Because he's a monster that will never stop. He needs this power. He'll only come back stronger and seek us out later."

Aaron stood up to face Enatt, "You don't know that!"

"Yes, I do. I was connected to his mind, and I know that it's him or us."

"You just want revenge!"

"He has to DIE!"

All Aaron could see was the Prince Adept. That horrible fat old man cackling with vile evilness. He wasn't going to end up like him. He wasn't going to let this happen. Aaron punched Enatt in the face and set him hurtling to the floor with a loud thud and a scream from Nakinee. He then knelt beside Yslawna again and begged. "Yslawna, there are always other ways. Don't fall into this trap. Don't go down this path. You and I, we've both made mistakes, but we're doing better now. We're doing good things now. Please don't kill everyone. We won't come back from this!"

Yslawna continued playing for a moment and then slowed the song into a soft finish that was seeped in sorrow and misery. She looked down for a while and then up at Aaron. "Okay."

Surrounding the tomb was a large sea of slaves alongside Casadarious, who was easy to pick out from the mob.

"You said we could leave!" Aaron shouted down.

"You can," Casadarious pointed towards the entrance of the Mausoleum. Aaron glanced over at the other side of the tomb, where a wide, empty space led to the exit.

But before Aaron could even consider whether the open path was a trap or not, Casadarious howled in pain as Nakinee plunged a dagger deep into his back. The horde of slaves shrieked and wailed as their only connection to sanity crumpled in on itself. Aaron watched as the mob began tearing into each other like animals in such a sickening display of savagery that forever burned itself into his nightmares. Nakinee disappeared into the maelstrom while Yslawna desperately tried to play another song that failed to gain any weight or power over the mob. Eventually, the two just bowed their heads and looked away, trying not to hear the cries of agony around them.

CHAPTER SIXTEEN

The Silent Angel

"You asked if I'm doing the right thing. I asked myself that very question when I first looked into their sick, lifeless eyes. All I know is that we have to survive."

"What is survival though?"

-Casadarious Markelm, High Commander of the Order of the Golden Band

-Inegos, Watchman of the Order of the Golden Band

2,470 years after the opening of the seal.

The group quietly passed under the Mausoleum entrance, away from the grotesque carnage. Enatt didn't want to look for Naki-nee. They gave a few token calls, but looking at the slaughter that sprayed across half of Casadarious's village, they knew that there couldn't be any survivors. They staggered out of the Mausoleum and over to the small black fence guarding the entrance. Aaron collapsed against its thin iron bars and pulled off his unusually tight, smothering helmet. The air was bitter and nauseating as always, but he didn't care this time. He just needed to breathe. He let his helmet slip out his hand and fall to the side as he took breath after haggard breath that fogged in the frigid cold. Yslawna slid down into the snow beside him with a soft thump while Enatt leaned on the black fence a little distance away to gaze blankly at the surrounding darkness. The three of them sat for the longest time in a slack-jawed daze, completely overwhelmed by the nightmarish scene that they just walked away from.

"I feel like that could have gone better..." Yslawna sluggishly commented.

Aaron slowly nodded. He glanced over at Yslawna. Her breathing was heavy, and her head was rigidly fixed on that ghastly entrance that loomed out of the black abyss stretching around them.

"I recognized that song," he weakly remarked.

She didn't say anything and continued to stare at the entrance.

"It's the Gated Waltz," he persisted through another labored breath of rotted air. "I didn't know it could sound so... distorted. You're not doing well, are you?"

"You can tell by the song?"

Aaron nodded again.

She leaned back against the cold metal fence and admitted, "You're right, I'm not doing well at all. In fairness, though, I think I'm doing better than him." She weakly pointed to Enatt, who hadn't looked away from the darkness or said a word since the Mausoleum. "That song was inspired by someone I loved," she explained with a crushing heaviness that began to strangle her voice. "It's smart of you to judge my wellbeing on its tenor."

Aaron didn't know what to say or how to keep the group moving. Before he could do or say anything at all, Yslawna stood up while muttering to herself, "Just take one day at a time..." She offered Aaron her hand, which he took to help himself stand up. "Arragg! You're heavy," she groaned as she pulled him and his ridiculous suit of armor to his feet.

"It's saved me about three times now." He meekly countered.

"It's missing something, though." Yslawna dug around her bags and produced a thin strip of golden cloth, which she softly tied around Aaron's arm. "Congratulations, you're now an official member of the Golden Band."

"What? Why?"

"For your acts of profound compassion and wisdom in the Mausoleum. You stopped me from taking a path that would've destroyed me. I owe you deeply for that. At this point, there'd be a big ceremony, but…" she glanced at the unpleasant blackness around them and said, "We'll have to do that another time in a nicer place."

Aaron looked down at the tiny golden ribbon, which unexpectedly filled his chest with a swelling pride. He looked up and said, "Thank you, Yslawna."

She patted him on the shoulder and then pulled his helmet out of the snow and handed it to him. Aaron, Yslawna, and Enatt ambled out through the small, black gate, which Yslawna gingerly closed behind them.

Enatt walked a few steps out and pointed up to a tall, slender building peeking through the darkness. "Casadarious's ship is in the hanger that overlooks this area," he stated with a soul-crushing apathy.

Yslawna pulled the group together and laid out her plan. "I think we should keep Casadarious's idea of using the labyrinth to enter the palace. Almerin had a key, so all we need to do is fly the ship to his tower to get it."

The thought of entering Almerin's tower to search for that key made Aaron sick, but it did seem like the best plan so far. He knew that Casadarious also had a key, which was waved in their faces, but no one wanted to bring it up. They had no idea where the unfortunate puppeteer was buried amidst the slaughter they left behind. They didn't even know how many pieces of him were scattered around the Mausoleum. Almerin's tower was the best plan.

"I agree," Aaron said with a weak thumbs up.

Enatt gave him a blank stare while Yslawna's expressionless veil was unusually quiet.

"Why do you have your thumb up," Enatt asked.

"I, uh…" Aaron shook his hand to discard the motion. "It's something from my culture."

Enatt sputtered a little, trying to understand what other culture he could have possibly come from.

"Okay," Yslawna cut in. "Time to move."

With splintered constitutions that hung only by threads, they marched onwards and began ascending the dreary, musty stairwells of the tower until they reached their ship. They stepped through a dented metal door and into a hanger, where they stopped in awe as Yslawna and Enatt's lanterns washed over a sleek, silver vessel that sat atop a metaphorical cloud of hopes and dreams. It twinkled in the light as if someone had plucked a shooting star straight from the night sky and placed it right in front of them. Enatt ignored the gorgeous creation completely, bypassing it to go open the hanger doors while Yslawna and Aaron swooned over the ship. They brushed their hands across its smooth, gentle surface and took turns remarking how clean and shiny it was. Even if their excessive attention to the ship stemmed less from its beauty and more from a need to focus on something other than their recent traumas, it was still a remarkable creation.

When Enatt reappeared, Yslawna turned to him and started launching a barrage of questions, "Where did he find it? How fast does it fly? How did he keep it in such good condition?"

Enatt didn't answer. He just said, "The entrance is over here. Let's go."

Yslawna glanced over at Aaron as Enatt opened a door and meandered into the vessel. They both had the same understanding, visible even through their masks. Enatt might not last long. He was deeply and profoundly damaged. As they followed their psychologically wounded friend into the vessel, Yslawna and Aaron couldn't help but marvel at its glittering interior. A bright red carpet rolled majestically through gloriously silver hallways adorned with colorful pictures and dazzling ornaments. Yslawna twirled around like a bewildered child, touching and looking at things, while Aaron became very quiet as he distractedly passed by each decorative ornament, trying with moderate success to push the slaughter at the Mausoleum to the back of his mind.

He peered into a nearby lounge and gasped at the fluffy sofas and chairs scattered decadently across the interior — chairs that would have been very useful in the stark bedroom Casadarious had provided for him.

He indignantly turned to Enatt, "Didn't Casadarious say no luxuries? What is all of this?"

"This was a time capsule to remember how things were," he replied with a misery that made Aaron sorry for even asking. "This ship was never supposed to be used, only preserved so we could remember what we were fighting to save."

Aaron glanced over at Yslawna, who had stopped to gaze at a picture of the music hall, unrecognizable to Aaron without the fog and rot spread across the city.

Aaron looked back at Enatt and asked, "It still flies, right?"

"Yes, but I don't know how to pilot it. I was hoping one of you would know."

"I can fly it," Yslawna answered, tearing herself away from the memories of the past and strutting over to Enatt. "Just show me where the controls are."

Yslawna and Aaron followed Enatt to a marvelously crafted bridge where a comfortable chair sat before a great window and a mighty steering wheel. Yslawna strapped herself in, flipped some switches, and the ship hummed to life. With little effort, it lifted away from the hanger and sped off to Almerin's tower. It punched out of the disgusting fog and floated up into the gleaming daylight, where it pranced for a prideful moment before snapping off towards Alme-rin's tower.

As they drifted across the sunny sky, Yslawna leaned over and asked Enatt, "Does the ship have a name?"

"The Silent Angel"

"That's a bit melodramatic... but I guess it fits. It doesn't shriek like my old ship did."

Enatt wordlessly stepped away from the conversation and meandered downstairs. Aaron watched him leave and then made himself comfortable in one of the plush chairs around the bridge. The warm sunlight beaming through his window and the smoothness and beauty of the Silent Angel caused a small, hopeful smile to visit him. They might actually be able to do this.

"Awhet would have given anything to see this ship," Yslawna thoughtfully remarked while brushing her hand over the pristine controls. "I still feel him around sometimes. I'm sure he's been helping us."

Aaron looked over at Yslawna and asked, "Do you think we're actually going to close the seal and end all this?"

"I'm sure this madness won't just end if we manage to close the seal. But it'll start to end, and we'll have a shiny new ship to go off and leave the city!" She caught herself before she could get too excited, "If we succeed, that is. Always be prepared for failure." She tapped a couple of times on the console as her suppressed excitement worked its way into her hands.

Aaron looked out the window at the beautiful sky stretching across endless possibilities and then looked back at Yslawna. She was dirty, ragged, emaciated with gangly limbs, and always twitched slightly when she wasn't actively moving. She was in complete con-trast to the delicate environment she sat in. She was a product of Hiri Handi now, and he wondered what she or Enatt would do if this ever actually ended. He decided to ask her.

"Yslawna?"

She turned and looked at him through her impassive purple veil.

"What would you do if this actually ended?"

She paused thoughtfully and then said, "I'd sleep a lot and eat food that didn't taste like mold. What would you do?"

That was a ridiculously simplistic answer, but he couldn't blame her lack of imagination. He felt the same. He just wanted to go home.

"I guess I'd sleep too and then find my way back home."

"If you ever manage to do that, would you mind if I came along? Nothing is left of my old home here."

Aaron gave a surprised smile. Yslawna's hatred of him must have waned, and he couldn't help but smile at that. "Yeah, that'd be nice. Maybe Enatt could come too… if he's not angry about me punching him."

"I doubt that he is. He has deeper problems than that. You might want to talk to him, though. He doesn't look good."

Aaron agreed and got up from his cushy chair with an aching groan. He descended back down into the luxurious mansion of a craft, pausing periodically to look at the splendid art while scanning each room he passed for his new acquaintance. He finally stumbled across Enatt in a little bedroom, sitting atop a vibrant blue and gold bed. Enatt looked up and regarded Aaron and then bent his head back down.

"I just want to be alone for a while. I have some things to work out."

"Do you want to talk?" Aaron asked, taking off his helmet and hoping the gesture would be interpreted as a sign of empathy.

Enatt cast Aaron a startled glance and said, "I guess Hiri Handi hasn't treated you well either."

Aaron was taken aback for a moment before he realized how much of a toll the city had probably taken on him. "No, it hasn't."

Aaron sat down beside Enatt with a heavy sigh filled with all the trauma the horrible city had heaved upon him.

Enatt quietly looked down and opened up by saying, "I still see their faces…. the ones Casadarious made me execute. And I still feel his presence, even though he's dead. It's like he's a part of me now, and I just want to claw my chest open to tear him out."

"He's not a part of you, and he never will be. You just need time to heal." Aaron didn't know if any amount of time would actually fix Enatt, but it would certainly dull the wounds.

Enatt looked at Aaron with a broken gaze that only Jalmi could match and said in a hushed voice, "You don't know what it was like to be controlled that way. To have his fingers in my brain, washing away my memories and trying to soothe me by making me believe it's a good thing. I can't get that out of my head!"

"Yslawna has this thing I've seen her do," Aaron paused as he tried to put her odd behavior into words. "She seems to take each day at a time and then takes that time to focus on enjoying the small things that happen around her. It doesn't sound like much, but allowing ourselves to drown will only lead to…. well, drowning."

Enatt was quiet as he considered Aaron's words.

"Why don't you come upstairs?" Aaron invited. He got up and stood by the door. "There's a beautiful view outside that we could all use right now."

Enatt closed his eyes and turned away, "I'll see later. I just want to be alone right now."

"Alright," Aaron turned around and began to meander back up to the bridge. He left Enatt's door open as an inviting gesture, but he heard the door slide shut with a light thump as he walked away. He crossed a small mirror on his way back to Yslawna and leaned in to look at his face. Tired, fearful eyes in a ragged, dirty face stared back at him. Enatt was right; Hiri Handi hadn't treated him well.

He returned to the bridge and looked around. Yslawna was still piloting, and the gorgeous cityscape, only gorgeous from afar, was still drifting past.

"He didn't want to come up," Aaron announced with defeat in both his voice and lethargic movements. He collapsed back into his chair and resumed staring out at the view.

"He's damaged like we all are. We'll just have to talk to him again later."

Yslawna's voice had a slight waver of uncertainty. It was only slight, but Aaron caught it and knew what it meant. Enatt might never come back. He might have died along with Nakinee in that accursed tomb.

Then Enatt marched up the stairs and stood on the bridge. Yslawna and Aaron spun around to greet him.

"Good to see you, Enatt!" Yslawna said with what Aaron thought might be a beaming smile under her veil. He couldn't help but smile too. Enatt gave a stark nod and sat across from Aaron at the other end of the room to gaze out the window until they finally arrived at Almerin's tower, which slowly melted out from the indistinct backdrop of the city.

"Here it is," Yslawna announced as she pulled some levers to slow the ship's speed. Aaron got up and stood behind her as they gazed through the crystalline window at that majestic tower, which filled Aaron with dread and self-doubt. Terrible images of him reaching down to retrieve the golden key of the labyrinth from Almerin's shredded corpse swirled through his imagination. It made him physically ill, so he sat back down with a mild whimper while Yslawna pulled the ship up to the tower.

The floating manor they had the privilege of traveling in extended a working ramp which the group used to effortlessly step onto the snow-covered bridge.

Before them was the tower, no longer bathed in the soft moonlight but out in the harsh vividness of the sun. It almost seemed older to Aaron, more worn and weathered, but he wasn't really sure. At its entrance were those two statues, frozen forever in that one instance of time where a simple door and an inability to open it halted all of their terrifying might and fury.

"Looks like our friends are still here." Yslawna pointed ahead as they walked up to the tower gate.

She glanced backward with concern as neither Aaron nor Enatt answered. Both were too enveloped in their own problems to muster any sort of clever remark. They stopped before the pale blue gate, and Yslawna turned around to bring Enatt fully up to speed with their plan to use the labyrinth to enter the palace and close the seal. Aaron just gazed up at the tower while they talked. Their words drifted further and further away while the weakness in the pit of his stomach grew with each moment he contemplated entering that enormous tomb. He didn't know why he felt so weak. He'd seen many corpses throughout this nightmare. Maybe it was because he'd known Almerin. He'd heard the sound of his voice and seen the utter fear in his eyes when the old man resolutely declared that he'd never leave his tower. Maybe it was because he felt guilty for taking the suit of armor that protected his home and for abandoning him during the sanctuary battle, or the fact that his mutilated body might somehow foreshadow his own demise. Maybe it was all of it...

"Are you ready?" Yslawna lightly jostled his arm, and he lurched back in terror.

"S-sorry. Yeah, I'm ready."

She looked at him, her mask once again concealing either concern, disappointment, fear, or all of them mixed together. She just looked at him and said in a slow, calming voice, "Okay, we'll start this cautiously then."

She directed the three of them as they heaved the statues aside and into the icy snow. Then Yslawna opened the makeshift door and paused a moment before poking her head inside to take a look.

"First room seems clear."

Enatt marched in first, brandishing a thin side sword and a makeshift buckler. Yslawna turned back to Aaron and motioned him forward.

He couldn't move. It was humiliating and cowardly, but his feet simply refused to budge. "I…" He struggled to even get the words out as Yslawna walked up to him and placed a firm hand on his trembling shoulder.

"It's okay, we can handle this. Why don't you guard the door to make sure nothing sneaks in while we're inside."

Aaron gave a short nod, and Yslawna rushed into the tower to join Enatt.

He shut the door and stood facing the pale blue gate as a light wind whipped across the small bridge.

He wondered if Yslawna and Enatt would find the creature or if it had hidden away somewhere else. Maybe it was back in the labyrinth. Was it too much to wish it would get hopelessly lost there and maybe fall down a pit, too? He stood vigilantly guarding the entrance in the blistering cold until Yslawna finally opened the door and stepped out with Enatt, who had armed himself with a shiny new spear and a long, pale blue shield. She approached Aaron with a notable apprehension in her step and said, "Be glad you didn't come."

"Why?"

She hedged slightly, "Uh… not much was left of Almerin."

Aaron's gaze started dragging down with the hellish scene his imagination was able to concoct when Yslawna suddenly caught his eye with the delicate golden triangle she held in her hand.

"He won't die in vain, none of them will."

Enatt stepped forward and held out his new brass-colored spear. He angled it downward and proclaimed, "For the tie that binds us."

Yslawna drew her thin silver sword, placed the blade atop Enatt's spear, and repeated the mantra, "For the tie that binds us."

Aaron looked at the two weathered knights, drew his own single-sided, twisting yellow and blue broken sword, placed the shattered tip on Yslawna and Enatt's weapons, and repeated the mantra, "For the tie that binds us."

CHAPTER SEVENTEEN

The Whispers of New Life

"For the tie that binds us," the mantra of the Golden Band refers to an old story in which a spiritualist performed *astral projection* and left her body far behind to ascend into the cosmos. While exploring the far reaches of space, she was tethered by a golden band that tied her to her physical body so that she would never lose her way. It is said that not only are we connected to our bodies by this golden tether, but that the same tether connects all life together and binds it to the same universal power of love. The Order of the Golden Band, having fallen into utter despair upon the loss of love and the rise of absolute evil, adopted this mantra to constantly remind themselves that no matter the darkest places they might walk, a golden tether will always guide them home.

-From the Book of Worlds.

Yslawna, Aaron, and Enatt marched through the academy and toward the labyrinth with a renewed resolve. They wound through the old passageways that teased Aaron's nerves with its shadowy corners and dark phantoms that seemed to scurry just outside the limited vision of his visor. They retreaded the path to the sanctuary until they finally came upon that same dark wood door with tarnished hinges and peculiar etchings.

Yslawna stopped before opening the door and looked back at her two companions. "Since the monster wasn't in Almerin's tower, it's probably going to be in here. Be prepared for that."

They both nodded, and she turned back and jostled the grimy old doorknob, which refused to budge.

"Oh," Aaron suddenly remembered, "Almerin used a key to get in."

Enatt glanced over at Aaron with a frustrated sneer and said, "That would have been good to know before."

Aaron sputtered out some form of defense while Yslawna looked up and down at the old door to size it up. She then kicked it with a brutish force that tore the lock off entirely, stunning Aaron and Enatt, who turned quiet.

The labyrinth unfolded before them with its featureless grey brick walls and closely trimmed grass floors. The entrance had changed, though. Aside from the same delicate glass fountain dripping water into a crystalline basin, they now stepped inside a vast hall lined with intimidating corridors and a few broken columns scattered around the periphery. They pensively scanned the area for danger until a new door quietly manifested behind them and then slammed shut with a loud crack that sent the battle-hardened knights scrambling.

"I don't think the labyrinth liked that," Aaron breathlessly remarked. They pushed aside the possibility of an irate labyrinth and maneuvered to a nearby wall where Yslawna whispered something to the triangle. She pressed it against the bricks, creating that vibrant yellow line of life and safety that would almost certainly see them to their destination... Aaron hoped. They set off down a right-hand corridor and began their trek. At Aaron's suggestion, they followed Almerin's old tactic that seemed to work last time. Enatt led with his massive shield and spear while Yslawna stayed in the middle to manage the group and keep a hand on Aaron's shoulder, who volunteered to watch the rear, having a minor amount of experience doing it before. They obediently marched through the twists and turns that the line directed them through while keeping diligent watch for the monster that was undoubtedly skulking around the same passageways.

They crossed under a dull grey bridge that stretched out above them, turned a corner, and then found themselves in a wide field of short stone obelisks.

"I don't like this," Aaron nervously whispered to Yslawna. They kept their formation, with Aaron watching the rear as they trudged by the obelisks. Each was featureless with a shimmering gloss that slightly reflected the lights built into the walls and ceiling. The obelisks were arranged close enough together to be mistaken for graves, which made them even more unsettling.

"Stop!" Enatt shouted.

Before Aaron could even ask what was wrong, Yslawna briskly spun him around and pointed at a hulking collection of roots and vines twisted together in the vague form of a person. It lumbered out from a passageway ahead, carrying what looked like a body in its arms. The group scattered behind the obelisks for cover and waited for the thing to charge at them.

It didn't. The collection of vines hefted the body to an open grave, deposited it as softly as a tree monster could, and then left the way it came. The group waited to see if the creature was coming back. After a few cautious moments, they left the cover of the obelisks and approached the pungently odorous grave.

"He was of the Golden Band," Yslawna pointed to the contorted mess below them. "He has the colors and armband."

Aaron took a quick glance at the corpse and then stepped away. He couldn't tell if it was the same body he found with Almerin when they went through, and he didn't want to look close enough to check. "Is it fresh?" he asked through a wave of nausea.

Yslawna leaned closer to the grave, "No, it's pretty old. Looks like someone is doing some cleaning around here."

"Who would care about cleaning this place?"

Yslawna waved the group away and back into their positions. "I don't know, but I don't feel like asking the walking tree. We should keep moving."

They marched on past the obelisks and into another corridor, leaving the field of graves behind. As they maneuvered down the increasingly narrow path, a familiar smell that Aaron thought they had left behind at the grave began to waft over the group. It was something ghastly that grew in pungency until they finally stopped.

Enatt was the first to catch it, "What's that smell?"

They looked around but couldn't identify a direction.

Aaron shuddered, "It smells like another body up ahead."

"Let's keep following the line," Yslawna directed, "and keep our guard up."

They pressed onwards, deeply concerned that the smell was worsening until it couldn't be anything other than a rotting corpse.

Then, they stepped around a corner and stopped.

"What's wrong?" Aaron asked with a readied flare of his sword for anything that might jump out at the rear.

Yslawna patted his shoulder and pointed to the path ahead of the group, "Looks like we have a trap."

Aaron turned around and stood on the tips of his toes to peer past Yslawna and Enatt. There it was, another ragged body decomposing in the open light of the thin corridor. It sat right in their path, right under the line.

Aaron stared at it for a while before asking, "How are we going to pass that?"

"Passing it isn't the issue," Yslawna answered. "Stepping over corpses is easy."

This statement concerned Aaron.

"Stepping over corpses with monsters hiding inside them," she pointed to the body, "is another matter."

Aaron glanced over at Yslawna with utter terror mixed with disbelief, all of which was hidden under his mask but profoundly projected into his voice when he asked, "Is that a thing?!"

Enatt looked over at Aaron with concern, "You can't sense them?"

"He hasn't had that training," Yslawna answered without taking her eyes off the trap.

Enatt shot Aaron a disappointed scowl and protested, "That's basic information. This armature is going to get us killed."

Yslawna smacked Enatt on the head with a whack that echoed across the passageways. "Focus!" she barked. "If he doesn't know, then teach him."

"There's a particularly nasty type of beast," Enatt rubbed his head while explaining, "that likes to hide in corpses. One is over there and will jump out and attack if we try to pass by."

"Then how do we—" Aaron stopped mid-sentence when he noticed Yslawna mixing some chemicals from her bag.

"You just have to know the right weapon. Get behind me," she ordered without looking up from her mixtures.

Enatt cautiously stepped behind her while she combined some more concoctions that began to foam and smoke. She then tossed a couple of empty vials to the floor and swished around a bell-shaped bottle filled with a startlingly yellow liquid. It frothed angrily as she swished it back and forth while mentally measuring the distance of her throw. She capped the vial, swished it around a couple more times, and then tossed it onto the corpse, which burst into a terrifying blue inferno. Aaron looked away as the body, which was supposed to be lifeless, twisted and screeched. He hoped it would just burn away, all of it. The fire lasted around two horrible minutes until it finally withered into a pile of black ash.

"Everybody stay aware," Yslawna motioned the group together as they all retook their positions. "There's probably going to be more traps ahead."

They set off again, stepping over the cindering ash and continuing along the line's trusted path. They walked and walked for what seemed like ages in the claustrophobic, grey corridors. They marched through twists and turns, open spaces, and tight passageways until everything began looking the same. Even the occasional thin trees or broken columns were all similar in form. The columns especially confused Aaron, for there were never any intact ones, not a single one. He pushed the question to the cluttered space at the back of his mind so he could focus on watching out for the creature he knew was undoubtedly hiding somewhere.

And then they stopped.

Aaron turned slightly while keeping his eyes on the rear and asked, "Are we there? Is it over?"

"No," Yslawna weakly replied. "It's not over."

Aaron spun around and took in the large circular room with a wide, pleasing glass fountain in the middle, dribbling crystal-clear water. For a moment, he didn't know what the problem was until he looked around the edges of the room. There were no other exits. The line brought them to a dead end.

Aaron froze as he tried his best to stifle all the fears he'd been stuffing down. The line was a lie, and they were trapped. Aaron stood in this petrified state of confused fear while Yslawna sauntered over to the fountain to gaze into the water, and Enatt began pacing back and forth as he muttered angrily to himself.

The room, although a harbinger of doom, was peaceful and relatively protected with only one way in or out. Aaron curled up across from the entrance and ducked his head under his arms as he tried to think of what to do next.

Yslawna looked up from the fountain and caught Aaron's attention. "Aaron, could you come over here?"

He lumbered upright with an aching groan and stood next to Yslawna, who asked, "Are you alright?"

"N-no, not really."

Yslawna slowly nodded, but he couldn't tell what she was thinking. "We need to solve the labyrinth using the old way," she explained, "using psychic premonitions."

"What does that have to do with me?"

"Enatt and I are… damaged. You're not. You're the only one who can reliably navigate the maze."

"Wait!" Enatt turned to protest. "He just demonstrated that he doesn't have any training. He couldn't sense the monster before. How is he supposed to solve the maze, especially a maze that's this warped?"

"He's right," Aaron admitted. "I can't really sense much of anything."

"I've been doing this for a long time," Yslawna sighed while digging some pills out of her bag. "I always come prepared."

Aaron didn't like the fatalistic tone of her usually cheerful voice.

Enatt took a step forward and gawked in disbelief at the pills. "That's… barbaric! You can't give him those."

Aaron didn't like that either. He lifted his visor and looked to Yslawna with profound worry.

"Aaron," she said. "These pills will help you navigate the maze. You're not as broken as me or Enatt, and they'll give you a temporary sight to guide us to the palace."

Aaron waited for the 'But' he knew was coming.

"But," she continued. "They're gonna screw with your head, make you see things, and then your body will scream in agony as you purge the substance from your system."

Aaron blinked his eyes a couple of times in disbelief. "*WELL, GIVE ME THE PILLS NOW THEN!*" he exclaimed with as much sarcasm as he could possibly muster.

"I wouldn't ask if I knew another way, believe me."

"I'll take it," Enatt said, stepping forward and extending his hand. "I'm damaged but not broken, and I've been trained for this. You can't push this on Aaron."

Aaron looked over at Enatt with more respect than he had before. But his eyes... Enatt's eyes were still glazed, and his temperament was erratic. Yslawna always seemed to have a method to her madness, and she offered Aaron the pills for a reason. He couldn't risk failure because he was afraid. He couldn't stand any more lives on his conscience.

He looked back at Yslawna and, with part of his brain shouting, *don't do it, you fool*, he extended his hand.

Yslawna gave him two ugly red and white speckled pills and a thermos to drink from while Enatt shook his head and stepped away.

"You're going to see phantoms and monsters," Yslawna warned. "We'll always be right next to you, even if you can't feel or see us. We won't let anything hurt you, so... don't swing your sword around trying to chop things. You could hit us instead."

He shook his head, shoved the pills into his mouth and swallowed them, choking slightly on the milky drink.

"You ok?" she asked again.

"Yeah, what do I do?"

"You think about the palace and let yourself be guided. Let me know when you start feeling pain, and I'll stave off the effects until we reach the end."

"Alright," Aaron stepped toward the room's exit with worry. He didn't feel any different, and that was probably a bad thing.

"I don't feel any —" He paused mid-sentence as the world began to weave and bend in a sickening way that reminded him of that ungodly wooden heart.

"Just take it slow," Yslawna stood up as Aaron stumbled against a wall.

He tried to say, I feel like everything is spinning, but the only sound that drooled out of his mouth was "Errrhhhggg."

He looked around as the room suddenly had a disgusting blueish tint. Yslawna and Enatt's voices became more distant. What was he doing again? The palace! He focused on the palace and felt a pull in a random direction. He followed the pull out of the room, hoping that his companions were following along because he felt too sick to look behind and check. He staggered through random corridors with the picture of the palace in his mind guiding him.

He turned a corner and stared straight at Almerin, covered in blood and gore. Aaron looked away. He couldn't face what he did and pushed past the old man. He hoped Yslawna and Enatt were still following. He turned back to check and stumbled into a wall.

They weren't behind him.

He gasped for air as he tried to recall what Yslawna had said. She said they'd always be next to him. He hoped that was true. He pushed onward, feeling sicker and more disoriented. He turned a corner and stared straight at Jalmi's parasite. It was a disgusting gremlin, and he was glad it was dead. It suddenly leaped at him, and he shrieked while wrestling with the beast. He threw it off and glanced around but couldn't find any trace of it.

Aaron shook his fist at the nothingness that had attacked him and tried to scream curses but only managed to garble out a slurred noise that was not dissimilar to a goat.

He continued on but slipped and fell to the ground. It was surprisingly easy to stand back up. Maybe Yslawna and Enatt were helping him after all. He didn't know, but he continued on anyway.

He turned another corner and looked straight at a twisting corridor of nightmares that dared him to even try and pass through. He slumped against a wall and wailed as his veins suddenly began burning. Someone handed him a drink, and he slurped it down, hoping it would relieve the agony. It did, and the wretched hall of hell began behaving like a normal passageway again.

He pressed on, turned a corner, and stood face to face with Almerin's killer, that monster with the hanging jaw. He screamed and flailed as it grabbed him and pulled him down a dark passageway.

Yslawna said not to swing his sword....

He curled up into a ball as the monster tried to tear into his armor. Suddenly, it screeched and stopped. Aaron stayed curled on the ground for a while as a cloud of commotion stormed around him until it screeched again and showered him in a horrible liquid. He staggered up, covered in the new substance that he didn't want to inspect, and continued on.

The halls bent and weaved in disapproval as he teetered onward with a fading determination. He didn't like this. He didn't like any of it. He felt sick, and it burned every time he coughed. Could he even stop if he wanted to? Would Yslawna even hear him or care?

He turned another corner and faced Awhet, mangled and broken as the giant monster had left him. Seeing this man broke his heart. He didn't mean to kill him. He didn't know he was being tricked. Aaron pushed past the grisly specter and pressed on. He didn't know if he was crying. He didn't know if he was capable of it anymore. Everything felt twisted and wrong.

He slipped to the ground and laid there for a while, gurgling gibberish, when a light ahead of him opened up and invited him in. He crawled forward, confused, sick, and afraid of everything. He neared the light and stood on his knees as it looked down at him.

"Are.... you god?" he burbled.

"No, I'm the labyrinth," it replied with a gentle, androgynous voice.

"Can you take me to the palace?"

"You want to close the seal?"

Aaron hesitated before he remembered that this was indeed his goal, "Yes, I do."

"That would destroy me."

"Then… come with me," Aaron sluggishly opened his satchel and showed it to the light. "I keep that big tree's heart in here. I'm sure you could fit too."

"You'd keep me safe and find me a new home?"

"Yeah, of course! Come with me. I've always got room for new… friends."

He suddenly stumbled into a solid door that swiftly opened by itself and carried him inside. He collapsed onto the ground, where he heaved and vomited so thoroughly that he truly felt like he was going to puke up his guts. Everything burned, and he collapsed, shaking as Yslawna slid off his helmet and patted his face with a wet cloth.

"He did it. He actually did it!" Enatt exclaimed, genuinely impressed by Aaron's drug-fueled, manic endeavors.

Aaron coughed and looked up at Yslawna. "We made it?" he weakly asked.

"Yeah," Yslawna answered while pulling out a flask of water. "We did. Just rest now." She helped him drink a few sips and then rested his head on a folded yellow tablecloth she'd brought with her.

Aaron wondered if he was going to die here. If Yslawna had chosen him as a sacrifice for his lack of skill and was now letting him drift away gently into oblivion, or whatever sort of afterlife awaited him. Reincarnation seemed to be a thing, so maybe he could come back somewhere nice. He closed his eyes and hoped he wouldn't die. If he was going to die, though, at least it wasn't a monster that got him.

CHAPTER EIGHTEEN

What We Choose to Be

He was in that dimly lit room again, lined with the unpleasantly striped dark red and blue wallpaper. The air still reeked of smoke and sweat, and the large leather chair he sat in still strained his lower back.

The Prince Adept sat opposite him, breathing in his drugs and bellowing out smoke like the exhaust pipe on a broken truck.

"Ah, god!" Aaron screamed. "I'm in HELL! I'm in hell because of YOU!!!"

"We're the same person," the Prince Adept grumbled between puffs. "Just different masks. And you're not in hell. You're in an ethereal plane you created specifically to speak to your past life."

"Ah, god!" Aaron scrambled to his feet, not listening to the old man. He began to pace back and forth, blithering out prostrations to God and whatever saints he needed to appease to get into heaven.

"You're not in HELL!" the old man shouted, collapsing slightly into a coughing fit.

Aaron stopped, "I'm not?"

"No!" the old man coughed a few more times before regaining his composure. "You're about to come face to face with your... rather unfortunate choices."

"You mean your choices!" Aaron shot back.

"No," the old man said with a fat finger pointed at Aaron. "Your choices, the choices you committed in your lifetime."

"I didn't do anything wrong!"

"You did when you released my old husk, the Prince Adept."

Aaron froze. Almerin had mentioned something about that. "But..." he stammered in confusion. "Almerin said I was tricked, and I barely even remember what happened."

"You were brought to this world by a cult who wanted to restore the romantically distorted memory of their delusional empire by releasing their divine monarch," the Prince Adept explained while circling his hand in an exasperated flare. "You didn't question. You didn't dig deeper. You just followed along and undid the world... again."

"Well, what do I do?"

"Do what's right," the old man said between another puff of smoke. "Whatever you decide to do, remember that the easy path is what led me right where I am."

He coughed a few more times as if to demonstrate how miserable he must have been while alive.

Aaron didn't know what to do or say, so he just stood there until the Prince Adept pointed to the door and said, "You'd better go back to your friends unless you actually do want to leave for the afterlife."

Aaron spun around and bolted for the door.

He groggily awoke with a miserable groan. Part of him wanted to go back to sleep, while another part was terrified he'd end up with the Prince Adept again in that ugly, smoke-filled room. He slowly looked around as his eyes readjusted from his horrible hallucinogenic trip. He was in a dazzlingly gorgeous sitting room with lavish, vibrantly colored furniture neatly arranged in the most pleasing manner possible. A stunning assortment of most, if not all, the colors of a rainbow danced together in a mixing harmony across the splendid walls. Enatt stood off to the side next to a dead body that was sprawled across the otherwise perfect red sapphire floor while Yslawna leaned over Aaron in her characteristically unsettling way.

"You're awake!"

He jolted, first at how close Yslawna was to him and then at the dead body on the floor.

"What's that?" he pointed at the knight who wore terrifyingly familiar armor.

"The palace is guarded with humans," Enatt explained while disrespectfully kicking the corpse with the tip of his foot. "Apparently, the Prince Adept has found a way to spread his disgusting influence outside the city and has summoned help."

"This is good, though!" Yslawna enthusiastically chimed, still leaning close enough for Aaron to smell her nauseating breath. "Humans are easier to fight than monsters, which might mean that the Prince Adept underestimates us."

Aaron sat up and gazed at the body with grave concern.

"Can you walk?" Yslawna asked, waving Enatt over to help Aaron up.

With both their support he unsteadily rose off the ground and braced himself on a glittering blue desk, panting slightly from the effort. "Please, don't ever give me that drink again."

Enatt cast Yslawna a concerned glance while she soothed him. "Don't worry. We'll find another way out of the palace."

With a subtle, disturbed sigh, Enatt stepped away and peeked out a dazzling golden door to look for more guards. Aaron distractedly watched him as a bizarre memory from his hallucinogenic trip suddenly returned.

He brought something with him...

Aaron cautiously grabbed the top flap of his satchel and then pulled it up. A glaring light exploded across the room with so much brilliant force that the three of them were utterly blinded and stunned.

Yslawna shouted, "CLOSE IT! CLOSE IT!" while shielding her eyes until Aaron was able to frantically shut and buckle it closed. The group stood in complete confusion, blinking their eyes to ease the stinging pain as they tried to comprehend what just happened.

Enatt lowered his hand from his face and quietly asked, "What was that?"

"Uhh…" Aaron hedged as he remembered with sharp clarity what had happened. "I think I put the labyrinth in my bag."

"What?"

"I… uh… talked to it. Don't look at me like I'm crazy. It's in the bag!"

"But…," Yslawna struggled as she tried to wrap her mind around this bizarre concept. "Why is it in your bag? And how?"

"I don't know. I spoke to it and asked for directions to the palace. It said it'd help me if I took it out of Hiri Handi. Look, is this really the strangest thing to have happened to us?"

The two just stared at Aaron.

"Well," Yslawna finally spoke after an uneasy silence. "I guess we have the labyrinth with us. Try not to open your bag, please."

Aaron remembered that it was the same satchel that also contained the wooden heart. He'd have to figure out how to deal with that later.

Enatt peered out the door again to see if anyone came to investigate the noise. He turned back and said, "It looks like no one heard us." The group then cautiously slid into an equally lavish hallway with Aaron staggering slightly behind, tired, sick, and bewildered.

They stood in a magnificently lofty hall, polished and shined as if nothing terrible had ever happened. Radiant blue walls, white ceilings, and golden tables painted the corridors in an extravagant display of opulence. With the decay of Hiri Handi and all the monsters he'd seen, Aaron expected the palace to be a horrific den of hellish nightmares, not an actual palace.

Yslawna led a few steps before stopping at an intersection, which echoed with cautious footsteps. She quietly listened to the soft thumping and then held up one finger. Aaron took this to mean one guard. She motioned everyone to step back against the wall as she picked up a small object from one of the golden tables and gave it a low toss across the corridor, ending in a small clank.

Footsteps suddenly pattered closer, and a man called out, "Jargal, is that you?!"

The man came too close to the corner and, despite cautiously standing in the middle of the corridor, Yslawna leaped out and stunned him with a silver bolt of magic. The man barely had time to shriek before she dug her sword into his throat and pulled him to the ground. Aaron watched in horror as Yslawna and Enatt dragged the body around their corner and out of the way so no one would easily find it. They were careful to not to allow too much blood to leak onto the ground.

"Ok!" she said with sickening joviality. "The armory is this way. If we can, we should stock up on weapons before approaching the seal."

Aaron just nodded. Any suitable words escaped him as he looked down at the slack-jawed corpse.

Enatt wiped some blood off the floor with a white rag from one of the nearby tables as they crept down the now tainted hall. They made their way further into the palace through several intricately decorated corridor junctions, one of which had two patrol men who thankfully meandered past them. They finally reached a corner that veered towards a massive, reinforced brass door covered in etched depictions of battle and glory. To Aaron, the garish display really couldn't be anything other than the armory. One guard stood outside while several voices echoed from behind the door.

"This is perfect," Yslawna whispered. "We'll lure the guard over here, finish her off, and then ambush the rest when they walk out."

Aaron wanted to protest. He wanted to ask if they really could just kill people like that. These were not monsters. They were human! But he hesitated too long, partly because the growing empathy he had for these guards startled him, and he feared somehow being discovered as one of their agents, which a horrible feeling told him he might very well be.

Yslawna moved closer and used her sword to tap a couple of times on the wall. The guard took a few steps away from her post and shouted, "Who's there?"

They didn't answer, and the guard, being cautious and wise to the dangers of Hiri Handi, called for help, "Hey guys, something's over here!"

She diligently stared down the amorphous noise Yslawna had created while the great brass door groaned and squealed open, allowing a second guard with a hefty winding gun to slip out and ask, "What did you hear, Letra."

"A tapping over there."

The second guard stepped forward and then paused as he thought better of it. "Commander," he shouted. "Something's over here!"

"This isn't good," Yslawna whispered as a whole troop of footsteps marched out of the armory.

The commander, in battle-worn armor and a cracked helmet with a thick visor, stepped forward and pensively surveyed the scene before asking, "What did you see?"

Aaron's ears twitched in terror as he recognized that voice, that cold and desolate voice that pulled him back to an equally cold and desolate castle perched atop an anemic mountain.

"Light! Light is the most useless of miracles! What good can you possibly do with that?" Commander Adoni berated Aaron as a frail, flickering ball of light twinkled atop the thin, pale branch that Aaron held in his hand. A branch from a sacred tree that had been used for centuries to suss out an individual's magical inclinations.

Aaron stood under that wide, half-dead, sacred tree in the snowy courtyard relegated to only those of royal admission. Only the Royal Order of the Sky, the monarch's personal vanguards, and those dedicated to teaching them were allowed into this holy, squarish, and otherwise unremarkable slice of the mountaintop. Aaron's comrades stood off to the side.

A woman with an icy, bitter face.

And a man painted with the agonizing brush of a recently lost love.

Aaron looked up at his mentor, who gave a deep sigh. "Light won't be useful for much other than a candle, but we can still pull out other magics from you. It just won't be as easy."

Yslawna broke Aaron's trance by mixing some vials into a familiar angry yellow liquid. Aaron recognized the color immediately. If she tossed the frothing vial, then the whole platoon of guards would burst into flames. Aaron caught her arm and whispered, "I have a plan. Do you trust me?"

"No," she plainly answered. "But I'm always up for trying something new. Go for it."

Aaron stepped out from behind the wall and courageously marched to meet the clamoring formation of guards who quickly arranged themselves into a firing line. Yslawna and Enatt followed on his flanks and stopped before the platoon. The men and women who guarded the armory gazed upon the three filthy, blood-soaked fighters, and their confident searing glares twisted into looks of utter terror.

Yslawna, who stood in a sprawling stance that made her seem more like a spider than anything human.

Enatt, whose spear, shield, and dead eyes were reminiscent of a scorpion eying its prey.

And Aaron...

Aaron, whose once brilliant colors were now just a greyish monstrous shell that took on the form of death itself. It was not three valiant knights who stood before the guards but three ghastly specters of Hiri Handi. Three phantoms of the death and horror that had made its home in this maelstrom of evil. The looks of terror struck Aaron in the deepest part of his heart.

He pulled off his helmet and let it clatter to the ground. He had a chance to settle this without bloodshed. He had no idea if it would work, as most things seemed to blow up in his face, but he had to try something. These were people that he knew, even if the memories were vague and disjointed.

"AARON!" Adoni belted in shock. "You died! How..."

"Don't do this," Aaron abruptly launched into his plea. "The Prince Adept is a monster. I've seen firsthand what he's done in Hiri Handi. He's created a hellscape nightmare that he's about to bring on your home."

Commander Adoni was at a loss for words. He lifted up his visor with a rusty metallic click and sized up Aaron through a scarred, harshly aged face with dull brown eyes and lips dragged down into a permanent scowl. Had the commander been anyone else, Aaron would've found no hope in laying the truth out. He remembered Adoni, though. He remembered that behind that scarred, harsh face was a surprisingly contemplative mind. Aaron knew he wouldn't offhandedly dismiss him.

"Ecrea's mercy, you're alive!" Adoni cheered. He crushed Aaron in a wide-armed hug that took him completely by surprise. This wasn't what Aaron expected.

Adoni looked Aaron in the eyes like a father might do to his lost son and fiercely repented, "We've made a terrible mistake, Aaron. We didn't know the Prince Adept would try and murder you.

He's a monster, and now he's on his way with the rest of our army to the Forge Bastion to consolidate power. He has everyone under his sway, but you're alive! The reincarnation of the Prince Adept is ALIVE!"

Aaron trembled. The cat was out of the bag now.

"We now have just cause to start a coup," Adoni jubilantly continued. "We'll return to the Forge Bastion, show everyone that you're not dead, and proclaim the other Prince Adept to be a pretender. Hopefully, we'll sway enough to do this without bloodshed, but if we don't, then we'll certainly sway enough to start a sizable rebellion. It's a miracle that you're alive. A miracle!"

Yslawna and Enatt quietly watched the bizarre scene unfold as Aaron nervously stammered and stumbled over himself in an attempt to say anything at all.

"I have some questions," Yslawna interjected with one very strong finger pointed up.

Adoni regarded her with visible uncertainty and answered, "Alright. If you're a friend of Aaron's, then I guess we should make introductions."

"You do that," Enatt said, placing a firm grip on Aaron's shoulder. "We need to talk." His voice was as firm as his grip, and Aaron knew there would be no moving forward until he explained himself.

Enatt guided Aaron past Yslawna and the guards and into the armory, away from the others. He stood by the door as Aaron stepped inside the massive cascading hall of weapons and armor, not dissimilar to the library if Jalmi had replaced all the books with guns.

Aaron spun around as Enatt shut the door, which locked with a heavy thud.

"Enatt?" Aaron's stomach sank as he stared into the man's cold eyes.

"Are you the Prince Adept's reincarnation?"

"No," Aaron quickly lied with an unpleasant knot twisting his insides. "They thought I was, but it was a mistake, and I... well, didn't dissuade them."

"I figured. That makes this more difficult."

"What? What do you mean?"

"We're going to the nexus of the world. All of the power the Prince Adept held was pulled from that spot. Anyone with a fragile mind will be tempted to do the same. You're weak, Aaron. You'll try and claim that same power."

"No!" Aaron fiercely contested. "And I'll even stay away from the place entirely if it makes you feel better."

"The group out there wants to put you on the throne as the new Prince Adept."

"So what! That doesn't mean anything. Enatt, don't do this. This is insane!"

"Aaron," Enatt readied his spear. "Yslawna is dealing with your friends outside. I have to deal with you. We're so close now. We can't take chances. No one can enter the seal but me and Yslawna."

"That doesn't make any sense! ENATT?!"

Enatt propelled years of suffering into a sharp thrust of his spear at Aaron's head. The man had cracked, and all Aaron could do was garble out half-formed pleas as Enatt launched a flurry of jabs that he could only back away from.

"YSLAWNA!" Aaron finally managed to shriek as he back-pedaled from the madman's assault. Enatt made a strong, vicious strike at his unarmored face, which Aaron was only barely able to fend off with a deflection of his sword. The blade refused to cut through Enatt's spear, but Aaron was able to toss a sharp blast of light into Enatt's eyes to stun him and buy enough maneuvering space to disengage. Aaron wasn't foolish enough to push any sort of advance, even if Enatt was blinded. The skill gap between them was as wide as a canyon, and all Aaron could do was buy time for Yslawna to come save him.

Fortunately, Enatt wasn't aware of Aaron's utter lack of fencing skills, and the burst of light gave the appearance of advanced training. He allowed them both to slide back into a cautious defensive lull to study the other's movements. Aaron was shaky and uncertain; Enatt was aggressive and twitchy. Aaron retreated too far and gave his adversary enough space to make a play. Enatt suddenly dropped his spear and shield, and for a moment, Aaron thought he was giving up. Then, in a flash of motion, he reached to the side and pulled a winding gun off the wall of weaponry. There was no cover. Aaron had to run.

Enatt slammed back the charging wheel and fired, pounding a bolt of energy into Aaron's side. Had Enatt aimed, he could have easily taken off Aaron's head. As it was, though, Aaron poured energy into his suit, which dulled a blast that would have ripped half his torso apart in a bloody splatter across the whole room.

He ducked behind a shelf and grabbed a nearby rifle while clutching his side, which gushed blood and burned in agony. In one smooth motion, Enatt wound his gun and fired again before sliding behind his own shelf for cover. The shot thankfully missed, and Aaron kept low as Enatt fired stray bolts to keep him pinned.

The pain was sharp and terrible. Breathing hurt, and his hands were shaking. He thought he heard pounding on the armory door, but it was hard to tell through Enatt's shooting. Then something clear danced across the room and wrapped around him.

Music.

One of Yslawna's songs, something with a soft melody, circled around his head and began easing his pain a little. Enatt was wrong. Yslawna was still on his side! It wasn't much, but he was able to think and move again. As the song rhythmically intensified, he wound his gun, waited for Enatt to fire, and then quickly returned the shot.

He missed, and Enatt didn't even seem dazed as seconds later, he fired again through a plume of smoke ejected from the burning core of his gun. Aaron flinched as the shot blew past his head. Going back and forth wasn't going to get him anywhere. He took heavy breaths and closed his eyes to listen to the song. The melody wasn't like the Gated Waltz. It was catchier and more energetic. The music cleared his mind, allowing him to go back to that horrible bowman riding atop his giant bird, where he fired spears into the Dancing Star. He caught that monster by firing at the same time, but Yslawna was impaled by that...

Aaron wasn't paying attention and let his head drift too close to the edge of his cover. A lucky shot from Enatt clipped the shelf, with the residual explosion catching part of his ear and sending his mind whirling. Now his ear was bleeding; his side was gushing blood, and Enatt was firing shot after shot.

He took rapid, heavy breaths as he prepared to do something stupid. He had Yslawna's music this time, and he didn't have that before. Aaron charged his gun and then quickly reached over and grabbed a shield off a rack before Enatt could decimate his arm. He waited until the rhythm of the music synched with his movements and then tossed the shield and stepped out. Enatt fired at the shield, giving Aaron a small window to shoot him while he was exposed.

Aaron stepped out and, in those two seconds, looked Enatt in the eyes one last time. They were terrifying — merciless, vengeful, spiteful. Above all, though, they were human. Had Aaron been more hardened from battle, more callous, and more prepared, he would have pulled that trigger without a second thought. Enatt was trying to murder him. This was self-defense and completely justified. Hiri Handi had whittled him down, though. Almerin's death, Awhet's death, Jalmi's death, Yslawna's near death, and Casadarious' death all affected him. Even Landala's death, something he had never witnessed, affected him. So much suffering, so much pain, and agony, all summarized in Enatt's hateful eyes. Aaron let the barrel of his gun slip to the right and fired at the wall. He just couldn't do it.

He slid back behind his shelf as Enatt furiously wound his gun and pounded Aaron's cover with shot after shot. Aaron just closed his eyes as the ear-shuddering crack of each bolt filled the room with smoke and doom. He didn't see any way out of this. He looked up to the arched marble ceiling and thought about praying. He used to pray to God, but everyone here seemed to pray to Ecrea. Maybe they were the same thing. He didn't know. Whoever was above him was probably tired of hearing him beg to the high heavens. He couldn't count how many times he frantically prayed while at the mercy of some abomination, and at this point, he didn't know what else he could possibly say to God or Ecrea. He wouldn't mind one last candy bar, though. He sifted through his bags as each shot tore away his cover bit by bit.

One left! He delicately unwrapped the Omos bar and bit into its wonderfully gooey center. He savored the delicious bite until an explosion suddenly rocked the entire armory. He peered around his cover and watched Enatt hurtle away the cindering wreckage of his gun while screaming, "MY EYES!"

Enatt struggled with scorching burns across his entire face as Aaron nervously looked down at his own aged, timeworn rifle with a sense of dread.

Enatt unsheathed his side sword and blindly stumbled closer to Aaron, who quickly wound his gun, despite the risk, and fired a stray shot.

"Stay back!" Aaron shouted through a mouthful of Omos candy.

Enatt froze in confusion. The primal growls and the hateful contortion of his face made it clear he wanted to kill Aaron despite being horribly blinded and at the complete mercy of his enemy.

Aaron wound his rifle and fired at the wall again. "Get on the ground, or I'll blast your goddamn head off!" Aaron's mouth was unimpeded by candy this time, and Enatt was left with a choice. Give up or die.

Enatt relented, slowly got on the ground, and tossed away his sword.

Aaron tried to get up, but his injury was taking its toll now. He repositioned himself to get a better view of Enatt, leaned against a wall, and took another bite of Omos. Yslawna's music had stopped, so he settled in for a long wait, hoping she would eventually open the door with magic or something. He moved to take a third bite but shrieked as Yslawna suddenly leaped out of some loose panels in the ceiling, landed with a loud, graceless thump, and then viciously suffocated Enatt with a chemical cloth.

She stood up from Enatt's incapacitated body and looked at Aaron, who was slouched against the wall, bloodied and gasping for air. She stared at the candy bar in his hand and asked, "Is that an Omos bar?"

Aaron looked down at the candy. It was a beautiful piece of heaven, but he also didn't want to bleed to death. He gingerly wrapped it back up with a sigh and offered it outward.

Yslawna took the candy bar, broke it in half, and gave part of it back to Aaron. "To help with the pain."

Aaron chomped on the bar before she could change her mind. "Do you hate me again?" he garbled through aching pain and a mouthful of candy.

"Nah, you do make things needlessly complicated, but I can't say my life is boring when you're around." She unpacked her medical tools, took off his chest plate, and began to work on the shot to his side and ear while asking a very pointed question. "So, who are your new friends?"

Aaron looked away as he tried to think of a good way to explain them. "The short answer is that they pulled me from my home by mistake and thought I could release their savior, the Prince Adept."

Yslawna quietly nodded. "So, what's the long answer?"

CHAPTER NINETEEN

The Forge Bastion

The Long Answer

Aaron stood atop the cragged, brittle stonework of the battlements which wrapped around an anemic mountain like a ring on an old, withered finger. The thundering canons above him reverberated through the fortifications and under his feet, which quaked unsteadily. They were massive guns, ancient relics from the old empire, carved out of metals nobody could fathom and tucked into hollowed out caves. Apparently, there used to be twelve guns. After all this time, only four still worked. These four were strategically maintained to give fire support across almost all of the landscape around them. They fired nonstop, every day and every night. At first, the constant calamitous pounding nearly drove Aaron insane. As the months crawled on, though, it eventually became a barely passible background noise.

Aaron stood atop the battlements, clad in a theatrically ceremonial garb to encourage the troops and boost the morale of the human wall that fought off horde after horde of raging barbarians, all united under the same religious banner of hatred. He was a prop, a figurehead. He was a simple chess piece for a war he didn't understand in a world he didn't understand. All he knew was the people of the mountain generally treated him with accolades, while the people outside wanted to rip his arms and legs off. He had no power. He never made any decisions, and that was fine. He didn't really care about the politics of the realm. He just wanted to find a way home.

The horde began another charge, and the Bastion troops readied. The riflemen on the walls fired first, thinning out the numbers with the ear-cracking pops of their guns. Then the archers let a hail of arrows shower over the battlefield, followed by the guards at the bottom who lowered their pikes and steadied their footwork before the fanatics hurled themselves into certain death. This was one of the few holes in the fortifications that had yet to be repaired, a gaping wound in the ancient walls guarded by a mishmash of townsfolk armed to the teeth with spears, glistening armor, and hardened by years of relentless fighting. The charge was hopeless, but it didn't stop the barbarians from trying. After a bloody effort, the horde retreated and regrouped far over the snowy ridge that sat in one of the bastion's blind spots.

"I've been told that they don't actually care about winning anymore," Commander Adoni said with a foul grimace at the slaughter. "Our spies say it's part of their religion now. They need to attack our home. It's a rite of passage for them. Any one of us who dies will assure them a place in the afterlife."

A group of black-garbed monks stepped out a heavy wood door in the lower courtyard and somberly trudged over to the most recent slaughter. Their job was to clear the bodies away after a failed attack.

"I'm ready to go in now," Aaron said with a glance at the door back into the bastion, unsettled by what the monks were preparing to do.

"We'll go when they've finished." Adoni pointed down at the monks. "It's a terrible job they have, and they need to know that we support them."

The monks hefted the dead invaders onto hand-crafted stretchers and, one by one, carried them into the depths of the mountain, deep into their dark and dreary monastery. Aaron was brought to the monastery only once. It didn't have a name, nor did the monks, who forwent their own names upon joining. Down in the depths below the bastion, and the small village that was nestled underneath, was a terrible place that prepared the dead bodies into food for the mountain dwellers. It was explained to Aaron that the horde surrounding them cut off most food sources. Only small amounts could be procured by the Rocs and their riders, which were then divvied out to the royalty and leadership. While the leaders ate small but wholesome meals, the town and army were fed the cooked bodies of their attackers, a secret the monastery kept under pain of death.

It was a horrifying codependent relationship that had developed between the mountain dwellers and the horde. The horde built an entire religion out of purging the remnants of the old empire, a religion that united their vast lands against a single nightmare, and the mountain dwellers survived on the sustenance that was provided by the horde in the form of reckless, hopeless attacks. Watching the last monks enter back into the mountain with their bounty made Aaron sick to his stomach. The guards around Aaron watched with equal unease. The guards, despite having ample reserves of that strange, suspicious meat available, were sickly and thin. Though the secret was kept on pain of death, rumor still circulated among the villagers not to eat the meat.

"They're done," Adoni announced. "We can go back now."

Aaron eagerly followed Adoni back into the bastion that awkwardly jutted out of the mountain. They ascended a dreary stairwell until it spat them out into a large banquet hall where the leadership had gathered for their morning meal and planning. A large fireplace radiated a healthy orange glow that enveloped the frigid room with warmth and an odd feeling of comfort.

This meeting was far from comfortable, though, with officials shuffling about in agitation and a servant already pulling out Aaron's religiously built, stiff-backed chair at the end of a long, wide oval table. He thanked the servant with a thin smile and a nod. It was all he could muster today.

At the head was Empress Emeya, flanked by two flags of a white, interweaving diamond dotting a blue background with a gold fringe and dressed almost entirely in blue, white, and gold — colors that represented the second empire, which was swiftly crushed after several mediocre decades of rule. She was technically just a baroness, only reigning over this mountain castle, but she kept the title and a laughable claim to a shockingly large swath of land. Dark brown hair trailed down the sides of Emeya's face, tracing sharp hazel eyes set deeply into robust but bitter features with lines too deep for her age. She was older than Aaron, but not by much, and had taken the throne far too early in life after her father was murdered by cultists, an event that happened before Aaron's arrival. Looking back, Aaron realized it was Emeya's callous apparition that he met in the sanctuary. Telling him that *he was never the one they really needed.* A chilling statement that was reflected all the way back at the bastion in the short stoic glance Emeya afforded Aaron from across the table.

Aaron replied with an equally short, nervous smile.

Sitting next to the Empress was her younger brother Mattane, the first blood-splattered apparition he encountered. He had a gentler, artisan mannerism about him that contrasted with his harsher older sister. Unkept blond hair drifted over a thin, bearded face with heavy, sleepless shadows under his pale blue eyes. He was younger than Aaron, but not by much, and was still grieving the loss of his wife, who was recently cut down in battle. Although Aaron wasn't able to save her, he did manage to recover the body so she could have a proper burial. Mattane felt deeply indebted to Aaron, even though the act was not so much out of bravery but simply a series of unfortunate circumstances.

Aaron watched the Empress, situated at the opposite end, as if they were equals. He sat in a dangerous position, and he knew it. He was brought to this land by mistake, but the leaders here couldn't admit it to their already crestfallen subjects. They wanted to summon their god-emperor, the Prince Adept, but they got a scrawny nobody named Aaron Hodges instead.

At the time, it all seemed like some horrible mistake. Looking back, though, it was clear the mountain dwellers succeeded in resurrecting their monarch, just not in the form that they wanted. To keep hope in the people's hearts, Aaron played the part of the Prince Adept with the leaders, weaving a thin story about his power being locked away in the cursed city of Hiri Handi. He would pretend to be their God Emperor while the Empress and her court would hatch a desperate scheme to release the actual Prince Adept, or what they thought he was, from Hiri Handi. After that, Aaron would be sent back home by the God Emperor's unrivaled powers, or so he was told.

Aaron didn't know what was going to happen or if he would even make it out of this alive. At any moment, Aaron could denounce the Empress and call for a revolution. The generals knew he was fake, but the villagers didn't, and that meant he was a threat to the throne. Aaron knew any revolution he might ignite would fail miserably, but the bastion was sitting on a knife's edge with the horde right outside the gate, and the Empress was as cold as the endless snow around them.

Aaron was handed a plate of meat and mashed vegetables with meager seasoning. He sipped from a silver cup and watched the Empress from across the table as she ate and conversed with her advisors. She tossed him another short glance before returning to her business. Her advisors were probably talking about him.

She was probably going to have him killed, which was why he made arrangements in case he had to escape. Aaron looked over at Mattane, who returned his anxious stare with a reassuring nod. Aaron had expressed his fears to Mattane, and he agreed that Emeya had the capacity to order Aaron's murder after the real Prince Adept was recovered. If Aaron promised to disappear forever, then Mattane would help Aaron escape. During their upcoming expedition into the cursed city, Mattane would stay by Aaron's side, and should the Empress call for his death, Mattane would quickly volunteer. He'd use a fake dagger along with some trickery and false blood. A few of his loyal friends he got assigned to the mission would help haul Aaron's body away and then let him escape. The Empress would have Aaron's death, and Aaron would make his way out of Hiri Handi and vanish into the snowy wastes atop his Roc, which the old priest Hodei, a friend of Aaron's, would "accidentally" let escape. Aaron was pretending to be the Prince Adept, which meant he had to ride a Roc and preside as the head of the Royal Order of the Sky. The months he spent forming an unbreakable connection to his Roc is a tale for another time, but it is sufficient to say that their bond was deep, and once he was able to leave the city, the great bird would eagerly carry him far away. The scheme was flimsy at best, but it was the most any of them could do. Aaron would vanish, and the Prince Adept would return to power.

Once everyone had finished shuffling into the room, Commander Adoni, sitting as the right hand of the Empress, stood up and seized everyone's attention with a sharp rap of his knife against a hard iron cup. "Inheritors of the Itzalla Empire, Empress Emeya will address you."

All eyes turned to Emeya. She lethargically stood up as if the weight of the endless battle outside was dragging her down and flatly announced, "We are going into the cursed city of Hiri Handi." She waited a moment for the full impact of this statement to resonate with her court. To the mountain dwellers, Hiri Handi was considered the physical manifestation of Hell itself. It was one of the few sentiments that that horde agreed with. The difference was that the horde felt the Prince Adept was the master of their equivalent to Hell, the Devil, while the mountain dwellers saw him as the prophet of their moon goddess, Ecrea.

"All of you know the dangers we will be walking into," Emeya continued. "You know the old legends, and our scouts have confirmed that they're probably all true. We will be descending into the land of death and lost souls. If we succeed, then the power of the Prince Adept will be restored, and all our enemies will burn and suffer for what they've done to us. If we fail, then our souls will be locked in the cursed city forever. I can't give you a profound, inspiring speech. All I can tell you is that we no longer have a choice. If we stay here, then the horde will eventually break our defenses and kill us all. A pilgrimage into the cursed city is our only hope. We live or die tomorrow."

One of the advisors raised his cup to Aaron and shouted, "For the Prince Adept!"

The whole table did the same and bellowed, "FOR THE PRINCE ADEPT!"

Aaron spent the evening gathering all the things he might need for a very long journey. After making a third pass over his supply ledger, he climbed up a seemingly endless spiral of stairs with a heavy heart. He might not ever go home. He might be stuck in this medieval wasteland forever, and the realization sucked all his strength out. He stood at the top of the stairs and opened a thin wooden door that heaped a stinging gust of icy wind across his face. He tossed a thick scarf over his mouth and stepped out onto the highest peak of the mountain, a wide plateau where the Rocs would rest. The space was carved out by centuries of these great rare birds who had made this mountain their home. It was the reason the castle was built here in the first place.

His Roc, he affectionately named Shenandoah or Shen for short, was a great blue feathered bird with a splattering of green coloring that was distantly reminiscent of the great river Aaron spent many of his days at. Drowsy blue eyes watched him miserably saunter over, and she pulled in her wing to let him curl up beside her. He laid down with a huff and watched the sky rise above him.

He could leave now, flee before they all set out for Hiri Handi, and never look back. He'd never be able to go home, though; Hiri Handi held his one and only chance. He looked up at Shen's big blue eyes, and she nuzzled her head into his shoulder.

She wanted him to flee. She didn't communicate with words, but Aaron could clearly understand her thoughts and feelings from their psychic bond. He knew she hated the idea of Hiri Handi, and she wanted them to flee far away.

Aaron rubbed her head and sighed, "I know Shen. I know."

Looking back, Aaron felt selfish. Going home might mean abandoning Shen somewhere in that frigid world. He told himself that she'd be alright, but deep down, he honestly didn't know. What he did know was that she was still waiting for him. Even though Aaron's plan had gone horribly wrong, he could feel a faint sense of her somewhere outside, waiting.

None of the Rocs could enter Hiri Handi. The energy was too chaotic for them to tolerate. After they settled the Rocs in a camp nearby, the expedition marched into the city. Hodei must have done his part in releasing Shen because Aaron still felt her life. Aaron wasn't so lucky.

They carved their way past monsters and danger until they marched across the sovereign roads into the palace, which eagerly opened its doors to them. They stood before a broad throne where a shadowed husk of a creature pointed at Aaron. Its guard moved like lightning and cut into Aaron with a swift strike that echoed across the vast, empty chamber. Aaron's sword and body were broken. Everything went black after that.

CHAPTER TWENTY

The Heart of the World

Yslawna hauled open the heavy doors of the armory and greeted Commander Adoni with a short wave. "Everything's okay now. You can come in."

"What happened?"

"It's, uh…" Yslawna pressed her finger against her forehead as she tried to come up with a simple way to explain Enatt's bout of madness, but she gave up. "Why don't you just come inside and see," she beckoned him to follow and stepped back inside the armory.

Adoni and a few guards followed her up to Enatt, who was horrifically blinded and thoroughly tied to a shelf. He didn't struggle or say anything. He just sat with his head lowered. Aaron was leaning against a wall, bloodied, battered, and a cautious distance from Enatt.

Yslawna pointed at Enatt and explained as delicately as she could, "He was already fragile to begin with, but meeting all of you pushed him over the edge. The Prince Adept ruined his life after all."

Adoni looked at Aaron, blood still painted across his half-ear and cheek, and then back at the blind prisoner. "Well, there's only one thing to do then." He grabbed a winding gun from one of his soldiers and hefted the barrel at the madman.

"No, stop!" Aaron and Yslawna shouted.

Adoni looked at them both skeptically. "If he's vengeful, then the best thing to do is kill him now while he's weak."

"That's not what we do," Aaron growled.

Yslawna stepped up to Adoni and stared him down. There was something inherently unsettling about someone in a mask staring at you, especially if it was clearly antagonistic. Yslawna's presence was also not quite right if you took the time to really look at her. It was not something obvious that you could easily point out, but it was there and added to her intimidation when she wanted it to.

Adoni sized her up and lowered his gun. Maybe he could challenge Aaron's judgment, maybe even Yslawna's, but he didn't want to go against them both at the same time. He exhaled and handed the gun back to the guard behind him. "So, what do we do with the traitor then?" he grumbled.

Yslawna took a long, hard stare at Enatt's pitiful state. "We bring him with us," she declared, "and take him out of Hiri Handi when we've finished. Hopefully, the fresh air will help his mind."

Adoni stiffened up with a sturdy glare at Yslawna. "Aaron," he sharply asked. "Who is this woman?"

Aaron got up with a groan and staggered over, "She's in charge, so do what she says."

Adoni skeptically eyed Yslawna, who responded with a sarcastic tilt of her head and a solid pat on the shoulder before stepping over to Aaron.

"Do you want to see something amazing?"

Aaron nodded.

She led him over to the back of the armory and up to a conspicuous heavy silver door marked with the wide etching of a bird of prey.

"You can't get in there," Adoni hollered from behind. "We tried. Guns don't blow through the thing."

Yslawna pulled a silver key out of one of her bags and held it up triumphantly. I've held onto this for a long time. She smoothly opened the door and stepped into a wide tunnel of glistening suits of armor arrayed in rows stretching all the way to the end of the room. Each was sleek, distinct, and vividly colorful with intricate detail.

"You and I get the first pick," Yslawna announced with an enthusiastic step inside. "Although your armor might outclass everything here. None of them are made with the same metals as yours."

"I guess you get the first choice then," Aaron distractedly answered. The suits of knightly armor were so shiny and intricate that he couldn't help but gawk at each one. It did feel strange that what he assumed to be the armory of a formal military would be so individualistic. "Why are they all so different?" He asked while eyeing a stunning blue and silver suit with a wide plume on the helmet.

"These were crafted for specific members of the Royal Order of the Sky, who tended to be assertive and even egotistical. They were nicknamed the Royal Vanguards because they loved to jump into a fight first. I'll have to find one my size. You too, if you want something weaker but dazzling."

"My armor's dazzling," Aaron warmly protested. "It just needs a good clean... maybe several cleans."

"That's true. Your armor was stunningly radiant before you cocooned yourself in garbage." Yslawna moved down the rows of armor, taking her time to pick out sets that might fit her alarmingly emaciated physique. She picked out several possibilities and then waved Aaron outside so she could change. After a moment or two, she stepped out in an agile, burning red suit with gold highlights that accentuated a fierce presence. "It's not my colors," she explained while patting the sturdy metal bands on her arm, "but it'll work for now."

After she had her pick and Aaron a chance for his, she invited Adoni and his companions inside to find whatever they could use. The group marched out of the armory, armed with radiant new suits of knightly armor. The helmets of these suits were angular, as seemed to be the style of Hiri Handi, and fitted with glowing eyes with selectable colors.

Yslawna's glowed a light purple, while Adoni's silver and yellow suit was a sharp green.

Despite being somewhat jealous of the selectable eye color, Aaron kept his old, battered, filthy suit and was careful to collect his grungy helmet before leaving for the seal. His suit had saved his life several times now. He wasn't going to risk anything untested, even if it was astonishingly polished.

They faced no resistance while making their way to the seal and soon found themselves at the gargantuan white and purple doors, gloriously adorned with enameled religious depictions and flanked by gruesome blood stains splattered across the entire entrance hall.

Aaron felt shaky, and his heart pounded apprehensively. This was it. This was the entrance to the seal.

There was a heaviness around them as if the doors were subtly warping the air, and Aaron could almost make out faint, unsettling whispers rattling from the other side. A guard handling Enatt set him down against a wall. Enatt's head cocked up as if hearing the whispers and shouted, "Yslawna, don't let them inside!"

"Quiet!" The guard smacked him on the head.

Yslawna hesitated, and Aaron knew what she was thinking. They had to fight whatever was inside that room, but if the seal really was so powerful, could it tempt any weak-willed fighter they sent inside? Aaron tapped her arm, and she turned to him.

"It's your call, Yslawna. However you want to handle this."

She looked back at Adoni and his guards, armed and ready for battle, then back at the entrance to the seal. "Just Aaron and I go in." She flatly announced.

"That's insane!" Adoni fiercely protested. He took a step forward and pointed to the door. "The Prince Adept's guard is in that room, and he's a beast of a man. I've seen him myself. You'll need all of us to bring him down."

"I've made my decision." Yslawna's declaration was as unyielding as the marble floor beneath their feet.

Adoni looked to Aaron for help, but he just grabbed two rifles from the guards and said, "Stay here with Enatt and make sure nothing comes up from behind."

Adoni shook his head as Aaron handed Yslawna one of the rifles. She inspected the gun and wound the charging wheel back and forth. "It's a good rifle, but remember to count to three after firing, so the core doesn't overheat and well… She gestured over at Enatt, and Aaron got the message.

The two embattled knights of Hiri Handi started to move toward the doors, but Adoni caught them with one last ditch effort. "This isn't a good idea," he pleaded. "Why do we even need to do this? We can leave the city now, can't we? We should leave for the Forge Bastion."

"Only the Prince Adept figured out how to safely leave," Yslawna answered without taking her eyes off the great doors before them. "You try to leave before the seal is closed, and I can't tell you what will happen. We need to do this, not just for our sake but for everyone's. The seal has been leeching the life out of the world, and it needs to stop."

Adoni relented and stepped back. Yslawna and Aaron pushed the heavy, blood-soaked doors open. They stepped inside, then quickly heaved the doors shut before Adoni could change his mind and slip in. Aaron wasn't sure what he had expected to see in this room. Pillars of light, gates to other bizarre realms, or even floating magic symbols. He was somewhat disappointed.

It was a large, plain, circular room lined with columns built into the walls, made from white brick. The floor had a massive purple spiral dominating the center, drenched in fresh blood.

Aaron gazed into the spiral and started to feel his mind being stretched across the very planet itself. He quickly looked away before it pulled his sanity to pieces.

Yslawna tapped Aaron and gestured to a figure waiting at the other end of the expansive, empty room. "There's Bakar, the Prince Adept's bodyguard."

With a name like Bakar and the rank of bodyguard to the Prince Adept himself, Aaron expected to look at a behemoth of a being. However, just like the seal defied his expectations, across the room was instead a willowy thread of a man... or thing. Its head was bent down, and it stood unnaturally still with not even a shudder to breathe. It was clad in cracked white and purple armor that hung loosely to whatever withered husk was inside. Tattered ribbons and broken metals adorned its chest. Its head was covered by a feathered helm, cracked and dented, and its regal gauntlet clutched a twisting blue and yellow sword broken midway down the blade. Beside him was a rotting corpse garbed in yellow robes. It felt familiar but only distantly, like someone else's memories. It was probably someone the Prince Adept murdered. Aaron didn't really want to think about it, so he glanced off to the side and caught a glimpse of a broken shard.

It was the rest of his sword. He didn't even have to see much of it. He felt it.

"This is it," Yslawna murmured, taking the time to talk since Bakar seemed to be in no rush. "Bakar was known to be fast. We'll try to pin him down with our rifles first, then we'll resort to swords if he gets too close."

"What about your music?" Aaron asked, pointing to the black metal case Yslawna kept slung across her shoulder.

"Magic is going to be too unpredictable in here… I can even feel my skin prickling. I'd rather not try it. In fact…" She gingerly set the case on the ground beside the intimidating door. "It'll be easier to fight without it."

Yslawna looked over at Aaron, and he nodded. There was nothing left for either of them to say. This was it. With heavy breaths and weapons drawn, they began advancing.

"BAKAR!" Yslawna hollered across the bloody mess of the seal.

Aaron separated and walked along the side of the room to flank Bakar in case he decided to charge.

"How's life been treating you?" Yslawna continued, "Read any good books?"

Bakar didn't answer.

They stopped a great distance away from the creature, Yslawna directly facing him and Aaron to her far left. "Do you remember the love of your life," she pressed for some sort of reaction, "your heart and soul, Casana?"

Bakar finally bent his head up, uttering a squawky growl.

"She was a pretty girl. Why don't you go look for her! I think I saw her back at the Library. We'll take care of the seal while you're away. You don't have to worry about anything!"

Bakar screeched and began to charge Yslawna.

The two knights fired the second he moved. Their guns rattled with a booming thunder that rippled through Bakar, spluttering gushes of horrific black blood.

Aaron's gun spewed smoke from its core. He counted to three, "one… two… three… and slammed the charging wheel forward. He trained his gun on Bakar, who staggered forward with a horrific screech.

Yslawna fired first, pounding Bakar in the chest. Aaron pulled the heavy metal trigger of his gun, and his ears rattled as another booming cloud of smoke exploded out of its core, bulleting through Bakar's neck.

The creature screeched and gurgled before dropping to one knee. Yslawna and Aaron wound their guns and launched another barrage at the mass of sputtering agony.

Bakar collapsed.

They paused and watched to see if the creature flinched.

It didn't.

Aaron lowered his gun slightly and suggested, "Maybe we should burn it, just to make sure."

Yslawna gave an approving nod and then quickly staggered back as Bakar's body exploded in black tumorous growths, sprouting new malformed limbs from his mutilated form.

They launched another furious barrage with their guns, but the mass of horror shrugged it off and tried to slam Yslawna with one of its arms. She almost managed to dodge the blow, but it grazed her enough to send her sliding across the room.

Aaron gawked in terror as the thing turned to him. It lurched forward, dragging itself toward him in a cataclysmic aggression that shook the whole room. All he could do was fire a stray shot and run.

The monster didn't even flinch as the bolt slammed into what could generally be called its body. Aaron tried to regroup with Yslawna but tripped as one of the creature's arms grabbed hold of his leg and yanked him back toward its pulsating center mass. He shrieked and frantically hacked with his sword until a lucky blow severed the tendril before it had a chance to pull him any closer. He quickly scrambled to his feet and cried as the monster continued to drag its horrible self towards him. He tried running to Yslawna again, but the monster suddenly maneuvered between them, as if reading his thoughts. He chaotically fled before the thing could get any closer to him.

Yslawna limped back into the fight and heaved a chemical firebomb at the creature, which landed unfortunately close to Aaron.

The explosion knocked him onto his side but managed to engulf the monster, igniting it into a burning mass of horror. For a moment, Aaron thought the bomb had done it, but the monster started dragging itself toward Aaron again with an undaunted determination. And it was now on fire…

"THROW ANOTHER ONE!" Aaron screamed.

"That was my last one!" Yslawna cried back.

Aaron hollered startling profanities while running from the creature in the circular room.

Yslawna darted over to her music case.

The monster continued pursuing Aaron.

It finally got close enough to grab him with several flaming arms and began dragging him closer while he hacked at its burning limbs with all the force and energy he could muster.

Music suddenly started playing. It was energizing at first, allowing Aaron to target his strikes and cut himself free.

It quickly changed, though.

It sounded like the music was being pulled and distorted by the seal, which dragged out the sounds until they warped into something hellish. It cut into Aaron's head like a knife, and he screamed as his brain felt like it was being put in a blender.

Yslawna stopped, and the sudden halt only made it worse.

Aaron felt like the room twisted upside down and then tossed him in a twirling somersault. He lifted his visor and vomited.

Yslawna slumped over, lifted up her helmet, and vomited.

The monster quivered and shrieked while backing away from Aaron and lurching toward the source of its agony, Yslawna.

This was his chance. Aaron charged the monstrosity and poured a ludicrous amount of energy into his sword. He ran up behind it and shot a wide beam of blue terror out of his broken blade, piercing through the monster and causing it to screech and gush putrid black blood. It furiously hammered Aaron with one of its arms, sending him hurtling across the room. He didn't have enough energy to pour into his armor, and he took the full blow as he slammed into the far wall with a shattering crack.

He could barely breathe, let alone speak, and his eyes struggled to stay open. He watched from the floor while the beast flailed around, hemorrhaging copious amounts of blood. Yslawna used the monster's confused agony as an opening and charged it with her sword. She stood atop the burning abomination, her armor protecting her from the brunt of the fire, and viciously hacked its limbs and body, pounding it with strikes. It was hard for Aaron to stay focused; the room kept fading in and out, but eventually, he saw the beast stop moving.

Yslawna hopped off its carcass and ran over to Aaron, both of them drenched in the monster's black guts.

"Is… it over?" Aaron moaned.

"Yeah, it's over," she knelt down beside him. "How bad is it?"

"Pretty…," it hurt to even speak, "…bad."

She rummaged through her bags and pulled out a purple flask. "Drink this. It'll help if you have internal bleeding. I can properly inspect your injuries from inside the ship once we get back."

Aaron nodded and gulped down the drink as best he could. It tasted like lighter fluid, but he managed to not spit it out.

"Can you move?"

Aaron tried to move his legs, but they wouldn't budge. He looked up at Yslawna and muttered, "I'm just going to lie here for a while. Can you close the seal?"

Yslawna stared at him for a moment before saying. "Sure, don't worry about anything. Once I start the ceremony, it'll pull us both in, so you can help from right here."

"Okay," Aaron mumbled. "You go do that. I'll be here… Just resting."

Yslawna took one more look at him, her helmet concealing the emotion that her silence clearly conveyed. She was concerned. She left and began placing some candles around the room, along with some crystals from her bag. Aaron didn't understand the bizarre chants, strange movements, or exaggerated gestures. He just closed his eyes and tried to jostle his leg a little to make sure he could still walk. He couldn't even move it, so he closed his eyes and soon found himself being pulled away to sleep or some form of half-sleep.

There were broken doors everywhere, shattered like open wounds gushing with the blood of the planet. There was so much power here. Unbelievable power all concentrated in this very spot and so easy to take. Aaron quickly turned away. He wasn't going to fall into that trap. The Prince Adept had impressed upon him well enough. Yslawna, Almerin, Landala, Maalen, and many others he didn't recognize were hammering away, closing the holes, so Aaron decided to follow their lead and do the same. He took some time to help craft a few doors, and although they weren't particularly nice, they were serviceable enough. He helped put the doors in place and hammered away with his comrades. Before too long, the broken passageways were sealed. A new opening was necessary, though. Yslawna and Aaron walked a far distance away to a place with many doors, but most of them were tightly shut.

They couldn't open the doors themselves because the distance was too great, but there were people there. Not many of them, but a few who happened to be listening. Yslawna and Aaron told them what had to be done to truly restore balance. Magic had to be sealed away in the moon realm and opened in the sun realm.

The handful of men and women who were listening understood and set off to open the new doors.

Aaron woke up with Yslawna standing over him again. He didn't jolt this time, though. She was a welcome sight.

"How bad does it hurt?" she asked.

"It's barely manageable."

"Can you move?"

He tried to jostle his legs again, but they still wouldn't budge. "No... I can't."

Yslawna bowed her head and placed her hand on his shoulder, "We can try and heal the damage when we get back to the Silent Angel. The ship has a good medical room.

"How am I even going to get there?"

She sighed, "It's a shame because it's a very fine suit of armor, but you're going to have to lose it. I can't carry you otherwise."

Aaron looked down at his suit. Despite the filth and grime, it had become a part of him. It saved his life many times and probably even saved him from more severe injuries when he hit the wall. With a heavy heart, he looked up at Yslawna and sighed, "Okay."

She helped him out of the armor, retrieved his sword and the shattered tip that Aaron pointed out, and they left the sealing room to regroup with Adoni and his guards. Aaron took one last look at the dirty, battered suit as Yslawna carried him out. It had belonged to someone else originally. Estrin might've been his name, but it felt like such a long time ago. Aaron quietly thanked Estrin for keeping him safe. He couldn't be sure, but Aaron thought he felt the armor smiling as he left. He was probably becoming delirious from the pain...

Yslawna, Adoni, and his companions carried Aaron through the mostly abandoned palace and back through the labyrinth, which had become noticeably darker as if the little life left in it was waning. Thankfully, there was still enough light and life to use the golden line, which mercifully worked this time, to quickly guide them back to Almerin's tower, where their ship waited patiently for them to return.

They brought Aaron to a little medical room, where they laid him down on a stiff table with many frightening instruments and unsettling buttons. Yslawna tended to him with a variety of drugs to dull the pain and manage any internal bleeding.

Aaron watched Yslawna read over some tiny luminescent screens, and he asked, "Is there something you can give me? To help me get my legs back?"

She looked up from the screens. The angular, blood-splattered helmet she wore was off-putting, but the soft, faintly glowing purple eyes were calming, even when she said, "Not without invasive surgery."

Aaron looked away with a nervous breath and asked, "Is that going to be hard?"

"It's certainly not my specialty, but I might be able to pull it off if all the equipment is here… and maybe a manual."

This didn't make Aaron feel better.

"We'll have to do this after we leave, though. The city's only going to get worse until… well, I'm not exactly sure what will happen here."

"Wait," Aaron leaned up as much as he could and asked with eyes as wide as dinner plates, "Are we actually leaving?"

Yslawna tilted her head in a way that suggested a deep smile and began looking around the room while muttering, "Let me get you a mobile chair. I want you on the bridge for this."

All of them gathered around the bridge; Yslawna was at the helm skillfully guiding the ship, Aaron in the copilot's seat with his surprisingly cushy wheelchair nearby, Adoni and his companions twittering over the marvel of a ship they found themselves in, and even Enatt who though still tied up and blind was given a comfy seat to experience this moment. They set off.

Aaron leaned forward and watched the city skirt past, the horizon looming ever closer.

"We're going to try to leave the city," Yslawna announced with an equal mix of nervousness and excitement in her voice. "I'm not sure what will happen, so brace yourselves."

Aaron's fingers dug into his seat as the end of Hiri Handi finally came into view. A wide border wall that soared up into the sky marked the edge of all their nightmares and terrors, all of their mistakes and failures. Beyond sat the manifestation of their hopes and dreams in the form of a vast, endless expanse of majestic snow and mountains that seemed to stretch on forever like a blank canvas on which absolutely anything could be written.

Aaron was so taken by the scene that he barely had time to react when Yslawna shouted, "This is it!"

He closed his eyes and clenched his teeth as he prepared for the universe to send him one last cannonball to obliterate everything. That's how it would work, he thought. It'd be right at the end where the universe got its last laugh.

The universe didn't laugh, though.

They passed through the border and soared across the open skies above an unknown country with endless possibilities ahead of them. None of them spoke, and none of them knew what would happen next, only that they were finally free.

Pronunciation Guide

Aclamartom *(AK-lah-mar-tuhm)*
Adoni *(A-doh-nee)*
Almerin Arnaz Telith *(AL-MƏR-in) (RN-az) (TEL-ith)*
Asier *(AH-shər)*
Asontzo Ilseea Delis *(A-sont-so) (ILL-see-uh) (DEL-iss)*
Awhet Ebarria *(AY-wet) (EE-bar-EE-uh)*
Bakar *(BA-kar)*
Casadarious Markelm *(CA-sa-dair-ee-uhs) (MAR-kelm)*
Casana *(CA-sa-nə)*
Ecrea *(EE-kree-uh)*
Eleseney *(EL-se-nee)*
Emeya *(EH-mee-ah)*
Enatt *(EE-nat)*
Enekoat Arzako *(EE-nee-coht) (AR-za-koh)*
Estrin Geanta *(EEST-rin) (JEEN-tah)*
Hiri Handi *(HEER-ree) (HAHN-dee)*
Hodei *(HOH-deye)*
Isrina *(IS-rin-ah)*
Itzalla *(IT-zahl-uh)*
Jalmi Yabeen *(Jal-mee) (YAH-been)*
Kaeta *(KAY-ee-ta)*
Landala *(lan-DƏ-lə)*
Maalen Recean Balerri *(MAY-leen) (REE-san) (BAL-ər-ee)*
Marceon Ecra *(MAR-see-awn) (EE-cruh)*
Mattane *(MA-tah-nee)*
Mistakoen Ordina *(MIS-ta-koh-en) (OR-dee-nah)*
Nakinee *(NA-ki-nee)*
Posiid *(POH-sid)*
Yslawna *(YIS-law-nah)*

www.ingramcontent.com/pod-product-compliance
Lightning Source LLC
Chambersburg PA
CBHW030646020726
47493CB00006B/1896